Bittersweet Manor

Bittersweet Manor

A Novel

TORY McCAGG

SHE WRITES PRESS

Published 2014
Printed in the United States of America
ISBN: 9-781-938314-56-8
Library of Congress Control Number: 2013951192

For information, address:
She Writes Press
1563 Solano Ave #546
Berkeley, CA 94707

She Writes Press is a division of Spark Point Studio, LLC.

This book is a work of fiction. Any similarities to actual events, places or persons, living or dead, are coincidental.

Cover photo by Peyton May Seaver.

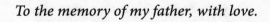

To the memory of my father, with love.

If you bring forth what is within you,
what you bring forth will save you.
If you do not bring forth what is within you,
what you do not bring forth will destroy you.

—Gospel of Thomas, verse 70

Contents

Children

Young Adults

Maturity

Entitlement

If it blew down in a hurricane. Or if it were struck by lightning and burned to the ground. If the house, home to the Michaels clan for three generations, were destroyed—what a relief. But no such luck. It would have to be a willed event on Emma's part . . . and would her family survive the loss? The house had always been a safe haven, a familiar setting that, in her mind, evoked love and nurturance, even if the reality left her empty. What if by giving it up—not through a natural disaster but a real estate transaction—she was giving up what the house symbolized: her family and her past?

Did she even care?

Emma wondered this as she walked into the Poquatuck Village assisted living facility and headed for her grandmother's apartment.

"She's gone!" the attending nurse announced to Emma.

Of course. She had disappeared. Again. Her beeper bracelet lay on the bed, but Gussie herself was gone. While the Harbor View staff searched the premises, Emma surveyed her grandmother's room—touched the crushed pillow on the bed, the rumpled sheets. Where might she have gone? The old graveyard, as she had the last time she had "gone for a walk"? Impossible. Two years ago, Gussie was still driving, whereas now . . . Gussie's wheeled walker didn't do well in April mud.

A whiff of her grandmother rose up, stark in the back of Emma's nose. Camay soap, Jean Nate body powder, molasses. Gingersnaps. Emma and her grandmother used to bake gingersnaps together, rolling the soft, spiced dough into balls with their bare hands, then through a drift of white sugar. She could almost feel her grandmother standing next to her. Could almost hear her saying, *You wouldn't dare.* And her grandmother would be right. Emma's determination to sell the family property dissolved into concern for Gussie, whose absence left room for breathless imaginations of what life would be without her. Even Gussie's Queen Anne desk suggested dearth. No bills to be paid. No robin's egg blue stationary. No chair to sit in and stare out the bedroom window at the view. At which thought Emma turned to leave. She knew exactly where her grandmother had gone.

Emma hurried out of The Harbor View and ran to the town docks. Maneuvering the sidewalk, with its sheen of black ice, she worried that her grandmother might have slipped and fallen. She picked up speed down Gold Street, heading to the harbor and the fishing pier. Then a moment of relief, because there sat her grandmother, profiled against the horizon, her posture straight, her chin up. She was staring across the gently ruffled water of Poquatuck harbor to the peninsula, and the family property, across the way. Emma cursed and resumed her race across the playground to the gazebo. She had somehow to protect her grandmother, who would be upset looking at the house. It was so different.

Stepping up into the gazebo, Emma paused to catch her breath through the knot in her throat. She reassured herself. Her grandmother was alive. She was fine. On the surface, anyway. Though upon closer inspection, and with foreboding, Emma saw a chilling likeness. Nostrils flared. Eyes wide and glassy. Her grandmother looked exactly as Emma's father had years before. Emma had not known then that she was seeing the resemblance backwards: that her father was looking like his mother. Instead, it had taken until now for Emma to see what they shared: fear. Of loss. Of mortality. Of what would their legacy be.

In so short a time, so many changes. For the first time in years, Emma had known exactly what she wanted: freedom from her family's expectations. Minutes before, at The Harbor View, she had intended to reject all that her grandmother had given her and to ask for her imprimatur on that decision. She had come for her grandmother's support. Now, instead, Emma would have to help her grandmother. As Gussie shifted her attention to her granddaughter, Emma wondered if she had the strength.

"You're back," Gussie said, her voice quavering. "I'm glad. I've been wanting to talk."

"Me too, Gram." Emma sat on the edge of the bench, as close as she dared. The fishermen shouted to each other as they stacked lobster pots and coiled thick ropes into neat piles on the dock. Terns screamed and dove. A solitary sailboat's halyard clanged against its mast.

"That clanking noise never happened in the old days," Gussie said. "Boats had wooden masts then. We owned a lapstrake-planked rowboat that Winston bought early on in our marriage. He used to row me into the village with the children. I can still hear the plunk of the oars into the water as Winston pulled us to shore. He was proud of his strength. I suppose I was, too."

Emma considered her grandmother, the matriarch of the Michaels family. Faded, hazel eyes; tousled, short grey hair; skin soft as a calf's on a feather-stuffed pillow. At eighty-seven, Gussie exuded beauty and formality. It was easy to imagine her as the young woman who had overseen the work in her garden, involved herself in church duties, and raised her children—and eventually her grandchildren, too. All those ages, child to adult, were layered and shifting like sand on a beach exposing seashells and sea glass, secrets of the depths. Were there secrets? Gussie looked at Emma sideways.

"You wouldn't happen to have any gingersnaps in that satchel, would you?" she asked.

"I didn't know I was coming to see you," Emma said.

"You didn't?" Gussie flushed with offense. Emma sat up, reminded of her strict, not her weak, grandmother. "How did you end up here, then? Just happening by, after absenting yourself for months and months?" Gussie paused to look about them, her spine stiff. "Certainly, I wasn't expecting you. In fact, I assumed I would never see you again. I'm not young anymore, you know. I could die any day."

"Especially if you catch pneumonia walking around in the cold without a coat," Emma replied and stood up.

"You're already leaving?" Gussie asked, and again that tremulous voice, the vulnerability.

"No, Gram," Emma replied, bending to kiss her on the cheek, grateful for the opportunity to do so. Her grandmother was right. Emma had taken a terrible risk not coming sooner. What if her grandmother had died? Then what would Emma have done? She shivered and took off her oversized peacoat. "Put this on. You're cold."

Emma tried to cover Gussie, who pushed her away.

"I'm perfectly fine. I survived an entire winter without your ministrations."

"You don't have on socks. You have goose bumps, and your lips are purple."

"Don't be insulting." Gussie sat up. "Fresh air and exercise. That's what everyone says I need. I intend to stay out here and enjoy this superb weather."

"I guess we do what we do for good reasons, even if, from a distance, it looks foolish," Emma said, earning a sharp glance from her grandmother. Maybe it was better not to point fingers.

"Watch the seagull dirt."

Gussie pointed to a dribble that lay on the shoulder of her argyle sweater.

"Oh." Emma set aside the coat. "At least it brings good luck."

"That, Emma, is an old wives' tale made up to make a weeping, mortified five-year-old girl feel better."

Emma rummaged through her knapsack, removed a roll of toilet paper.

"Conner told me that when a bird shat on me on our first date."

4

Emma began to clean the sweater. "I took it as a good sign. I guess I was wrong."

"About what?"

"Conner. My boyfriend. You never met him. Too bad. You would have liked him."

"Why the past tense? I'm not going anywhere. You can bring him to visit anytime."

"We broke up. He's my ex, as of last night." Emma's chin trembled, her throat tightening to the extent that she could not express how afraid of the world she would be without him.

Gussie shifted her contemplation from her sweater to Emma. "Fortunately, one survives such losses," she said.

"I know," Emma replied. "You have only to keep breathing, right? Even if you don't want to."

Gussie didn't respond. Emma had not expected her to. Because it was true. The heart kept beating, the lungs expanding and contracting, though the chest was compressed and the soul contorted. In and out. Every breath fanning the pain of living. What could words do to alleviate that? "Why did you remove your beeper bracelet, Gram?"

"Shackles." Gussie looked back to the house.

"You get disoriented, remember? You have to keep it on so we can find you."

"How can I get lost in a one-bedroom apartment?"

"When you leave it."

"I suppose I know the village well enough."

"I suppose you do. It's more for the staff. They're looking for you."

"They should look where you looked," Gussie replied with a familiar crispness. "How did you know?"

Emma shrugged. "This is where I'd come," she said.

"This is where you came. Home. It's fascinating, isn't it, to look in instead of out?"

Gussie indicated the property across the way, cloaked by a striated white mist that hovered just above the ground. Her father,

Mr. Willard, had bought the land nearly one hundred years before, at the turn of the twentieth century. He had built a house on the gently sloping fields. Cows grazed on the stony granite ledge that, over centuries, had been covered by sand, soil, grass, and slowly, with habitation and plantings, by bushes, hedges, and trees. Small chunks of the property were sold off and built up. What was left Mr. Willard divided and handed down to Gussie and her brother. Gussie's brother sold his share and moved West. He never came back.

Gussie stayed. She and her fiancé, Winston Michaels, built a house in the year of their engagement and marriage, 1929. There, their children were born—Auggie in 1930, Livy in 1931, and Alyssa in 1936. Gussie and Winston had rebuilt what was destroyed of the house by the Long Island Express hurricane, that "annoying bit of weather," in 1938. The repairs and additions had given the house, with its wraparound porch and abbreviated L-addition to the front, a hodgepodge look.

Soon after the work was done, Gussie's parents died, suddenly and relatively young. The Willards' house was sold, leaving Gussie to maintain what was left of the family's holdings. Days and evenings—hundreds, thousands of them—she and her growing family had sat on the porch, enjoying the property with its sinuous paths. They all led to the beach that overlooked the harbor to the village. There had been less and less of a view each year, given the overgrowth of trees and bushes. Gussie had moved to the assisted living facility in her eighty-second year, leaving the property to be dealt with by her children. The result: Emma inherited her father's share, the house. There it was, modestly exposed and sandwiched between the scar left by Livy's house to the south and Alyssa's to the north.

"The distance," Gussie said, "allows one to appreciate the details."

"Do you miss it, Gram?" Emma asked, hesitant because what if the answer were yes?

"Why would I?"

"Usually when people lose what means something to them, they miss it," Emma said, irritated by her grandmother's composure around a subject that so jarred her. Or perhaps her grandmother was better at hiding feelings, having had years of practice. But then, so had Emma.

"I haven't lost a thing." Gussie straightened the skirt of her dress and patted her purse. "You're the one who's tried to, and unsuccessfully. You remind me of your father. Auggie used to rail against the house, too, but he's always come back. We all do."

"I'm not back," Emma said with a lift of her chin and more confidence than she felt. "I'm selling the house, and I've come to ask—"

"Crying wolf!" Gussie scoffed. "At Thanksgiving, you intended to move in. Then a big to-do and you left in a snit, not to be heard from since, other than sending off a slew of letters telling everyone you'd put the house on the market and not to contact you. Spiteful, ridiculous threats. We're family, Emma. You can't divorce us."

"I thought I might try."

"A Sisyphean task."

Emma tossed the wad of toilet paper into the trash can a few yards away, then draped her coat over her grandmother's shoulders. How true—it was a Sisyphean task, because here she was, right back where she had been four months before, resentful of and alienated from the person she felt closest to: her grandmother.

Not closest to. Most understood by.

Or, if not understood, connected to by history and the house. Which exposed the rub. Her grandmother might recognize the connection, but not the need to be free. She would never agree to sell the house.

Sitting down on the bench, Emma crossed her arms, wishing she had stayed on the train. If she had, she would be arriving at New York's Penn station now, losing herself in the masses of people, each with his or her own dreams, horrors, and history. Were hers so much better or worse?

"My favorite color in the world is the sunrise over the village as seen from the house," Gussie said, taking Emma's hand and squeezing it, as if that would make it all better. "The mix of yellows and reds and oranges burnishing the houses and the harbor. The peace of knowing the children are asleep, safe. With the slow dissipation of the fog, the rising anticipation of the day and all it holds."

"That's not a color, Gram."

"A feeling, then. A place. It would kill me to lose that forever."

Emma narrowed her eyes at her grandmother.

"Not if you keep breathing. Remember? One survives such losses."

"My point being, you missed a lovely sunrise," Gussie concluded with that clenched-jaw smile that had formerly been reserved only for her husband. "The storm clouds looked like billowed steel, tinged with pink and yellow."

"How did you see it from the house?" Emma asked.

"I dreamed I was there. It was good to be back. Isn't it? Good to be home again?"

Emma studied her grandmother. She, too, had dreamed of the house. The dream had been full of varying shades of fear.

"It's not my home anymore, Gram."

"It most certainly is. You should be grateful to have it."

"Shackles."

"Nonsense. Our situations are entirely different. No comparison." Gussie paused. "You make the house sound like a curse."

"I feel cursed. Last night when Conner found out I own that?" Emma indicated the land, the family house, with a nod of her chin. "He looked at me as if I'd morphed into a monster."

Gussie gave Emma a shrewd look.

"How long have you been dating?" she asked.

"Two years. One month. Two weeks and three days."

"And he didn't know you own the house?" Gussie asked after a long moment. Emma hesitated, shook her head. "Then why the surprise? That's what you wanted, wasn't it? For him not to know you. Or us. My goodness. Why such secrecy?"

"I knew if he found out, exactly what happened would. It's awful. He thinks I'm rich."

"We aren't so terribly rich."

"Gram, look across the way. The house exudes wealth. Owning it suggests privilege. That I'm entitled."

"Of course, you are."

"I know, but it's not as if I had a choice in the matter."

"You certainly know how to look a gift horse in the mouth."

"Gift? It sucks up every dime I have. I'd give it up in a heartbeat, if I could."

"Then why don't you?" Gussie snapped. She sat up, alarmed. "But you won't. Imagine giving up all we've been given. You love the house. Just like your father. You just don't have the sense to appreciate it. Entitlement needn't be a bad thing. It's what you choose to do with it."

"Choose, Gram?" Emma asked with a flare of resentment that curdled into shame. Why punish an old woman for the past?

"Yes. All you need to do, Emma, is decide what you want to do." Emma only stared at the ground. She had decided, and once again it was the wrong decision. Gussie prodded her. "You used to dance."

"Yes, Gram. I used to dance," Emma said, annoyed and trusting that her grandmother would leave it at that. Gussie did. Emma couldn't. She remembered too clearly the last time she had dared to dance, truly dance, with her heart: years before, in the cabin that her grandfather had built out behind the garage as a study for her father. She had used it as a dance studio. Its hard wood flooring worn down by age. Its picture windows opening to a view of the harbor and village. Sun had flooded the room as Emma tapped the floor with a toe. Exacting and absolute, she had raised her arms. Left hand gently touching a wall, right arm lifted out. Feet into fifth position. With her weight on her left foot, she had glided her right leg straight out to the front, heel up, toe pointed. Slowly, she slid her foot to the right, stretching. And then to the back. *Battement tendu*. Repeat. Heart cringing. Stop thinking. Balance. It was about balance, not turning, she had reminded herself as she broke away from the wall and pirouetted around the room. Bare wood against slippered feet. Around and around. Each turn a petal from a daisy. Do I. Do I not. Stop . . . ping. Bending backwards, stretching as if reaching, debating, her body expressing soul as she twisted and turned. Every movement had felt right. She would never have believed then that it would be for the last time.

"I dreamed last night that I was a tree," Emma said. "It had been raining for days and the earth was loose and mucky. I was all excited by the idea of walking. Like an Ent in those Tolkien books. My leaves shivered as I pulled my roots up out of the ground, one and then another. I lost my balance. Instead of walking, I toppled over. I lay in the mud and what leaves were still exposed rustled in the breeze."

"That will teach you not to try to be an Ent when you are a tree," Gussie said dryly.

"Have you never wanted to escape yourself?" Emma asked. "Be someone entirely different?"

"No," Gussie said, though after having said it she appeared to think about the question. "How can you hope to be different, if you don't know who you are?"

"But I do know who I am. I'm my family, trapped in old behaviors. I can't seem to escape them. For all my privilege and entitlement . . . I'm lost. I have trouble telling the difference between what I want and what I think is expected of me, and end up doing things that seem right at the time but turn out to be all wrong. Nothing feels true anymore. Sometimes I suspect that I'm killing myself day by day, holding back, not living for fear of life. I worry that one day I'll realize that I've been dead all along, or might as well have been, but it'll be too late. My life will be spent, wasted, and I want to do so much."

Gussie didn't respond at first, staring out at the breakwater, the piles of granite that stretched across the mouth of the harbor and ended in a strip of beach with a high-tide mark of salt and sun-dried seaweed, black and crunchy on the sand.

"Years ago, on my eighteenth birthday, my tutor said the same thing to me that your Conner said to you." Gussie paused, as if distracted by a thought or, perhaps, by the seagull that had landed on a pylon and was screaming, its head thrust forward, an open maw. "*'Gussie Willard, you're entitled!'* Lawrence said as he led me to the enormous chestnut tree. Do you remember it, in the old graveyard off Bittersweet Lane? It was neglected even then, the gravestones all enmossed and pitted, leaning every which way. I did not consider it a morbid place to spend my birthday. On the contrary, it promised quiet and beauty, hope. An opportunity for a lesson on gravestone rubbing. Or, given neither of us had brought pencil and paper, on remembering the dead. We sat down under the chestnut tree. Lawrence allowed me a puff of his cigarette. I told him entitlement need not be a bad thing. It's what you do with it."

Bridge of Sighs
1926

"Of course I'm entitled," Gussie said as she leaned her head back against the tree, dizzy with the smoke and their delightful discussion of the travels they would take now the Great War was over. The cathedrals of France, what was left of them; the Forum in Rome; the canals of Venice; the Ponte dei Sospiri. "Does that make me a bad person?"

"No, a lazy one." Lawrence looked at her with a vague smile. "You act as if life owes you. You've such grand expectations, Gussie. Your situation allows you opportunities most of us can only dream of, but it holds responsibilities, too. It requires sacrifice."

"Exactly," Gussie replied, ruffled by Lawrence's reprimand. His professorial air made her feel inadequate when, in fact, she was as good as he was, if more ignorant. But that was why he was there. To teach her. "I have to deserve all I've been given. It's a moral imperative. And I am not lazy, Lawrence. I've done everything my parents wanted me to. I even took lessons from a silly tutor nearly twice my age, and far more attractive than they've any idea about." She tossed a chestnut hull at him, keeping the nut for herself. She rubbed her thumb against its red-brown smoothness. "Why not a trip to Europe with said tutor as instructor and guide? I deserve it."

Lawrence picked up the yellowish-tan hull, pricked his finger with its burry exterior.

"Sweet dreams, Gussie. If you hold too tight, expect too much, that's how they are destroyed."

"Don't be melodramatic. Besides, it's the other way around. If you don't hold tight enough, you lose everything."

"Your parents will never agree."

Gussie was quiet for a moment, balanced between respect for her parents—their umbrage at other people's poverty and lack of lineage—and her love for Lawrence. She prayed that, if and when the balance tipped, she would make the right choice.

"You're as stubborn as they are with your assumptions." She plucked an imaginary leaf from his forearm so she might feel his warmth. "They wouldn't mind half so much if you'd accept some sort of dowry."

"Never, and it's you who wouldn't mind half so much."

"It would make everything much easier."

"It's not about ease, is it? If something is worth having, you need to work and—"

"Sacrifice," Gussie said, finishing his sentence. She threw the nut to the ground. "Why purposely give up what's been given to me through God's grace and Father's hard work? If I use the money well, why is it evil?"

"Gussie, you're getting ahead of yourself. A chaperoned trip to Europe would be challenge enough for your parents. Save marriage for when you're of age and free to choose for yourself."

"I'll ask them about the trip tonight."

"Like you asked them if it would be okay to take this walk?" Lawrence teased.

"All right." Gussie took the cigarette from him and put it between her lips. She sucked smoke into her mouth, holding it for a moment before inhaling it into her lungs and then letting it out slowly, making smoke rings.

"I won't ask. I'll tell."

"Don't, Gussie," Lawrence said, abruptly sitting up and taking her hand. "Please. They'll suspect something, and prevent us from seeing each other."

"Nonsense. We live in the same village. Just on opposite sides of the tracks. Though as my mother's Cousin Lucinda used to say, here there is no wrong side of the tracks."

"Let's leave travels for the future. Now is the time for you to apply to college. Educate yourself. Learn to think."

Gussie removed her hand from his, peevish because he always did that, said something that left her feeling not quite right.

"I'm not so silly as you suggest, Lawrence."

"I don't think you're silly at all. It's just that you act so surprised when things don't go the way you want them to go. It's because you don't think of the consequences, only of the ideals."

"I thought that's what you wanted. Aren't I your will-o'-the-wisp, a devilish dream you will catch against all odds?" Gussie tried to smile, but, instead, her chin trembled. "You frighten me, Lawrence. I'm not sure what you want me to be."

"Yourself, of course. You've a good mind. Use it. Think."

"I do think, Lawrence, very hard and very deeply. My favorite thing to do is to sit and think. I have thought long and hard about this. I intend to talk to them about the trip tonight so that tomorrow we can start to plan the itinerary. Now that is decided, educate me," Gussie demanded with a toss of her chin. "Tell me about this tree."

Lawrence stared at her for a moment, his eyes traveling, like touch, across the lazy lid of her right eye, the smooth fullness of her face, unmarked by worry and flushed with a confidence of strength that she sensed he didn't think was there.

"Genus *Castanea.*" She watched the words being formed on his lips, reading them so she might never forget. She intended to understand everything he told her.

"Latin for sweet chestnuts. There are eight or nine different species within the genus. This one is a *Castanea dentata.* An American chestnut. Symbol of abundance, fertility, and love." Lawrence's tone of voice caused her to blush. "It's doomed."

Gussie blinked.

"Excuse me?"

15

"The chestnut blight." Lawrence stood up. "You've heard about it. *Endothia parasitica*. The fungus killing the American chestnuts. Soon they'll all be gone."

"But not this tree." Gussie rolled up onto her knees and turned around to touch the deep ridges of the gray-brown bark.

"Look here. And there." Lawrence pointed at the orange-fuzzed sores and cankers on the tree. "Sad. It's a relatively young tree."

"But how awful. No more conkers."

"Conkers come from horse-chestnut trees, Gussie. An entirely different genus and species. *Aesculus hippocastanum*. Unlike these chestnuts, horse-chestnuts, or conkers, are poisonous to eat, though they've medicinal capacities."

"Well, I guess we'll just avoid those, and eat the sweets while we can." Gussie put a chestnut in her pocket, and another. She began to collect the nuts on the ground around them. "How do you know so much?"

"I read a good deal, and have excellent retention."

"Weren't we talking about dreams?"

"Ah, dreams," Lawrence said and squatted down to be at her level, near her as her hands nimbly picked up the choicest nuts. "Picking up chestnuts from the ground means you have the ability to make your lover think that life without you would be unbearable." Gussie paused for a moment, then smiled, and, rather more self-consciously, continued her collecting. "Sweet chestnuts signify love. Horse-chestnuts signify money and healing."

Gussie sat back on her heels and looked at him, her hair falling out of its bun, framing her face with an auburn halo flecked with red-gold.

"And if I dreamed of sitting under a chestnut tree?" she asked. "What would that signify?"

"Good times are on the horizon."

Gussie laughed. "So then, I will dream of today, tonight. Isn't it lovely? Life has such potential."

"Potential is all very well," Lawrence said. "It's what you do with it."

"Exactly. I am going to do great things." Gussie looked around them, at the moldering gravestones. Mary Edith Talcott, age 4, buried next to Henry Wood Palmer, beloved husband of Mabel White Palmer. The entire Woolenworth family held down by a five-by-seven-foot boulder but *Alive for Eternity with the Lord, Our Savior.* Gussie trembled, her heart fluttering at the idea of mortality. To think that she would be old and die someday, and what would be left? Kneeling before him, she looked to Lawrence. "Mother says I shouldn't be so excitable, that women don't change the world, men do. When I mention great women, she informs me that I'm not Joan of Arc. But I might be. I have hidden talents. I feel them bubbling inside me. These dead, forgotten people here? I'm different from them. It will matter that I existed because one day, I am going to discover something terribly important. It will change the world."

Lawrence studied the bark of the tree. Gussie preferred it when he studied her.

"I sound exceedingly self-centered, don't I?" she asked, wanting him to contradict her, or at least help her to be better. "I don't want to be overly proud, Lawrence. I know I've loads of room for improvement. And there's so much out there. So much to do. It's quite overwhelming. And do you know? When I hear other girls say how wonderfully perfect they are, I feel quite helpless. I can just picture them in their limited worlds, knowing limited people. I could sob. I am so afraid I'm just as little."

"You have only to listen to your heart, and act."

Gussie looked away, flummoxed, because if she allowed herself to listen to her heart, she knew exactly what she would do, which was entirely the wrong thing.

"Gussie!" Lawrence and Gussie, startled, looked over to the road. Her mother was waving to them, standing next to their new Ford Model T sedan. Her father glared from the driver's seat. "What in heaven's name are you doing? Come here."

"I'll tell them tonight. I swear it." Gussie blinked rapidly to be rid of the tears that had gathered. She waved to her parents as she walked towards them. "We've been on a constitutional, Mother. I needed to rest."

"We wondered where you'd gone off to," Mrs. Willard said as Gussie approached. Together, they waited for Lawrence to join them, returning his jacket to its rightful place: on. "It's well past the hour, Mr. Finer. I trust we won't be billed for the extra time? Get in the car, Gussie. Mr. Finer? We will see you tomorrow as usual."

Lawrence shut Mrs. Willard's door for her. They all nodded to him. Mr. Willard depressed the left floor pedal. The car lurched forward.

"We were discussing geography," Gussie said from the backseat. "I was saying how much it would help to physically go to the places. A kind of mnemonics."

"Fascinating." Mr. Willard's left foot let up from the pedal as he pushed the floor lever on his right forward. The car roared into second speed.

"To travel," Gussie said. "See the world. Lawrence was telling me—"

"Are you referring to Mr. Finer?" Mrs. Willard asked, looking back over her shoulder.

"Yes. Of course. Mr. Finer was describing the Trevi Fountain."

"Has he been there?"

"Why, no. I don't believe he has. But he reads a great deal and has a wonderful memory. Which isn't the point, Mother. The point is, I have to see the world if I am to save it."

"I think it is an excellent idea, Gussie," her father said. Her mother looked at him, her eyes wide.

"You do?" Gussie said.

"Of course," her mother agreed, looking forward as they approached their house, a Colonial Revival, built in the year 1902 by the Willards. It had been a bracing time in their marriage, before the children, when Mrs. Willard, fifteen years junior to her husband, had opined too much on women's rights and architecture.

It was a period that she blushed to remember, though Mr. Willard enjoyed ribbing her about it on occasion. "It will expand your horizons. You'll meet people, see places, be seen. To make your way in the world, you must be known."

"Yes," Gussie said, relieved but vaguely disappointed that there had not been more of a *contretemps*.

During the next day's discussion of the itinerary, Lawrence added his comments and suggestions. As always, he was withdrawn and respectful in her parents' presence. Gussie missed that he wasn't sitting, as he usually did, in the seat next to her; unwittingly, her parents had sat on either side of her, leaving Lawrence to stand at the opposite side of the table, reading the maps and the travel books upside down.

"I do not know what we will do without you, Mr. Willard," Mrs. Willard said to her husband, who disliked travel more than the idea of being without his family; he would endure a bachelor's existence. "I hear the roads are treacherous."

"You'll travel by train for the most part," Mr. Willard assured her. "They've reasonable schedules and accommodations. Not American, of course. But you'll be in Europe. There will be sacrifices."

"Mr. Finer will be there to drive us, Mother," Gussie reminded her as she collected her notes, preparing to write them more clearly.

"We are letting Mr. Finer go, Gussie," Mrs. Willard said. Gussie tossed Lawrence a triumphant glance. His expression—somber, deathly pale—corrected her. Her mother was using *to let go* as a euphemism. "We won't need Mr. Finer's assistance. We will be with our own there. The Glenns. The Fitzwilliams. They will help us on our way. Of course, I will write a recommendation, Mr. Finer, before I leave. You have been quite patient with Gussie."

Stupid, stupid Gussie, Gussie berated herself as she watched him bow, thanking her parents for their generosity. He excused himself, saying he was late for his next lesson, which Gussie knew was not true, and how dare he leave her like that, alone!

They were never alone again. He was not able to advise or help her. Gussie tried to back out of the trip, pointing out the expense and the stress on her dear mother, the loneliness of her poor father, but her parents pushed her forward, called her a will-o'-the-wisp, disliking the way she shifted and changed with the wind. They had made the decision together, and at her instigation, hadn't they? She must stick to it.

Thus Lawrence was *let go* a few weeks before the trip began. His absence gave Gussie plenty of time to shop, to pack, to rue the day she had ever heard of Europe. Under her mother's watchful eye, she sat on the sun-bleached log that had washed up on the beach and stared out to Fisher's Sound, the Atlantic, the future. After all, this was a determining moment in her life. Whatever she decided would be what she would be: the impoverished wife of a tutor or a sophisticated world traveler and heiress. There was no question. She would come back educated, more of an equal to Lawrence. Because the fact was, sometimes she did not feel in control of her own life with him. She needed Lawrence so desperately. Maybe it was safer to leave. To grow up and be her own woman. By the time she returned, he would have made sufficient money to support them. Thus she convinced herself that leaving him was the right thing to do.

Passing

As an enormous, blue-gray, amoeba-shaped cloud ate the sun, Gussie dozed on the bench. Emma sat next to her, comforted by the view's familiarity and her grandmother's presence. For a moment. Because how be comforted by a view of the past that had such power over the future? How gain succor from a woman whose life appeared to have unfolded as a series of "should-dos," when that was how Emma felt her own life evolving? Emma did not know. The only thing she knew for certain was that for months—years—she had felt like one of those child's puzzles in which all the pieces, no matter how you put them, fit, forming amorphous shapes that can be round and whole or reaching out, stretching to the distance but without enough pieces to come back around and join up with the beginning.

The beginning was so far away. When someone else had taken care of what needed to be taken care of. No worries other than the hope for a bedtime story read by her father unfulfilled. The comfort of her mother's arms around her, tsking that there was nothing to be afraid of, she was there. There, there. Working. Never here. Emma had learned to comfort herself by seeking security from place rather than people. All she wanted was home. A forever home.

Emma looked across the harbor at the house. Once upon a time it had been her forever home. Now? A magnetic repulsion. She pushed it away even as she grasped for it. To reject. To cling. Which action would hold off the rising panic that made it so uncomfortable to sit still? She lifted up her legs onto the bench and hugged her knees. By shrinking physically, she hoped to shrink her breathless discomfort, the growing suspicion that by selling the house and leaving Conner she was doing what her grandmother had done: rejecting what maybe she needed.

Proven the night before.

Conner and she had been reading the newspapers and paying bills at the dining room table. They lived in the house that they had renovated together, the fifth house that Conner had owned in his eleven years living in the same district. The neighbors prided him for having single-handedly "brought up" their neighborhood by buying a house, renovating it, then selling it for enough to buy another house and pay himself a modest salary. To their horror, however, the new assessments were pushing their own homes out of their price range, which had caused Conner to switch his contractor's cap for one of advocacy for the downtrodden. What sense did it make, he asked, penalizing people for maintaining their property? Tax the rich with their two and three houses, not the poor and middle class. Emma had agreed with him because it was true, and because she preferred flour to plaster dust; if they weren't renovating the house, she was free to put down her Stanley Wonder Bar and take on more hours at the bakery where she had just started working.

"Who's Thea?" Conner asked. Emma blinked. A rush of adrenaline. The world in slow motion.

"A friend. Why?"

"She called on the home phone. You must have left your call forwarding on. She said she needs the answer to the question, and that she'll call back if she doesn't hear from you."

"Thanks for the message." Emma sat up, teary-eyed. "That's what I love about you, your messages."

Conner rolled his eyes and then asked, "What's the question?"

". . . Thea's going to start a studio. Wonders if I'll help."

"What kind of studio?"

"Probably yoga. Gymnastics. A little dance. She remembered

I have business experience, and I'm athletic." Emma shrugged. "It might be fun."

Conner studied her as if debating whether to pursue that line of questioning. Instead, he returned his attention to the paper. "There's an RV in Lincoln. Do you want to go look at it tomorrow?"

"Excuse me?"

"If we're going to travel for a year or two, we need a vehicle."

"No."

"What do you mean 'no'? You were totally into the idea last November. You dragged us all over creation looking at RVs."

"That's me. Give me a goal, and I'll get it done," Emma said, because it was true. The problem being that the goal was sometimes counter to what she wanted. She always forgot to include that in the process, with the consequence being reactions like Conner's: confusion. Maybe even irritation.

"You wanted to do this, Emma."

"No. You did." Emma girded herself, defensive, because she might have given him the impression . . . When she had come home from Thanksgiving with her family the previous November, the idea of a home on wheels had held an appeal. They would be home no matter where they traveled. Too, if he insisted on selling their newly renovated home, then the movement of the RV would match the anxious pitch of her heart. She'd needed the change over and done with, and so had pursued it with fierce determination. Obsessed, she had spent hours looking up possibilities in the papers, online. He'd had to remind her of their budget: RVs without all the gewgaws. She'd found a good match, but they'd arrived too late: another buyer had shown up, cash down.

Rich people, Emma had cursed. They could have everything they want.

All at the distance of November. Half a year ago. Anything could happen in that amount of time. A person could find her forever home in that amount of time.

"Diesel fumes make me nauseous and generators are too noisy.

Besides, I can't afford to travel." Emma reached for a pencil, relieved by the excuse. If a person didn't have the money, there was no choice.

Conner's chair squeaked as he leaned back and peered at her from beneath his bushy brows. The first time she had seen him, at a wedding of a mutual friend, she had thought he was a troll king. A tank of a man, intimidating, silent, and drop-dead attractive in his tuxedo, though she found him more approachable in his work clothes. She wished they could go back to when he hadn't known her. She had not felt so threatened, at risk of exposure every moment.

"Where does your money go?" he asked. "You work like a dog but you're always broke."

"School loans."

"Seems crazy to have spent that much on horticulture school and then not use the degree." Emma didn't deign to respond. "Do you not remember that we decided last November that it would be fun to take some time, after we sell this house, to drive across the country? A week before Thanksgiving. You agreed. You took the ball and ran with it. You dug up your garden beds, rolled out a new lawn. Better curb appeal, you said. The house would sell faster."

Emma slouched. Of course she remembered. Only she had tried to forget.

"Why not keep this place?" she asked. Conner frowned at this next apparent hiccup.

"It's a rat warren, Emma. That's what you called it the first time you walked in. You said it made you claustrophobic. It's a huge colonial sieve."

"We insulated it. It's comfortable now. The colors are soothing."

He opened the newspaper to the foreclosures section, making it clear to Emma that he wasn't in a negotiating mood. "This neighborhood is getting too expensive."

"You mean safe?" Emma snapped. "Do you miss the bullets flying past your ears?" He didn't respond. Emma noted how difficult it was to maintain a steady breathing pattern. "I don't want to sell it, Conner. I've gotten attached to this place."

"Just because you want something doesn't make you entitled to it. Renovating and selling houses is how I make money."

"I thought it was different this time because I was helping you. I thought maybe we'd be able to settle in for a while. Why else would I have tolerated all that plaster dust and paint?" He didn't respond, and a falling sensation came over Emma. "My opinion doesn't count? I don't matter?"

"I don't do settled, Emma. You know that. Settled makes me crazy."

"You're always saying how great it would be to come home to a clean house and a cooked dinner."

"Who's going to cook and clean? You? You're home even less than I am."

Tears welled in her eyes. His words brought into reality what until now had been only a background distraction, something that maintained the ripples in her life, like the waves rolling up on the beach she had used to play in as a child, jumping up and down to keep her waist well above the water. Those waves had apparently been tidal. They had pulled her in, deeper and deeper, and now she was in over her head.

"I'll buy you out," she announced. His look of bafflement melted into a bemused smile.

"You just said you don't have money."

Emma slapped the table with her palm, resentful and frustrated because it was not fair. All her money was tied up in the family house, which still hadn't sold.

"Even if you did have money," he said, "I can't afford to give you a deal."

"I don't want a deal. I'll be able to pay whatever you want. Just don't sell it out from under me. I only need a little more time."

Though maybe she needed more than a little. Who could say? What was supposed to have happened—the immediate sale of the family house to a rich family with four or five children who would enjoy the property as her family had before them and let her visit on occasion—had not. The family had failed to materialize. Worse, no one had even looked at her family home. According to the real estate agent, it was the season. No one buys houses at Christmas time. Nor, apparently, in January, February, or March. Emma had initially priced it at twice the assessed value. (The house and property were unique. To sell it for less was laughable. Stupid. A waste of her inheritance.) After the New Year, her real estate agent had suggested they lower the price from astronomical to reasonable. And still nothing.

"What's time going to get you, Emma? A lottery ticket? What's so special about this house all of a sudden?"

"Quiet and calm," she said, her voice raised, as if louder would have an impact on what felt inevitable. "A sunny breakfast nook. Cozy couches in front of the fireplace."

"We only have one couch."

Emma stared at him, taking a moment to think, to realize that she was not describing their Providence house but the house that had been her grandmother's. She had never noted the likeness before. Both were Sears Catalog houses. Similar layouts. And the paint colors. Emma had chosen the same colors that her grandmother had chosen so many years ago. The main difference was the view, not of the ocean but the backyards of neighbors, and the sounds, not seagulls and foghorns but sirens, traffic, and garbage trucks. "If I stay here, I'll be able to focus on what I need to be doing."

"What's that?"

Emma stared at him, stymied.

"I don't know. That's what I have to figure out. What I'm doing with my life." Emma reached for her datebook, stared at it. Nothing had changed. She'd had four months to "figure herself out." Four months of constant motion. Denial. Avoidance of Thea's offer. Emma's outrage at Thanksgiving had died back down to helplessness and resignation. She had no control over her own life. She was the same as ever, and why did nothing change? The ship's clock chimed. "Look at all the to-dos I haven't done. All those papers that still need filing. I need to slow down, Conner, not drive across the country. I'll never accomplish anything if I don't sit still."

Conner studied her. She wasn't sure she wanted to hear his response. In fact, she knew she didn't. He reached for her hand as if that would soften his words.

"Everything you do keeps you from sitting still, Emma. What are you avoiding? You were excited about the RV trip. You said the distance would give you perspective on your life, remember? It would help you to see what you were missing. The fact is, Emma, you keep distracting yourself wherever you are, and then . . . it's as if you expect success to come to you. You have to stick to something and work at it if you're going to succeed."

"Don't be sanctimonious." Emma stood up and went over to the counter to deadhead her geraniums. "I know what hard work is."

"I know you do. You trained for a marathon and then stopped fifty feet from the finish line because someone was about to pass you. As soon as anything gets challenging, you give up, and then wonder why you feel like a failure. It's as if some terrible flaw is going to appear. If you'd only think what—"

"I do think." Emma tossed the floral flakes into the compost bin. The inflection of her voice sounded to her just like her Aunt Livy. She wished she could go back to Livy's house and have tea with her and chat. Was that too much to ask?

"Mumpsimus," Conner said. "It's a good word, isn't it? *Some be too styff in their old Mumpsimus, others be too busy and curious in their newe Sumpsimus.* Henry the Eighth's Christmas speech."

Emma glared over at him.

"I don't know what it means," she said.

"An erroneous notion clung to."

Emma scoffed. "Where do you pick up this stuff?"

"I read a lot and have excellent retention. Emma, you have a way of looking at things and won't change them. As if change will kill you. You create a world, full of rules, then live there, trapped."

"You should talk. You've rules, too."

"But I make them consciously. I know I'm hyperkinetic and that I have to use up my excess energy or I'll go a little bit crazy. I need to keep things just so because it's the way I get through a day. I like things to happen the way they are supposed to happen. If they don't, I'll have a bad day and I don't like having bad days. Like that cabinet over there. The door is lopsided. I've been staring at it all night, thinking I'm going to have to fix it before I go to bed. Which means I'll be up—"

"I know how you are," Emma snapped. From their first conversation, she had known. He presented facts, step by step, with absolute confidence and an almost childlike naïveté. He held no nuances. Mathematical to a fault, he looked at a situation and took it for its face value. Just so, he was who and what he was. Honest. Hardworking. Exacting. Endearing. By the end of their second date, she couldn't imagine not having him to guide her. "My point is, you're as unwilling to change. You won't even consider staying still."

He looked at her with his direct stare, his blue-gray eyes taking her in, assessing her words and whether they lined up with the facts.

"You're right, Emma. We both do the same thing, over and over. The difference is that you're surprised that you get the same result."

"You're the surprised one." Emma flushed to tears. "I'm the same as when we met. I haven't changed."

After a pause long enough to suggest that he thought otherwise, or that maybe change would be a good thing, he said, "It's as if you're on an elevator that goes only from the tenth floor to the penthouse, never below. You never slow down, go deep. I hardly know you."

"You aren't alone," Emma said. She returned her attention to the checkbook. She added six and five and carried the one. "Someone left a box of hissing cockroaches on the sidewalk. Upside down. We're going to be invaded."

"They aren't hardy," Conner said.

"What is that supposed to mean?" Emma asked, insulted by his insinuation that she couldn't deal with life's challenges.

28

"Hissing cockroaches are from Madagascar," Conner said. "They don't survive cold."

"If they come into the house, they won't be cold. Wingless, three-inch monsters." He didn't respond, leaving her uncertain of what to say. Her heart fluttered. His silence suggested rejection. What if selling the house were his way of saying good-bye? "Well, as Gram once said, the best families have cockroaches." Still no response. Panic warmed her chest. She looked around the kitchen. What would she do without Conner to help her wash the dishes and clean the house when she was overwhelmed by clutter? And at night? All by herself? She would have to stay indoors once the sun set. The problem being, where would indoors be without the house?

The phone rang. Conner got up from the table.

"I suppose cockroaches are better than Monitor lizards," Emma said to his back.

"Monitor lizards eat cockroaches," he replied.

"I'm not home," Emma said as he answered the phone.

"Emma isn't home," he said in response to the caller's inquiry. A pause. "This is her fiancé." Emma relaxed. He still thought of himself as attached. He even admitted their engagement to a stranger. He nodded. Looked at Emma. Frowned. Turned his back.

"Okay. I'll tell her. Her house is being shown tomorrow."

Emma knocked over her chair running to grab the phone from him. She took the rest of the call from her real estate agent, trying to ignore Conner standing next to her, as the agent told her a woman had looked at the house for her boyfriend, who wanted to see it. If the land passed inspection, he would make a cash offer with no contingencies, and wouldn't it be nice to have so much money? The lurch of reality. A sense of doom. Emma hung up the phone.

"What house?" Conner's voice was clipped. Emma's vision tunneled. Her self seemed to pitch forward.

". . . Gram's house. Mine. Across from Poquatuck Village. The taxes are killer. That's why I'm always broke."

Conner stared at her. She wondered why he didn't say anything, and why she had said so much, though she knew. Why not tell all? The subterfuge was over.

"And you're selling the house," he finally said. "Which is how you'd have money to buy this one."

"If it sells. The guy tomorrow is the first person to look at it and it's been on the market for ages. I can't believe that no one has snapped it up." Emma hesitated because her disbelief at that moment was more that someone might buy it, and then what? "Waterfront property doesn't come up very often anymore. I radically lowered the price a couple of months ago. You know what they say: there are houses for sale and people who want to sell houses? I didn't want to sell before. I was asking for twice the assessed value."

"Which is?" Conner interrupted. Emma couldn't bring herself to tell him exactly.

"Over a million. Maybe two. So, I'll be rich if this guy buys it. I'll be able to buy this place." Emma tried to laugh, make light of her words. Judging by his expression, Conner wasn't amused. She changed tactics. "I didn't tell you I owned it because men find it threatening to be with women who have money. Or you might have stayed with me just for my money. I'm one of those people you hate because they have money they didn't earn. You wouldn't have given me a second look."

"The only reason I've ever said anything about money is because you go on socialist rants about greed and immorality. I don't care how much money a person has. I accept people as they are."

"And how am I?"

"Apparently, I've no idea."

To fill the void created when he pulled back, his face expressing doubt rather than trust—hurt, not confidence and acceptance—she said in an unconvincing voice, "We could always move there after we sell this place. People would kill to own that house."

"People don't kill for houses."

"Some do."

"Most don't."

"Whatever. A lot of people would like to have my luck. They wouldn't have to work. They could enjoy life, instead of it being a chore."

"Do you enjoy life, Emma? It seems as if life is a chore for you." Emma held her breath because he was right, and what she needed was the reassurance of his arms around her, for him to help her. Instead, his tone of voice kept her at a distance. "You race around free, scheduling your time down to the last minute, and don't allow for any breaks, as if by doing all the time you'll somehow justify your existence. You take a Renaissance art class but get irritated by all the Christs and Marys, then sign up for a family tree course that you don't bother to attend. And your garden. It was going to save the world until you dug it up last November without a second thought. Nothing seems to matter to you. You get no satisfaction out of anything, Emma. That's not a life most people would kill for. Why did you lie to me? I can't believe you didn't tell me about a house."

At which point Emma left him. She went upstairs to bed, where she lay much like a snake, coiling tighter and tighter because she felt threatened. Her skin prickled. Shamed, she listened to Conner washing the dishes, fixing the cabinet door. A deathly silence suggested to her that he was looking at the things that she had brought into their lives, claiming to have picked them up for a song at yard sales: her grandmother's French Provençal sideboard and Ming Dynasty fire screen; Livy's thumbnail-sized ivory elephant; her grandfather's Georgian oak desk with drawers, full of seashells, that she opened on occasion just to smell her past. A past of privilege that Conner despised because he believed it was better to live in virtuous poverty than in undeserved wealth.

Or was it her who believed that?

How dare believe anything else? Wasn't that why she kept busy, never sitting still? To somehow earn what she had? Incessant movement had become her way of life because to be still suggested laziness. And failure. And just below failure, at the core of her, shame. Conner was right. She was avoiding something with all her busyness and distraction. She had to avoid the fact that, with all the opportunities her privilege afforded her, she had never accomplished what she had set out to do. She had worked so hard as a girl to be good enough, only to find out that she wasn't. The mortification of that failure created a fear of failing again, and a sense of having no ability to overcome that fear. She was left only with what had been given to her, and a hope that self-flagellation and relentless activity might mitigate the risk that came with her good fortune: that of losing it. Because without it, what was left?

The rustling of papers. The sliding open of file cabinets. Conner was doing the filing she had avoided for months. Emma sat up in bed wide-eyed—not with gratitude, but rage. Resentment of his organization and calm counterbalanced the mortification of her incapacities and hypocrisy. Exposed, she rejected. Another self-preservation tactic: better to attack than to explore the raw fear of needing. She needed Conner, which meant, according to her circuitous logic, that he would leave her. Unless she left him first.

She decided she would return to the family home. For the same reason she always had: to hide there. Protected. In the way prisoners are protected in their cells. And, like a prisoner, terrified of what life would be if she were freed.

When Conner got into bed, they lay silent, back to back, until Emma couldn't bear it anymore. She turned around.

"Do you not want to sell this place?" she asked. He didn't respond. "If you want to stay, it's fine with me. It's not too late to keep it."

"We're moving on, Emma. Just like you said you wanted to when we discussed this months ago."

A hot flush of horror overwhelmed Emma.

"You would have stayed? If I had said I wanted to stay? Is it my fault?"

"Yes, it is your fault," he snapped. She cringed, having hoped for a denial and words of comfort. Instead? "You keep changing the rules. As if you have no clue that others might count on you, or be affected. I don't like surprises, Emma. I invested all my resources in this house and in our relationship. When I brought up the idea of selling this place, your only response was to say you were going to your family's for Thanksgiving, and then you ripped up the garden. I figured you didn't care. Not about this place. Maybe not about me. And then you started on the RV. We spent weeks researching possible road trips in a goddamned RV, the idea of which is anathema to me. Surprises around every corner, but that's what you wanted. I've thrown everything up in the air for you, and now I find out you have some mansion, not an hour's drive from here, that I know nothing about. You've taken no risks, invested nothing. Everything I thought you were, I'm not sure of anymore. I can't trust you. I have to get up early in the morning, even if you don't. Good night."

A deadening silence fell on the room. Both curled themselves into self-contained balls. He didn't trust her? She couldn't blame him. She didn't trust herself, the despicable she who had deceived him. Though he was wrong about one thing. She had risked with him. She had risked by daring, one last time, to commit to another person, to trust him with her self. She had been whatever he wanted her to be. She had spent months sledgehammering, lugging sheetrock, plastering, and painting. Working for his approval. Wanting what he wanted—which, it turned out, was what she wanted. The problem being, she hadn't known that. And now? It was over, and what was life but a long, frightening stretch of nothing?

As she lay there next to Conner, she sought safety. Past fantasies, people, places. Anything that might comfort her until she fell asleep. She dreamed she was going to her grandmother's. To the house. She ran down circuitous paths. Familiar, yet alien. Everything overgrown. The vines catching her clothes, chasing her, encircling her. She had to get to the house. But when at last she did, it was locked. Dark and empty. She had returned too late and it began to rain. Her arms became tree limbs, her legs its trunk and roots.

Emma woke in a sweat. Conner snored gently, his eyes moving rapidly under their lids. She forced herself up. An old habit. Action and activity to avoid . . . discomfort. Pulling her suitcase out from under the bed, she removed a pink binder, which she left on the kitchen table for Conner to find. She ran out of the house and down to the train station, where she caught the next south bound train.

Thus, Conner's discovery of Emma's deception had precipitated her homecoming. Though this homecoming was different. This time, she knew her return was not the answer. Something had to change, because Conner was right about another thing: people wouldn't kill for her life. Though they might die of it.

On the dock, with her grandmother's head resting on her shoulder, Emma thought how all that had happened across the harbor had been remembered, denied, or forgotten, and thus had been passed down through the generations. Would it be possible to sift through the past and find its meaning—perhaps a means, however subtle, to change? At which thought the amoeba-shaped cloud consumed the sun entirely and Emma's temporary contentment warped into panic, because changing would mean letting go. She would lose everything. Not least her relationship with her grandmother, who would never forgive the betrayal of a sale.

A phone rang. An old-fashioned ring. The kind that rang in houses before answering machines and cell phones, computers and the Web.

"Hello?" Gussie startled awake, looking about her, wide-eyed and confused. "Hello?"

"It's my cell phone, Gram," Emma said, looking at the caller ID. Conner Sheffield. Emma wondered if he were calling to say goodbye or to ask her to come back. She wanted to go back.

"Your beau?" Gussie asked. She adjusted herself, patted her purse to be sure it was there. Emma nodded, pressing the ignore button.

"It's confusing, Gram," Emma said, overwhelmed by the breathless conviction that he wouldn't call again. "Sometimes I think I don't need him. He can be so in the way, stepping on my feet, eating all the apple pie without a thought that I might want some, billowing the covers when he gets into bed so I get blasted by cold air." Emma hesitated, realizing she had over-shared. This was her grandmother, after all. One need not flaunt the specifics of *living together*. "The reality is, I don't know how I would function without him, and now I'm going to have to because he's dumping me and I resent the hell out of him because what right does he have to have that kind of power over me? It's ridiculous. Because I really don't need him."

"Men are like dogs. They're a sort of company, but when they're gone you have to wonder what all the to-do was about."

Emma glared at her grandmother.

"Livy said you cried for days after your dog Whiskey died. She said you missed him terribly."

A pause. Silence for Emma and Gussie to contemplate the emptiness dogs and men had filled, and then left, in their lives.

"Must you jiggle your legs like that?" Gussie admonished. "You're worse than a pogo stick."

"I'm not comfortable being still."

"It's healthful to sit still for a time."

Emma stopped her movements and lifted her chin. She skirted the outer reaches of the feeling that breathed within her, threatening as a green tornado sky. The relentless pressure to be doing. The breathless discontent with everything she did. It was all an avoidance of her inner chaos, a vortex that pulled her inward. She hadn't the strength to fight anymore, though what her other option was she had not yet figured out. She only knew that if she went to the source of her disease . . . that would be what Conner would challenge her to do if she stayed . . .

She didn't dare. She jumped up and began to pace.

"Do you know why I never told Conner about this place, Gram? I met his family this past February. Conner wanted to introduce me, show me the house he'd grown up in. It's the size of our living room. No art. No books or travel memorabilia. It's all about sports and the price of hamburger with them. His mother hinted that they didn't have money and how a loan would come in handy and apologized, over and over, for the casserole being so small, they hadn't expected so many people. It was just Conner and me. The television was on full blast, and his father was shouting at it as if that would affect the outcome. You should have seen his expression when I said something about a hole in one. He looked . . . just like Conner did last night when he found out about the house. Stunned."

Emma stopped, remembering the awkwardness she had felt when Conner's father had patted the seat next to him and begun to explain the details of the game to her, the skills of this or that player, their names and stats. Conner had watched like a kid hoping his present will be accepted, and Emma hadn't known whether it would be until they were leaving and his father had clasped her hand and leaned over, looking her straight in the eye. He had said, "Don't worry. You're smart. You'll learn the difference between golf and football." And all Emma had wanted, as Conner's mother had slipped the last piece of blueberry pie into her purse, was to stay and learn what she had never learned.

"The weird thing, Gram? I felt comfortable. I could sit around and do nothing, for all they cared, and it would be fine."

"Why would you want to sit around and do nothing? That's a waste of time and education."

Emma glared at her grandmother.

"I thought you said it was healthful to sit still."

"That depends on your intent."

"My point is, I didn't tell him about here because he and I don't share expectations."

Gussie contemplated Emma.

"Are you afraid he won't pass, or that we won't?"

"Oh, he'll pass," Emma said, noting her use of the future tense. She imagined Conner stepping into the house, evaluating the architectural flaws and her cabinetry choice, echoing the comments of her family after the renovations. No one had appreciated what she held out to them, the only thing she felt she had to offer: the house. Would Conner view it as a gift, or a flaw? "I'm the one who won't pass."

Gussie picked at a piece of fluff on her skirt.

"We set very high standards for ourselves in this family, and beat ourselves up when we don't live up to them. You might not be who you want to be, but that doesn't mean you aren't perfectly fine as you are."

"Hard to believe."

"For pity's sake! Where did you get such a negative opinion of yourself? Your privilege should allow you to rise above, Emma. Instead, you hide who you are and where you come from. Just because you've a degree of money."

"It was different in your day, Gram. Then it was a class thing. You were born into money. There it was, no questions asked. Now, no one talks about class. It's all very democratic. You meet people and one of the first questions they ask isn't who are you but what are you. *What do you do?* A friendly, get-to-know-you question that flummoxes me every time. If I say '*Nothing*,' people look at me strangely. I mean, if you don't have a job, earn money, how do you survive? So I lie. I make up stuff that I've done, pretending to have earned what I have. It's humbling. I drift along, spending money I don't deserve and worrying about how I'd survive without it."

"You do wallow in your ideas. Entirely of your own making, and beside the point. Why do you care what other people think?"

Emma studied Gussie. The aged quality. The frailty and vulnerability. She wondered what Conner would think of her. Gracious, with an old-school formality and pride, or repugnant because so untouched by the poverty around her?

"It's a family trait," Emma said. "We pass. The problem is, passing leaves a person alienated. Black or white. Rich or poor. They aren't what they claim to be, but have divorced themselves from what might connect them. Their heritage. Maybe their culture or community. Maybe even their selves. Like Uncle Ed. He was from a different class, always careful not to expose his less-than-upper-snuff upbringing. Alyssa says he didn't care which sister he married. He wanted the imprimatur of the family. I wonder, when he looked in the mirror, who did he see? Who he presented himself to be, or the person behind the deception? Did he dare to admit, even to himself, that maybe he missed where he came from? But how dare give up that mask, because what if the truth doesn't pass? Like I didn't pass with Conner. Everyone wants to be acceptable."

"Ed was perfectly acceptable. As are you. Only you do everything you possibly can to make yourself not acceptable. Last Thanksgiving. What in heaven's name happened that was so terrible?" Gussie demanded. "Why did you leave and not come back?"

Emma looked away.

"I've no control over my own life here, Gram."

"You have more control than you've any idea about. That's what privilege gives you. The money to determine for yourself. Exactly as you said. Most people have to work for a living. You can do what you will. Anything at all."

Emma looked at her fingers, flaked with dried bread dough. Her jeans, clean but for the permanent stains from construction work. What did she will?

"Did you do *anything at all*, Gram?"

Gussie did not respond immediately. Emma contemplated how teary eyes ran in the family. All those unwept tears had to spill out sometime. She rooted out a packet of Kleenex from her knapsack and offered it to her grandmother, whom she had always thought of as . . . her grandmother. Gram, in control and understanding how the world worked and why. An adult who had followed rules and expectations that defined how a person should act, without taking into account the individual. Certainly, Emma had never imagined Gussie as a young woman who had been given choices that didn't feel like choices, and opportunities that felt like curses because the should-dos were so different from the want-tos.

"As you said. It was a different time," Gussie said. "Women got married and had babies. In that order. There was no question. There were rules. If you broke them, the consequences were enormous. It took me a while, but I came to recognize that my parents had a clearer perspective of my life than either Lawrence or I had. I had to get away from him."

"Because they were afraid you'd marry him?"

"Marry him? I would never have married him. His incessant questions would have killed me."

Emma started. "But I thought—"

"So did I at first," Gussie interrupted. "But life was a test with him. I was supposed to know the answers, or, at least, think about them. I didn't fit his mold. He used to criticize, in a very quiet way. He would tell me how to be and how not to be. I felt uncomfortable with him. I realized I needed to know myself before getting involved with someone who thought he knew best. I would never have been happy with him."

The slight dip in Gussie's voice, the lack of air supporting her words, left Emma with the impression that her grandmother was not convinced. Or was that Emma's imagination? After all, if it were true that Gussie had wanted to leave him . . . Wasn't that how Emma felt with Conner? They were worlds apart, and she wasn't comfortable with the differences because his idea of a vacation was camping out in the middle of nowhere, whereas Emma thought of New York City and plush beds that have mints placed on the pillow each night. Those kinds of preferences expose a person. Emma would have been embarrassed to have Conner know that about her. Though Emma knew it about him. With that thought, Emma had an awful recognition. It was bad enough to feel ashamed of one's expensive tastes and habits, but deeper down and more damning was the feeling of superiority; not a fear of being rejected, but one of rejecting.

"When I returned from Europe, I knew I had nothing to be ashamed of. Lawrence did," Gussie said, articulating what Emma would not have dared to. "At my homecoming party, I met your grandfather. Winston was in top form, dancing with all the girls, dressed to perfection, startlingly powerful and tall. I was hypnotized by his blue eyes. I hardly noticed Lawrence standing there, holding that bouquet of white lilacs. They're symbolic of first love, you know. He had frozen them the previous spring. Romantic thought, isn't it? White flowers glistening with ice, held up as an offering. Unfortunately, they were brown and limp. Not quite the thing. Nor was Lawrence when I introduced him to Winston. He was all wrong. It must have been the traveling. I'd had months and months to think about Lawrence, until he wasn't himself anymore. I still respected his intelligence. He was a fount of information, but the reality of him? Shabby, and a tad short. I felt embarrassed by him, and he knew it. When he asked me to dance, there was a look in his eyes, as if he were daring me. And Winston was watching. I refused. I didn't dance with either of them. I preferred having them following me with their eyes, admiring me. I felt in control of the situation. I knew exactly what I was doing."

Gussie abruptly leaned over to pick up . . . maybe it was a granule of sand to rub between her fingers, to feel.

"Sometimes, Emma," she said, sitting back up, "even when you have everything you need, life doesn't give you what you want, no matter how desperately you want it. But you can't live for wishes and dreams. Then you'll only be left with the memory of wanting. Strange, memories. How clearly you can see something and yet, not. Places. People. You don't even know you need them. You assume they will always be there. You can feel them right here in your heart, but then one day you've only got what you had, because they're gone. They died, and you can't change a thing. Lawrence, for instance. Lawrence Finer. He died this morning."

Gussie's voice cracked. Emma's eyes widened, alert, as she touched her grandmother's arm. She debated whether to clarify the fact that Lawrence had died seventeen years before. A heart attack during the blizzard of 1978. His wife, Kitty, had been trapped in their house for two days. Would it make a difference to her grandmother when it had happened?

"It must be awful," Emma said. "To lose a friend."

"A dear friend," Gussie said, blinking rapidly. Her hands lifted slightly, as if to shrug. "Dead. Hard to believe. Poor Kitty. I'll have to tell Kitty."

"Gram, Kitty's dead."

"Oh?" Gussie tilted her head slightly as if listening for something as she looked out before her. The breeze picked up, creating little waves on the water. The flags on the boat flapped and snapped. The halyards clanged and the church bell gonged the half-hour. "Ah, well."

"Sad," Emma said, moving to be closer to her grandmother. "Dad used to say that when he'd talk about some tragedy. Mrs. White's Pekinese dying, jobs lost, homes sold." Emma paused to let those last two words sink in, because they had to get back to the point: the house would be sold. Wouldn't it? "He'd pause, and then say "Sad" and shake his head, so you couldn't tell if it were sad or something to take with a grain of salt, because what's to be said? Catastrophes happen. Life goes on."

"Awful to think, being powerless to stop the catastrophes," Gussie said. She pulled a thread of her dress hem. It unraveled, an inch, two, six inches before Emma put a hand on Gussie's to stop her. "Isn't it fortunate that they don't feel the same?"

"Who?" Emma asked.

"The poor," Gussie said. "They're not so sensitive as we are."

"Gram!" Emma pulled back. Her grandmother had always been 'politically correct.' On the surface, anyway. "You used to be furious when Gramps said things like that. You said it was the biggest sin of all, to be blind to others' pain."

"Did I? Well, I suppose it's protective, raising oneself above. If I had thought for one minute that Lawrence felt as I felt. But I knew he didn't."

"It helps to think so," Emma said. "But it's not very sympathetic."

"Shared expectations is the key. You must marry the person with whom you share expectations. Then you need not worry about acceptability."

". . . So why did you marry Gramps?"

"What?"

"No one could understand why you married him. The two of you were opposites. He was stiff and proper, a staunch Republican, with no intellectual interests, whereas you were . . . more liberal."

Emma narrowed her eyes, thinking about the differences she had always assumed, and wondering if the tension between them had nothing to do with politics or opinions.

"Winston and I had similar upbringings," Gussie said. "New York. Newport. Strict. Both Protestant, of course. Everyone liked Winston. He had quite a sense of humor. I liked him because, with him, there were no questions. Everything was simpler with Winston, safer. He and I were popular, invited to all the right parties, always racing about, never still."

"Conner says I do that. I race around so much, he doesn't know me. I guess I haven't let him know me."

"You young people think too much," Gussie said. "In the old days, we lived. We didn't worry about too much alcohol or food, or too little exercise, or not knowing each other. We just had fun. Good fun, Winston and I. That time Whiskey left all those messages on the stairs."

"Messages?" Emma asked.

"A euphemism we used for accidents. Whiskey was an adorable mutt—short-haired, short-legged, and blond. Such a personality! Even Mother liked him, excepting that he tended to relieve himself indoors. It was the night of our engagement party. Winston was dressed in his tuxedo, I in a tight-fitting, white silk gown. The guests would be arriving at any minute. My parents were busy overseeing the final preparations. Messages everywhere. Winston and I set to our task. I got towels and vinegar and began to clean them up. Winston let out the dog, then helped me. We were a sight, the two of us. I could hardly bend over in that dress. Then Whiskey, small but solid, came barreling back in and knocked me over. I couldn't get up. We were both in stitches."

Emma tried to imagine her grandparents in their youth, carefree and happy, maybe even loving, compared to how she had known them—tense, her grandmother looking grimly resolute whenever her grandfather entered the room.

"I laughed until I cried," Gussie said, staring thoughtfully before her. "The fact is, I chose him. I wanted my own life. If Winston did nothing else, he did give me that. And he built the house." Gussie looked over at Emma. A bright smile. "It arrived in the mail!"

Winston Builds a House
1929

Winston Michaels was engaged to Gussie Willard. They were to be married on May 25, 1929, and he was building their house on weekends, when he wasn't in Providence, where he had begun his new job at the bank. He was a teller, but Gussie knew he would go places, and the pride with which she looked at him gave him confidence that he would succeed. He was determined to, as the house got put together, piece by piece, with the help of the laborers Gussie's father had hired. They worked during the week. Progress was rapid under Winston's weekend guidance. He still found it hard to believe, as he hammered and measured, that such a beautiful, rich woman would be his, particularly given the rumors about her tutor, Lawrence Finer. A scrawny, bookish type. But when she came back from her European trip—extended twice and lasting well over a year—Gussie had met Winston and accepted his attentions, his company, his proposal.

Despite her parents' ambivalence—Winston was not what they had hoped for for their daughter, but who would be?—or perhaps out of relief—Gussie was twenty-two, nearly past the marrying age—her parents had gifted them some of the family land.

Stone walls marked off pastures and property lines, and a wooden gate placed across Bittersweet Lane divided "the farm," owned by "other people," from "the Point," which was owned by the Willards.

The Willard house, where Gussie had grown up, sat just inside the gate, close enough to keep watch, daring those blasted cows to come through and tromp Mrs. Willard's vast flower gardens and specimen bushes, but far enough away to be respectable. Gussie and Winston's house site was a few hundred yards farther in. The house, fully framed but not yet enclosed, stood in the midst of an open field of lowbush blueberries, sea roses, and grasses. A birch copse to the east and giant oak to the west, a view of Fishers Island Sound to the north. The house, called "The Honor" (Sears Catalog number 3071, 1926 model, arriving, *"already cut and fitted,"* in thirty-thousand pieces) was oriented to the south, towards the Willards', but the household activity would be directed toward the back of the house, drawn there by Gussie's wraparound porch. Which was not numbered on any of the thirty thousand pieces surrounding Winston, nor was it detailed in the specs. Winston was sure he had mentioned it on the order form. As he studied the house plans, laid out on the plywood flooring of what would be the kitchen and held down by various sized stones, he saw not one line that might be construed as a porch. He frowned, irritated. How inconvenient of Gussie to want a porch, and not a chair on the lawn.

"Winnie?"

Winston started at the sound of her voice, embarrassed to have been caught thinking so dismissively of her porch. Had she gleaned his disloyalty? He looked over to where she stood on the wide granite stone that was to be the first of the steps to the front entrance. She was hatless and wore black, strapped pumps and a light gray, low-waisted dress, its hemline fashionably uneven and dropped to the knees. The dress was far shorter than Winston thought proper, but Gussie had a stubborn streak. Once they married, of course, he would see her skirts fall and her long auburn hair held back in a loose bun.

Her chin held up, hazel eyes bright with excitement, a white-toothed, irrepressible smile on her face, Gussie held her hands behind her back as if hiding something, laughing, breathless. Most likely she had run, as she always did, most of the way from her parents' house. And what a ridiculous thought! Of course he would build her that porch. With his own hands and whatever it took. Thus he promised himself and her as he walked toward his intended. Almost insecure because the sight of Gussie, so clean, made him conscious of the dirt and sweat on his work clothes: a dingy white undershirt and tan slacks, a tear on the right knee. But, too, he was aware of their mutual admiration, and what a handsome couple they made. She was steady and capable in her way, but next to him—six feet, four inches tall, lean, and muscular—her frailty became apparent. She leaned toward him, appreciating the strength of his arms; his promise of relative independence and freedom; his humor, if not his wit.

They walked together around the house site, assessing the work that had been done, and how so, finally turning to the endless horizon. Rather, she looked out to sea, while he studied the russet gold of her hair, the elegant slope of her nose, her ear. He wanted to whisper in it, to kiss her curved neck, expose the collarbone, the full breasts. She shivered.

"You're cold," he said, only now noticing the chill of the air and her coatlessness. He took a step toward her, to share the heat of his body, then stopped. He dared not touch, for fear of smudging her clothes.

"Oh, bother the chill. Guess what?" She turned to look up at him. He imagined that this would be how she would look when she first announced herself pregnant: excited but shy, hesitant, proud; a warm, happy vessel that it was his duty to protect. "Winnie, I got the letter from Radcliffe."

"Who?" he asked, blinking. Gussie's smile faltered, but not a crease or flaw appeared on her face.

"Radcliffe College. For women. Cambridge, Massachusetts," she added, as if hoping that might tweak a memory. "I've been accepted."

"Accepted for what?" he asked, as patient as she was as he watched her, fascinated by the way her face reflected the light of the day, their love.

"To attend, of course," she said, her cheeks flushing. Their apparent softness, the smooth texture of her skin, overwhelmed him. "Isn't that lovely? Just like Cousin Lucinda."

In response, he embraced her, passionately, and for the first time she let him kiss her full on the lips, she kissing back.

"Winnie," she said, finally pulling away, glancing around them, still held in his arms. "Mummy and Daddy say it's okay, if you do. They'll pay for it, of course."

"Don't be ridiculous," Winston said, dropping his arms. "Absolutely not."

He turned to the house, set his feet apart, his arms crossed. Gussie stood next to him, viewing his profile, hesitating before reaching up to touch the breadth of his shoulders.

"Winnie," she said. "Daddy says if you say yes, he'll pay for it, so it's nothing to do with you not support—" She stopped. "The money is there. It's not about our not having the money."

"Of course it's not." Winston glanced down at her, surprised.

"Oh, good," she said, letting out a deep breath. A laugh. She stepped back and twirled herself around, arms stretching out, sleeves fluttering in the breeze. "I thought, at first, you weren't going to—"

"Wives don't go to school," Winston interrupted, loudly, firmly. Gussie froze, her back to him. Her arms slowly lowered as she turned toward him.

"Why not?" she asked.

"Too busy."

"Doing what?"

"Whatever it is you women do. It's a puzzle." He indicated the stacks of finished lumber. "Thirty thousand pieces, and not one of them for a porch."

And so he broke the ice. They had not spoken of it for weeks, their *words* while choosing the house. They had been sitting at the library table of her parents' living room, the elders in the background overseeing the young couple's negotiations. Gussie had initially picked one of the most expensive plans. The Magnolia. A colonial-style, ten-room house with a sunroom, a den, a porch and terrace, plenty of bedrooms. But there was something about it that Winston didn't like.

"What, Winnie?" Gussie had asked.

"I don't know. A gut feeling. I don't like it."

"You did at first. Remember? You liked it best, and then I agreed."

"Maybe it's too expensive."

"But—"

"No."

And so he rejected The Magnolia, along with Gussie's other suggestion, The San Jose.

"A Spanish bungalow, Gussie? We live in America."

"It is American-made."

"I want it to look American."

They had paged through the catalog. Too small. Too big. Awkward floor plan. Rejecting one, and then another, never in accord. Gussie's parents—the missus at her drop-front desk writing letters, and the mister next to the fireplace, reading the news—leaned more toward Winston's taste than Gussie's.

"What about The Lexington?" Gussie asked.

"Too expensive," Winston said, again trying to keep her in a reasonable price range.

"If you want cheap, why not The Willard?" Gussie snapped.

"Don't be unreasonable, Gussie," her mother said, sharply. "You made your choice."

Gussie looked at her mother, over to her father, who pretended deafness by rustling the page of the *Poquatuck Advertiser*.

"Two bedrooms, Gussie?" Winston whispered. He gently touched her hand, delicate and small, soft as it twisted around to grasp his. She turned to him, her eyes searching his as he explained, reassured his little bride. "We'll need a bigger house than that, won't we? And to have to add on? By that time, I'll have moved up at work, more responsibilities. I won't have the time that I do now."

Gussie nodded and sat back in her chair. Her hand slipped out of his. The catalog slapped shut.

"You're right, Winston. I don't mean to be unreasonable. All I really want is a sunny room to read in, and a porch."

"Then let's go with The Honor," Winston said, returning to his first choice.

"We talked about that one, Winnie," Gussie said, her smile small and tense. "It's even more expensive than—"

"Gussie!" her mother hissed, slapping the desk in exasperation. Gussie startled, paled.

"There's no porch," Gussie said.

"I'll special order it," Winston promised, moving to cut off Gussie's view of her mother. "That's how it works. You can adapt the house to your needs. The porch can go right here, off the living room. See? There's your fireplace, too. To keep you warm in the winter. There will be plenty of firewood. I'll see to that."

She did not look at the proffered floor plan.

"Winston," Gussie said, standing, as if hesitating. "I am sure that will be most appropriate. I need a rest. Please excuse me."

After she left, her parents had joined him at the table. They'd agreed that The Honor would be perfect. A Colonial Revival-style home with a modern touch. Just as it said in the catalog, it would "make a favorable impression" with its "inviting front entrance" and "big, handsome windows and decorative trellis." Winston filled out the order form and, at his future in-laws' insistence, added storm doors and windows. Now here they were, months later, with no porch, and Gussie looking at him with the strangest expression on her face.

"What?" Winston asked, with a gruffness he had not intended.

"I thought you would be amenable to the idea," Gussie said.

"I ordered the porch, Gussie. I know I did. Fortunately, a porch is easy enough to tack on once the house is built."

"You've always agreed education is important. I thought taking a class or two would be interesting." Gussie's voice rose, as if she were trying to be heard from a great distance. "It won't take much time, and you'll be at the apartment in Providence during the week. You'll be at work. You won't even notice."

"But I would know. Everyone would. And I'd worry. You traveling to such a big city."

"That's what I've done these last years, traveling in Europe."

"Not alone."

"But—"

"I'd be ashamed of myself if I let you do it."

Gussie's back stiffened, her chin lifted.

"Ashamed? You wouldn't want me to be ignorant, would you? With nothing to say or think about?"

And the way she said *ignorant*, with an ever-so-slight curl of her lip, of disdain, reminded him of that Lawrence fellow, and her travels, and how, sometimes, she would talk about things he had no idea about. Not that he cared. But he sensed that she did. He had to admit, she made him nervous, staring at him that way. As if he weren't quite what she thought he was, and she would cut him as she had that Missy Grendel on the street the other day, just because she didn't come from the right side of the tracks. Of course, time and children would help.

"You're not ignorant, Gussie," he said, because she wasn't. He had never hidden from her who or what he was: more brawn than brain, preferring sweat, sore muscles, and calluses on his hands to books, pens, and ink. She knew. He was absolute and unchanging. Strong. Physical. And so, abruptly, for reassurance, Winston moved to put his arms around Gussie, to remind her of his merits and capacity. She stepped back, shook her head, shivering.

"But I am, Winston," she said. "Quite ignorant. I've so much to learn. I'll have to make adjustments. Being a wife is different from being a daughter. There are choices to make. Decisions once under one's own roof. Things will be very different, won't they be? Once we're married and have our own lives to lead. But it's chilly. I'm deathly cold. I need to rest."

Gussie turned and ran, occasionally tripping on the uneven ground. A delicate woman, subject to chills and full of silly ideas. School. Spanish Bungalows. Porches. They endeared her to him. Her idiosyncrasies kept him on his toes, and gave him something to think about as he returned to his hammer and measuring tape, building their home, piece by piece, with close attention and care. He wondered how she would decorate it. What they would name their children. And imagined laughing, confessing to her, perhaps after some intimate moment, how he had felt on this day: the recognition of the devastation her scorn would bring, and a happiness so great that it was close to dread.

New York City
1936

Seven years, three children, and one miscarriage into her marriage to Winston, Gussie saw a greeting card in the pharmacy. The image was of a woman sitting in a chair, her chin in her hand, staring out the window. The word *You* was in the upper left corner, and *are* in the middle, and *so* in the lower right corner. Inside: *boring*. Gussie quelled an urge to buy the card and hand it to Winston some evening. She imagined it though. Cocktail hour. They would be in the living room, she in her mother's Victorian mahogany armchair, clutching the card, and he in his Queen Anne wing-back chair, stirring his drink with his pinkie, ranting about those damned Roosevelts. When she could bear it no longer, she would stand, walk over, and hold the card out to him. She would watch him read the note. What would his reaction be? His eyes looking up from the card, blue eyes that lightened and darkened with the day, the night.

Her heart gave way even in fantasy. It wasn't his fault but hers. There was something wrong with her. Certainly she didn't want to offend, only to be free of him. He was, after all, well-intentioned, if entirely oblivious to her inability to breathe fully in his presence. He was so like her parents. Worse, because there was no escape. She had chosen him. And now he had lost his job. Again. It was up to her to support the family with the dwindling inheritance that she had received, along with the furniture, upon the death of her parents. They were gone, leaving her with him, who was not holding up his side of the bargain. What good was he if he didn't do what he had promised to do? Support her. Take care of her. He was to brighten her day, alleviate the tightening of nerves, her yearning for something, she didn't know what. Nothing helped. Not even God seemed to hear her.

Gussie decided to go visit friends in New York City. Plays on Broadway. The Metropolitan Museum. She would stay with her friend Sally Merrill. Together, they would expand Gussie's horizons. An entirely acceptable plan. It was summer. The children could stay home and play on the beach while Winston did whatever it was that he did. She would escape, if briefly, the claustrophobia of her life. The activity and movement would do her good.

Winston thought it was a wonderful idea, a second honeymoon.

"Honeymoon?" Gussie repeated, staring at him, her world lurching again in a direction that she had not intended.

"Obviously I'll come along," Winston said, and he looked at her as if to say he knew it wasn't obvious. Because he must recognize that she wanted to get away. Escape. He wouldn't condone it. "It's not appropriate, a woman traveling alone to New York City. Besides, we've not had much alone time since Alyssa was born."

He stepped toward her. The idea of his touch repulsed her.

"You're right, of course," she said, turning away. "It will be a wonderful experience for them to see Manhattan."

"Them?"

"We can't leave the children, Winston. Alyssa cries when I am in the next room. Imagine if I were all the way in New York City. There would be no peace."

"No, of course not."

She allowed her brow to rise slightly, certain that he now felt quite as disappointed as she in the plan, but just as determined to see it through.

The trip did not begin auspiciously. Winston refused to stay at

Sally Merrill's apartment, and then got lost looking for the hotel. The babysitter never arrived. They had to bring the children to the New Amsterdam Theater after having missed dinner with the Leonards, whom Gussie hadn't had the pleasure of seeing in years. The lights dimmed. No sign of Sally, who had been offended by Winston's refusal to even have tea. Alyssa fidgeted and whined in Gussie's lap until Winston, who had no interest in the play, took her out to the lobby. Sandwiched between Livy and Auggie, Gussie gave her full attention to Cyrano de Bergerac.

Gussie restrained herself until they arrived back at the hotel. Until the children were tucked into bed and the lights were out. Then she broke down, weeping uncontrollably. Winston was beside himself.

"What's wrong, Gussie?" he asked. She could only wave him away. "You give entirely too much merit to such fictions," he admonished, stroking her long hair, smelling it. "They are supposed to be pleasant distractions. What did you expect, dearest?"

"More than you can imagine," she dared to say, and blew her nose with a handkerchief.

"I knew we shouldn't have come," he said.

"You're right," Gussie said, laying her head on her tear-dampened pillow, thinking how different everything would be if she'd been free to come alone. Winston squeezed her shoulder and there was a hint to his touch, a testing to see if she were . . . amenable.

"It's too stimulating for your nerves," he whispered in her ear.

She sat up and away from him, her eyes tearing again.

"On the contrary, I haven't felt this alive in years," she replied, and then she left him. She locked herself in the bathroom, lay down in the white porcelain bathtub. She could control herself there. In the bathtub she could stop the thoughts, her feelings, from overwhelming her.

The next morning, Gussie determined to do exactly what she had intended to do: everything. The family would just have to keep up. Walk miles from the lower to the upper reaches of

Manhattan, ending at Grant's tomb. Gussie wanted to see the transitions of the neighborhoods, the variety of rich and poor, the blood moving, not sterile and trapped. Then the children would go to Central Park.

Cumbersome things, children. Miserable and fretful in the heat. Auggie six, Livy five, and Alyssa one. They made slow progress. Livy insisted on running off, rushing back to tell them what was up ahead, while Auggie informed them that the park had been built on land that had been the home of hundreds of poor people. Free blacks. Irish pig farmers. German gardeners. Gussie wondered where he got his information from, and his questions! For instance, had poor people less rights than the animals in the zoo, and wasn't it interesting that the animals were displaced, too? It seemed silly. Why couldn't they all live together? Gussie didn't answer. She only listened, relieved by his intelligence.

Hot dogs and hot chestnuts for lunch, eaten in the shade of a tree, and then into the cool of the Metropolitan Museum. Gussie stood, frozen in the vast atrium entrance, unable to decide what to see first. So many choices. She wanted to see it all, spend the day. But Livy had to "spend a penny," and then Winston said he would only stay an hour. At which point who should appear but Lawrence Finer. And why not? He lived in the city, taught at New York University, and it was the most natural thing in the world to see him, talk to him, comparing one to the other, self-conscious as she introduced the children. She knew he disliked children until they were of an age to think and reason. It was kind of him to pretend pleasure at Alyssa's chubby cuteness. Granted, she was an exceptionally pretty child.

"It's hard to know where to begin," Gussie said.

"At the beginning, of course," Lawrence said, smiling. "The Greeks and Romans."

Winston, bored by the surroundings and glad for the arrival of an escort, excused himself and took Alyssa to find something to eat.

"If this were an army museum, he would be here for hours,"

Gussie said, embarrassed by her husband's apparent philistinism. It reflected on her, and how to counter the appearance, if not the fact?

"We went to see *Cyrano de Bergerac* last night," she said. "I found it bracing. Hopeful in a devastating way."

"Yes," Lawrence said, studying her. She blushed. "I was sorry to hear about your parents."

"Were you?"

"Mummy?" Auggie pulled at her hand.

"Later, dear. Go look at the jugs with Livy. They are ever so old. My father worked himself to death. He was a very hard worker, Lawrence. He earned every penny."

"Yes."

". . . Mother never forgave herself that trip to Europe."

"Oh?"

"Father visited, of course. He met us in Rome and stayed for a month. He preferred home. We were gone a terribly long time."

"Yes. Why did you stay away so long?"

"Mother knew she wouldn't make it back to Europe, given Father's dislike of it, and wanted to see as much as she could. I daresay it was freeing for her to be away. But poor Father. Left by himself, all he had was work. So he worked, and died of a heart attack at fifty-seven. I think Mother died of the guilt."

"She was all heart, I'm sure," Lawrence said. Before Gussie could react to his wry cynicism, he continued. "Auggie, what do you think of that painting? The creature there is a cyclops. A giant with a single eye in the middle of his forehead. Polyphemus is his name, and he was in love with Galatea, the young nymph there. He is gazing at her hopelessly because she doesn't love him. She loves someone else."

"Sad," Auggie said. "Does the someone else love her?"

"Yes. Acis."

"Good for her. Bad for Polyphemus." Auggie stared up at the painting, thoughtful.

"One can't help one's heart," Gussie said.

"Besides, Polyphemus wasn't a very nice fellow," Lawrence

57

said, and proceeded to tell the story of how Polyphemus trapped a crew of men in his cave, eating them one by one, until the leader of the crew devised a plan to blind the cyclops and they escaped; but Polyphemus called to his father, the god Poseidon, for revenge, which resulted in the continuing adventures of Odysseus in a book that Auggie should read, *The Odyssey.*

And so the hour passed. Gussie enjoyed seeing the children and Lawrence interact. To her relief, he seemed to enjoy himself. She listened as he imparted his knowledge to them, and thought how educational it would be to have him around all the time, challenging the children—and her. It had been a long time since she had had the stimulation of new ideas and information. She craved that stimulation and felt shocked by how much she had forgotten. Her French idioms. She had struggled so hard to be proficient in French. If only she could remember the poems they had used to recite to each other, surprise—and, perhaps, please—Lawrence with her retention and intelligence.

But to articulate anything in that intimate language was beyond her now. The children pulled at her for such base things as food and toilets. Physical and emotional, not intellectual, demands. The fact was, Lawrence's presence shone a light on all she had not done that she had hoped to do. If only she could stay. Gussie could have spent a lifetime in the cool clarity of history and art. But Winston returned with a shrieking Alyssa. *Adieu.* She was swept off by her family into the claustrophobic heat of a summer's day in New York City.

Sweat dripping down the back, clothes sticking, people bumping, irritable. They headed back to the hotel, marching along Fifth Avenue with the rest of humanity, the noise and activity. Gussie looked up as they approached Saint Patrick's cathedral. The round stained glass window. Tall, white spires stretching to the sky. A single cloud slowly passing. The building swayed as if it would fall. An illusion, she knew, but one that added to her anxious recognition of life's brevity, and her regret that she might have already missed the opportunity to really do something with her life.

The last day, while the children napped, she claimed to be meeting a friend in the lobby. Instead, she returned to the cathedral, walked up the stairs into the cool embrace of its interior. Inspiring, its representation of human potential. Work and purpose twined together in the worship of God. This was where she needed to be. To recover herself. Her rapid footsteps echoed. She knelt on a bench, hoping for peace and reason. She needed to sit still, her forehead pressed against clasped hands. Her mind was too full and too empty. Gradually it slowed enough to note the organ playing, softly, a familiar hymn. She had sung that hymn in her own Episcopal Church, and were they so different as to have caused murder, rape, and torture? So many people dying in the name of God, and what was God but love?

A hand touched her shoulder. She started. A priest. With the gentlest of gazes. He joined her in the pew, and they talked. About faith. Architecture. The history of Saint Patrick's cathedral. Together, they stood up and slowly walked through the church's interior, he detailing the sculptures, pointing out features of the woodwork, the spirit of the stained glass. A full turn, then another. Refreshed by the confidence of a worldview so certain in its hierarchy and the way of the world, she was ready to face her life again. The priest walked her out of the building, back into the glare and noise of the city. He blessed her as they parted, he turning back, she forward, looking up to find the children waiting for her at the bottom of those stairs. Auggie and Livy pale, Alyssa shrieking in her carriage, and Winston standing there, doing nothing, on the assumption that Gussie would. And was her independence to be so curtailed?

"What are you doing here?" she asked, her voice trembling, all the heat and frustration returning because what was marriage if not the ability to trust one's partner? "How dare you follow me."

"Catholic, Gussie?" Winston asked, his voice a hiss, his eyes wide and teary, and she couldn't tell if he were angry or afraid. "You would give up your soul?"

"That would be my choice, wouldn't it?" she asked as she picked up Alyssa, whose sticky, hot skin radiated heat.

"Can we get our ice cream cones now?" Livy asked, stepping between them, white as a sheet but smiling. Winston and Gussie studied each other, wordless, as Auggie joined Livy. The children looked up at them, waiting for everything to be okay.

"Come along," Gussie said. The corners of her lips twitched into a makeshift smile. "If he said you could, who am I to say no?"

In silence, they walked in search of ice cream, Livy and Auggie racing ahead and asking total strangers where they might find their grail. They finally did. Gussie went into the store to order, while Winston stayed out with the children. A fan blew hot air at her. It smelled of fried fish and fudge. Parched, Gussie watched the two customers at the counter eating their hot dogs and fried clams, and how anyone could eat in such heat and confusion, she didn't know. She balanced the sundaes and cones, headed out.

Winston was talking to a young woman in a light, floral dress. Working class. Plain. Cool. The woman didn't look at all warm, whereas Gussie knew how undone she, herself, appeared. Self-conscious, she handed Livy her strawberry sundae, checked the carriage to be sure Alyssa was still breathing. Flushed red and tear-stained, asleep.

"Where's Auggie?" Gussie asked as she handed Winston's sundae to him.

"Gussie, this is Gloria," Winston replied, smiling at Gloria, who blushed and curtsied. "Gloria is my boss's secretary at the bank. She's just been saying how terrible it is, my being let go. She says I was one of their better clerks."

"It seems to me, Winston," Gussie said, ignoring Gloria, molten heat within her as Auggie's chocolate ice cream cone stuck to her hand, "that you don't have a boss at the bank anymore. Where is your son?"

"With the carriage," Winston replied with a nod of his head.

"No, he is not," Gussie said.

Winston glanced around. Without another word, he went off in search of Auggie, leaving Gussie alone with the girls. She took short breaths of fiery air. Shivered in the heat. Stared at this Gloria as horror buffeted her like waves crashing down on a shore, drowning the question of a secretary with one asking how far would a little boy go? All she could do—as she had learned to do over these last years—was scream in silence.

She saw them approach from half a block away, Auggie's arms gesticulating as he talked to Winston, who was smiling broadly.

"Here we are!" Winston said, triumphant.

"What are you smiling about, young man?" Gussie asked Auggie, infuriated by his self-satisfaction. So like his father.

"I found the tallest building I could find."

"Didn't I tell you not to go anywhere without us?"

"You're silly, Mummy," Auggie giggled. "I know you can take care of yourself."

"You think so?" Gussie asked, her throat closed, and her hand in a fist.

"Gussie, he's back," Winston said. "Our little adventurer, right, Auggie? How about an ice cream?"

"Here's his ice cream," Gussie said, her words clenched as she held out the crushed mush of sugar cone and chocolate ice cream.

"I'll get you some napkins, Gussie. And for Auggie—"

"Nothing. There's a depression going on. He missed his chance. It's time to go home. I need to go home."

To sink back into its comfort and familiarity. Routine. Gussie realized that Winston had been right. New York had been over-stimulating for her. Frustrating. Unhealthy for her to challenge herself so much. She would struggle for her life in other, small ways. Churches and secretaries fell to the background, denied if not forgotten. And Gussie cut off her hair. Winston was devastated, but what could he do? She knew he adored her long hair, but it was a bother to take care of. She did not want long hair anymore. Who else in their set still had long hair? She would be free of it. Though she saved it, a rope of burnished red, dead strands.

Failed Expectations

Shouts and the dying off of power drills announced the start of a coffee break for the builders renovating the village's old velvet mill into high-end condominiums. A couple of teenaged boys walked toward the gazebo where Gussie and Emma sat but, upon noting them, turned around. Emma tried to move her toes, numbed by the cold.

"It's a shame," Gussie said, "that a decision made by such a young, ignorant girl should have such ramifications."

Emma fidgeted. Which young girl was she referring to? The young Gussie, or Emma? It dawned on Emma that she, herself, could no longer be described as young. Thirty-two was an adult, whether she felt like one or not. The days slipped by, and one day she would be her grandmother's age, looking back at the person she had been today, and the consequence of her decision: homelessness. Not a physical homelessness, but an existential one, of never feeling settled or comfortable, one of loss and perpetual seeking. A life of anxiety and fear because where to go if not *home*, and where would home be if not Poquatuck Village and the house? Without Providence and Conner? And yet, wasn't that what she claimed she wanted? To be free of the entanglements of the past? Wouldn't keeping either of the houses be coddling herself?

Or was holding on to them being true to her nature? Her dislike of travel, her craving for routine.

Why did both giving up and holding on feel so unacceptable?

Emma consoled herself. At least she wasn't deluded. She knew she didn't know what she was doing.

"The morning of my wedding," Gussie said, "I woke up early, well before the sun. I snuck out of the house and walked to the old graveyard. Lawrence was there, asleep under the chestnut tree. I woke him. He thought I had come to stay. I stayed for some time." Gussie hesitated for long enough to suggest something more than nothing. "But then I left him. What would people say, after all, if I didn't show up at the church? I could never embarrass my parents. I promised, though, that if anything . . . untoward came of our meeting, I would leave Winston. I believed that, even in the car as Winston and I drove away from the church and I looked at him and realized he was a complete stranger. I didn't know him at all. And so the promise to Lawrence helped. It gave me confidence that things would turn out fine. It was in God's hands."

"So Lawrence is my grandfather?" Emma asked, digesting the information.

"Wherever did you get that idea!" Gussie sat up in alarm.

"You just implied as much."

"If he were, I'd have left Winston, just as I said I would," Gussie tsked, blushing. Emma had never seen her grandmother blush or flustered. "You don't think I would do such a thing, do you? On my wedding day?"

"People do."

"Not us."

"Aunt Alyssa did."

"I beg your pardon?"

"Nothing," Emma said, surprised Gussie didn't know about her Aunt Alyssa and Uncle Ed. "It was just a story I heard, like the one you just told me. Who's to say if it's true or not. It doesn't matter."

"The truth most certainly matters," Gussie said. She glanced sideways at Emma, as if assessing the direction of their conversation. "You need to know what I wouldn't do. Otherwise, you might make me into someone entirely other than who I am. It's not just what we do at the time. It's why we did what we did, and how our actions are seen and remembered."

"Then I don't understand why you would tell me something happened when it didn't. Or that something didn't happen when it did."

"You've no right to judge me," Gussie snapped.

"I have every right."

"What I did made sense. It was a different time. Aspects of it might be regrettable, but there they are, and here you are. I don't want to leave a wrong impression."

"You said it doesn't matter what other people think."

Gussie looked to the house, Emma to the breakwater, their intentions misunderstood by the other because Emma assumed Gussie wouldn't let go, and Gussie that Emma would. Neither recognized that they were each working hard to do the opposite. That their intentions were to accept the unacceptable.

"Press your palms together," Gussie ordered. Emma obeyed. "Now bend your middle fingers and put them back to back. Put the knuckles together. That's right. Keep the other fingertips and the heel of your hand pressed together. Now then. This is a Chinese explanation for why the wedding ring goes on the finger that it does. Each finger represents a part of you. The thumbs are your parents. The index fingers your siblings. The middle fingers are you. The ring fingers are your life partner. The pinkies are your children. Try to separate each finger in turn. Do you see? You will separate from your parents. From your siblings. From your children. But you can't separate from your life partner. The ring fingers can't be separated, and neither could Winston and I."

"A game with fingers shouldn't be the determining factor on how to lead your life, Gram."

"It's what I have believed."

Emma moved, or tried to move, the various fingers.

"I believe me," Emma said, testing what it felt and sounded like to believe. To suspend doubt and trust that she might have the answer.

"What?"

"The middle fingers can't be separated either," Emma said. "In a relationship, you have to recognize that. You're together, but you can't lose the connection to yourself. I guess you knew that when you left Lawrence. That's what you said, isn't it? You had to know yourself before you could be with him. He tried to mold you, right? Whereas Gramps didn't challenge you in the same way."

"On the contrary," Gussie said, and her eyes were bright with the memory. "There was a weekend. Lawrence stopped by for a drink. Nothing new or unusual about that. I think he'd been away for a while. As he left, he turned to me and commented on what a lovely home Winston and I had. I said, '*Yes, of course. But it is just a house.*' He shook his head. '*It's a home.*' The simplest comment, and everything changed. That one word gave me a jolt. Home?

"The next morning, I walked out to see Winston. He was clearing the drive of snow and ice with the tractor that he had retrofitted to be a plow. There was to be a party that night. Auggie had come home from school. It was Alyssa's twelfth birthday. We were all together again, and Winston was looking fit and handsome, and what had I expected of him, after all, but exactly what I had? Together, we had created a home. '*How do you do?*' I shouted up to him. '*Fine,*' he said, staring at me as if he had more to say but was unsure how to say it. '*I'm glad, Winston.*' I headed back toward the house. '*I've tried my best, Gussie,*' he called after me. '*I've tried.*' I turned back to him. '*Of course you have. We both have.*' And for that short February day, I felt hopeful. But when I came home from church the next morning, he didn't know what to do. The fool. He had ruined everything. There was nothing he could do."

Gussie fell silent, her eyes quivering with tears.

"About what?" Emma asked.

"That woman," Gussie said.

"What woman?" Emma asked, studying her grandmother, who looked directly back.

"Ask Alyssa," Gussie said, sharply. "She was there. All the children were. God only knows what he hoped to accomplish, bringing her to the house."

"I'm confused, Gram."

"You stopped me in the middle of a thought," Gussie snapped as a lobster boat chugged into the harbor. "Now I've forgotten."

"I'm sorry," Emma said, not sure whether the flush in her grandmother's cheeks was a blush or a fever, or if the story were a memory or a dream. In either case, Emma felt the frustration of not grasping what she had been told as Gussie fretted, pulling the coat more tightly around her neck.

"Gram, why don't we go back to the apartment and have a nice, hot lunch?"

"Gruel."

"We should at least tell them where you are."

"Should! I've had enough shoulds. All my life, shoulds and should-haves. But what else could I have done? How was I to know? He disappeared."

"Who disappeared?" Emma asked again, and with concern.

Gussie glared at Emma. "Auggie," she said. "Who else? On our family trip to New York. All I could do was scream. But, of course, I wouldn't have. Imagine, standing on a street corner in New York, screaming. People would have thought I was crazy. I was only angry. I was so alone. He had left me alone with those lilacs, covered with melted chocolate ice cream."

"Gram?"

Gussie stared at Emma.

"That wouldn't make sense, would it?" Gussie said. "The lilacs were at the engagement party. Whereas the ice cream was Auggie's. He came back, so proud of himself. He had no idea how disappointed I was in him. Just like his father. That's when I decided to send him to boarding school."

"Dad was only seven when he went away?"

"Six. Advanced for his age. I insisted. I had to get him away from Winston. Without work to distract him, he started meddling in what wasn't his purview. Trying to control what he couldn't control. Those cold showers were the last straw. Every morning, Auggie hunched over, his skinny shoulders pelted with ice water. Winston bellowing at him to stand up straight. Attempting to make a man of a six-year-old. Such nonsense. I couldn't bear it. I drove Auggie to the school. His blond curls were plastered to his face with tears. He waved good-bye." Gussie raised a hand. Her fingers bent toward her, curling and uncurling, more a gesture to say come back than good-bye. Her hand dropped back into her lap. "I cried all the way back home. But I knew it was the right thing to do."

"How did you know?"

". . . It felt safer."

"I guess, in theory, if you give up what you need, then you don't have to worry about losing it," Emma said, remembering her departure that morning. The rebellion and claustrophobia she had felt at the idea of facing Conner. She had left him for the same reason she had put the family house on the market. A visceral rejection that had made perfect sense. Until the call from the real estate agent saying there was a buyer. The wave of panic, hearing those words, was remarkably like the one she had felt as she stepped onto the train that morning. She had not felt joyous and free of the house and Conner, but rather a terrifying premonition of loss and death. A helpless, fathomless sadness that it was over.

"It's not that simple," Gussie said. "In fact, it's complicated. A kernel grows, creeping its way through your life, determining, if you let it, your path. It becomes habit too quickly. When I went to Europe, I knew in my heart that Lawrence would come get me. I didn't understand that money mattered quite so much. Or if it did, I assumed he would borrow it. Figure out a way to save me. Every day, I expected him to show up. Every day, I hoped and trusted. I counted on him, and he failed me. I had chosen to travel, but I blamed him for my disappointment. I had known that year would change me. I just didn't know how. I was a different person when I came home. Oh, yes, all the new clothes and knowledge were all very well. But surviving had taken something out of me. I no longer had the energy to challenge myself. It was easier to settle. Be home. Not question. I resigned myself to doing small things. Tiny steps, not the leaps and bounds I had dreamed of. What a disappointment I was to myself! I didn't notice to what degree until that trip to New York. It was there that all the bitterness and resentment over how my life had unfolded came out. I had disappointed myself, and I laid the blame on Winston. He hadn't challenged me. He hadn't helped me to grow; rather, he had encouraged my complacency. I couldn't let him ruin my children too."

"No," Emma replied.

"Hopes and dreams, Emma. We all have them. But, too often, things don't go according to plan."

They sat silent. For comfort and to comfort, Emma put an arm around her grandmother, gently holding her, protective, because it was crippling, the giving up on the surface of what was vitally important deep down. Emma had tried to escape, but there it was still. Whatever her choices, there was that dark vortex, waiting for her plumb line.

Together, they stared out at the stark grays and blacks and whites, the patterns of waves, rocks, and beaches, horizons against which questions seemed irrelevant. Not just the why of it—why stay, why leave, why love—but the how, how to hold on, not push away.

Children

Nature vs. Nurture
February 29th, 1948

The echo and din of Boston's South Station. Seventeen-year-old Auggie ran as best he could, cutting through the crowds of bustling tourists and commuters as he did his studies: with speed, focused determination, and a great fear of failure. He must not miss his train to Poquatuck. Heart pounding, he lived out the nightmare he had been having for weeks. The clock ticked, relentless, as he remembered what he had forgotten (Alyssa's birthday present) and wondered what he had brought (far too much). Shouts and whistles as Auggie burst through the doors to where the lineup of trains huffed. One was pulling out. Was it his? No. The *Yankee Clipper* remained at Gate 4, its monstrous pair of DL-109 engines black and belching smoke in preparation for departure. Auggie sprinted and reached the passenger cars just as the conductor was about to board. He helped Auggie toss his bags in and lift himself up. A sharp whistle, and the conductor shouted. With a jolt, the train pulled out of the station, heading south, taking Auggie home for the weekend.

Auggie bumped down the aisle and settled into a seat on the left side of the car for the water view. He stared out the window, his legs still moving up and down, his Oxford shirt damp with sweat, chilling. It seemed a long time since he'd been home. He had planned to work on his paper, "Self-Determination and the Palestinian Question," during the first hour of his trip, before indulging in the labors of Agatha Christie's Poirot, but the train pulled into and then out of the Providence station and still he stared out the window, imagining what one imagines of home: the security and comfort of the living room, its soft couches and chairs, the fire crackling as he and his mother talked over tea and gingersnaps. His bedroom, small and smelling faintly of mothballs. His sisters arguing and gossiping. The bark of his father's voice as he shouted up the stairs, ordering Auggie to come be of assistance instead of dreaming over his books. For all Auggie's dreams, he never felt quite right, and all he wanted was to be acceptable. The train progressed down the tracks as Auggie fought a too-familiar twist in his gut, a dark suspicion of his deficiency. To feel so bad, he must be bad. Though he tried so hard to be good. He reassured himself by thinking of his January exams. They had gone brilliantly, though the A minus on his English term paper niggled and his Palestine paper would have to be good. Without emotion. He was having trouble focusing it. There was so much to be considered, all that blood and politics, and how would he make amends to Alyssa for forgetting her present?

The train slowed to a stop. Auggie started. He had dozed off. The train had arrived at the Poquatuck stop. He hurriedly gathered his briefcase, his brown Gladstone, and his duffel bag, anticipating the sight of Livy and his mother, who would be picking him up. Exiting the train, he stepped down the stairs, directly into a puddle of slush. He looked at his soaked shoes, then up.

"Auggie!" Behind the dinging gates, waving, was his father. Disappointment wafted over Auggie, and dread. He stood straighter and walked over to his father, set down his bags. A firm handshake. The father and son stood eye to eye, but Winston, solid and strong at forty-five, dwarfed his son, who had still to fill out and own his body.

"How was the trip?"

"Uneventful." Auggie did not bother to look around. Of course they hadn't come. The girls were preparing for the weekend's events: the Club party and Alyssa's birthday. Auggie's eyes stung and his head ached with exhaustion. He needed to eat and to take a nap. If he were a child, he could be carried, nestled in his parent's embrace.

"I left the car for your mother in case she needs it," Winston said, expressing what was as close to an embrace as he was capable of. "We'll walk."

"Ah." Auggie nodded. The train huffed, pulled forward and away. Auggie's attention was not quite so rapt as his father's; he was more concerned with his luggage, the four or five reference books he had, at the last minute, dropped into his duffel, and the two-mile walk ahead of them.

"Carry your own bags," Winston said, marching off at a sharp clip, showing by doing as any decent parent would. "You'll be eaten alive as a recruit looking the way you do. You've got to build up those muscles."

Auggie very nearly replied that the draft had yet to be reinstated, but that would cause an argument, and besides, all signs pointed to Congress passing the bill that would require all eighteen-year-olds—which, as of March 15, would include Auggie—to register, making him liable, at age nineteen, for twenty-one months of service, followed by five years of reserve duty. The thought of having to give up his studies in favor of running around a field with a gun and a rock-filled knapsack gave Auggie a queasy feeling. He picked up his bags, the Gladstone and briefcase in one hand, the duffel slung over his shoulder, and contemplated the word *luggage*'s etymology.

They headed down the railroad tracks. Breathing white clouds, blinded by a brilliant blue sky and the sun reflecting off the water, ice patches on the ground. Auggie's bags bumped against his legs. Their conversation was stilted and careful, both father and son wanting to get along and so avoiding any topic on which they might disagree—which, too often, included even the weather. Family goings-on were relatively safe. Livy's excitement about the Club party, her superficial concerns about boys and makeup, at which subject—Auggie didn't understand why their father wouldn't let Livy wear a bit of lipstick; all the girls did these days—they delicately moved on to

Alyssa, the "leapling," who was *to the moon* about finally having a *real* birthday to celebrate. Her third, actually, and why the perpetual dissatisfaction? Father and son agreed: Alyssa seemed always to need just a little bit more than she got.

This rare accord brought them to the crossing, where they stepped off the tracks and headed down Bittersweet Lane. Auggie's bags felt heavier and heavier, but he would consider it a failing if he stopped to shift hands. His father maintained a good pace as they marched past the potter's field, a dead chestnut tree in its midst. Vines had crept up it, and weeds and brambles had grown over the gravestones.

"We've spring cleaning to do to prevent that overgrowth from happening on our own property." Winston pointed out, then listed the tasks: The fencing around the blueberry bushes needed to be mended. The ruts and holes in the drive had to be filled. The stones and boulders that had surfaced during the frosts had to be removed from the field and added to the rock pile behind the garage.

"I've cleared a new path near the garage," Winston said with a hard frown back at his son, who wore no gloves and was struggling to keep up. Winston worried about Auggie. He lacked in masculine interests. As a boy, he had always preferred dolls to soldiers and books to football. What would become of him in the army? Winston had voiced his suspicions to Gussie, who had met them with such deafening silence that he knew not to mention them again. But he could think them, and he would until the boy filled out and showed a bit of muscle. "There's a clearing to maintain."

"Yes, Sir," Auggie said. "I look forward to it."

Satisfactory to both: The idea of crisp air, the stretch and strain of muscles as they hacked and pulled. The vibration as the ax struck wood. The resistance, then release, of a root from the earth. The two left off any further talk as Auggie, breathless, tried to keep up with his father's march, which had slowed markedly.

"You're the best birthday present I could ask for!" Alyssa shrieked as she ran up the gravel driveway toward them, practically knocking Auggie down with the force of her hug. Bundled in a beige coat and hat and a bright red scarf, she took Auggie's briefcase with gloved hands. He stretched his fingers, shifted his duffel to the other shoulder.

"You look terrible." She studied him matter-of-factly with her clear, hazel eyes. Her too-long bangs caught her eyelashes. "You must be working too hard. Mummy is furious that Father didn't take the car. So am I, Father, because it means you didn't bring me a present."

"I brought you your brother," Winston said gruffly, but his eyes were light, belying the sternness of his tone. Alyssa was his favorite, in part because she had taken up where Auggie had failed: she adored her father's gun collection, his toy soldiers, and to work outside with her father and big brother was her definition of heaven, because the tension that usually existed between father and son retreated under her banter and diplomacy. She was, in her own words, their savior, and she elicited from them a happy promise that they would, all three, work outside the next day.

Content, they followed the length of the driveway, Auggie answering Alyssa's questions about his studies (had he mastered them?) and friends (were they eligible?). Auggie enjoyed Alyssa, appreciating her grounded sensibleness, something their sister Livy, even in her most "matoor" moments, lacked. Too, he knew Alyssa would give a biased but complete assessment of the home front once their father was out of hearing—which he was soon enough, falling behind them to tussle with a vine that was climbing a forsythia bush.

"It's lovely having you here, Auggie." Alyssa skipped a step or two. "You make everyone happy."

"Do I?"

"Of course."

Auggie did not dare ask, "Does *everyone* include Father?" Rather, he asked, "Anything I should know about?"

"It is my third birthday, about which you have said nothing."

"You are going to be twelve. Most children want to be thought of as older than they are, Alyssa."

Alyssa rolled her eyes.

"Age is just a number, Auggie. Of course I am older than three, but birthdays don't count if they don't land on the actual day. It's like celebrating Christmas in June. I think it's mean that my family refuses to recognize that. Though you are here," she added. "It is very nice of you to come specifically for my birthday party."

Auggie refrained from reminding her that, in fact, he was there to escort Livy to the Club party; why cast shadows on Alyssa's sunny mood? She tilted her head to the side in thought.

"As to what you should know about, other than the gun incident—"

"That was an outrage on Father's part," Auggie interjected.

"Don't be so quick to judge, Auggie. It was Livy's own fault, bringing her boyfriend up the trellis that way. Father's been a lamb, otherwise. Everything has been quite peaceable. Except at cocktails, when he tends to go off on the Frogs and the Commies. It's a miracle Mummy has any teeth left, she grits them so. Professor Finer is coming for drinks."

"Professor Finer?" An anxious thrill ran through Auggie. Professor Finer didn't like children. Auggie's mother said they made him nervous, that he preferred to talk to people who could think and reason. Which was why Auggie held a special place with Professor Finer, being quiet and bookish, rather than a flirt (Livy) or a rambunctious tomboy (Alyssa). But Auggie rarely had the opportunity to really talk to Professor Finer. Only on social occasions and in letters, and always with Gussie as the connection. Auggie hoped he was now educated sufficiently to converse with Professor Finer, preferably on the subject of self-determination. But would he pass?

"Mummy knew you'd be pleased," Alyssa said, lowering her voice to a whisper. "She wanted it to be a surprise."

"I thought he was living in England."

"Now the war's over, he is considering his options. Mummy read part of his letter aloud to end the to-do. You know how jealous Father is of any letters that come in. Excepting bills. There is simply no privacy, nor secrets," she said as they came around the curve of the drive, now in sight of the house. "Mummy will be murderous if I don't tell her you've arrived."

Alyssa abruptly dropped his briefcase and ran off. Auggie stopped where the driveway ended in a cul-de-sac, in the middle of which was a lawn with a magnificent chestnut tree presiding over five crab apple trees. Lining the circular drive were plantings of forsythia, rhododendron, birch, and white pines. Like a clock, from eleven to two, the graveled area of the drive enlarged to a rectangular parking area. At twelve, the garage. A stone wall led to three o'clock, where stood the house and his mother's shade garden. As Auggie looked about him, he thought that the house had a tired, morose appearance. The mountain laurels framing the garden to the right of the house appeared dead, the arborvitae dried out. Brown grass. Patches of dirty snow and mud. Winston came up behind Auggie. He took off his gloves and roughly put them onto Auggie's hands, grumbling about his son's lack of preparedness, that he had to be more forward-thinking.

"This way," Winston ordered, picking up the bags and swinging them lightly as he strode forward. Auggie followed his father toward the garage, to the side of which was a new, three-foot-wide path that led to an unfamiliar clearing and structure.

"It's for you," Winston said, indicating the approximation of the cabin that Auggie had sketched the previous summer. At the time, Winston had penalized him for drawing when he was supposed to have been chopping wood. Ten by twelve, of pine, with a porch— onto which Auggie stepped. He opened the door. The cabin smelled of sawdust and paint. Built-in bookshelves lined the lower half of the walls to the right. A dictionary and horseshoe crab on the long pine table before him, above which were picture windows opening out to the harbor and village. An oil lamp with the wick newly trimmed. To his left, a wood-burning stove, a neatly piled stack of wood, and a rocking chair with a blanket.

"Isn't it a wonderful place, Auggie?" Alyssa asked, breathless from her run and clearly feeling terribly athletic, enjoying the way her hair flew behind her and her muscles stretched. In acquiescence, Auggie took his briefcase and duffel from their father and began to unpack his books. "I helped to frame it last September, and we've been working on it ever since," Alyssa told him. "Father bought windows that were too big—he knew you'd want lots of air and light—so he had to redo the shelving. He hadn't thought ahead, right, Father? The paint color is good, too. It's not sterile."

"It's perfect." Auggie looked behind her to Winston and smiled. "Thank you."

"I half-think Father likes you best, Auggie," Alyssa said with a glance at their father, who had reddened and was busying himself brushing a speck of dust off the bookshelf. "He only made me a silly old dollhouse for Christmas. This is much better. You can really use it."

"Auggie? Alyssa?" Gussie shouted from the kitchen. Winston and Alyssa both startled, exchanged looks, at which point Auggie realized that his mother disapproved of the cabin. How disappointing. Auggie looked around him, regretting the place before he had even had it. "Where is everyone? Winston?"

"I was to tell you lunch is ready," Alyssa whispered as the screen door to the kitchen slammed shut, the tap of their mother's feet coming down the wood stairs to the gray stone path leading to the gravel of the driveway. They hurried out of the cabin and down the new path to meet her.

"There you are!" Gussie smiled as she stopped in the middle of the drive. Her brown hair was short, and its permanent wave was disheveled with work and rush. She wiped her hands dry with her apron before holding out her arms to welcome Auggie. "Why are you out here? It's freezing. You look like a raccoon, Auggie, entirely done in. Come inside. You need something to eat and a nap."

She hugged Auggie, who, for all his height, abruptly felt like a child with only his mother to protect him.

Silliness, of course. Even when she had left him, years before, at that damned school, she had known he knew what he had to do. Study. Take long walks. Sleep. By the time he entered Harvard, he was used to the heavy emptiness he woke with every morning. He joined the debate club, had friends who enjoyed talking about the same things he did: philosophy and logic. He got lost in his mind. It wasn't lonely there. Though now, with his mother's arms strong around him, there welled a great sadness in his heart. Nonsense, again. Why sad? He was home, safe.

They all walked back to the house, into the kitchen, where Auggie and Winston sat at the round children's table. Sky blue, with matching chairs, it was the perfect size for three- and four-year-olds. No one living in the house fit that description anymore (excepting Alyssa's of herself), but Gussie had hopes for a future full of grandchildren, and so both men sat scrunched at the table, knees at chin level but enjoying the warmth, as they ate the baloney sandwiches Gussie had prepared for them. She stood at the stove, stirring a pan of milk and Bosco chocolate syrup, while the teakettle heated up on the stove.

Gussie poured the liquids. Marshmallows sizzled as they melted in hot chocolate, and the citrus fragrance of Ceylon tea joined that of the angel cake fresh out of the oven. Alyssa amused them with a detailed account of her day-before-her-birthday's menus—breakfast, pancakes with loads of butter and maple syrup; lunch, banana splits and not a single vegetable; and dinner, lamb and mint jelly, with an enormous chocolate cake drenched in caramel and fudge for dessert—and then the list of guests who would be in attendance, including a set of Irish twins, the use of which term earned Alyssa a stern rebuke from Gussie. Alyssa continued: Lauren, the older twin—by eleven months, which meant the use of said term was perfectly acceptable, even if it had been slightly pejorative in the stone ages—was also a seamstress and, Alyssa supposed, partly a friend of Livy's. The point being, Lauren, more Alyssa's friend than Livy's, had a brother who had been adorable at first, and so was invited to the party, but then became a pest and tease, and so now was not. Lauren had vowed to sew him up in the remnants of Livy's dress material. A lovely, velvet blue. The dress's neckline, Alyssa noted, plunged far more than was warranted given Livy's less than ample bosom. At this, Gussie cut short the raconteur and sent Auggie off to his nap.

He woke up to the sound of voices. His eyes adjusting to the dark, he sniffed and smelled not the rancid smell of his roommate's dirty socks and T-shirts but the back-of-the-nose smell of the ocean molded into the carpet and clothes, and the coals of a fire burning. A train whistle in the distance reminded him of his trip, and his tender palms of the walk home. He smiled. His sisters whispered outside his door, arguing who would wake him, until their mother's library whisper called them downstairs. Alyssa's heavy footfalls masked Livy's ballet steps. The front doorbell rang. Shouts of hello. Professor Finer! Auggie threw back his covers and fumbled to put on his bathrobe. He hurried out into the hallway to go to the bathroom.

"Auggie!" Livy stopped her progress down the stairs. Their mother's handsome features, softened and youthful, smiled at him through the wooden spokes of the railing. He leaned down to kiss the top of Livy's shiny, reddish-blond head of hair. "I wanted to wake you, Auggie, but Mummy wouldn't hear of it. I cannot believe we have to sit through an entire cocktail hour. I intend to be bored to tears. I've so much to tell you."

"Soon," Auggie promised as he shut the bathroom door to her adoring face. Shaking with chill and the rush of anticipation, Auggie removed his bathrobe and turned on the shower. A glance in the mirror proved his father right. He was scrawny and had little muscle to show for himself. A kick of dread. *Boot camp.* He stepped into the tub. Cold water blasted out of the shower. He braced until the water warmed, turned soothing, scorching, cleansing. He decided to ask

Professor Finer his thoughts on Palestine, and if he had read the transcript of Bertrand Russell and Father Copleston's debate on the existence of God. Had Professor Finer wondered, too, at Bertrand Russell, who had been entirely in the right until Copleston asked how Russell distinguished between good and evil. *By my feelings*, Russell had said. Auggie groaned: a ridiculous response from which Russell's argument had never recovered, and what had Professor Finer thought?

A blank. Auggie wasn't sure what Professor Finer would think, and so he went about imagining ways of posing the question, which would have to be made in between the conversational platitudes of the rest of his family, whose presence would be frustrating given all Auggie needed to discuss with Professor Finer. The man's presence stimulated Auggie, challenged him to stretch his mind in a way that discussion with his peers—and, more obviously, his family—did not. When Auggie asked a question, Professor Finer knew exactly why the question had been posed, and he would look at it from afar and then say, yes, that is pain, that is love, that is fear.

Auggie had many questions, not least about conscientious objection.

When he came down the stairs into the living room, his family had settled on the couches and chairs around the fireplace. Even Winston had broken routine and sat, not in his chair on the other side of the room, but with the others, his body dwarfing the seat he occupied. Opposite him, at the hearth, stood Professor Finer, lithe and of middle height, his brown hair lightly salted. Gussie sat on the couch to his right, closest to the fire, wearing her best smile in an attempt to counter her disappointment that she would not be having her evening bourbon with its three tablespoons of frozen lemonade because Professor Finer had brought a bottle of wine. Well-intentioned. Rather dear of him. But she did enjoy her cocktail.

"I overslept," Auggie said, joining them. "I hope I didn't miss anything."

"Not a thing," Lawrence said as they shook hands. His hand was warm and dry, his embrace reassuring. "Welcome home."

"You too," Auggie replied. "Or do you consider England home now?"

"I suppose home is where the heart is." Lawrence smiled, his eyes bright as, with a glance at Gussie, he returned to the process of opening and pouring the wine. A rustling of movement as the Michaelses adjusted themselves to that thought. Home. The heart. Gussie reached for a Ritz cracker and studied it before placing it in her mouth and allowing it to melt like a communion wafer.

"I don't understand why you went to live in some foreign place like London," Winston said. The corners of Gussie's lips tightened in disapproval.

"The army took him there, Winston," Gussie said, accepting the glass of wine that Lawrence offered her. "Just like it took you to North Carolina."

"It's not foreign to me anymore," Lawrence said. "It's been five years, and difficult ones. But I love it."

"I vowed never to leave home once I came back. I'm here to stay," Winston pronounced. He glared at Auggie, who remained standing next to Lawrence. "Give the man some space, Auggie. You're looking at him like a lovesick puppy."

"Father, you are impossible," Livy said, standing and moving to the opposite couch, leaving Alyssa frozen in her seat, unsure of whom to comfort, or how.

"Winston," Gussie said, pale with rage. "You sound just like my father."

"Good," Winston barked, his chair creaking as he leaned forward for a handful of nuts. He surveyed the room with grim satisfaction, as if enjoying his role of pariah and the concomitant attention, which he would not otherwise have received.

"I find one of the pleasures of travel is coming home again," Lawrence said, sitting down on the low-cushioned bench in front of the fire and indicating the seat next to him for Auggie to sit, too. "There is nothing like coming home, is there, Auggie?"

"No. There isn't," Auggie said, still breathless from his father's words but consoled by Lawrence's understanding. The fire heated his back.

"Don't get too comfortable, young man. You're off to the army soon," Winston said. "The boy is going to be eaten alive if he doesn't fill out."

"Winston!" Gussie said, her voice a clipped rebuke. Winston sat back in his chair.

"Bullies don't bother me, Father," Auggie said with a confidence he didn't feel. "I make myself too useful to them, reviewing their homework, making sure it looks about right but not so right the teacher will know the fellow didn't do the work."

"And, in the end, you teach them the theorems and equations that they hadn't wanted to bother to learn," Livy said, smiling.

"And it doesn't even hurt," Alyssa followed up, and speaking from experience. The women all looked at Auggie with pride. Lawrence gave him an appraising look.

"Are you signing up?" he asked.

"I suppose I'll have to." Auggie slouched, abruptly and unutterably depressed.

"You aren't so privileged that you would avoid your duty, are you?"

"No, of course not," Auggie said, embarrassed to have given such an impression. "I only meant, my studies are so interesting. I hate to break them off."

"What would you want to do, were you free to do anything?" Lawrence asked, as if there were a choice. Auggie hesitated. His mother looked at him expectantly. They all did.

"Learn languages. Study different cultures. Other people. Learn how we might all live together peaceably."

"The army will be perfect for you," Lawrence said. "Study Russian. With that qualification, you'll get an interesting assignment.

Especially given you already know, or can guess at, the Romance languages."

"My counselor at school was suggesting a Turkic language," Auggie said.

"Knowing a Slavic language will give you an edge," Lawrence countered.

"I could take lessons this summer." Auggie sat up. He felt suddenly a good deal better about the whole thing. He had never considered there might be an option beyond the gun aspect.

He could make it through any physical training, so long as he knew that intellectual pursuit pended.

"The wine has rather a distinct smell," Gussie said, preventing Winston's response to his son with a hard look. "It reminds me of—"

"Manure," Lawrence said, sticking his nose into his glass and sniffing deeply. "Barnyard. The French love it. An acquired taste."

"I prefer a good Chablis," Gussie said.

"Yes," Lawrence replied, with a smile. Gussie flushed. She held her glass out to her son.

"Would you like to try it, Auggie? It's lovely. A Bordeaux."

Gussie handed her glass to Auggie, who wondered if she wanted him to taste it or spill it; clearly, she didn't like it, or she would have allowed him his own glass. Auggie looked to his father, who had, just as clearly, not bothered with manners and stuck to gin. Gilby's on crushed ice. Two fingers. Twice. Gussie shut her eyes, as if by not seeing, Winston would not be lifting an olive out of his drink with his right-hand pinky. His gold class ring with its garnet clinked the glass. A sniff. A sip. Auggie passed the wine to his sisters.

"I smell licorice and blackberries," Alyssa said, and wet her lips with the wine, acting the part of ingénue, though her siblings knew perfectly well that she had had a run-in with a bottle of whiskey over the holidays. Livy took the glass from her.

"I think it's magnificent," Livy said to gain the same look of approbation from Lawrence that Alyssa had elicited with her candy and fruit remark.

"May I have a glass, please?" Livy addressed Lawrence directly. If he acquiesced, her parents wouldn't deny her.

"I was about to recount an experience I had a few weeks ago," Lawrence said as he obliged Livy, with no reaction from either parent. "I was at a cocktail party, in a room full of strangers, and I noticed a familiar-looking woman. Apparently I was staring, because she asked to be introduced. I explained to her that I felt as if I knew her and wondered if we had met somewhere, and just at that point—your wine, Livy. But smell first. Get it in your nose. You'll gain more appreciation that way—she reached over to deadhead a mum." Lawrence snapped his fingers. "'Gussie Michaels,' I said. She looked at me with an odd smile. 'My second cousin,' she replied. Her name is Katherine, Gussie, though she goes by Kitty now."

"Katherine? My goodness," Gussie said, brows raised. "I haven't seen her in years. She is the daughter of my mother's Cousin Lucinda, who went to college and then eloped with a Frenchman."

"I've never heard that story." Livy sat forward, her face bright with curiosity and luxurious with the half-full wineglass in her hand.

"Because I've not told it," Gussie said. "It's base gossip, and scandalous. Mother used to hold it over my head. If I did anything wrong, *you might end up like Cousin Lucinda, penniless in France,* the insinuation being that her cousin had had to resort to the depths of Sodom and Gomorrah to survive, which she had not. She married her Frenchman and had two children. I always rather admired her for doing what she did. But at such a cost. Cousin Lucinda was never welcomed by the family again. Terrible."

Gussie looked down at her lap, the wine, sighed.

"Was it terrible?" Lawrence asked.

"I used to feel quite threatened by Katherine," Gussie replied after a brief hesitation. "She showed up looking far prettier than I could ever hope to be. We played in the sandbox and had an awful row over a pail. I'm sure it was because I thought she'd come to replace my grandmother, after whom she'd been named. It was our grandmother's funeral. Cousin Lucinda had come home to pay her respects, maybe hoping things had changed. Which they hadn't, in no small part because she expressed no regret."

"Perhaps because the only thing one can do with regret is regret it," Lawrence said. "Best to move forward, and hope to do better."

"Yes," Gussie agreed, and took a sip of wine with an expression that brought to mind Socrates' death. "She must be quite something now. Beautiful, of course. Cosmopolitan, educated."

"She's all that," Lawrence said. "So would we all be, given her heritage and life experience. She grew up traveling, exposed to all the main European capitals' culture and variety. So much of it destroyed by the war. She's jaded, but I sense a softness at the edges. It's amazing, Gussie, how alike you two are. Your intonations and syntax, your gestures and bearing are nearly identical."

"Fascinating," Gussie said.

"Aren't things like gestures and the way one speaks learned by being with one another?" Alyssa asked, using her fingers to get the cherry out of her Coca-Cola.

"Alyssa!" Gussie said. "For pity's sake."

"I want to get to the cherry," Alyssa said. Upon closer inspection of her mother's expression, she lifted her fingers out of her drink, reddening to the point of tears. Livy moved to sit next to Alyssa, reaching for an unused knife from the cheese board. She fished for the cherry in Alyssa's drink.

"Katherine's mother and mine grew up together," Gussie said. "They had similar habits, which they apparently passed down to their daughters."

"Cousin Lucinda must be where I get my streak of wildness," Livy said.

"You just don't like rules," Alyssa replied, accepting the proffered cherry.

"Why let anything stand in the way of my being free?" Livy

asked. "All I need is a Frenchman, preferably a tall one. One who is interesting and nice, like Professor Finer. Then I'd kick my traces."

"Just try, young lady," Winston grumbled, reminding the Michaelses of the midnight hour, a shotgun, and the shouts and running steps of one of Livy's beaux.

"The dramas we play out!" Gussie smiled at Livy, who had thrown herself back into her seat, arms crossed and glaring at her father. "They seem earth-shattering at the time, but they are moods, Livy, not facts. One lives through them, learns, and moves on. Truly, having one's freedom is all very well to talk about, but the reality is not as easy as you make it out to be. Rules are made for a reason."

"Don't be so old-school, Mummy," Livy said. "A room of one's own and all that. Rules are confining. We should be entirely free to do what we want."

"But what you want is not necessarily the best thing for you, Livy," Gussie chided.

"How do you know that, Mummy?" Livy asked.

"I wonder if we can ever be free?" Auggie interrupted. He watched Lawrence to discern any reaction he might have, good or bad. "What if people's learned behaviors eventually become innate? As with Mummy and her cousin sharing so many tics and traits. Or the Russians. They've a whole history of authoritarian regimes, and though they tried to throw off the yoke, the Russians—or Soviets, as they call themselves now—have yet more of the same. They might have jobs and housing, food, but they don't have their *freedom*. It leaves me wondering if the Russian people are not able to be free."

"That depends on the definition of freedom. One people's freedom is another's oppression," Lawrence said. "Just look at Palestine."

"I'm writing a paper on Palestine," Auggie said, leaning forward. "Centuries of Christians and Jews and Arabs taught to hate and fight from birth. Why all the conflict, when they all want the same thing, self-determination?"

"Because they also want the same land," Alyssa said.

"So share," Auggie snapped, frowning at Alyssa. "And don't interrupt."

"We are a freedom-loving nation," Winston grumbled.

"Auggie isn't criticizing, Winston," Gussie said.

"I'm only wondering if how we are is inevitable," Auggie continued. "Do habits and attitudes, that were familial, become societal, part of a people's nature? And if so, is it possible to overcome our ancestry, or does it doom us?" Auggie asked, unintentionally meeting his father's eyes. "Are we trapped?"

Winston stood up, quite suddenly and to everyone's surprise. He stepped forward and grabbed Auggie's hand, turned it palm upward.

"No calluses," he said. "You'd be shot in one of your Commie countries."

"Winston!" Gussie said.

He dropped Auggie's hand, turned away.

"You certainly seem to know a great deal about things I know nothing about," Winston said, picking up his cocktail glass. "But about what I do know, you are entirely wrong."

"What do you know?" Gussie asked, her teeth clenched tight as she smiled.

"That the only solution as you go along is the American one: be your own master. Even in a very small way. Then your errors are your own and your good fortune is yours forever."

The phone rang. Winston excused himself. The floor creaked under his weight as he walked out to the dining room and kitchen. The air palpably relaxed as Winston's voice on the phone verified that he was well out of the way.

"Be your own master," Lawrence repeated, thinking about the words as he said them. "Then your errors are your own and your good fortune is yours forever. He is right, you know, Gussie."

As Lawrence spoke to Gussie, the color rose in her cheeks. Out in the kitchen, the phone was hung up, the freezer door opened and closed. "I'm thinking about my cousin," Gussie replied. "And what Auggie is saying. When you children were born, from the very first day, I knew what to expect of you." Gussie looked at her children. "Auggie had a quiet calm about him; Livy was sensuous and awake; and Alyssa was either shrieking or so soundly asleep that nothing would wake her. They've been the same ever since."

"But that's just personality and tendency," Auggie said, discomfited by the idea. "You can't know what we will do in a situation. It denies us our free will."

"Exactly, Auggie," Lawrence said to Auggie's relief. "There are certain inevitabilities. Inherited diseases like Huntington's. But there are an infinite number of variables, such that, even if we are determined, we can, at least, imagine ourselves free and try to act accordingly, so that at the end of our lives we can look back and be certain we've led a good life, one that we don't regret. However, people must be taught, and must challenge themselves, to look outside of their boxes. That is why I have a problem with rules. With rules, a person doesn't have to think, only obey. Rules don't allow a person to change, and the tighter you hold on to them, the smaller the chance of success at being your own person."

A brusque movement on Gussie's part, and her hand knocked over her wineglass.

"Oh, dear. I've broken it." She knelt on the floor and began to pick up the glass shards. Everyone moved to help. "No, no. I don't need help. Thank you. Ridiculous. All this space and we're all in one little corner. It's only one of our wedding glasses. Funny."

Winston returned. Gussie looked up at him, shrugged.

"I get so nervous and jumpy sometimes when entertaining, even close friends like you, Lawrence. As if I won't pass. I wonder why I bother."

"Because you're happiest when you entertain, Gussie," Winston said, setting down a full, old-fashioned cocktail glass on the side table next to her. A refreshing whiff of bourbon. She sat back down in her seat, handing the pieces of the glass to Alyssa to dispose of. Winston touched Gussie's shoulder lightly. "When you are happy, the world is happy."

"I wonder if that's possible, Winston—happiness," Lawrence said. "People aren't happy. It's not in their capacity."

"That's not true," Livy said. "I'm happy. Sometimes."

"That's right, Livy. We all have our little problems." Gussie picked up her cocktail with both hands. "Basically, though, we are happy."

"Is that the point, happiness?" Lawrence asked. "Isn't the point of life to learn and grow, challenge ourselves to do uncomfortable things because they might ultimately lead to a greater happiness?"

Silence, and Auggie had the feeling that Lawrence had directed the conversation to a path that would leave the rest of them behind—though not, perhaps, his mother.

"Happiness is a roof over one's head, family, and sufficient food to feed them," Gussie said. "Happiness is home."

"A compromise, then," Lawrence replied, lifting his glass. "To happiness, and other more important things."

"Gussie," Winston said, interrupting, still standing, not joining them. "That phone call. I have to go help a friend."

"So late?"

"How long is your paper to be?" Lawrence asked as the married couple's discussion continued in undertones.

"Ten pages."

"Have you considered, Auggie, that self-determination, the history of Palestine, and free will might be a broad subject for a ten-page paper?"

"But it's all so interesting," Auggie flushed.

"It could be a lifetime's work. Come to my house tomorrow. We'll refine the topic while I pack."

Auggie agreed.

"But you're to work outside with Father and me!" Alyssa interrupted. Auggie glanced at his father, who was putting on his coat and scarf in the entry foyer. Again, their eyes met.

"I'm afraid tomorrow is the only day possible," Lawrence said. "I leave Sunday at noon."

"We'll not take the whole day," Auggie said as his father walked toward the front door.

"Lawrence," Winston said, his voice gruff. "Safe travels."

"Thank you. Be well."

"God bless."

"It's important I do this paper right," Auggie said, his heart sinking as he looked out to the darkened foyer where his father stood—tall and robust, but wasn't there a hint of a stoop, the tiredness of age in his posture? Or was it loneliness and rejection as he adjusted his hat and stepped out the door alone? Auggie returned his attention to Lawrence.

"I am surprised that you're leaving so soon," Gussie said as the door clicked shut behind Winston.

"There's no time like the present, Gussie."

"Is it safe to go?" Gussie asked. "The state of the world is so tenuous."

"It always has been." Lawrence looked into his wineglass and then at Gussie. "I find that it's hard to leave at first, but once you've made the break from routine, you gain a refreshing perspective."

"I can imagine," Gussie said, sipping her bourbon. Her eyes closed, briefly, and she sighed. "I suppose that the way you appreciate what you have is to lose it. If only for a while. It's hard to imagine losing it forever. Too awful to think of. That there might be no redemption."

"Just like there was none for your cousin," Alyssa said, her voice clear and sharp. "She was positively struck from all family records."

"Mummy," Livy said, glaring at Alyssa. "Rules are made to be broken. I bet Cousin Lucinda was perfectly happy most of the time, which, as we have already discussed, is the most anyone can hope for. After all, there are other more important things." Livy paused, as if unsure if she had made her point. "Why not have it all? Look at Princess Elizabeth and the Duke of Edinburgh. They seem really to love each other, and they got married, even with all the rules they have to contend with. It's quite romantic and lovely, and no reason for it not to happen again and again. I don't think we're doomed at all."

The clock on the mantlepiece chimed seven. Lawrence excused himself. Gussie suggested Auggie walk him to the stone gates, to get some fresh air before dinner.

The two men discussed the ways of the world until they stepped onto Bittersweet Lane, at which point Winston drove past them, slowing the family station wagon to frown at them. They waved him on.

"Father can be difficult," Auggie said, staring at the red taillights.

"He's always been that way."

"Always?"

"He hasn't changed a bit. His intentions are good."

Auggie didn't reply at first.

"I've a photo of them," Auggie confessed. "On the back is written *Winston and Gussie, 1932*. Mother is dressed in a long white gown, a fur stole, and Father in a tuxedo. They are covered with snow and laughing. I suppose they'd had a snowball fight on the way home from a dinner party. Mother's cheeks and eyes are aglow, and her arms encircle Father's neck. She looks up at him as if he were her knight in shining armor."

"She loved him."

"But how? If he hasn't changed?"

"I met your father's parents once," Lawrence said. "His father, your grandfather. He was an interesting enough fellow, but your grandmother didn't have a kind word in her. A strict, no-nonsense woman. Whereas Gussie was so warm and generous, supportive of him. She believed in him. I would be willing to hazard that Winston had never heard the words *I love you* until your mother said them to him. He worships her."

They reached the stone gates. Lawrence looked up at the stars.

"That explains his actions," Auggie said. "Not hers."

"Think of our earlier conversation, Auggie. Our nature. What we are born with, whatever that may be, yet we live in the context of our learned behaviors. They give us a certain perspective, determine how we go about making decisions. Our work is to raise ourselves above. We mustn't let ourselves be trapped in rote ways of thinking and judging. Your father is a simple man married to a complex woman, and you have your mother's expectations."

Lawrence held out his hand to shake.

"Take that into account, Auggie. I will see you tomorrow at eleven."

Lawrence walked into the darkness, and it was as if Auggie had been thinking of something quite wonderful and then there was a distraction and the wonderful thought was gone, leaving an emptiness he wasn't quite sure how to fill.

Late the next afternoon, Auggie returned from Lawrence's to find his mother staring out the window, unmoving. Auggie approached her, looked out the window to see what she was looking at: Winston, tussling with a winter browned vine.

"Your father will never win." Gussie shook her head with a mix of condescension and pity as she returned to frosting Alyssa's birthday cake. "He will die and the bittersweet will grow up and cover whatever small mark he has made in the world."

"Isn't that what happens to us all?"

"Some rise above. You will. You'll leave something substantial, like Lawrence. Working on things beyond the menial."

"I suppose so," Auggie said. "Though the menial serves its purpose. It was the sweat of slaves that built the pyramids, not the whip that drove them."

Gussie glanced at him as if surprised.

"Would you rather have worked in the fields today?" she asked. Auggie's heart skipped a beat, and his face flushed.

"It would have been a different day," Auggie replied.

"Yes, it would have been." Gussie studied Auggie for a moment, during which he held quite still. "We are lucky to have all we have. Lawrence wasn't so lucky. I hope you appreciated your time with him. He has so much to teach you."

"Yes. Everything is clear in my mind now," Auggie said, able to breath again, if tentatively. "Silly, how confused I let myself get."

"You're only trying to get in all your ideas. Give yourself more time and room. You'll figure it out."

"Exactly what Lawrence said." Auggie felt again the pleasure of Lawrence's validation, and an urge to get to work on his paper. He had to get those ideas down, or he might forget them, and then what would he be?

"I'm terribly glad you spent the day with him. He is an excellent mentor. Under his tutelage, you'll succeed in making something of yourself."

"I'll try, anyway."

Gussie didn't respond, leaving Auggie to wonder if she had not heard him, or if she thought the answer too clear to be bothered with. She swept up another scoop of frosting with her knife and spread it.

"It was good of him to take the time," she said. "Poor man. He doesn't have anyone like you, Auggie, to take care of things when he's gone. There's a good deal to do. A trip requires suitcases and packing up things."

"Yes," Auggie agreed.

"Unless you leave everything as it is. Sometimes that's the best way."

"I suppose," Auggie replied, not sure at all that that was true.

"You have to get ready for the Club ball. I want you and Livy to be well out of here so that Alyssa can preside over her party. I had hoped it would distract her from the one she can't go to." Gussie sighed, smiled wryly. "Our plan didn't work this time."

"Where is Livy?" Auggie asked, uncomfortable at the reminder of his complicity. Sometimes it felt wrong, not being direct. Going about things in a way that others didn't have all the facts for their decisions. Though he supposed there had been no choice with Alyssa. She was too young to go to the Club ball, and she did deserve a birthday party.

"I've not seen her all day. She is dying to talk with you," Gussie said in a tone that stopped him short. "You'll need to support Livy. She is quite fragile."

"Is she? I sometimes wonder if that's just a role she's playing."

"If so, she's convinced us, and perhaps herself, too. She needs your help, Auggie."

And the tears in her eyes left Auggie wondering, as he walked out of the kitchen to prepare himself, whom she was talking about, and if his father was right in doubting whether Auggie would be strong enough.

Grand Illusions
March 1, 1948

*I*f not this weekend, it would be too late. Livy felt it in her bones as she looked into the mirror that hung above her dressing bureau. She looked deep into her own eyes and determined that her mother would run off with Lawrence, but not before Livy, herself, had escaped. Because if their mother left first, Livy would have to stay and take care of everyone. A horrific thought. Which was why someone would have to discover Livy at the Club ball tonight. Or fall in love with her. Someone rich and fun. Whomever he might be, he would whisk her away. Livy took a deep breath to relax the torrent of butterflies the thought unleashed. Did she dare?

Livy sucked in her checks, lowered her eyelids. Voluptuously. Barefoot, she turned. The skirt of her dark blue velvet dress swirled. Its dart-fitted bodice extended down to the full, just-below-the-knee-length skirt. Short puff sleeves. A V-neck and—Livy turned to see—a V-back that a man could admire right down to the adorable bustle she had tacked on to hide the fact that she had no bottom to speak of. She had to admit, the dress was perfect; telling but not *too*. She lowered her shoulders to emphasize her collarbones, turned sideways, and lifted her chest. That, unfortunately, was not *too*, either, even with the wad of toilet paper's boost. To mollify herself, she lifted one of her long legs.

Lovely and coltish, with fawn ankles. The movie cameras would adore them, if ever they had a chance, and there was no question that she would dare! She would run away that night and wouldn't give a hint to Auggie, though he had been her compass, moral and otherwise, ever since the mishap of the previous summer—an escapade at a neighbor's that had resulted in the disappearance of a rare wine collection and Livy's being grounded for the rest of her life. She had vowed after that that all her decisions, without exception, would depend on his rationale and reason. Which was exactly why she couldn't consult him this time. He might convince her to do otherwise than leave. Livy didn't want to be convinced otherwise.

Livy walked over to the closet, on the door of which hung a full-length mirror. She presented herself to the mirror, curtseyed deeply, and then, in exact imitation of Lauren Bacall, tilted her chin and looked up into it. A knock on the door.

"Go away, Alyssa," she snapped.

"It's Auggie."

"I've been waiting ages for you." She rushed to open the door. "Come in."

"What's taking you so long?" Auggie asked, stepping in, dressed in his tuxedo, his hair brushed back. He looked almost exactly like Perry Como. "It's nearly seven, and we are supposed to walk to the club."

"My hair is being impossible. Alyssa, scat! I want to talk to my brother alone."

"He's my brother, too." Alyssa frowned in the doorway. "Mummy told me to tell you that your dinner is quite cold."

"I can't even think of food or my dress will bust."

"I thought you'd just spent weeks fitting it to you," Auggie said, finally noticing the dress.

"I made it ever-so-slightly too small," Livy said. "It's quite slimming, don't you think?"

"It's lovely," Alyssa said from the hallway.

"Thank you, Alyssa, but you are skulking."

"I'm not." The door slammed in Alyssa's face. Livy returned to the dresser, cleaned just that afternoon with Murphy's oil soap. Her perfumes. Lipsticks. Various hand, face, foot, and body creams. All alphabetized according to make and color.

"You're a lucky devil, not having to live here." Livy picked up her silver hand mirror and matching brush.

"What's wrong with here?" Auggie asked, so quietly she hardly heard him—but, of course, she did, and so she replied.

"Simply everything." Livy bent over, flipped her hair, and brushed it toward the floor, the blood rushing to her head, rejuvenating any cells that needed rejuvenating. "Rules everywhere. Alyssa to spy. I will tell you right now that I won't be stuck here when Mummy leaves." Livy stopped herself. Mum's the word! She stood up and turned to Auggie, who leaned up against the windowsill. He stared out, though there was nothing to see but his reflection, it was so dark. Livy felt, quite suddenly, tearful.

"Auggie," she said, needing to tell him, because he would understand. He had to understand. "I spent the day in the bathroom."

"You always do," he said. "It's the only room besides Mummy's with a lock."

"Auggie, listen to me," Livy said sharply. She hadn't meant to be so sharp. "I only wanted to tell you. I was all showered. My hair brushed. I was ready to face the day, but I couldn't get out. The door wouldn't open. I yelled and hit the door with my fist. Shouted out the little window. No one heard me. No one helped. It was frightening, sitting there all by myself for hours on end."

"I'm sorry I wasn't here," he said. "I should never have spent so much time with Professor Finer."

"It's not that," Livy said. "You would have saved me if you could. I know that. Strange, though. I half-suspected Mummy heard me but couldn't be bothered to come."

"That's your overactive imagination. She'd never do such a thing."

"I know." Livy gave him a quick smile and then came as close as she dared to telling him everything. "Mummy knows what it is to be trapped. It was only how I felt. In that little room with no escape but that tiny window and a two-story drop. Do you understand, Auggie?"

"I'll check the lock and make sure it's working all right."

"Yes. Do. That would be lovely." Livy gathered herself. A teaching moment. She had to learn to cope with these silly feelings of neediness by herself. "I'd hate for that to happen to anyone else. I was perfectly fine, of course."

She studied herself in the mirror, admiring how her eyes glistened. If only she could draw up tears the way she used to, holding her eyes wide until they began to water. It had been effective in her youth. It would be helpful to her in New York. At her auditions. On Monday! She shivered, thinking what a different person she would be in forty-eight hours. The maturing she would endure.

"It was terribly romantic, wasn't it?" Livy hinted irresistibly.

"What was?" Auggie asked, startled.

"Mummy and Professor Finer last night, of course. Didn't you hear him as he was leaving? 'You've a beautiful view, Gussie,' he said, staring at her, not at the view, and Mummy said, 'Yes,' looking into his eyes, not at the view. He leaned toward her and her eyes closed. She held her breath, waiting for their lips to touch. Instead, he whispered in her ear, 'We'll never be happy without each other. Come away with me.' Mummy opened her eyes, tearful, as he gently kissed her neck just below the ear—"

"Which side?" Auggie asked, pleasantly enough. "Left or right?"

"Left," Livy replied, knowing perfectly well. "She shivered and promised to leave with him tomorrow at noon."

"You made that up entirely out of whole cloth." Auggie burst out laughing. "You see too many movies."

"On the contrary, it happened, if not in so many words," Livy said, brushing her long hair. "He quite clearly asked her to run away with him, if you were paying any attention whatsoever. Love and heartbreak. It's what makes a person feel alive, isn't it?"

Auggie rolled his eyes.

"Professor Finer will always love her, Auggie." Livy looked at him via the mirror as she twisted her hair up into a bun. "She just has to snap her fingers, and he'll come back to her."

"Don't be ridiculous. He is enamored of her cousin Kitty. You heard him talking about her last night."

"The ideas you come up with, Auggie! I should have gone with you today to see him. I am much more sensitive to subtext than you. Didn't you notice how Mummy flushed when he said how alike the two of them are, and how comfortable he felt with her cousin? Or how Mummy broke the wineglass when he was telling her to break free of Father, break the rules, be her own master? We have got to encourage Mummy to snap her fingers. She thinks she's made her bed and resigns herself to sleeping in it. I'll never do that. If my husband doesn't meet my expectations, I'll divorce him and find another."

"The world is your oyster?"

"Absolutely." Livy smiled. "What do you think of these, Auggie?"

She held up a string of pearls to her long, pale neck. Auggie looked at her, frowned.

"They're Mummy's. Does she know you have them?"

"Of course not. She's too busy with Alyssa's party." Livy fastened the clasp and admired herself. "Do you think she enjoys sex with Father?"

"That is something I would prefer never to think about."

"Don't be a prude."

"I'm not being a prude. It's distasteful to think of that in regard to one's parents."

"Conceptually," Livy said, applying a rose lipstick. "I don't imagine it either. I merely wonder if Mummy is satisfied. It would be such a sad thing, to go through life unsatisfied physically. When she leaves, we'll have to be far more patient with poor Father."

"What do you mean, when she leaves?"

"You don't think she'll stay forever, do you? What do you think of this lipstick?"

"The color's a bit strong."

"It's perfect." Livy pressed her lips together.

"You don't need lipstick."

"That's like saying I don't need clothes, Auggie. I've got to wear lipstick to cover me up. Besides, Lauren Bacall, Ingrid Bergman, and Judy Garland all wear Max Factor makeup, and look where they are."

"Where?"

"In the arms of Humphrey Bogart, Cary Grant, and Gene Kelly! Come stand next to me."

Auggie joined her and they studied themselves in the mirror, he in his tuxedo, new and already a tad too short in the pants leg, and she in all her elegance.

"We look marvelous," Livy said, clapping her hands in anticipation. They would take over the dance floor, sweeping past all the plain girls and wowing all the men. "I'm as beautiful as Mummy ever was, aren't I?"

"You're different."

"Meaning?" Livy tried to smile into the mirror.

"You're perfectly pretty."

"But not beautiful," Livy said, and watched the tears gather, brightening her eyes, reddening the whites. She mustn't break down entirely, as she wanted to, or her nose would go all red.

"Do you sometimes wish, Livy, that Lawrence had been our father?" Auggie asked—to change the subject, she knew. Livy looked at him.

"Nevah," she said, after a long pause. For effect. Like Bette Davis. Her words short and clipped. "We wouldn't be us."

Livy wrapped an old tartan scarf around her neck to hide the pearls, and then the finishing touch: perfume. Adrian's *Saint & Sinner*. Only enough for herself, and the man who would whisper in her ear, to smell.

"The three telltale signs of a lady," she said, quietly affirming her commitment to lipstick, perfume, and pearls.

"I suppose Father isn't so bad," Auggie said as they walked

downstairs together. "He might be able to get me intelligence work in the army. That's what he did for Lawrence."

"That would be lovely." Livy patted her brother's shoulder, pitying him his illusions.

Alyssa's guests had arrived—fifteen thirteen-year-olds—and Gussie, flushed and distracted, was in the kitchen with them, all chatting and gossiping. Livy and Auggie shouted their good-byes over the din, donned their coats, mittens, and rubber boots, and hurried out the door, leaving Livy's dinner plate untouched next to the sink.

Cobalt blue sky. Waning gibbous moon. Crisp night air. Ice and snow crunched beneath their feet as Livy noted a certain sadness inside herself. Would this be the last time she walked the gravel drive? She glanced back at the house and had to admit the comfort and reassurance that its bright lights in the darkness gave her. She imagined never returning and felt a twinge of pity for her mother, left to cope alone.

Livy corrected that thought. Her mother, too, had options. She could leave. It was not Livy's fault if her mother didn't take life by the horns and live. What Livy had to do was meet the challenges of her own life, which meant taking her opportunities as they came. Now. This was her time, her evening. She could only hope the high heels she had chosen were the right ones. She lifted one of them out of her coat pocket. Black patent leather was not quite blue velvet, even in the dark.

"Strange, how peaceful it seems," Auggie said. "Everyone is so relieved to be done with the war, yet the violence continues. The fighting in Palestine. Gandhi's murder."

"Gandhi. Yes," Livy said. She stuffed the shoe back in her pocket and picked up her pace to keep up with Auggie's. "It was so sad. Mummy and I wept for a full week afterwards."

"One could argue the fall of a certain . . . civility in his murder."

"It is ironic, isn't it? Nonviolence dying violently."

"It will make a martyr of him," Auggie said. "His ideas and followers might get civilization farther up the cliff."

"Cliff?"

"Toynbee's theory. Did you happen to read the article on it in this week's *Life* magazine?"

"I didn't happen to, no." Livy smiled thinly.

"He has a fascinating theory on history. He describes the world's various civilizations working their ways up a cliff, toward the yin of God's perfection. It's a constant struggle, and the ones who are still struggling pass the dead and the dying civilizations. Five civilizations are still struggling up, and all show signs of destruction."

"What a cheerful thought."

"It is. Because if the civilizations face their problems creatively, they might save themselves. There's hope. Unfortunately, humans have a tendency to take the short-term, selfish point of view. We'll more likely go extinct. Not a bad thing. The world will be better off in the long run."

"This little fit of negativity is rather dull, Auggie."

"It isn't negative. It's realistic. I find it interesting to think about— the passages of whole civilizations, and we think any small decision on our part makes a difference. As if we matter."

"Clearly, you were not paying attention this Christmas when we watched *It's a Wonderful Life*." Livy trotted to keep up with those damned long legs of his. "One person can make all the difference in the world."

"However much you like Jimmy Stewart, Livy, he is no Gandhi."

"Everyone can't be," Livy said, pacing her words to her steps. "We can do our part. Just like in the war. Some people don't need to be quite so riveting. Some people are happy just being, however insignificant they are. Of course," she added after a pause, "that wouldn't be us."

"No?"

"We've so much opportunity and potential. There is only the sky to limit us."

"And perhaps ourselves," Auggie said.

"Nonsense. How can we limit ourselves when we're limitless?"

Auggie stopped abruptly. She smiled, patient as the day is long, though it was too irritating, the way he went from walking rather too fast—she did not want to arrive *shining*—to a dead halt. They had to arrive, after all.

"Where does it come from?" he asked. "The expectation that we're so special? That we're entitled to succeed?"

"I suppose it's just how it is. Our good fortune. We've no excuses. You're to be a brilliant scholar, and I a famous actress."

Auggie stared at her for a moment. "What if we're not? What if we're just wasting ourselves on dreams, giving ourselves airs and expectations that we'll never fulfill? Sometimes I think we're just deluded."

"Speak for yourself, Auggie!" Livy said, furious at him for articulating what she spent so much time trying not to think about. That kind of thinking caused wrinkles, premature aging, which was the one thing she could not afford at this juncture. Livy turned to directly confront her brother. "There is the difference between us, Auggie. You think up these dreadful ideas and then worry them to death."

"At least I think."

"I think, too." Livy cuffed his heavily cloaked shoulder with a mittened hand. "All the time I think. It breaks my heart, sometimes, to think that each and every one of my thoughts isn't recorded so future generations might think with me. I can hardly keep track of all my thoughts, some of which might even be deep enough for you." Livy paused, momentarily devastated by the vast distance that had risen between the two of them. "You've no right to judge me, Auggie. You've no idea what it's like being me, whereas I know exactly what it's like being you. That's how I know I'll be successful. I can entirely understand other people's hurts and pains and yearnings and desires. Because I feel so deeply. That's just how I am. And if it is the case that I don't think, then you don't feel. You hold everything at a distance, inspecting and analyzing. I worry about you, Auggie. It seems the only things that make you truly happy are your books and studies. As if the ideas you think about are more real and significant than people. But if ideas are so terribly important and our day-to-day decisions don't matter, if our dreams are to be discounted as nothing, if the only thing that matters is what we accomplish, then why do you waste your precious mortality on those novels and mysteries that you read?"

Auggie looked at her and she knew exactly what he was thinking: Livy is overwrought again. Working herself up into an emotional tizzy about nothing. But it wasn't nothing. What was life if not feelings?

"They're a relief," Auggie said.

"Exactly. And what you don't seem to understand, Auggie, is that my film-watching is like your book-reading. Films are a means to get out of one's life entirely. It's vicarious living. When you are stuck in your own, grinding existence, you see alternate ways to get out and have hope that life might hold something more for you. For me. They let me know that I am going to do things with my life. Nothing is going to stop me. Some day, soon, I'm going to be discovered."

"Success won't be handed to you. They aren't going to come and find you."

"Do you think I don't know that?" Livy snapped and began to walk. "I intend to work hard. My point is, it's difficult to progress here. There is no one really good to teach me. You have your college professors. You've Lawrence Finer. I have no one to advise me."

"What about the director for the senior play that you're leading in? You had nothing but good things to say about him in your last letter."

"He's an amateur. Mummy came to a rehearsal and was quite horrified. She suggested I decline the honor. She doesn't want me to embarrass myself."

"You won't embarrass yourself. You'll have great fun."

"No. Mummy is right. I'd forget my lines."

"Is that what she said?"

"What does it matter? It was a silly high school play. I'm meant for something bigger. This is my prime. I mustn't waste it."

As if on cue, a train whistled in the distance, approaching from the north. They both started, looked at each other. Livy grabbed Auggie's hand and they ran, she tripping and slipping but supported by him as their footsteps sounded on the snow, squeaking. They rounded the last curve of the road before the railroad tracks, laughing with excitement as another blast of a horn sounded, in the distance but not too far now. The train would be going by the Poquatuck Tennis Club, then over the bridge, slowing for the sharp curve. They could see where it would pass, and stopped a few yards from the gates, which had begun to ding, red lights flashing. They stared up the tracks. Livy thought how in her parents' day, it was possible to wave down the train. It would have stopped and she could have stepped up and away, bringing Auggie with her.

"It's an I-5 Hudson!" Auggie said, and he looked just like the five-year-old Livy always remembered him as, all innocence and glee in the moment. Such a brief moment.

The engine sped *The Merchants Limited* into view, steam plumes rising into the crystalline air, white against black. Two engines, a luggage car, three, four, five passenger cars, full. She could see the people in the lit windows, reading, chatting, and eating, and, as they clattered past, she had an urge to run after the train, to escape to New York City, where life would be entirely different and her brother wouldn't look so sad. The train left a chilling, buffeting wake. An owl hooted.

"Trains are quite satisfactory." Auggie checked his wristwatch as the evening settled back to quiet. "So timely and dependable, getting a person from point A to point B. Enabling them to cover such distances."

"Yes, especially in the snow. These boots are ruining my stockings."

"Why don't I carry you the last bit, across the bridge?" Auggie suggested. "Father would be pleased to think I had, perhaps, worked my muscles, and you'll be more fit to dance."

"Do you think you can bear me?"

"I can try," Auggie replied with a quiver of a grin, and she felt a twinge because she had not meant to offend him.

"I only ask because I've grown so much. I'm not the little girl I used to be." He lifted her up with more ease than she would have guessed. "You are a dear, Auggie, and perfectly strong. It's lovely you have been rowing this year, even in winter."

"It's peaceful on the water."

"I think Professor Finer is right." Livy looked ahead of them as Auggie carried her up the tracks, stepping on the cross ties, across the water beneath them, the moon's path out to sea broken by the breakwater. The stars above, shadows of clouds passing by. "If you learn another language or two, which you seem to do in your sleep, you'll not have to worry about physical strength. The Army will use you for something smart. You'll be free of Father. That's what we need to do to fulfill our potential, is to get away."

Auggie didn't respond to what she was suggesting. Livy decided to tell him, so he would understand the next morning why she had done what she had done. There would be no going back for her. Whether he thought so or not, each person's decisions did have an effect. She would have hers.

"Mummy should never have told you to quit that play, Livy."

"She didn't. Not exactly. I did it of my own accord. I've no intention of ending up like her, you know. It breaks my heart, seeing her waste her life."

". . . Do you think she's unhappy?"

"I certainly would be."

"Sometimes I think that if it weren't for us, she'd leave him," Auggie said. "That it's our fault."

"It's Father. She should have divorced him years ago. Imagine the life we would have had! We'd have traveled the world. Lived in all sorts of different places. Instead . . . how she tolerates him, I will never know."

"It's more *why*, isn't it?"

Livy studied Auggie. Could it be that he really didn't know?

"It's different for you, Auggie, dear. You're a man. You're expected to and must go off, make your own way in the world. That's your cross to bear. For women it's different. It takes a great deal to throw up our role in life. It is easier for me to do it now than it is for Mummy. It will take courage for her to do it. We must help her to leave. The only way for us to get what we want is for Mummy to get what she wants."

Auggie frowned.

"What about Alyssa?" he asked.

"Alyssa is resilient. She's fine with Father. She adores him but is embarrassed to let on. They go off and cabal, clearing land, having a gay old time. He'll spoil her rotten, such that not even she will be able to complain. She'll be happier without us."

"You've thought this all out, haven't you?"

"Absolutely. It will be perfect." They arrived at the other side of the bridge as Livy broke her news. "I can't stay, Auggie. If I do, I'll never leave."

". . . Sad," he said, his pace unbroken, as if nothing had changed. As if he had not heard what she had just said. "All those people fighting on the other side of the world for a right to a home, and we go around complaining about ours. We take it for granted, but what if we were to lose it? What if it were taken from us?"

"We'd fight for it," Livy said.

"Why fight for something you want to escape?" he asked.

Livy stared at him. His face looked nearly unrecognizable these days, he'd matured so. The soft, fuzzy roundness of childhood had been replaced by an acned angularity. His nose, which had seemed too big for his face over Christmas, quite suddenly fit. And his brown eyes suggested a deep intelligence, a playful wit. Though he did still have a bit of the lost puppy look to him.

"Poor Auggie." Livy touched his cheek, gently patting it. "Everything is a life and death struggle for you. Why not just acceptance of things as they come? You must try, we both must, to be fun and lighthearted. We survived the war. We are not starving, or having to shoot people. Nor are we dirty, though we are a bit cold. Awful things happen, but here we are, young and at the start of our lives, with all our potential. We're going to a party. Let's just enjoy it. Please? We can think about losing everything tomorrow."

"Ah, Scarlett," Auggie said.

"My dearest brother."

Auggie set her down and they walked, hand in hand, to the path that led to the Poquatuck Tennis Club's parking lot, at the edge of which Livy used Auggie as a balance while she changed her fur-trimmed boots for her high heels.

"This is going to be lovely," she whispered as Auggie escorted her into the club.

The entry hall served as the coat closet, with racks full of coats and piles of boots. Another set of doors opened to what usually served as the large, circular dining room but now had been positively transformed into a dance hall, complete with a big band. Livy stood at the doorway while Auggie hung up their coats and swayed to "Imagination," picturing herself in the arms of Frank Sinatra.

"It's magical," she whispered when Auggie joined her. "Isn't the band marvelous?"

"They're okay."

"Expectations," Livy sang as they stepped in and took a walk around to see who was about and what fun there was to be had. Couples on the dance floor. Singles watching. They stopped to greet acquaintances, went out to the porch and joined the crowds of people standing around a bonfire, smoking, sneaking a drink. Exactly as she'd imagined it. There stood Mary, Sarah, and Joanne. Not her favorites, but she left Auggie for their company. A lit Chesterfield, smoke coming out her nostrils. A drink. Gin. How adult she felt, her life ahead of her and all sorts of men about, such that she proclaimed, behind the smoke of her cigarette and to her new best girl-friends in the world, that she intended to meet a fellow who would take her to New York City, whoever he was, married or not, anything to get away. The pearls? Given to her by a jealous admirer.

When the bottle was empty, Livy wandered back inside and watched Auggie dance, as always, with the wallflowers of the party. He did adore to dance, and he was so tall now, surprisingly graceful as he waltzed and whirled them about.

"My turn, Auggie." Livy tapped him on the shoulder when the song ended. "Lead me right past that fellow with the black hair. Don't look. In the corner there, by the band."

Off they went, the real start of the night. Jitterbugs to waltzes, the band was divine, no matter if Auggie thought them amateurish. She danced all night. With Mort and Henry and Jonathan and Michael, and in between dances a sip of whatever was offered. The belle of the ball. Cheeks flushed, eyes sparkling, a dab more lipstick as the night proceeded, the lights dimmed, the glitter, the movement, blurred, and she would sing! She would take initiative. She approached the bandleader, not the least bit nervous, only savoring the moment. This would be her break to stardom.

"Livy." Auggie touched her elbow. She startled, smiled, quite surprisingly lost her balance, but there he was to catch her.

"Isn't this lovely?" she asked, leaning against him. "I'm about to—"

"You should eat something. You've had too much liquor."

"Don't be ridiculous," she said, standing up straight. "And I certainly will not eat anything."

She brushed him away and walked toward . . . she wasn't quite sure. She had meant to do something, but she kept moving, smiling, wondering at life. If she were a boy. Not that she wanted to be a boy, because—Max! Right in front of her with his solid shoulders and round, bright red face. He asked her to dance. Max, the boy she had grown up with, practically. He was a photographer now. Living in the City! They'd known each other forever, and she admitted to him with a cavalier laugh that she had always imagined . . . *things* might happen between the two of them. She'd never thought he cared, but somehow, tonight, he did. Hadn't he been looking at her all night? And here she was in his arms. They flew about the dance floor like two sparrows, and around and around, and ended up, somehow, in the shadows of the coatroom, kissing. It was a dream. Luxurious. She adored him, and he said he loved her, too.

"Livy!" Her name. Shouted in the distance. Max was all tangled up, then suddenly breaking away, saying he would call, and gone as the swinging door of the exit creaked shut. In his place, her father. In his work clothes. The music dimmed, and everyone—she knew it!— was watching. "Livy Michaels, you're coming home this minute."

She lifted her chin and, concentrating very hard, walked away from him, across the terribly uneven floor. Bumping into the dancers, and how could they think of dancing at a time like this? Where was Auggie? Her arm caught on something. Her father's hand.

"Father?" she said, trying to control her outrage. Her voice trembled. "Why are you here, and dressed like that?"

He dragged her across floor and out to the car.

"Father, this my night. It's not fair. You're ruining everything."

"You're drunk," he said.

"Why are you doing this to me? Where is Auggie? Go bother him."

"Your mother cooked you a fine dinner." Winston opened the car door for her. "You're going to eat it."

"No, I am not," Livy said.

"Your mother is not your maid, young lady."

"She might as well be a maid, married to a janitor the way she is."

Winston slapped her across the face.

"You brute!" Livy burst into tears of mortification.

"Get in the car."

"I'll never be able to face anyone again as long as I live." Livy moaned and dropped into the car. The seat felt astoundingly good. She wanted to die.

Winston slammed the door shut and walked around to the driver's seat. She would kill him. No, it would take too much effort. The car lurched forward. A wave of nausea came over her. She groaned and curled up in her seat. If only she could sleep. Everything whirled. Her father lectured, his words unintelligible, irrelevant to her life. She was too sick even to weep. She had to concentrate very hard until, when finally the car stopped, she opened the door and vomited. Bitter. Bile. Her father's cooling hand on her forehead, patting her back, making a soothing whispering sound. She spat, weeping, shivering, heaving again, a shuddering breath. Her father handed her his handkerchief. She wiped her face and blew her nose.

"I hate you," she said.

"Let me help you," Winston said, gently lifting her up in his arms. She was too exhausted to protest. He carried her in the front door, so as not to interrupt the shrieks of Alyssa's party, ongoing in the dining room. Upstairs, he set Livy down in front of her bedroom door. She reached for the wall to balance herself.

"Mummy?" she mumbled, eyes closed.

"Busy. I'll bring you up your dinner."

"No."

"Livy, you'll feel better if you eat."

"You can't make me eat. Go away. I never want to see you again. Mummy is going to leave you, and I'm glad. I'm going with her. We all are. YOU ARE GOING TO DIE ALONE!"

He was gone. She stumbled into her room, to the bureau, and stared at herself in the mirror. The whites of her eyes were brilliant red, brightening the blue iris, but her nose and face were a sight. How did those movie stars look so good when their lives were falling apart? And then Livy noted the absence of her mother's pearls.

A roll of toilet paper, toothbrush and toothpaste, a flashlight from the hall closet, an extra pair of underwear. Perfume, lipstick, a burp of bile. With shaking hands, freezing cold, she took off the dress and shoes and added them to the stuffed pillowcase. She put on a pair of jeans, a long-sleeved Oxford shirt and heavy wool sweater, and sneakers because her boots were still at the club and clearly her only option was to run away.

She pushed open the glass window and tossed out the pillow. The cold air braced her as she pulled herself out of the house, clinging to the trellis and the rain gutter. Well-used to this exit, she shimmied to the ground, picked up her pillow, and ran down the path to the beach. As fast as she possibly could, stumbling, convinced she was being followed, she ran. Forever. It seemed like miles and miles. She arrived, breathless, on the beach. She was alone. She raised her hands above her head. Reaching to the sky. Desperate for a sip of water. Parched and queasy. This was what it felt like to be free! Very cold. Heart beating hard. Ill as ill could be. If only she could lie down on her bed . . . but she would never go back.

The tide was ebbing, the ocean gently lapping at the frost-coated sand. She looked to the end of the harbor. The club was still lit up. The music, voices, laughter carried across the harbor. How could the party have continued as if the entire world had not changed? Odious people. They were probably laughing at her. Years from now, when she returned, they would not laugh! By then, this night would be buried beneath the memories of the wondrous people she would have met, the rich parties she would have attended. She turned to look up the path leading to the house, her chin lifted. Strange. A vague fear. A pang of regret, maybe doubt. But why?

"You're home."

A voice from the darkness startled her awake. Alyssa.

"What?" Livy said.

"You're home before midnight." Alyssa stepped onto the beach to join her. "Auggie isn't back yet."

"He's a boy, free to do whatever he wants. Why aren't you at your party?"

"They've all left. I'm stargazing. What are you doing?"

"Running away," Livy said, defiant. Alyssa hesitated.

"Why?"

"Because I'm an adult. I can't live here forever. I should be off on my own. Independent. Free of this place."

Alyssa stared at her, wide-eyed, pale, doubtful.

"If you're leaving, may I have your silver mirror and brush?"

Livy hesitated. She had forgotten to pack them! But she dared not go back.

"I suppose so."

"Thank you. I'll consider them a birthday present. If you're leaving because of Mummy's pearls, Father found them when he was hosing down the driveway. It's disgusting, Livy, vomiting in the middle of the drive."

Livy didn't answer. Pearls found?

"Where are you going?"

"New York City. Where else?" Livy replied, with a growing sense of doom. "I'm going to be a lady of leisure. I'll have a penthouse apartment and all sorts of lovely clothes and men knocking at my door, just like a movie star."

"You'll need money to do all that. I bet you don't even have enough to get there. Trains cost money, and if you ask for a ride Mummy and Father will find out and they'll never let you out of their sight again."

Livy sat down abruptly. Only due to the wave of dizziness that had come over her, not because Alyssa was right.

"It's stupid to run away without a plan," Alyssa added. "Why not wait?"

"If I wait," Livy said, her voice harsh against the painfully enormous knot in her throat, "Mummy will leave and I'll be trapped here forever."

"Mummy's not leaving."

"Of course she is. Tomorrow, with Professor Finer."

"Impossible. Tomorrow is my birthday. We've all sorts of plans. She can't leave. Nor can you. Just look at the sky."

"Velvet sky," Livy said.

"No. Just sky. Why is it always a velvet sky to you? Velvet makes me think of dresses, not constellations. Far simpler to call it sky. That's what it is, after all. Then I know what you're talking about. That's Orion." Alyssa pointed up, then made a fist as if she could measure the sky. Livy tried to see it. "There's his dog. *Canis Major*. It looks like a dachshund."

"I don't see it." Livy's eyes filled with tears of frustration.

"Look. It's right there. See that bright star? That's its nose."

"I prefer real dogs." Livy stood up and brushed the sand off her. "Not silly stars."

"Major or minor?" Alyssa asked, looking at her. "Is it a big or little dog?"

"I can't tell," Livy said. Hadn't she already confessed that she couldn't see the damn star dog?

"I hope it's big. Little ones are yippy."

"You're smart, Alyssa," Livy said. "So is Auggie. Whereas I feel as if I'm a failure."

"You're perfectly smart in your own way."

"I don't feel it. I do badly in school. In everything I do. Without boys, I'd go crazy. At least they like me for who I am."

"Of course they do," Alyssa said. "You're lovely."

The church bell in the village tolled midnight.

"It's my birthday, Livy," Alyssa said, sounding doleful.

Why had she said anything about intelligence and boys, Livy wondered, exposing herself to her baby sister who idolized her? It was Livy's job to take care of Alyssa, not the other way around. A yowl from somewhere in the darkness. Violent rustling. A fight was going on, right there near them, they couldn't tell where. Shrieks from a doomed animal, and Livy had to save her sister, if not herself, from the terror.

"Run!" Livy shouted. Both girls sprinted back up to the house. The sound of their footsteps through the grass and heavy breathing spurred them to run faster. Alyssa, laughing, ran ahead, leaving Livy behind, who tripped. Her leg twisted. She lay on the ground, in tears, unable to determine which pain was greater: that of her leg, or the fact that she would not run away tonight.

"Help! Save me!" she shouted, and wept, telling herself that soon she would take her life into her own hands. Soon she would be free and independent. If only someone would help her.

Birthday Wishes
March 2, 1948

The sun was a boor the next morning, nudging and tickling Alyssa with its brightness. She had forgotten, again, to shut the shades, and how nice it would be to have use of the back bedroom, which was closer to the bathroom and dark and cozy in winter, cool in summer. As it was, she endured the heat and light of the front one, and decided that the first thing she would train her puppy to do would be to close the shades. Because her parents were giving her a puppy for her birthday. It had to be a puppy, because an adult dog would have grown up without her to train it. It wouldn't bond with her or depend on her in the same way.

She surfaced from beneath her quilt and pillows, rolled onto her back, and stared up at the ceiling. She had promised herself to be as happy as could be on this of all days, her birthday, yet she had to admit she felt disappointed. Livy had ruined the surprise. Alyssa never got to be surprised.

The ship's clock out in the hallway chimed three times: nine thirty! The day was nearly over. Alyssa threw back the covers and got up to dress. Pancakes? She sniffed the air, listened, because this room did have its benefits: being at the top of the staircase, one knew who was up and what was cooking.

She burst out of her room, glorious and three. After checking to be sure Livy and Auggie weren't in their rooms, she raced downstairs. Living room, empty. Dining room still cluttered with the remnants of the previous evening's divine party. Kitchen, no one. She paused to listen. The tick of the grandfather clock. She ran out to the garage, then the cabin. Shouting hellos. She searched down at the beach, up to the driveway's end, before finally returning to the house mortified and offended. If she had had any idea the day she was born that twelve years later, to the day, her family would desert her, Alyssa would have . . . she didn't know what.

In the kitchen, she found their note. "*Livy broke her leg. Gone to hospital. Back by 11.*"

Alyssa smiled. They had gone to pick up her *present*. It was almost too much to bear, the ticklish anticipation.

At ten thirty, she heard voices coming up the back stairs and into the mudroom. The kitchen door opened to Auggie, still in his tuxedo pants and dress shirt, and Livy, on crutches, in one of Auggie's old Oxford shirts and a pair of jeans, the right leg of which had been freshly hacked off to make room for the cast that reached up her entire left leg. No puppy.

"Where have you been?" Alyssa asked, frowning.

"Didn't you see our note?" Auggie asked. Alyssa didn't answer as the fact sunk in that they had, in fact, *gone to hospital.*

"What happened?" Alyssa assessed the cast, envious of the attention it would get Livy.

"Well, Holmes, it looks like I broke my leg, doesn't it?" Livy said. "Saving you from the monsters in the woods."

"It was a raccoon fight," Alyssa said, eyeing Livy's cast suspiciously. "Your leg was perfectly fine last night on the beach."

"I broke it saving you from the murderers. I saved you at great risk to myself, whereas you left me to die." Livy swung out of the kitchen, her siblings following behind.

"I didn't," Alyssa protested. "I went to bed. I thought you'd gone up the trellis like you always do. I would have helped you if I'd known."

"A likely story. I'd still be out in the woods if Mummy hadn't come and found me. Where is Father? He disappeared too. Typical. He's never around when you need his help."

"Last I knew, he went for a walk. He and Mummy had an argument about your stealing the pearls. He wasn't here when I woke up. No one was," Alyssa added pointedly.

"I did not steal the pearls."

"You were dead to the world when we left, hidden under all those covers," Auggie said. "We tried to wake you. I thought you were pretending, with all the ruckus Livy made."

"I was stoic relative to the agony I was in," Livy retorted as she lowered herself into their mother's winter seat on the couch nearest the fireplace. She winced as she tried to get comfortable. "Auggie, would you build a fire? Thank you. Alyssa, get me aspirin and water."

"Where is Mummy? I thought she wasn't going to church today," Alyssa said, unmoved.

"Who said anything about her going to church?" Livy asked.

"It's Sunday. My birthday. If she's not at church, where is she?" Auggie snapped a stick of kindling. Alyssa smiled. Needing no other answer, Alyssa ran upstairs. Puppies love to gnaw on sticks. Their mother was picking up a medium-sized dog. A pretty dog. Perhaps one of those smart, collie-looking sheepdogs the Ellises owned. Alyssa grabbed the aspirin and hurried back downstairs.

"Odd to think of Mummy gone, isn't it?" Auggie was saying in a hushed voice. Alyssa froze halfway down the stairs.

"You didn't believe me last night when I told you. It was clear as day to me though. They're off on the noon train."

"I'm glad for her sake. I've always imagined Mummy was a Dorothea to Father's Casaubon, tolerating the intolerable. A martyr to our cause."

"The difference being, Father hasn't the consideration to die, and society isn't what it was. Mummy is free to leave, as today demonstrates," Livy said. "Would you put a pillow under my leg, Auggie?"

"We'd a nice chat while we waited for you in the hospital."

"I'm glad my leg served some purpose. Thanks. That's lovely. What did she say?"

"Nothing. I mean, we neither of us spoke to it directly. She did say she has no regrets."

"Perhaps, but she certainly wasted no time dropping us off just now. We must remember to tell Alyssa she apologized."

"Apologized?" Auggie asked.

"Didn't you hear her? *Tell Alyssa I am sorry. I'll be back.*"

"Someday."

"It's a lesson to us," Livy said. "I've always thought she adored this place, but she's giving it up with hardly a snap of her fingers. Exactly as I intend to do as soon as I get this ugly cast off. I'm going to plan it out very carefully. Father won't be able to stop me next time. Laws, I don't know which hurts more, my leg or my head. ALYSSA?"

"Here I am." Alyssa stepped down the stairs, slowly. She walked heel to toe, as she used to as a child when contemplating one or another hurt. Step by step, she would try to make sense. Who was the *they* that their mother was leaving with, where were they going, and would there be a dog or not?

"Why are you talking as if Mummy isn't coming back?" she asked, handing Livy the aspirin.

"Your pajama top is on backwards."

"She promised me pancakes. She would never go back on her promise."

"Why don't I make the pancakes?" Auggie said.

"Because Mummy is to make them," Alyssa replied.

"If you aren't having breakfast, you should do your math homework," Livy said.

"Math? Today?" Alyssa asked, stunned. Her eyes filled with tears. Not a single happy birthday, and now math! "I'd rather die. I hate math. A squared plus B squared equals C squared. Why should I care?"

"Because it will teach you to think logically," Auggie said.

"I already do."

"You'll be able to prove it. You have to learn how to present your argument, if you're to win your cases as a lawyer."

"I'll just do what your Agatha Christie does, not showing her entire hand, so you're left guessing until the end. It's not fair how she does that."

"Fair smair. You'll have to deal with the consequences of not doing your homework, not us," Livy said as Alyssa sat down on the couch at her feet. "Ow! You practically sat on my leg, Alyssa. Move."

Livy kicked her off the couch to the floor.

"May I write on your cast?"

"No. It hurts."

"A cast can't hurt."

"It can if I kick you with it. What are you staring at?"

"How could you be so stupid, breaking your leg on my birthday?" Alyssa scowled because two plus two equals four, and wasn't this exactly how things worked out every time? Promises broken. Alyssa faced the crackling fire while her siblings settled into the couches on either side of her. The creak of snow pressing into gravel caught Alyssa's attention. She jumped up and ran to the window.

"I don't recognize the car. Father's in the passenger's seat," Alyssa reported. "I think he has a dog! No. It's someone. A girl. He's waiting for her to come around from the driver's side. He's . . ." Alyssa blinked and felt a lurch, as if she were in a boat that had scraped up onto a seaweed-covered rock. "They're hugging."

Both Livy and Auggie looked over at Alyssa, alert.

"He's taking her by the elbow, leading her up the front sidewalk. They're coming in."

Alyssa stepped back. Livy pulled herself into a sitting position. Auggie stood up. They all three looked toward the door that led to the entry hall and their parents' room as the exterior door opened and shut.

"Thank you for coming," Winston said, his voice strangely kind, with none of its usual gruff defensiveness. "I couldn't bear it here alone."

The door between the front entry and living room swung open and the woman stepped into the room. Red hair, freckles, brown eyes. She wore no makeup. A fitted black coat, unbuttoned to show a simple blue dress with a floppy lace collar. She paled upon sight of Livy on the couch, Auggie holding a poker next to the hearth, and Alyssa.

"Winston!" she said, her voice sharp and alarmed. Their father came in, towering above her. He paled, touched the woman's shoulder.

"Come," he ordered.

"No," the woman said. "The bell's been rung. I'm not a pet to be ordered about or hidden anymore."

She stepped farther in and surveyed the room as one might a house one is about to claim possession of, assessing what will stay and go. Alyssa looked at the room too, judging it as this stranger might. The furniture needed upholstery. The green carpet had faded to a color remarkably like overcooked string beans. Magazines, books, and opened mail littered the surfaces. The dining room, through the doorway, was still ravaged by the previous night's birthday party. Two teenagers looking tired and disheveled, and Alyssa, who said the only appropriate thing that could be said.

"How very kind of you, Father. A maid to clean up and do the dishes for this afternoon's birthday party. Mother will be delighted."

"Alyssa!" Winston said sternly.

"What, Father?" Alyssa asked. "If not a maid, who?"

Silence, excepting Auggie's strangled breath as he sat back down on the edge of the couch, clutching his knees and staring at the woman, who moved to sit.

"Not there." Winston stepped forward.

"That's Mummy's summer chair," Alyssa explained, watching as her father assisted the woman to his chair, off in the corner of the room. His touch and concern startled Alyssa to a recognition of the nature of their relationship. "As opposed to her winter chair, which is there at Livy's feet. Both are lovely because they are in the middle of things. From them, you can see all the comings and goings of the house, and the phone can be brought to your lap."

"Where is your mother?" Winston asked.

"Directly behind you," Livy snapped. Winston startled and turned, but there was no one. Pale and watery-eyed, he looked at Livy, pretending to be engrossed in an article, though anyone could see it was an advertisement for Kotex. The rip of a magazine page turning, exactly as their mother did when irritated. "You told me last night she was leaving and taking you with her."

"I never said any such thing," Livy retorted, her freckles disappearing in the flush in her cheeks.

"Livy broke her leg, Father," Alyssa said.

"Broke her leg?" Winston repeated.

"We've met you before," Auggie said abruptly to the woman. "The summer before I went away to school. In New York. Gloria. You worked for Father."

"Not exactly. I helped to get him a job after he lost his at the bank."

"We have you to thank that our father is a janitor?" Livy asked with a curl of her lip.

"He's a night watchman. It's a job," Gloria said simply.

"Have you children?" Alyssa asked, gathering the facts. She needed all the facts. Livy would run off when her leg was healed; Auggie would return to school. It would be she, Alyssa, who would be stuck with this woman, a cruel stepmother, punishing the real children . . . in favor of her own.

"That's a personal question," Gloria replied, flushing.

"Not really," Alyssa said. "Children aren't pets to be ordered about, or hidden, are they?"

"Hello! I'm home. Where is everyone?"

A door slammed shut. The one from the driveway into the kitchen. They all looked in that direction. The swinging kitchen door opened. Gussie entered the dining room, her high-heeled shoes clicking, sure and firm. Winston motioned to Gloria, who sat frozen in his chair.

"Alyssa, stop her!" Livy hissed, too late.

"How is the patient?" Gussie asked, stepping into the room. She looked beautiful, her cheeks red with cold, eyes bright and cheerful as she looked around the room, placing everyone. "I bought the eggs and cream for the birthday pancakes. I'm terribly sorry, Alyssa, being so late. Auggie, you look like you've seen a ghost. Whose car is that in the drive?" Gussie's glance settled on Gloria, who had stood up from the chair. "Hello. Have we met?"

Gussie smiled and began to walk forward, her hand outstretched to greet the guest.

"Gussie!" The sharp tone in Winston's voice, and Gloria's fiery blush, stopped her.

"Mummy?" Alyssa said. "This is Miss Gloria Wilson. She's the maid."

"Maid?" Gussie repeated.

"To serve dinner. We met her years ago in New York. She's the one who got Father's job for him."

"As night watchman," Livy added.

The bloom in Gussie's cheeks disappeared, leaving her pale and tightlipped. She put an arm around Alyssa's shoulder, who leaned in for the warmth, though her mother's hands were ice. Alyssa had to brace herself to support her mother's weight.

"Your car is blocking the drive," Gussie said, and propelled herself forward, toward the bedroom. She paused to look over at her husband, then retreated to their room. Winston glanced at Gloria, then followed his wife.

"It's my birthday today," Alyssa told Gloria to fill the silence.

"Mine, too," Gloria replied, staring after Winston. Alyssa blinked. On top of everything else, she would have to share her birthday?

"Alyssa," Livy hissed, her voice a command, her hands directing Alyssa to move into the entry hall. Alyssa obeyed.

"Do you like the cabin your father built you, Auggie?" Gloria asked.

"He didn't build me a cabin," Auggie said as Alyssa stationed herself outside their parents' bedroom. She looked back toward the living room, puzzled. Why had Auggie lied? Alyssa nearly returned to the living room to refute him, but then she heard her mother's voice. It hardly sounded like her, so shrill and imperious. It upset Alyssa to hear. Her stomach rumbled. She was famished, and, to stop what was coming, she put her hand on the handle of the door to open it, prepared to smile cheerfully and ask when would breakfast be ready. Instead she listened, and knew that she would die if her mother ever had cause to speak to her in such tones of outrage and unforgivingness.

"This is the person you helped Friday evening?" Gussie asked. "The one you had to see last night, in such a rush to go you couldn't help your own daughter, shrieking in the woods? How dare you bring her here?"

"You bring your friend here. Why shouldn't I?" Winston said, sounding as he had the week before when he had been caught eating one of two pumpkin pies.

"I beg your pardon? Friend? Is that what she is. A friend? I take that to mean you're not the father of her child? She is with child, isn't she? Even a fool should be able to see that."

"I didn't think it would matter if I brought her here. Livy had told me you were leaving. I thought you had left, and taken the children with you."

"You thought. But did nothing to prevent that? Instead bringing your *friend* to my house."

"I wouldn't force you to stay. If you love Lawrence, I won't stand in your way."

"Lawrence?" Gussie repeated, clearly puzzled, and then repeated the name with almost a laugh. She understood the miscommunication! Alyssa relaxed her shoulders. The to-do would be over now. They could eat. "Let me reassure you, Winston, Lawrence is a dear friend, a friend to us both. He, anyway, appreciates what you and I have created. A home. He would never go about destroying our friendship or our marriage with his thoughts or actions. He wouldn't dare."

"I've never done anything wrong, Gussie."

"Then why have you stopped going to confession?"

"It's not obligatory. And I've nothing to say. A sin is seeking one's own will over God's. I've never done that."

"For pity's sake, Winston." Gussie's voice held all the frustration of a foot stamped. "You can't afford one family. What are you going to do with two?"

"There is nothing I wouldn't do for you, Gussie," Winston said, and he sounded as if he were crying, which Alyssa knew he would not be. He was too tall and strong to cry. He was her father. "If you had only paid me a small degree of attention. A look. A kiss. But I get nothing from you. No warmth. No affection. All your attention and interest goes to the children. There's nothing left for me."

"This is my fault? My shortcoming, not yours?"

"I'm lonely, Gussie. Gloria and I are company to each other. She listens to me. I'm able to help her, whereas you don't need me."

The sound of a slap, skin against skin. Impossibly. After all, neither of Alyssa's parents was capable of such extremity. Emotions were kept in check. They had to be read. The flicker of an eye. The tension in a smile. Never a hand against a cheek.

"How dare you suggest such a thing?" Gussie said, her voice shaking. "Need you? When I so clearly can't depend on you? I'm not blind to your faults, Winston. I went into this marriage with open eyes, and with God as my witness. I had only hoped for something more than this. I didn't expect this."

"What did you expect, Gussie? I've never been able to figure that out."

Gussie's response was long in coming. Alyssa strained not to miss it.

"You don't know, Winston? Then you're right. You are no help to me. None at all." Gussie's words were so empty of expectation that, had they been addressed to Alyssa, she would have known there was nothing she could do. But they weren't addressed to her. Perhaps . . . was there something Alyssa might do? "To think I could have married anyone."

"But you didn't, Gussie. You married me. I'm the same person you married."

"That's the problem. You've not changed."

". . . I understand if you want a divorce."

"Divorce? You would leave me alone?"

"No, Gussie. I wouldn't take the children from you. Unless you didn't want them. If you want a second chance."

A silence that became an endless pause, a bumping against the awfulness of reality. Alyssa held her breath, as she did whenever she was driven past a cemetery, not wanting the dead to envy her life and steal it. Alyssa didn't want to die. Yet she was dying, a black sinking in her chest, unable to take a breath, a tunneling of vision as the recognition came to her that her mother would leave. She had only been waiting to escape. Livy had been right. Their mother wanted to be free of them. Live her own life. A sob escaped Alyssa. Her mother did not love her, and Alyssa could not bear the fragility of what had kept her safe and secure: the house, her home. Where would her home be? Who would take care of her? Where would she live? Would she have to call Gloria *mother*?

"Never," Gussie said. "You can damn yourself to hell, but not me. Marriage is a sacrament. Second chances don't exist. We will endure this till death do us part. But that woman must go. Get her out."

"You will always come first, Gussie," Winston said, and the bedroom door opened.

"I had damned well better."

Winston came out of the room looking old. His posture, usually so upright, was bent, his limp more pronounced. And his eyes reddened and blind. He didn't see Alyssa as he walked to the threshold of the living room and motioned to Gloria, who rushed to meet him in the entry hall. They left without a word. The roar of the car motor starting, the gravel grinding. The sound of the car faded. Auggie sat down on the couch and began to read his book, which, Alyssa knew, meant he was lost to her until he had regained control of the situation.

"Mummy has to leave immediately if she is to catch Lawrence," Livy said. Getting no reaction from Auggie, she looked to Alyssa. "Tell her it's nearly noon, Alyssa. Hurry."

Alyssa looked at Livy with her broken leg. Helpless and needy, and who was Livy to order her about?

"You can't force her to leave on my birthday."

"She needs to live her own life. We all do."

Heel to toe, left then right. Without knocking, Alyssa entered her parents' bedroom. Her nostrils flared. No matter how much the room was cleaned or aired, the smell of sawdust and rich earth remained, as if the bare wood floors held only the initial days of their making—oak trees and mills—rather than taking on the attributes of age and time. It was Alyssa's favorite room, more their father's than their mother's with its revolutionary guns hanging on the walls and the cannon paperweights and miniature toy soldiers populating his bureau and desktop.

Her mother had disappeared. She was nowhere in the room. Then Alyssa noted a strange sound. A long, high-pitched squeaking, then silence until a rush of air, as waves in a conch shell but louder, harsher. And again the high-pitched squeak. Following the sound, Alyssa walked slowly over to the bathroom, pushed the door open. Her mother in the bathtub, fully clothed, breathing in and out.

"Mummy? I'm hungry."

Gussie didn't respond.

"Mummy?" Alyssa repeated with a stamp of her foot. "Mummy!"

Alyssa kept shouting, her voice higher and higher, until Auggie came running in. He pushed past Alyssa, drew up short upon seeing their mother, then moved to kneel next to her. In the tub. Strange. He spoke to her quietly, softly, while Alyssa looked on. Gussie blinked, slowly turned her head to look at Auggie.

"Tell Livy," Auggie ordered. Alyssa did. In response, Livy told her to tell them that everyone was to come out to the living room so they could talk sensibly. Even as Alyssa announced this demand to Auggie and her mother, she suspected the distance to the living room might be too far. Auggie had only gotten their mother to sit on the edge of the tub. What was to be done?

"Alyssa, please change the sheets on your bed," Auggie said.

"What?"

"Do it!"

He had never spoken to her like that. It hurt her feelings. After all, she was to be the one left. Everyone else did the leaving. It wasn't fair. And why did she have to change her bedsheets on her birthday?

Alyssa returned to the living room.

"Well?" Livy demanded, sitting up in the couch, half-heartedly reaching for her crutches. Of no help whatsoever. Alyssa ignored her and went upstairs. She changed her sheets, then began to tidy her things. Bundled up the dirty clothes. She felt very responsible, doing chores without being told to. She was admiring her more mature self in her new silver hand mirror when Gussie and Auggie entered the room. Gussie closed the curtains. Auggie dropped an armful of their mother's clothes onto Alyssa's bed.

"You're to move to the back room," Auggie said, looking remark-ably pale and determined. "Take that laundry out of here. All your things."

"But why?"

"You prefer the back room," Gussie said as Auggie emptied a drawer full of Alyssa's clothes onto the floor. Alyssa's heart fluttered. Her mother did not defend her. Alyssa had no one to protect her. "It's too light in the morning for a late sleeper like you."

"It's cold and dank in the back room," Alyssa said. "I don't want it. This is my room."

"This is Mother's room now, Alyssa," Auggie said.

"Why doesn't she take Livy's room? Livy's is the best room."

"Because Livy has a broken leg," Gussie said as she headed out and down the stairs. "Put the lamp on the bureau."

"That makes no sense whatsoever. Livy gets the best of everything all the time, and I get stuck with nothing. It's patently unfair!"

Auggie slapped Alyssa across the face. They stared at each other for a moment, Alyssa's eyes tearful, more from shock than pain.

"I'm sorry," Auggie said. "Your whining hurts one's ears. Are you all right?"

Alyssa nodded.

"Good. Then let's get this over with."

Alyssa moved her things to the back bedroom, and assisted Auggie in moving their mother's things to Alyssa's old room. Livy complained that she couldn't help, wished loudly that she were in New York, and finally drifted off to sleep. When Winston returned, no one said a word. Everything was as it should be, except for the sleeping arrangements and that they had pancakes for tea.

Late in the afternoon, Alyssa found Auggie in the cabin. He was sitting at the desk, staring out at the darkening clouds over the village, lit up by the setting sun. Alyssa's first urge was to run and hug him. He looked so forlorn. Then she noticed he had packed up all his books and papers, and decided that it was she who needed comforting. He started when she stepped in.

"Why have you packed everything?"

"I'm going back to Cambridge," Auggie said.

"You're supposed to stay another night." He didn't respond, and so Alyssa asked, "What kind of dog do the Ellises have?"

"A Border Collie. Why?"

"Nothing."

"Is that what you wanted for your birthday?"

"Whatever I wanted, it wasn't what I got," Alyssa said with a tearful laugh.

"No," Auggie agreed, and Alyssa could tell by the way he looked at her that he did like her, even though he'd slapped her, and his hazel eyes were just like their mother's.

"I love you, Auggie," Alyssa said, in the hope of getting him to respond in kind. "You're the best brother I could ever ask for."

"I try, anyway," he said, with a vague smile that ended with a tremor.

"What were you thinking about just now?" Alyssa asked. Auggie cleared his throat, shrugged.

"That it's hard to understand why she stays."

"To prove a point, of course. She's in the right," Alyssa said, confidently, because she spoke from experience. "Why should she be the one to pack up and leave? It's much more comfortable to stay."

"Is it?"

"Of course. You know what to expect. For the most part," Alyssa added after a pause.

"Would she leave if I were here to mind things?"

"I think it would be lovely if you both stayed. Auggie? I'm not entirely sure I want to grow up."

"You've not much choice."

Alyssa thought about that.

"I don't mind the getting older part. It's having to take care of things on one's own, instead of being taken care of. It's tiring. I might try to be like Livy, not take responsibility."

"It's not in your personality, Alyssa. You're responsible even when you don't mean to be."

"Thank you. It is rather automatic. Maybe I'll be helpful to you, now you're the man of the family."

Auggie stood up.

"I had better be off."

"Aren't you going to say good-bye to Mother?"

"I'll write." Auggie looked around.

"This is positively the worst birthday of my life," she said as Auggie picked up his bags and prepared to leave her. A sense of panic came over Alyssa. She did not want to be alone. "Alone" led to thoughts of solitary confinement. She had read once that if ever she were imprisoned, put into a cell with no light, she should take a button, or some little something, and throw it out into the darkness. The only way to keep her sanity would be to throw the button into the darkness and search for it, blindly reaching out, and when she found it, to throw it again and search, and throw and search. The problem being, she had no buttons. She had nothing she might risk by throwing it away, no means to maintain control and sanity in her out-of-order world.

"Why don't I give you the cabin for your birthday, Alyssa? I'm never going to use it."

As if that would make it all better, Auggie kissed the top of her head and walked out, leaving her with what she had wanted but not with what she needed.

Dreams of Reality

To get anywhere in this life," Gussie said, staring ahead of her at the breakwater, "you have to be directed, focused. You have to know what you want, or you will find yourself very far from where you'd intended."

"What if what you want isn't the right thing to do?" Emma asked. Gussie raised a brow and looked over at Emma.

"Then you listen to your grandmother. That's why you're here, isn't it? To find out what you should do."

"Will do," Emma countered. "What I will do, as in want to, Gram. Should isn't going to work this time."

"Selfish girl. There is only one thing that will work. You'll move back here. Take ownership of the house."

"No, Gram," Emma said, as adrenaline flooded her body, tickling her knees, because Gussie's pronouncement threatened her. It returned Emma to a too-familiar and anxious panic of having to do what felt entirely wrong. After all, there was her grandmother, so absolutely clear about what had to be done. It was time to be doing it. Emma had never risked the consequences of not. If her grandmother was so certain of what was right, Emma wanting something else must be wrong. But as she sat with her grandmother, struggling to determine what the future would be, the consequence of not having listened to herself was revealed. The part of Emma that had been denied surfaced. It demanded recognition. She did know what she wanted, and what she wanted was valid. Only, for years, she had not dared to admit it. Not to her grandmother, nor to herself.

"The house is part of you, Emma Michaels," Gussie said. "Selling it won't change who you are. If you were honest with yourself, you'd keep it. You are wasting your good fortune, otherwise."

"You think that. I feel that. But my good fortune? I come here, hoping to enjoy it, and end up spending the time dealing with maintenance issues. Paying and filing the bills. Cleaning, painting, mowing. It's a full-time job. I leave exhausted."

"Complaining about having a beautiful house when so many go homeless," Gussie said. "As if you're entitled to have things work out for you. Why the insult when things aren't perfect? Life is full of troubles and trials. We must fight for what we love."

Emma glared at her grandmother, who was being no help what-soever, and judging by the clenching of her grandmother's jaw, the feeling was reciprocated. There was no connection between them, no sympathy.

"What if the fight breaks us?" Emma asked.

"Don't be such a victim."

"Collaborator, isn't it? With the best of intentions."

Gussie's chin went up, signifying her intention not to respond. Emma did not have that option. The contradictions within herself had become too glaring. She had tried to avoid them by separating from her family, and by hiding herself from Conner, but the fact remained that the world she was from was an integral part of the world she had created. Passing, as her uncle had tried to pass, no longer worked.

"You are just like your mother, Emma. A helium balloon in need of an anchor. That's what this house is for you. Nan's anchor was your father. Ever since he left her, it's been exhausting to see how she moves about, as if trying to escape. She's like a will-o'-the-wisp. You can't catch her for long. She's off again, leaving a cool breeze and a wish that she would stay behind. She stopped by last week."

Emma stared. She felt herself reaching out, grasping for what wasn't there.

"Oh?"

"En route to Boston. It was refreshing to hear of a life going on. We both wondered what you've been up to."

Emma reminded herself not to care. She did not care. Her mother had always done her own thing, leaving Emma to tag along or not. And how had they ended up here, not there? About to embark on *what was she up to*; talking about her mother, who had been the one to leave, not her father; and not about the house, which was, indeed, an anchor, and Emma attached by a too-short anchor line at high tide. Her grandmother had turned the conversation to more comfortable waters for herself, away from the house to Emma's parents. Gussie had a way of doing that. Keeping to comfortable waters, whereas all waters seemed to hold a degree of discomfort for Emma. A feeling of losing, or one of grasping to hold on. As with her mother. Emma adored her parents. Talking about them brought her closer to them.

"I've been thinking, Gram, these last months about why I started with ballet."

"You had terrible posture. I suggested ballet lessons to Nan."

"But it was so important to me. From the very beginning. Age seven and I was hooked."

"I knew you would like it."

"Mom and Dad had started dining at their friends', the Ballards', house once a week," Emma said, ignoring her grandmother's self-congratulations. It had been Emma's choice to begin ballet; Gussie had allowed it to continue. "It was their Friday night outing, and they toted me along because I could play with the Ballards' daughters. Twins, and older than me. Diaphanous, pale creatures. I was fascinated by them. They were taking ballet lessons. Each week, they taught me what they learned in class. We'd practice the five positions, listening to their ballet record over and over again, and then *pliés* and *battements tendus*. *'As through peanut butter,'* they would whisper with all the self-importance of nine-year-olds revealing a profound secret. I don't remember if it was the first night or the hundredth, but Mom looked at me and said, *'What a good little dancer you are, Emma.'* And I have a very clear memory of thinking, *She noticed me. I exist.* I spoke right up and asked if I could take ballet classes. Because I thought, if I worked hard enough, I'd pass. The classes were convenient, right near to where Mom and Dad taught. I excelled. The discipline of ballet gave me a sense of control. It was my anchor. Dancing, I was sufficient. I knew I was good enough. I was me when I danced. Which is why, one day, I found that I danced just for the love of it."

Gussie sat still for a moment. "Self-pity doesn't become us. Sit up. It's all in the posture. Lift up your chest and suck in the air."

A too-familiar knot formed in Emma's throat. A sense of curling in on herself. Was it so much to ask, an arm around her shoulder, a sense of intimacy and understanding? She debated leaving, but, after all, this was her grandmother, and they had business to attend to.

"Sometimes that feels beyond me, Gram, sitting up and breathing."

"Feelings don't make a thing real. You're as capable as the next person—more so."

"I'm glad you think so, Gram," Emma said.

"Of course I do. You should get out into the garden. That would soothe your nerves. Plucking the weeds. Planting the bulbs. That kind of work connects a person."

"I don't garden anymore."

Gussie's brows rose in surprise. "Silly girl. Why not?"

Emma held her breath. Like a slap to the heart, she could see Livy's crooked grin, her shining green-grey eyes and freckles, and hear her voice, gravelly from years of smoking but warm, holding. The two of them had gardened together the year Emma had lived alone at the family house. They had shared an unspoken emptiness, a loneliness they both coddled because loneliness, like hunger, they could embrace fully. It felt safer than fullness, which, like love and life, they had no idea what to do with.

"It hurts too much," Emma said.

"You're too young to complain about aches and pains."

"I had a garden in Providence at our house. Conner's." Emma hesitated, noting the flare of anger that distinction had caused. His house. Not hers. "The house has a big, sunny yard. It begged for a garden. I built raised beds, and filled them with soil from a local organic farm. I put in a strawberry patch and an asparagus bed. We ate two summers off the vegetables I grew. We ripped it out last fall."

Emma heard, again, the creak of the nails being separated from the wooden beds with a crowbar. By the time Conner had arrived with the sod, she had graded the yard with her garden's dirt and burned the wood in the fire pit. Her cheeks had been flushed with the heat of her activity, and with resentment, as she'd laid out the rolls of too-perfect green. Conner helped to puzzle together the pieces of sod, and she'd blamed him for her pending homelessness. He had forced her into destroying her garden, never considering her needs or desires.

Though how could he have, if she hadn't? She had participated. Without a word of protest, she had acted how she should, not how she wanted to. Sitting with her grandmother, Emma speculated when it had begun, the habit of not listening to herself, of prioritizing others' expectations of her over her own so as to placate her panicky need for acceptance. She forced herself to be still, to feel. From the garden to the RV negotiations, and further, to the heart of her rage and activity, her ambivalent travels.

The fact was, most of her life Emma had had a condescending attitude toward people who stayed in one place. For instance, her Midwestern neighbors as she was growing up. Her parents had traveled to France and Germany, the Soviet Union. Their travels, with and without her, had made being home seem philistine, dull. Emma considered herself special, superior having parents with such worldly lives. Their sophistication reflected onto her. She was cultured and privileged. Better-than because she had grand opportunities that none of her friends had. Other children envied her. It was good to travel.

Those had been her assumptions. Those assumptions became her skin. She understood her loss as not loss but as a bracing challenge to be met with an extra layer of toughness—justification, because otherwise she would have had to admit the pain she felt leaving home, and, upon her returns, the offense of the rejections of her best friends, who had moved on to other best friends. Forgotten her. At first, she had wept, and as she wept had sought ways to alleviate the hurt. She told herself how ridiculous it was to cry. Her friends must be jealous. Ignorant. She didn't want their friendship anyway, because they did not understand her. She was more mature than they. There was no reason to weep for them. She, who had the good fortune to travel, and the choice to be left behind. She did not want to be left behind.

In their first conversations about travel, Conner and she had talked about how settling was boring. Now Emma wondered whether it was boring or frightening, because those conversations with Conner had exhibited the same rationalization she had used as a child: bad was good. Pain meant growth and maturity. Travel meant not being left behind. She presented herself as an assured, confident traveler for whom a year in an RV would be a positive experience, an education. She acted, and he didn't see her fear. He missed the subtleties. Her enthusiastic, let's-get-this-project-done attitude covered over her delays. She called around to different RV companies, pushed Conner to go see the various buses, studied for her commercial driver's license. Activity was good. Selling the house was no big deal. And an early snow enabled her to pretend that her garden was still there. Until the spring. When Conner reminded her that the house would be sold. That the decision had been made.

"One day," Emma said to her grandmother. "All my work on the garden was gone in one day. It was a *Look on my works ye mighty and despair* moment." Emma attempted to smile.

"It's a shocking realization," Gussie said. "Our mortality. Of course, that's the wonder of gardening. Seeing the green shoots pushing up through the soil after a long, gray winter. It's satisfactory to know that life goes on after death."

"Not always. My garden is gone. The only thing coming up this spring will be dandelions and crabgrass. That's not satisfactory. It's insulting. A repeat of the past, Gram. All winter, I've tried to make it so that I didn't do what I did. Heart and soul, I want to go back. I pretend to myself . . . but then I'm overwhelmed by the reality. It's over and gone." Gussie held still. Emma indicated the land across the way. "I thought it would have sold by now. For years, everyone has oohed and aahed over it. How unique. How beautiful. You call it my good fortune. But owning it, I can't have what I need. A forever home. I thought that would be the Providence house, with forever not being long enough. I want to stay there, Gram. I want my things to remain exactly where they are, to be able to walk out of the house and be in the city and community where I've lived all my adult life. Finally to be in a home I can come back to and feel in my heart. The house exists in me. It lives and breathes, and Conner is going to sell it because he needs the money and I can't buy it because of this place. There's nothing I can do."

"The way you just described is how we feel about this house. This is our home," Gussie said. "If you give up this place, you'll have nowhere else. Neither will I." Gussie leaned over to confide. "I am not going back to that place for the decrepit and senile. It's a prison and it stinks. I can't breathe."

Emma braced for what she knew was coming.

"Where do you propose to go?" she asked. Gussie waved vaguely across the harbor. Her fingers were gnarled, the knuckles swollen, her rings loose and fallen upside down.

"The house is just waiting to be reclaimed. We'll live there."

Emma's heart skipped a beat. An abrupt flicker of excitement. She realized that her ambivalence about giving up the family house had been because she wanted to keep it, and why not? Her grandmother was right. She had always loved the house. Emma's imagination raced at the idea of the turmoil and activity. She tried to think which room and what furniture might be acceptable to her grandmother, and how they would live their lives together. It made perfect sense to return to the family homestead to take care of her grandmother. Again. She had done it before, adjusted her plans to her grandmother's . . . her father's . . . any and every significant person in her life. Maybe that was why she had been feeling so uncomfortable about the sale. She had been about to make the wrong choice.

And yet, even as she determined to stay, that other feeling returned, and it was hard to tell which was more vast and overwhelming: her wish to hold on to the property, or her need to reject its demands, which reached so far beyond herself.

"I go back in my dreams, Gram."

"So do I!" Gussie said. "Last night. I dreamed I had to protect it from some great danger. I ran along the wooded path from Livy's, down along the beach, back up to Alyssa's, the back of the garage, the graveled driveway. There it was. The house, still standing. I had been afraid it would be gone."

"Was it locked?" Emma asked, though she knew the answer.

"Yes. I had to peer in through the window. I could see the whole house. Dimly lit rooms empty, excepting the cobwebs."

"And a dead squirrel in the living room."

Gussie nodded. "I had come too late. I was so ashamed. There was a crescent moon in the sky. Venus. It was an hour before sunrise, and the outline of the moon was revealed."

"I had the same dream," Emma said as she felt the parallels between the dream, her race that morning to the gazebo, and that exact moment, sitting with her grandmother. The panic. The sense of being too late. The wish to rescue. "When I woke up, I imagined moving back."

"Wouldn't that be lovely!" Gussie clapped her hands together, flushing, eyes bright until a recognition came to her. "But we can't. Someone else owns it."

"I own it, Gram."

"Of course you do." They sat silent for the length of a seagull's call. "You could move into your father's old room."

Emma imagined what it would feel like to move back. Grocery shopping at McQuades, not Whole Foods. Walking the length of Bittersweet Lane, not Blackstone Boulevard. Driving to Providence to see her friends. Driving to Providence to go out to dinner. Driving to Providence to be in Providence.

"Dad's room isn't there anymore, Gram. It's like my garden. We can't go back to how it was, no matter how much we want to."

"We could try."

"I took the train here this morning," Emma said, bouncing her legs up and down for warmth and motion. She had to move things along. If the change was inevitable, then make it happen now. "Whenever I take a train I think of Dad. Always traveling coach and sitting on the left side of the train going south, the right side going north."

"For the views of the water," Gussie agreed, approving.

"The train flashed past all the small towns and marinas, the stretches of coastline, wetlands. We slowed for that sharp curve and trundled past Bittersweet Lane."

"The train stopped there," Gussie interrupted, "on our wedding day, to drop off our guests."

"I thought about that." Emma smiled. "I imagined them all dressed up in tuxes and gowns, laughing and singing as they walked to the house, just like we used to. I remembered how all of us—cousins and aunts and uncles, Mom and Dad, and you—would take our constitutionals. I could see us perfectly, there on the road, stopped at the dinging gates, waving to the train as it went by."

"So much for your little divorce. We are with you even when you cut us off."

"When the train stopped, I got off. I ran to the house along the tracks. I was just in time for my meeting with the real estate agent."

". . . You shouldn't do that," Gussie snapped, agitated. She slapped Emma's hand. Then grabbed hold of it. Emma noted how cold her grandmother's hands were, and how frail. They trembled, and it was Emma who had caused them to, and now what to do?

"They arrest people, now the tracks have been electrified," Gussie said, avoiding the point altogether. "Ridiculous. After all, a train isn't coming. Usually. And here you are."

"Running along the tracks, Gram," Emma continued, feeling relentless, cruel, but not daring to stop, "I felt as if I were in a time warp. Everything looks the same from the tracks. You can't see any of the development that's gone on, only the open expanse of the saltwater marshes, then the woods and wetlands. Bittersweet Lane is the same narrow, paved road it's been since I was a kid."

"Winding all the way to the stone gates with the old 'Keep Out the Cows' sign," Gussie said.

"And on to the second driveway on the left with the three mailboxes—yours, Livy's, and Alyssa's. As I ran, I thought about the old house. How we'd enter through the clutter of the back door's coatroom into the kitchen. Off that, the laundry room, smelling of Tide detergent, dirty socks, and wet towels."

"The maid's room was off the kitchen too," Gussie interrupted, flushed with remembering. "Mother insisted we have one, though we could never afford a live-in maid. Winston believed it to be too gross to live that far beyond our means, and I didn't want someone constantly under foot. Instead, the room was used on Wednesdays by the washwoman to iron and fold, and on Mondays and Thursdays by the cleaning woman to change in and rest. The maid's room became the boys' room. I turned a blind eye to the cigarettes and bottles of gin that were snuck in."

The two were silent, eyes closed, Gussie smiling, Emma discomfited by the certainty that old people feel the same as young. Call it soul or brain chemistry, the person's essence persisted, perhaps jaded, gradually, more or less guarded, but the same. Didn't Emma feel and know herself as she had been at eleven, when her parents had traveled to Europe without her; and in her twenties, when they had divorced; and now, when life and love promised once again to prove their evanescence?

"Every time I came into the house," Emma said, "I'd forage for a cookie or snack in the open-shelved cupboards, whether I was hungry or not. Then into the dining room with its sky blue, curved ceiling."

"Such strange acoustics."

"I can still hear Handel's *Water Music* introducing that *Henry the Eighth* BBC series. And how we used to spread the green tarp out on the living room floor for those lobster dinners. The New England mold smell. It's in the back of my nose even now. Like a sneeze."

"Yes," Gussie said. "In the heart's mind."

They sat quietly. Emma recalled how she had picked up speed down the driveway. Her running shoes cracking the April iced puddles. A salty mist dampening her hair and face. The smell of seaweed, low-tide muck. Dripping sweat, legs numbed by cold, nostrils flaring, looking forward to seeing the house—and then the lurching sensation when she did.

"When I came around the corner of the driveway today, the house wasn't white clapboard but red cedar shingled. It didn't have a black roof but a gray one, with a solar panel stuck between the dormers. The back door doesn't exist anymore. You have to enter where the kitchen sink used to be. I guess I've spent so little time there, the renovations haven't registered. It was a shock, to expect one thing and to see another."

"Bizarre," Gussie said, looking over at Emma, wide-eyed. "That happened to me this morning. I woke up and had no idea where I was, nor how I got there. It came back to me, eventually. It's an investigative process these days, remembering."

"That must have been upsetting," Emma said, moving from her own discombobulation of the morning to her grandmother's.

"I find it revelatory," Gussie said, her eyes bright, her cheeks flushed. "What the brain chooses to remember out of all the events of one's life, and how."

"For instance?"

". . . My father, teaching me a lesson. He said to me once, long

145

ago, before the village became a tourist attraction, before the children, when I was just a child, '*You, Gussie, are one of those girls who questions. Like your mother used to, and her cousin Lucinda.*' I felt honored by the compliment. Briefly. Because then he said, '*Don't,*' with a hard tap on my head. '*Don't question.*'

"Seven years old, but I remember that tap on the head and how it made me feel. Unacceptable. Heart-stoppingly not good enough—and what had I done? Mother and Father had caught me brushing my hair. Long, thick brown hair. I had a sickly complexion, plain features, and too much baby fat, so people tended to compliment my hair. Naturally, I admired it, too. I would stare into the mirror as I brushed it, watching it bounce and shine, an entity almost of its own, apart from me, something I didn't have to do anything for. It was just there and lovely. Good. A wonder until Mother and Father caught me staring into the entry hall mirror. They had just returned from a week in Newport, and, as Mother walked past me, I held my back straight, my cheek upturned, waiting for her kiss, cherished because so rare. I knew the smell of her powder and perfume would warm me with a blanket of approval. Instead, '*Stop looking in the mirror or we'll cut the hair off.*'

"'*But it's beautiful,*' I said, following her a step or two. '*Why shouldn't I admire it?*'—and then the rap on the head. I wept when Mother cut it off that night. But Father was adamant."

"Gram," Emma said. "I thought you cut it off after a trip to New York. You used to tell us how upset Gramps was, but that you had had to cut it because it had taken over your life."

Gussie looked contemplative, as if wondering at the flexibility of memory.

"One of life's mysteries," she said. "When I was a girl, my parents answered all my questions. I knew I didn't have to worry. I'd always have a roof over my head, and three meals a day. We've never been *rich* rich. Moderately wealthy. Money went farther in those days, too. But the money came with a moral responsibility. We weren't out of touch with its effects, and we had a duty to help others. My parents were quite strict about how far those responsibilities went. We respected that in my day. I tried to instill that in my children, and grandchildren. Respect and responsibility. There are certain rules not meant to be broken. Selling principle. Mortgaging one's home, never mind selling it, was unheard of. Worse than divorce. One small act and you would lose everything that made sense of the world. My parents made that quite clear. I could never reject them by doing something so wrong as selling the house."

Gussie concluded with a tone of voice that suggested others sitting on the bench might not be so correct.

"Selling a house doesn't mean you're rejecting the people in it," Emma said.

"It feels that way, doesn't it?"

Emma shifted her seat, uncomfortable with the turn in the conversation. Gussie lifted her face to the breeze across the water, her eyes half closed.

"When I married Winston, I thought I was gaining freedom from those rules. I imagined I could convince him about school, about travel, that my life would begin. All that energy. The ideas percolating. The hopes. Until the children. I hadn't anticipated children. They took over my life. Every day, every moment, I had an unconscious awareness of them. Auggie in his room, reading. Livy downstairs, lying on one of the living room couches, writing letters to friends, bemoaning her most recent grounding. Alyssa closeted in her room, trying on clothes. They existed in my heart. It was disconcerting when it turned out they weren't where they were supposed to be. I knew so clearly where they were, just as Winston did his tools. He used always to get so angry when a tool was borrowed and not put back properly."

"No one had much sympathy for him," Emma said.

"I could appreciate his upset. At least, I do now." Gussie hesitated, as if unsure of what she had uncovered. "Obstinate man. He was supposed to help me, but he couldn't even keep a job at a bank. He was plain stupid." Gussie paused. "It was disturbing, to have known deep, deep down that he was able, but in fact, he wasn't. I had only myself to depend on."

"Even if you don't want to, you have to," Emma said. "You can't count on others to help."

"God. We always have God. He used to play a role in your life."

"Apollo," Emma admitted. "But he never played a role in my life the way your god does, Gram. He's not my best friend."

"God is like family, Emma. You can't divorce yourself from Him. He's a part of you, like it or not. The question is, will you accept Him? Just so your family. And good fortune. There it is, requiring sacrifices most people have no idea about. Most people don't have our choices. Choices are not a bad thing. But their consequences. I neglected to think through the consequences, and then there I was this morning." Gussie held out her hand for Emma to see. Boney hands. Liver spotted hands. Wrinkled, aged hands. "This. Is. Not. Me." Gussie enunciated the words, then sniffed at the insult. "It's the strangest thing. To look old when you know perfectly well you are exactly the same person you have always been. But there are no familiar faces around you, and those that are left, the young ones, think you don't feel anymore. You no longer count."

"That's not true, Gram."

"Isn't it?"

"I'm here," Emma said, trying to smile, hoping that might suffice in the face of her grandmother's mortality.

"It's not the same. You're free to visit, but what, in the end, do we have in common?"

Emma gave a guppy's reply, her mouth opening, closing, but emitting no sound, only bubbles, wishes. She looked away, because wasn't that what she felt? There was no one who understood her. Except her grandmother, with whom she had thought she shared some basic something. If nothing else, a fathomless connection to the house.

"It must be lonely, Gram," Emma said, her eyes seeping.

"Not lonely. Just strangely alone. Another of the ironies of old age. Just when you've lost everyone and everything that ever mat-tered, you've not got the energy to keep busy and get things done. You can only sit and think about all that's gone by. It's an obscenity. You do the right thing, and then life! Other people and nothing to do but watch it happen."

Gussie sat silent for a while, seeming to shift through her thoughts.

"Lightning is fascinating, isn't it?" she finally said. "The time it takes for its effects to show themselves. A streak of brightness, jagged across the sky, and then you wait, holding your breath in anticipation of the crash and rumble that shakes the entire house."

Young Adults

Cold War Whispers
May 1954

The prospect of emerging from the army and returning home had been a pleasant one for Auggie, though it brought to mind images of ostriches burying their heads. His army years had been intellectually stimulating. Begun with a twenty-one-month sojourn to California to learn Russian, he had continued them with four years of service in Europe, translating, traveling, and tasting the myriad cultures. However, as his commitment to the army neared its end, the strain revealed itself. After such a long time of working to discern deceptions, translating lies into truths, between the lines and in the quaver of an eye he saw only artifice. He had seen what people would do to survive—if betraying one's humanity could be called survival—and so trusted no one, least of all himself. German ales, Italian pastas, Venetian mystery and seduction were pleasant distractions, but they didn't alleviate his sense of alienation. He wanted home, and felt only relief as the three o'clock *Merchants Limited* emerged from the East River tunnel into the Bronx; nothing matched the New York City skyline as seen from a train trundling over Hell's Gate bridge, if only because it prefaced the trip home, and home was a loving Arcadia.

Thus, ostrich images. The parallel of European and familial divides was not lost on Auggie. The Cold War tensions put his family's into perspective. In fact, he had found the home altercations amusing, and read with enjoyment Gussie's telling of "Daddy's upset at a fascinating conversation I had with Bill Schefers last night," which would be contradicted by Winston's accusation that "your mother carried on in a most unbecoming way at the party," a view decried by Livy as "another lovely dinner ruined by Father's baboon-ish manners," and by Alyssa as "Mummy and Daddy returned home in foul moods, entirely forgetting to let out my dog, and I got the blame." Auggie responded to each in turn, embracing his role of diplomat with dedication. Six years and a three-thousand-mile buffer zone helped. From that distance, even his father seemed manageable. Which was why, in a head-in-the-sand way and as the landscape transitioned from New York suburbs to Connecticut wetlands and beaches, Auggie trusted that everything would be fine. He had only to maintain perspective and a sense of humor.

He repeated this mantra as he disembarked at the Poquatuck station and began his walk home, duffel slung over his shoulder. He had taken an earlier train for exactly this: fresh sea air in his lungs, blood in his cheeks, legs stretching as he briskly made his way along the train tracks that paralleled the road to the east and intersected the harbor's end, and marshes. He breathed in its peace and calm, the smell of dried seaweed, the buffeting wind. He stopped to watch two egrets standing in snowy elegance in the midst of wetlands. A timeless scene, primeval, as the sun lowered toward the horizon and the mid-afternoon hour hinted at a cool night. He smiled to himself. The beauty of train tracks: one couldn't take much of a detour following them, at least not without a large and noticeable mishap.

He stepped off them onto Bittersweet Lane. He could walk it blind, the winding, narrow road, on either side of which was over-growth, wetlands, and every five hundred or thousand yards a drive-way: the McCormicks'; the Bob Whites' (as opposed to the James Whites, who lived in the Village); the Hendersons'. Auggie passed through the stone gates, glancing at the old shack to the right where old Dave Baron lived, a grouchy Marine who listened to no one and talked only to *Sergeant* Winston Michaels . . . who knelt at the head of the driveway. Dressed in sweat-soaked, dirt-covered khaki slacks and a matching shirt, Winston was planting a forsythia bush. The sight of his father stunned Auggie with a breathless memory: the border sign between East and West Berlin, printed in big, block letters in English, Russian, French, and German: **You Are Leaving the American Sector**.

He had not paid much attention to the sign when he had passed it, unless to note that he could understand all the translations. But his memory of those crossings was of haunting discomfort and yearning. He recognized now what he hadn't then: that however stark his fear of exposure had been, it had been balanced by his wish for success and acceptance. Stupid, given the incongruous goals and biases of the parties involved. And to laugh, that was the key. No reason to feel upset or anxious as his father stood up, a handsome figure, dauntingly tall and robust, his piercing gaze appraising Auggie as he approached. Auggie noted the sensation of butterflies in his gut, his age-old fear that he was not acceptable, the desperate wish that he would be. To think that his father could still have that effect!

"First Lieutenant Michaels!" Winston saluted his son.

"Hello, Father," Auggie replied, standing at a sort of attention. Thus ended their six-year separation. They deflected any awkwardness to the property. Auggie admired Winston's planting of a line of forsythia along the drive, which ended with a sapling magnolia, and three baby Hinoki False Cypresses. Behind them lay hidden the brambles, vines, and dead rhododendron that he had ripped out and replaced.

"I bought these for your mother." Winston gently tamped the dirt around one of the budding bushes. "It's a luxury, how time passes when you work at something you love."

"Yes," Auggie said, wishing his father's "work" had more viable economic consequences. Winston gathered the garden tools.

"How is your friend Pat?" he asked.

Auggie wondered at how such information spread. His father

must have heard of it from Alyssa. Livy and his mother wouldn't have bothered to tell.

"I've lost touch with her."

"I'm sorry to hear that. I would have liked to meet her. She sounded like a pleasant, simple soul. Probably why your mother didn't like her."

"She is German," Auggie pointed out.

"Better than Russian," Winston replied as they headed down the drive in military lockstep, thirty-two inch strides, one hundred-twenty steps a minute. "We have yet to recover from the expense of your mother and sister's trip to Europe last year. Two months was too long. They were with you only nine days. They should have come back immediately. Or perhaps I should have gone."

"The expense would have been greater if you had, Father," Auggie pointed out.

"Cost is not the issue."

"I beg your pardon. I thought you just said—"

"I held back for fear I might be a damper, but the loneliness and heartbreak I experienced taught me my error. If ever there is another such venture, I will go with her so that we can enjoy it together."

"You dislike travel intensely, whereas Mummy finds it nourishing to her soul."

"I am determined never to be apart from her again, and to be as loving and supportive of her as she is of me."

"But Father," Auggie said, caught by a breathless suspicion that there was something more behind his father's words, a protest of goodness against an as-yet-unknown accusation.

"No, Auggie. I will either do things with Mummy or they will not be done at all. Possibly we will miss a lot, but that is a matter of personal opinion. I am fifty-one years old. I see no reason to change, and I don't expect to. Now you are home," Winston continued, "we will set up something here. A family business."

"How will you have time for a family business when you've a job to attend to?"

"I quit."

Auggie stopped abruptly. "Quit?"

"Cousin Kitty's family is foul with money and unwilling to spend a dime of it for good work. I asked for a raise. They refused. I had no choice. It was a matter of self-respect."

"Self-respect? Kitty's father created that job for you, for God's sake, to help Mummy make ends meet. We'd have lost the house without Kitty and Lawrence's help."

"What you describe is charity. In fact, they are family, and family should support family."

"You've been lucky to have that job."

"There are endless other possibilities. I am full of ideas. A workshop in the trades I know, or a small store with universal gadgets. We will be our own masters, and have fun to boot. The whole family will contribute and benefit from our venture."

Auggie stared at his father, his mouth dry. "Father, as you know, I have been accepted into Columbia's history program. I am to start in the fall."

"An unwarranted expense." His father resumed his march down the drive. Auggie followed him.

"As long as the government will pay for part of my studies," Auggie said, trying to stem a rising panic. "I don't see what the objections will be."

"You'll do real work, not the pinko stuff you've been at, talking all kinds of languages no one can understand, going to places it's no one's business to be. All this goddamned Russian-fixed upheaval in Europe and the Far East. This State of Emergency. You need to take a real job, learn what it's like to work hard."

"You seem to underestimate my occupation these past years," Auggie said. "I might have traveled a good deal, but most of my time has been spent holding down a regular job with considerable overtime, well above forty hours. I know how to work hard. As to the economics of it, language and travel are my talents. Nowadays, it is easy to put them to use professionally. To further develop them makes all the sense in the world. It might cost something now, but it will pay off in the future. Mother promised you would help. I refused a job because of that promise."

"You'll work for me," Winston said as the house came into view. Auggie stopped, staring after his father, who continued on to the garage. Everything looked smaller than Auggie remembered. Provincial and shabby. Small in comparison to the chestnut tree that had grown up and now shaded the circular drive, where two women and a man were inspecting what looked like a brand-new, white Porsche Roadster. One of the women looked over toward Auggie and broke away, running toward him.

"Welcome!" she shouted and waved.

He blinked. Livy? The eighteen-year-old he had known had indeed become the mature city girl she described herself as in her infrequent letters. Her gait was no longer that of a clumsy colt. Her face had lost its roundness, her carriage the affectations of her fanciful adolescence. Black slacks, tawny mohair sweater, reddish hair up, her face cosmetic perfection. She no longer had to pretend jet-set glamour; she exuded it with a sway of confidence and allure.

"I hardly recognize you, Livy," Auggie said, laughing. He dropped his duffel bag.

"It's been forever," she said, throwing herself into his arms. He twirled her about, she light and slender as ever. She whispered in his ear. "Not to worry. I've got everything under control."

She stepped back, smiling. He could only hope she was right.

"My goodness, look at you. You're a man! Strange, isn't it, to be an adult, Auggie? I don't feel a bit like one." Arm-in-arm, they strolled toward the car, where Alyssa stood alarmingly close to a cohort of Auggie's from the army, Ed McClellan, who dated Livy.

"Livy?" Auggie started to ask, but she interrupted.

"Your postcard from Potsdam arrived only yesterday, Auggie. Your descriptions reminded me of a theatrical backdrop with all the houses shell-pocked, looking as if, if you touched them, the whole building would fall. Behind the walls, there was nothing."

"I wrote that postcard while eating a würst with rye bread near the Glienicker Brücke. I was thinking how humans are façades, hiding nothing."

"Hiding nothing because there's nothing there?" Livy asked, glancing at him with a brow raised and a prim smile. "Or because we've made such a to-do of things that shouldn't matter, or we are so obvious about things that we can't hide anything, in fact, why don't we come right out and say it?"

"I suppose all the above," Auggie replied, trying to smile as he focused on Alyssa, who looked the same as she had the previous summer in Europe. Voluptuous. Her hair, sandy blond, framed her flushed face with its high cheek bones and wide blue eyes that had a diaphanous ambiguity; one could only wonder at their shifting depths.

"Hello, Auggie," Alyssa said, reserved, as she kissed his cheek. She had not, apparently, forgiven him for changing *her* travel plans, an accusation that was patently true and fully justified. Auggie had had only a nine-day leave before he had had to report back in Frankfurt. With so many places in the world to see, why see the same ones twice?

"Mummy and I haven't seen them," Alyssa had fumed. The pout, fortunately, had only lasted a day or so, assuaged by Auggie agreeing to spend a day in Venice, and by the arrival of Ed, whose unexpected and fortuitous appearance had lifted the black cloud engulfing Alyssa.

"Do you know Ed McClellan?" Alyssa asked, reaching to clasp the man's hand.

"You know perfectly well I introduced you to him last year in the Piazza San Marco." Auggie nodded at Ed, who stood between Livy and Alyssa. He held himself far more comfortably in plaid pants, a yellow shirt, and loafers than he had in the regulation army togs Auggie was used to seeing him in. A wave of nausea—or was it nostalgia?—for his time in the army, when he had worked in concert with others and known the difference between good and evil. "I'm surprised to see you here."

"Your sister invited me." Ed held out a welcoming hand, a firm, reassuring handshake that left it to Auggie to determine which sister. "How's the transition to civilian life going?"

"Bumpier than expected," Auggie said.

"Auggie? You've the most bizarre expression on your face." Livy said, leaning against the roadster as she lit a cigarette.

"I can't imagine why." Auggie looked from one sister to the other, feeling a strange repulsion. The two did not complement each other. Separate they were lovely, but together they both suffered. Alyssa's blunt good looks gave Livy's more subtle charms a faded quality, a precious evanescence that, in turn, caused Alyssa's appearance to seem almost gaudy.

"I was just telling Ed how funny time is," Livy said, her eyes damp but clear, her voice lilting up, gentle and smooth. "It's been years since he and I dated, and yet I feel as if it were just yesterday that we talked."

"It certainly seems that way." Ed grinned at Livy.

"Eddy has only just arrived." Alyssa ran a finger along Ed's arm. "We had lunch together down at the beach. It was delightful."

"Delightful," Livy repeated, blowing smoke rings into the air. She smiled, her chin lowering, her eyes appearing to look more to the future than to those around her. Auggie reminded himself: humor in the face of low-flying feelings. Only he had forgotten how intense those feelings could be.

"Where's Mummy?" Auggie asked.

"I begged her to lie down," Livy said. "Which means she is probably upstairs doing what she asked Alyssa to do: clean the bathroom for the party."

"Party?" Auggie repeated. "What party?"

"As if I haven't worked like a steer all morning with Mummy," Alyssa said, "arranging flowers and keeping her away from Daddy."

"A steer? Stepping off the train from your dearest Radcliffe not four hours ago, and then off you went with Ed. Selfish creature," Livy said. "If heaven arrived, you wouldn't change your plans to see it. This party was your idea, and you've put the entire thing onto Mummy. She's a wreck."

"If that's the case, the party should be canceled," Auggie said. "This is my first night home. I don't want the distraction of a party."

"Don't go manipulating plans quite so immediately, Auggie," Alyssa snapped. "I had quite enough of that last summer when you ruined my one and only European trip. We are going to celebrate your homecoming and Mummy and Daddy's twenty-fifth anniversary, like it or not."

"You see? Alyssa won't hear of canceling." Livy knocked the ash off her cigarette. "We've gone over it for weeks—and now here are the caterers." They watched as a Woody station wagon drove around the driveway loop to the kitchen entrance.

"Caterers! I thought this family had no money left," Auggie said, exasperated and embarrassed by Ed's presence during the discussion.

"Last-minute cancellations are rude," Alyssa said. "It will be a much-needed distraction."

"Distraction from Father quitting?" Auggie asked. Best to call a spade a spade so they might discuss the necessary task of calling Kitty, again, to ask her to intervene on their father's behalf. "I do think it would be best to discuss the family finances later. I'm sure Ed has other things he'd like to hear about."

"Oh, Ed knows everything," Alyssa said. Auggie held his breath. Ed shrugged.

"Right place, right time," Ed said in his own defense and with an awkward smile. A bellow from the garage; Winston in search of his hatchet. Ed excused himself to explain its absence. As he loped off, slapping the behind of one of the caterers as he passed her, Auggie wondered what the attraction of him was to women.

"Money is the least of it, Auggie." Livy stared grimly over at the garage.

"It's too awful," Alyssa said, her face transformed by concern. Auggie experienced the familiar sensation of his defenses relaxing, only to be raised again in a rush of adrenaline. "Mummy hasn't slept in a week."

At which point, his sisters whispered the details of their father's most recent abomination: he had pilfered their mother's money to buy *that woman* a house. It was only found out because of an overdraft at the bank. The check to the church. Their mother was mortified. Everyone knew. Their father had asked for a raise—double his salary—in hopes of repaying it. Kitty's father had been so insulted, he'd fired Winston instead.

"And," Alyssa added. "There might be a love-child."

"Alyssa, you've no idea what you're talking about." Livy flushed. "Sneaking about, spying on Mummy's and my conversations."

Auggie's gut twisted, as it used to at sensitive meetings for which he had been translator. He had had to maneuver through tensions blindly, deciphering the unspoken agendas, the mines that could blow up at the slightest provocation, unaware of the exact facts but feeling the strength of their power and danger.

"Has she called a lawyer?" Auggie asked.

Both his sisters looked at him blankly.

"What on earth for?" Alyssa asked, her clear blue eyes and smooth complexion exuding an innocence that gave Auggie's heart a turn.

"You don't know our mother if you ask that, Auggie," Livy said. "She's made her bed and will be damned if she doesn't sleep in it."

"But that's pure stubbornness."

"Her life is her family and this house." Livy shrugged. "She'll do nothing to lose them."

"That's exactly what she's done, isn't it?" Auggie asked.

"On the contrary," Livy said. "Because of her, we stay. She has us, every one of us, by the chin hairs."

"Speak for yourself," Alyssa said as the front door to the house slammed open.

"Glory be, it's Auggie!" Gussie cried as she hurried down the entrance path towards him. He tried to step forward to meet her, but all he could do was stare at the change. The vigor and bloom that his mother had exhibited in Europe, the real joy and satisfaction in everything they had seen and done, had withered. Black shadows around her eyes gave her face the sunken appearance of a skeleton. Her hair, overly permed, was a brittle halo around her head, and even without knowing *it* he would have noted an underlying distress, a plea in her outstretched arms. Her powdery lavender smell enveloped him as they embraced, and his shoulders and arms tensed to hold her up, as they had on so many other homecomings.

"You're home," she said, standing back, at which point Winston shouted from the garage for the bartender to move his bloody car off the grass. Her spine stiffened and she gave a grim smile. "Welcome back, my dear boy. How did your train ride go?"

To cheer his mother, he started to tell her about the remarkably beautiful dwarf who had sat next to him on the train, how grotesque he had felt next to her with his long, unseemly legs, and their conversation about perspective and how to overcome one's "shortcomings" rather than hiding from them. But something caught in his throat. All that had passed. A wish to go back . . . to when? He didn't know. There was only confusion, and a sickening sensation of emptiness. It filled him with a vast and yawning terror, and an overwhelming need to be taken care of, even as he was called upon to protect. He gasped, drowned for lack of air, and his mother held him as he sobbed. She whispered age-old assurances, promises made to a child, that everything would be all right, there, there, and here was Ed back from the garage, looking on with concern. Nothing had changed.

"I'm sorry." Auggie struggled to regain control. He had to think. About shards. Pottery shards. How a slave thousands of years ago made a clay pot, painting it with pictures of his king of kings, and both slave and king were dead and the only record of them was the work of the slave who made the pot for the king to piss in, and what significance had anyone in life? In the grand scheme of things, his presence made no difference. This crushing disappointment? Ridiculous. "I don't know what came over me."

"I do." Ed clasped Auggie by the shoulders and gave him a shake, reminding him of Ed's good fellowship and the bond they had held, a result of their working together in the army. "I nearly did the same when I got out. It's strange being back. The reality doesn't quite match one's dreams of it."

"I can imagine," Livy said, teary-eyed, as she stepped closer to Auggie and Alyssa took Ed's arm.

"It must be refreshing to let go," Gussie said, not one to do so herself. "Then one can look about, stand tall, and breathe in these May days. Thank goodness for them. I appreciate you wanted to walk home, Auggie, but now you've ruined the surprise and are overtired to boot. Try to lie down. Girls, see that he does."

With a slight lift of her chin and a kiss for Auggie, Gussie returned to the house by way of the kitchen, where Winston could be heard ranting about something. Auggie looked at his sisters. Alyssa leaned possessively on Ed. Livy held herself apart, pretending indifference.

"Intolerable," Auggie said, and picked up his bag. They proceeded up the bluestone walk and into the entry hall of the house. The sisters held a brief debate. More a tug and pull. Who would do what with whom? Auggie listened, watched, felt the tensions. He did as he did when in the process of learning a language for which he knew the grammar and general vocabulary. He tried not to translate but to follow the gist of the tones and phrases within the context, and felt as he did just before fluency, when the words begin to make sense and he gets the idea, if not the details. The words flowed through him, becoming distinct, and suddenly a rainbow shimmered into existence and there lay the path to understanding. He should not have come back. It was not safe here. His family needed so much. Granted, their need gave him purpose, but it took from him a vital energy. There might be nothing left for him. He told himself to hide, deep within himself. He had only to remember the way out.

The sisters left to help their mother in the kitchen, leaving Auggie in the living room. Smelling the spring flowers picked from the garden. Studying the furniture pushed to the periphery. Small round tables, on each a white linen cloth and a miniature vase of violets, primroses, and Siberian squill. Branches of forsythia, viburnum, rhododendron, and mountain laurel stood in enormous vases in each corner. A burst of laughter from the kitchen, and outside on the stone patio, a bartender was setting up a long, linen-covered table with an array of glasses, bottles of alcohol, vases of daffodils and tulips. Gussie's bleeding hearts—white and pink—in the garden. The cherry trees. In the distance, a mournful foghorn, and an osprey hovering in the sky over the harbor, diving for its prey. If he were not careful, he would never get out alive.

"How's Pat?" Ed asked, startling Auggie.

"Pat?" Auggie repeated the name he hadn't spoken in months, nor allowed himself to think about, and now twice in one hour. "You know perfectly well that's over."

"I'm sorry. She was a nice girl."

"You told me she was on the wrong side of it. You were quite clear that she wasn't all right."

Ed shrugged. "Maybe I was wrong."

Auggie didn't respond. He stared out the window, contemplating the innumerable rocks protruding out of the yard. Some were flat and contained, easily dug up and taken to the rock graveyard that Winston had created behind the garage. Others were the bulbous tips of boulders, intractable, inherently dangerous to lawn mowers. The grass grew up and covered them, cloaking them like unspoken secrets. He didn't want to know them. He wanted only to go back. He thought he could. He thought he would.

Showered and dressed, Auggie lay on his bed, reading. The house and patio below his room's window were packed with guests, the caterers wending their way through the crowd with platters of hors d'oeuvres: miniature cucumber sandwiches, stuffed mushrooms, shrimp with cocktail sauce. He could hear his parents' voices greeting the guests as they filtered out to the patio. Having spied, he knew that Winston was in a tuxedo and his mother in an orange-rose dress with too many frills. A triple-blossom camellia was pinned to her right lapel. Every time she looked around, she knocked it with her chin. Livy wore a sage-green fitted dress and Alyssa a flared red one, both pinned with single-blossomed camellias. Occasionally, he heard his name as someone asked for him, and then voices calling for him, but he had nothing to say. The very idea of going downstairs perturbed him. He concentrated on the words on the pages because he didn't want to face the task of social interaction. Such a bore, to be caught up by one or another of his family members, who would remind him of Mrs. So-and-So, so good to see you again; or introduce him to new friends from Providence, Boston, or New York, all young, bright, and employed, regurgitating nothing of interest.

A knock on the door.

"Are you coming down?" Livy asked.

"In a minute," Auggie said. The door handle turned and she stepped in, holding two drinks. She held one out to him.

"Not yet." Auggie frowned at the interruption and continued to read.

"Auggie, we are nearly an hour into the party given, in part, in your honor. You have to come have some fun."

"I'm having fun." Auggie turned a page. "There's nothing like Agatha Christie to keep one's attention."

Livy set his drink on the bedside table and walked to the windowsill to sit. She glanced over her shoulder, taking a bird's-eye view of the party. Auggie stared at the page.

"I asked Granny once why Mummy married Father," Livy said. "Apparently, Mummy wanted to marry him more than anything else in the world. She was *bound and determined.*"

"Marrying is one thing. Staying is another."

"She enjoys her martyr's role. She holds it above him. 'I am doing the right thing, and you are wrong. All wrong.' Don't look so worried. I already told you, everything will be fine. Mummy and I drove by the house yesterday. It's in Providence. A tiny little thing. Not threatening at all. Mummy seemed to feel much better about it. *'It's modest,'* she said. *'Not vulgar.'* That would describe the girl, too. Gloria. I would never have guessed she'd still be in the picture all these years later. Thank goodness she lost that baby."

"Mother should never have allowed for any of it."

"Given all the shoulds in Mummy's life, can you blame her for letting this one pass? It allows her to be as free as she ever can be unless she divorces him, which she will never do."

Auggie didn't respond. Livy gave him some time to digest the information.

"Now, you must stop wallowing, Auggie. Come down and distract Alyssa."

Auggie didn't move, caught between the two dramas—his parents' and his sisters'.

"Ed's too wild even for you, Livy."

"He won't be once we're married. It will be wonderful."

"You used to want to work."

"I still do. But a woman needs a husband."

"That makes no sense, Livy. Financial independence allows a woman the freedom to do whatever she will."

"Even Mummy thinks I should marry him. She's become ever so fond of him since you introduced them to each other in Europe."

"Oh?"

"Yes. She wants it as much as I do."

"And if she didn't?"

"It doesn't matter because she does," Livy said. "He's my escape, Auggie."

"You've already escaped, haven't you?"

"Have you?" Livy snapped. The two were silent for a moment, a moment in which Auggie thought of his mother's tête-à-têtes with Ed, and of Pat. Auggie and Pat had used to laugh. Just holding her hand had made him happy. He sat up abruptly and tossed aside his book.

"It's Ed's choice whom he marries, isn't it?" he asked. "We can allow him that much. Though what in God's name he's thinking, dating you both—and you, tolerating it?"

"I've forgiven him. We did break up a few weeks ago. Only a temporary break, but it was during that time that Alyssa asked him to the party. He said yes to get under my skin. You see? He's only toying with her. And she with him." Livy's eyes glistened with tears. "You've no idea what it feels like, Auggie, to have everything you put an eye on suddenly become exactly what Alyssa wants, even if two minutes before she's been denigrating it. She's a bottomless pit, wanting everything and convinced that she's got the short end of the stick. She didn't even remember about Ed until I said I was calling him up for old times' sake. *He's mine,*" Livy mimicked their sister. "My goodness, they exchanged a few letters since Venice. I've read them. Hers were superficial flirtation."

"Letters can be deceptive," Auggie said, thinking of the box he had shipped home, all the letters from the family that he had saved, labeled; he would reread them to find what he had missed. He had expected safety and comfort, clarity of purpose. Maybe someday. "Words misinterpreted. No body language to read. You can make letters and the people who wrote them say whatever you want them to. It's all in the interpretation."

"He's mine, Auggie. It's different this time." Livy hesitated, looking around her as she used to when she couldn't remember her lines for a play, as if something might tweak her memory. And then something would and she would twirl around. Triumphant, she would say her line. "I'm pregnant."

Auggie stared at her.

"For pity's sake," he said, with a shake of his head. "Just what we need on top of this parental feud. Does Ed know?"

"I don't want him to marry me because of that."

"It's the only way he will."

"I know. That's how Alyssa got him. She told him she's pregnant. Can you believe that? Lying to get him? So now I would sound ridiculous saying the same, wouldn't I? Please, Auggie. If Alyssa would just let him go, he'll come back to me. All you have to do is convince her that it's her idea to break off with him, leaving me with the dregs. Then she'll be right as rain. It's perfect." Livy walked over to kneel down before him. "Mummy doesn't approve of him for her, Auggie. She wants Alyssa to finish college and then marry a man who owns the newspaper, not the one who writes for it. Whereas I can marry anyone. Mummy doesn't expect much of me. I'm the stupid one. I might as well get married and have babies."

"What about your modeling career?"

"This is the first time you've ever called it a career. You see? Even you look down on me. Maybe I am just superficial. In which case, why not be happy? Auggie, dearest. If you'll only help. I have always sworn I won't end up like Mummy. I intend to worship and adore the man I marry."

"Do you worship Ed?" he asked.

Livy flushed. "Absolutely," she said.

Auggie allowed for a pause. "*Bound and determined*?"

"Yes," Livy smiled, her eyes bright with tears.

"Well, then," he said, taking up his drink. "Let us proceed."

Their mother stood at the bottom of the stairs. Her pearls glowed pink as she observed the party, her eyes watchful that the caterers were passing sufficient food, that the bartender was keeping the drinks flowing, that Winston, gallant and amusing, was keeping the ladies giggling and men amused with one or another of his stories.

"Hello," Gussie said as Livy passed by, giving her a kiss on the cheek. Auggie stayed by their mother, relieved to see she had loosened and combed her hair to give it a softer effect.

"What is it about not having something that makes it more desirable?" Gussie asked as Livy stepped into the crowd. "Your sisters are so threatened by each other, such that it's hard to know if they're doing things for themselves or in reaction to the other. They'll go to any lengths."

"Alyssa is claiming to be pregnant?"

Gussie's smile froze. "You heard wrong. It's Livy."

"Livy told me herself just now. She was quite clear."

"They need both to be put on ice," Gussie said, her smile ossified. Her glance passed over her husband to Alyssa, ending with a shadowed look at a couple standing arm-in-arm, occasionally leaning toward each other to whisper a comment. She indicated the couple with a nod of her head.

"You can see what a wonder marriage is when you look at Lawrence and Kitty," she said. "He dotes on her. I do hope, Auggie, that you will plan and hope and strive for nothing less than the kind of marriage they have, one of equals. Respectful. Make no mistake. Even then, it takes integrity, sacrifice, and hard work. Don't go for anything less."

"No, of course not," Auggie said.

"I shall love anyone you pick out to marry. You'll pick a sensible girl. Not like that dirndled fatty you were going about with last summer. Elsie, was it? She hadn't much restraint, eating all those pastries."

"Her name was Pat, and I found her refreshing," Auggie said, his heart caving in because, after his first introduction of Pat to Gussie and Alyssa, he had stopped calling her, and then Ed telling him that there were questions being asked about Pat and maybe it would be best to leave her alone had seemed to justify Auggie's neglect. Only now, from this distance, the shame of not calling equaled the shame of calling, and a gross irritation came over him because what right had his mother to comment on anyone's marriage, given her own choice?

"It's a mathematical equation, isn't it?" Auggie asked. Gussie looked at him, curious. "One plus one equals two. A divided by B over C. Livy opposing Alyssa over Ed. You opposing Father over—"

"Not now, Auggie," Gussie said, her voice sharp.

"Father is determined never to leave again, you know. He mentioned something about a family business? I suppose that means school is out of the question for me this year."

Auggie tried to sound neutral but heard the annoyance in his voice, and why not? After all, he had had opportunities for work that would have earned him money to pay for his education, but his mother had refused to hear it. She wanted him to enjoy his vacations, not work, and had promised him that his schooling could be paid for. And now?

"Your education won't be sacrificed to your father's . . . equation," Gussie said, putting her arm through his and leaning on him, heavily. He realized that she was not indifferent to his plight—rather, she was coping too. How selfish and suspicious of him to have thought otherwise. "You would do yourself a disservice staying here, Auggie."

"What of you?" Auggie asked.

Gussie shrugged. A lift of her chin. "I intend to mortgage the house to pay for your schooling."

"No," Auggie said, as a flare of hope burned into caution. "That is no compromise."

"What would you do? Self-education while tutoring as Lawrence did? He would have given his eyeteeth for money back then." The degree of pique in his mother's voice surprised Auggie. He wondered whether Lawrence's love for her had had a pecuniary aspect.

"I'll consider it an investment in you, Auggie," Gussie said, giving his arm a squeeze, girding them both for the future. "You'll work hard. I know that. You'll repay me one hundred-fold, starting tonight with your sisters. I want Alyssa to continue at college. A little trip to Europe to take care of things will suit her. You can take her to the places you denied her before. As to Livy, she has had her little job, but it's time for her to settle down. She seems to like the fellow. Who am I to affect that?"

"Ed doesn't have a say in this?" Auggie asked, trying to maintain perspective. He added a smile. For humor.

"He'll do the right thing. We've had some good chats. He likes our lifestyle. He wants to move up in the world. He could do worse than marry Livy."

His mother reached up to touch Auggie's cheek, her fingers cool against its heat. She smiled at him, tilted her head to study him. Ostriches? No. There was no hiding. Better to be a starfish, lose an appendage. It would grow back.

"I wonder what your equation is, Auggie?" she asked. "Whom do you oppose and over what?" She patted his arm. "Be sure to speak to Lawrence. He has been looking forward to hearing all about you. It gives me great pleasure. You both gain so much from the relationship. He is so nineteenth-century, and you so twentieth."

Gussie walked away to fortify a group of friends whose conversation had fallen into a silence that might become uncomfortable. Auggie took a circuitous route through the party, chatting with a variety of pretty girls with whom he reminisced about their mutual passion for each other and laughed at their childish loves; or hinted at what might be. He collected phone numbers. To his parents' friends, he told by rote of his army years and how he looked forward to them being part of his past, which they were, and avoided talk of the future by noting a single girl with whom it was his duty to converse, most particularly Alyssa. He attended to her whenever he saw she had a moment to look about. He wondered if it were necessary. The ease of her smile, the impish glee and wide-eyed innocence, allowed him to think that life would touch her like water does the proverbial duck's back. Certainly, nothing seemed to go too deep.

Auggie came up behind Alyssa and whispered in her ear, "Livy certainly seems sweet on Renny Jones. Look at her dote on him."

Alyssa turned her head slightly, studied her sister.

"Good. That leaves Ed for me."

"I don't believe for a minute that you're enamored of Ed. Your letters have been about Renny. Why are you suddenly ignoring that poor fellow, leaving Livy to steal him from you?"

"Renny is sweet but Ed's perfect," Alyssa said.

"You do give a wrong impression," Auggie said, frowning. "Talking about everything with the same level of passion, giving equal attention to all the Lincolns, Teds, Rennys, and Eds. Renny was perfect a month ago. How are we to tell which one you're collecting?"

"Maybe I'm collecting them all," she said with a chortle. She glanced at him sideways, her eyes growing wide and somber. "Ed likes us both. But possession is nine-tenths of the law. He's mine. He's all I ever wanted."

"You're infatuated."

"Infatuations are real."

"You're too young. A child, naïf."

"You should talk." Alyssa maintained her smile as her eyes narrowed. "Things go on right under your nose that you've no idea about. Ed said—" She stopped because Ed approached them, to the neglect of Livy, who was staring across the room, helpless to cross the divide by herself because in a conversation with Renny.

"I was just about to tell Auggie all the secrets of his old girlfriend, whom Mummy so disapproved of," Alyssa said, and her tone of voice, its touch of malice mixing with jovial lightheartedness, revealed her oblivion to her words' razor-edged strike on the heart . . . or maybe not. Maybe she and Ed were made for each other. "Renny looks bored to tears. I'm off to save him. Ed, would you please get me a drink?"

Alyssa left them to interrupt Livy and Renny's tête-à-tête. She pulled Renny over to another circle and introduced him around, leaving Livy to make her way to the bar, smiling their mother's tense smile. Auggie and Ed stood quietly.

"Ed?" Auggie said. "I don't appreciate your toying with my sisters' affections."

"A case of bad timing. It'll be over tonight."

"What about Alyssa's . . . problem?"

Ed flushed. "It's not mine. I've not done any of that with her. Auggie, you know me, right? I've always said, I feel pressured, I'm gone. Livy doesn't play games like that. She's exactly what I need. Fun and independent. She doesn't put any demands on me. Alyssa is too needy."

"Yes, she is," Auggie said, catching a glimpse of Livy, who looked young and afraid, helpless in the crowd. "You won't feel the traces so much with Livy, Ed. She'll let you get away with things Alyssa wouldn't tolerate."

"Exactly. She's got her work. And there's no talk of marriage or babies with Livy. She's just my style. She takes care of herself. I take care of myself. We have a great time together."

Auggie turned to look at Ed.

"Remember Stanley?" he asked. Ed's smile disappeared. His face became the stern, matter-of-fact one that Auggie remembered from their war years. Not so long ago.

"We agreed not to talk about that," Ed said.

"We should have told him. He should have known what he was going into."

"We weren't sure of him, Auggie. Remember? He could have wrecked the whole network, and it wouldn't have made a difference. He still had to go. He was following orders."

"If he had had all the information, he might have acted differently. He might have made it back."

"We did the right thing, Auggie."

"That's what you've said all along, but if the same were to happen to you? If you went into something without all the facts?"

Ed shrugged, raised his glass to toast. "*C'est la vie.*"

"Well, then." The two men toasted. The evening played out. Alyssa paid no attention to Ed joining Livy at the bar, where they stood so close it appeared they were pressed together. By the crowd, of course, as they waited for their drinks. Talked. Disappeared. The evening wound to a close. Auggie ended up on the patio. Neither sister in sight, but there were the Finers.

"Auggie!" Lawrence said. "Home must be a welcome relief after what you've seen. Your father has been telling us about the family business. I'm surprised. I thought you were going to Columbia University."

"So did I," Auggie said, with as wry a smile as he could muster. "Things have yet to be worked out."

"Auggie, I've a complaint against you," Kitty said, and Auggie looked to her with comfort, reminded of his mother by her rendition of the family's broad forehead and clear eyes. Her slight figure exuded energy and interest. Auggie wondered how she had adjusted to small-town life. "You wrote fascinating, humorous chronicles of the places you went, full of facts and descriptions, but never a word about how those places made you feel. I could have read a tourist book for all the information I got about what it was like for you to be in those Eastern Bloc countries."

Auggie hesitated, distracted for a moment by Gussie, who stood back to back with his father, each apparently unaware of the other's propinquity, though they were so close they seemed to lean against each other.

"Cloying," Auggie said, after a pause. "Always there was the sense of being watched and judged. The only way to feel right was by starving."

"I beg your pardon?" Kitty's smile quavered.

"Food was available, but why for me and not others? What had I done to deserve anything? Having access to things that would mean life and death to others. I determined to earn the sustenance, produce something worthwhile, which I felt I wasn't doing. So I learned to starve myself. If it's done purposefully, after a while, hunger is pleasurable and powerful."

"Hunger leaves me feeling rather weak," Kitty said, looking to Lawrence, who squinted at Auggie as if to divine what Auggie obscured.

"How is hunger powerful?" Lawrence asked.

"It teaches discipline. One learns to repel need, control what seemingly can't be controlled. The right and wrong of a situation you can't change. You see, Kitty, I used to think people feared death most in the world but I think there is a deeper fear. The loss of one's humanity. The evil of the Communists is their calculated destruction of the human soul, killed by constant fear and unceasing vigilance. Watching for the watcher. Never knowing if you are truly alone or safe, nor whom to trust. People betray their families and friends. I remember thinking on more than one occasion, if I come out of this with my humanity, I will have done something."

"Did you?" Lawrence asked.

"I don't know," Auggie said, trying to laugh, though feeling horribly close to breaking down as he had that morning. He wished he'd had more to drink, that he had told Ed . . . more. Auggie watched Ed approach Alyssa but did nothing to stop him as he led her, glowing under his attention, out the door. Now that he thought of it, this was not the first time Livy had gotten what she wanted, leaving Alyssa bereft but only because Alyssa didn't really care. Did she? She would be perfectly fine. "It's all a game in the end, anyhow. Certain rules that are made and broken."

"Life is not a game, Auggie," Kitty said. "It's the relationships we have, and the truth within them. How honest and true we are to ourselves."

"Which is what you were referring to in one's humanity, wasn't it?" Lawrence asked.

"Perhaps," Auggie said.

"Well," Lawrence said. "Come visit me and we'll discuss it. We promised ourselves an early night tonight, and here it is, already nine."

Auggie watched from the patio as the Finers made their way out, saying their good-byes to Gussie and Winston, who had taken their places at the door, standing next to each other, bidding *adieu* to their company. Livy arrived, sat down next to him on the patio wall, and lit two cigarettes, one for herself, one for him. They blew smoke rings until Ed came up. He glanced at Auggie, shrugged. Livy took his hand and they went in for a nightcap, leaving Auggie to go down to the beach, where Alyssa sat on a rock, raging and weeping.

"Oh, Alyssa, it's not the end of the world."

"But what am I going to do now?"

The question revealed to Auggie which sister had lied, and reminded him of his mother's advice.

"You want to be a lawyer, don't you, Alyssa?" he asked, sitting down. "The rules are changing, but they've not changed yet. Babies? Come, come. Make a sacrifice now and you'll be happier for it. Marriage isn't the only way to get away from here. Especially marriage to Ed. He got into all sorts of trouble when we were stationed in Frankfurt."

"That's what I like about him. He's fast."

"Then you should have known not to try to pin him," Auggie said, holding her by the hardened tone in his voice.

"I guess that's for Ed to decide." Alyssa lifted her chin.

"He has decided," Auggie replied, staring out at the water, black and reflecting the cool rays of the moon. "One has only to do the math. Whose child is it?"

Alyssa sat up, staring at him. She hesitated, flushed, then shrugged.

"You really should be put on ice," Auggie said.

"That's not nice."

Auggie thought about nice: a word or two from him and Alyssa could regain what she had lost. She would clarify to Ed the difference between need and want. But then Livy would be devastated. His mother would be displeased, which led to the thought of a *family business*. Not nice. Auggie determined that his job was to encourage. Ever the diplomat, he was to make the path to be tread appear light, easy, not despairing. Though the work left him ashamed. As if he were doing great wrong, so unsure he was of what was the right thing to do. How stupid he felt, not knowing.

"Do you want to know not nice?" he asked Alyssa, quite overwhelmed by a yearning to be understood and vindicated. Might she? "I've been having a recurring dream. I'm on the wrong train, but I can't find my bags. I have left them somewhere. I'm running through the train, trying to get off, but it pulls out before I can. I wake up, in my dream, and it's not the luggage I'm worried about. Rather, I am feeling the terror of the Jews, and the gypsies, and all the people forced onto trains, packed in, screaming all the way to the concentration camps, the gulags. And then I look around me, and I am in an apartment in East Berlin, and the people are living in the confines of their own homes, which have been divided into apartments housing strangers, and they're unable to relax or trust anyone because they've all learned that to save their own skin, they must betray those around them. There's no way out. No hope of escaping that pervasive, deadly mistrust of everything around them. They don't even trust themselves, and all I want is to go home. Then I realize that I am home. I wake up crying."

Alyssa stared at Auggie.

"What can I do to get him back, Auggie?"

He stood up and held out a hand to her.

"You and I are going to take a trip," he said. She shook her head. "We'll have a gay old time. We'll do everything you want to do, and when we come back, you'll be right as rain, ready to finish your schooling and move on to the next fellow."

"I don't want a next fellow. And I will not take a trip with you."

Alyssa ran off, leaving Auggie to look out at the village across the way and think about victims and collaborators; inhumanity; and how he had always hoped he would be the kind of person who would stand up for right and wrong. The type who was strong enough to call the woman he loved, accept her even if she weren't what she should be. A good person who could trust himself to challenge himself. Instead, he didn't dare to visit with Lawrence the next day, too afraid, too ashamed.

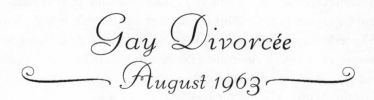

Gay Divorcée
August 1963

Livy and her four-year-old daughter, Joy, wended their way, hand in hand, through the white pine grove path connecting Livy and Ed's house to Gussie and Winston's. Barefoot, bikinied, and baby-oiled, mother and daughter enjoyed the shade, the soothing chill of the moss on the soles of their feet, the cushion of pine needles. It contrasted so nicely with what was to come: the intense, hot glare of the sun, and what could be better than that sultry heat to perfect the building of a sand castle, or cure a hangover?

"Mommy?" Joy called for her mother's attention. "When is Daddy coming home?"

Livy hesitated, then promised: "Soon."

Joy chortled and broke into a run, shrieking the thrilling news to all who would listen. Livy smiled, glad to have elicited such a happy response. This was her life! These would be her good old days, and they were good because even saying *soon* made Ed's return real and their last argument a thing of the past. She didn't even know what all the to-do had been about. She had only tried to kiss him good-bye.

Livy stepped out onto the sunlight-flooded lawn of her parents' property and up the slight slope to the house, where the adults and their littles were gathered. On the lawn played the children—Livy's own dear Griffin, seven years and four months, wrestling with Alyssa's Max, who shrieked "Seven years, eight months, and five days!" in defiance of Griffin's teasing. Alyssa's youngest, Julia, age four, weeded the garden with the help of her oldest brother, Gus, who had been born large, if "premature," on January 1, 1955. But who cared to do the math? Gus was a sweet boy, happy to teach the difference between weeds and thyme, his attempt at redemption for his erroneous pulling up of his grandmother's herb garden the previous spring. Gussie had been beside herself. As opposed to now, when she was orchestrating the day. Dressed in her faded blue-and-gray plaid bathing suit, she stood on the stone wall of the patio, directing Winston in cutting trees from the view.

"This one?" he shouted from down in the brush. A tree shook.

"No, to the right," Gussie shouted.

"Ed's coming back soon, Mummy!" Livy smiled up at her, feeling the warmth of the sun on her face. "Isn't that wonderful?"

"If you think so, dear. Winston! Next door to that one. To the right!" Gussie used both arms to direct him. The chainsaw roared. An entirely other treetop shook. "Damn his hide, not wearing his hearing aids."

Gussie climbed down from the patio wall and hurried off to stop him from cutting down the cherry tree. Livy sighed.

"Poor Mummy," Livy said with a mix of offense, amusement, and pity as she stepped up onto the patio. A branch fell, and then another, while Gussie shouted to be heard over the chainsaw.

"Why poor Mummy?" Alyssa asked, soft and buxom in an orange-brown plaid, two-piece bathing suit. She was studying her law books.

"Having to tolerate Father the way she does. He is her cross to bear."

"She's figured things out for herself, Livy," Alyssa said, pushing back in her white plastic rattan chair, her feet up on the stone ledge that bordered the patio. "She pretends he doesn't exist until she needs her view trimmed, or some firewood. I think she's more content than you think."

"Our generation is lucky. We know marriage isn't forever. We wouldn't tolerate his behavior. We'd get out of it if our husbands had another woman."

"Some of us would," Alyssa said. Livy bristled at the underlying criticism, knowing perfectly well Alyssa had a rather broad definition of fidelity herself. Poor Renny, trusting her the way he did, wanting to because he couldn't bear her loss. Livy knew how he felt. Granted, Ed was only on a business trip. He was busy with the story for *The New York Times*. And all the way in California! She shouldn't expect him to call her every hour on the hour. When he called, which he would, she would apologize and tell him that she had decided to go back to work, and that she missed him. She was desperately lonely and alone. That's all she had to say. Livy tossed her book—*Lady Chatterley's Lover*—onto a white plastic chaise lounge.

"Where is Nan?" Livy asked, reaching over to rock the family bassinet: an old laundry basket nailed to rocker feet and lined with sheep's wool. Eleven-month-old Emma slept. At peace. All swaddled and secure, surrounded by her loving aunts and doting grandmother. Gussie couldn't seem to keep her hands off Emma. *She'll do things when she grows up*, Gussie kept saying. As if the rest of them hadn't! Livy almost envied Emma all that attention, and wondered if their mother had paid as much attention to Livy and her siblings when they were littles?

"Nan is making iced tea, Livy," Alyssa said. "And I am attempting to study."

"How do you think she's doing?" Livy asked, lowering her voice.

"Nan?" Alyssa asked. "Fine. Why?"

"Auggie leaving her alone with us all day while he goes off to New Haven to work. It must be hard."

"We aren't monsters, Livy. It's lovely here. She can sun and relax with everyone around to help take care of the baby. I wish I'd had as much help."

Livy thought about Nan and her in-depth introduction to the family. Living in the house all summer. With all the whisperings. Livy found it comforting to talk about people and find out what everyone else thought, too, but she imagined it might be alarming if one were not used to it.

"Did you hear her suggest to Auggie that she go to the library with him next week?" Livy whispered. "She said they could keep each other company on the commute, have lunch together, maybe take a walk about Yale's campus to see what it's like. He said he thought that was an interesting idea."

"It won't happen," Alyssa said with a certainty that Livy shared. "He wouldn't bear the distraction. He likes to know that Nan and the baby are safe and snug with us. It's wonderful, isn't it, how enamored they are of each other? He positively lights up when Nan's around."

"Yes," Livy said. "I sometimes wonder who cheers her up."

"Emma, of course."

"She's not taken to motherhood the way you did, Alyssa. She's more like me that way. When Emma was born, Nan stared at her like she felt exactly the same way as I did when I had mine: you're presented with a wrinkly, squirmy, red being with eyes that go rolling about in their sockets, and told it's your responsibility for the rest of your life."

"That's what parenting is, Livy. Being the responsible adult," Alyssa said briskly. Livy bit her tongue. As if she didn't know what parenting was! She would not respond to Alyssa's patronizing. They each had their own way of life. They were entirely different. So different it amazed Livy, sometimes, to think the two of them were related. At which thought Gussie returned to her viewing podium and Nan returned with iced tea and sandwiches for all.

While the others ate, Livy watched her weight, and Gussie and Emma played their mutually adored pastime of row, row, row the boat. Eventually, Gus and Max insisted it was their turn and dragged Emma off in her basket to be the prisoner, trapped in their fort on the lawn. Julia and Joy were left in charge of interrupting the adults' discussion of whether President Kennedy would withdraw from Vietnam with the far more pertinent question of whether it was time to go swimming yet. At last, the requisite hour had passed.

Alyssa and Gussie raced the children down to the beach for a swim, taking Emma with them and leaving Livy and Nan alone. An opportunity for a nice chat. Livy adjusted her Gauguin-print towel on the chaise and checked to be sure a consistent film of baby oil covered her body. She lit a cigarette and watched Nan, hatted and sunglassed, scribble.

"How goes your work these days, Nan?"

"Slowly," she replied, her voice clipped.

"I beg your pardon," Livy said as the sharp edge of the smoke burned her throat. "I shouldn't be bothering you."

"I'm sorry," Nan said. She began to gather up her things: pencils, a dictionary, various papers. "I'm in a mood. It's unsocial of me to try to work with people about. But the sun is so lovely, and the breeze. I guess I wanted to have my cake and eat it too."

"You can. Sit yourself right back down," Livy ordered, lying back in her chaise and closing her eyes to face the sun. "I believe in eating one's cake. Work. Enjoy the sun."

Nan hesitated but acquiesced. Livy listened. The creak of a notebook being opened, the turn of a page. After a moment or two, the scratch of a pencil. Nan at work, content. Livy smiled and lifted her cigarette, drew the smoke in, let it out, smoke rings chasing smoke rings.

"It's only because you like company," she said.

"Excuse me?" Nan asked.

"I do, too. It gets lonely, doesn't it, when one's husband leaves?" Nan didn't respond. "I was thinking today, you must find this place a bit stifling. You've led such a city life. Living in New York, and Bombay. Here, you're rather stuck. No car, and not knowing anyone or where to go, and Auggie off in New Haven all day, every day. In theory, it sounds lovely. Loads of time to work and read and relax. But we can only occupy ourselves so much before the isolation overwhelms us."

"I'd like to have him around more," Nan admitted, after a pause. "He's much easier to tote than this enormous dictionary." Nan tried to laugh, cleared her throat. "I mean, to talk with, too. He gets so lost in his work, sometimes it's hard to get his attention. Not that I want to interrupt him. I know how important his work is to him."

"Yes," Livy said. "He needs his work."

Both women contemplated that thought. Livy rose up on her elbows to admire the trees growing up to frame the breakwater, colored by a white-blue haze of heat. The harbor's water, flat. A sailboat, trapped in irons. She puzzled: how capture the buzz of a whaler bashing against the wake of a lobster boat, and the shouts of the children, the caws of the seagulls opposing those of the crows in words, and in a way that conveyed a whole other meaning, too?

"I don't mind the loneliness." Nan's voice was stilted and abrupt.

"That's because you have your work to keep you company. I envy you. You're so together. A graduate degree. A book of poems published. Two years living in India. All that, and still your whole life ahead of you, knowing exactly what you want. You're so . . . interesting. Interested and interesting." Livy's chin quivered. She took a drag off her cigarette, blew the smoke out in a fierce stream. "Did you know, Nan, that I had to give up my job when I had my babies? It was the kind of work you have to be somewhere at a specific time for a specific number of hours. A real job. I wanted to make my mark, and was well on my way to making it. Imagine the career I might have had. Where I'd be now. All the fascinating things I would have to think and talk about. But Mummy and everyone encouraged me to stop work and take care of the babies. The irony is, I didn't want children. Not until I was thirty-five—and here I am, thirty-one with two of them! Isn't that too funny? It's a shame. I should never have given up my work. Whatever you do, don't make that mistake."

"No. I won't. I wouldn't."

"Of course not," Livy said, vaguely offended by Nan's tone. Livy stamped out her cigarette on the flagstone. She readjusted her towel, lowered herself back down, quite tired. "You don't have to. You make your own schedule. It must be freeing."

"That depends on your definition of free, Livy."

"Well, if I had my druthers, I certainly wouldn't get up at five the way you do."

"I get up so early because it's the only time I can get concentrated writing done. At least, I used to before Emma was born. My schedule isn't so free as it appears."

"But it's your choice to get up." Livy rolled her head towards Nan and squinted.

"If I don't, the work doesn't get done. Certainly, no one else is going to do it."

"I wouldn't get up," Livy said. "I'd stay up. It would be lovely. A good, strong Scotch, a pen and paper, writing until late into the dark and quiet of the night, up past even the crickets. I wrote a poem once. With a bit more tweaking, I bet I'd have gotten it published. What a different life that would have been!"

Livy sighed. Her eyes were heavy as the sun's heat soaked into her. The high-pitched chirr of the cicadas. A cleansing sweat. She touched her fingertips to her hip bones jutting up, the skin of her stomach, taut and freckled, smooth, hot. A heart tremor. She missed Ed. If she weren't so utterly exhausted, she would call him at his hotel and leave another message. A double entendre, like the ones she used to leave when they first dated. To think how young they had been! Children having children, and it was too awful how time passed and changed things. She wished she could again be the sweet, virgin girl she had been when they met.

Almost a virgin.

Innocent, anyway. Naive as the salty whisper of a breeze. It took off the edge of the sun's heat.

"I'm sorry you and Ed are having such troubles, Livy," Nan said in a quiet voice. "It's difficult, isn't it? To marry the exactly right person, only to find it's not what you'd imagined it would be."

"We aren't having troubles." Livy looked in surprise at Nan, who looked back, and even behind those glasses, Livy could see she was flummoxed. Livy laughed and reached over to give her sister-in-law a reassuring squeeze of the arm. "The family rumor mill at work. Ed and I have our moments, but we're fine. Making up from our fights is the best part."

"I'm glad." Nan stirred her iced tea with a finger. She didn't have the long, elegant fingers of the Michaels family, but hers had a competence and surety that Livy found attractive. "I heard that you were divorcing."

"Oh, that. I'm not sure it's quite the thing."

"Is that the point? I mean, if the two of you are unhappy—"

"Unhappy? Me?" Livy blinked. She thought about Ed's *cavorting*, their agreed-upon euphemism for his dalliances because the word *affair* was intolerable to her. *Affair* sounded too permanent and complicated. Like her father's *other woman* situation, which she would never countenance. Talk about humiliation and oodles of money out the window. Ed only had a penchant to step out. She had known that when they married. Just as she knew he was from a different background. She didn't hold it against him, no matter what he claimed. Why should that bother her? Excepting those Friday nights when he would drive up from the city, claiming it was the traffic that had kept him when she knew damn well he had stayed for a drink with some lady friend. How dare he keep her, Livy Michaels, waiting until well past the midnight hour! She should always come first. Times like that showed his low class, and she let him know it! At least, she had this last time, saying things she had never said aloud before. Hateful words. She wished she could take them back. But Ed had said such awful things about Auggie. It was one thing to tell her that he wouldn't have married her if he'd known she wasn't pregnant. (She had never suggested she was!) But to call Auggie a failure just because he had chosen to work in the Midwest rather than at an Ivy League school? She would not countenance that.

Of course, growing up poor, Ed wouldn't understand. Auggie's background allowed him to do whatever he wanted, which had been to get away from family. Auggie was good enough as he was and didn't have to prove himself, unlike some people, who married for money and pedigree. And there had begun the downward spiral. She would have to make up to him. If only because she could never give up their life together. They had too much fun. All the parties they went to, the dancing and drinking all night long with their beautiful, smart friends. Their travels to far-off beaches, where they enjoyed the cool sweetness of mai tais and margaritas; and to cozy winter chalets, warmed by scotches and hot rum toddies. The children, both birthed in a lovely epidural haze, hadn't gotten in the way at all. They had been fine in back rooms and coatrooms, and had only been left once or twice overnight in dirty diapers because she had been a bit too wet herself to change them. With Ed, one never had to sit and think, and he took care of all the piles of papers and bills which so overwhelmed her. Livy's job was to be happy and gay, and to make sure that everyone else was, too. She liked that job; she excelled at it, and the sun's heat was positively luxuriant.

"Ed and I are good together." Livy grinned sleepily. The black of her lids glowed orange and red. "Eighty-five. The perfect number for a marriage, and that's us. We aren't usually able to maintain perfection at one hundred percent, but we don't toddle along at fifteen or twenty percent either. The wonder of our relationship is that when one of us is entirely done in, at say ten percent, the other steps forward and carries the load. Then, maybe the next day, it's the other way around. A lovely give and take. We help each other."

"Yes," Nan said. "I suppose that's what marriage is, helping each other."

Livy shaded her eyes and looked over at Nan. A tendril of cloud covered the sun, giving a shadowy tremble to Nan's chin.

"I've an idea," Livy announced. "You were saying this morning that all you have to wear are those saris of yours. Let's go shopping tomorrow. There's nothing like a good shopping spree to perk up the spirits."

"What about the children?" Nan said with a quaver of a smile as she looked down at the ream of empty paper next to her.

"Mummy will take care of them."

"I wouldn't want to assume that. She might have her own plans."

"Nonsense. That's her role. We all have our roles."

"That doesn't mean you have to play them, does it?"

"Talk to Auggie about that," Livy snapped. "Our roles are what we are. It would be against our nature to do otherwise. For instance, I am the family screw-up."

"That's not a nice thing to say about yourself. I certainly don't think that. You only need to step up and you'll be fine."

"Step up? You mean get a job? The problem, as anyone will tell you, Nan," Livy said, with a pause to clear her throat of the sudden lump that had come up it, "is what would I do? There's nothing I'm really good at."

"What do you enjoy?"

". . . Drinking. I love to drink and throw a good party."

"You could be a caterer."

"I'm not a cook," Livy said, and to her horror she heard it. Her tone of voice. What Ed had accused her of: sneering. What a horrible thing to do, as if it would be beneath her to be a cook. She didn't really believe that. She was very democratic in how she viewed everyone. She would love to be a cook! "I'm not naturally talented that way."

"You'd have to figure out a way to hire people to do the cooking. You could be the overseer. The party planner."

Livy thought about that. It almost made sense.

"It's not very intellectual," she pointed out.

"We all can't be great intellects."

"Livy!" Gussie shouted from below. "I need your help."

Livy sat up and looked down to where her mother waved for her at the start of the path to the beach. She stood up, not wanting to leave quite yet.

"What no one seems to realize, Nan, is that I do have a job. Taking care of Mummy. That responsibility takes up all my time and energy. In turn, Ed helps me. Rather, he needs to think he does. He needs to think I need him, when, in fact, I only need to know he is there." Livy paused in her progress down the steps to her mother. "I am far more independent than he thinks I am. He thinks I can't do without him. What he doesn't realize is that I sometimes wonder *where* I would be without him."

". . . In New York City," Nan said. "Working."

Livy turned to find Nan peering at her through her huge, black sunglasses. She looked like a beetle.

"You play a role, too, you know, Nan. Auggie loves you in no small part because you kick the can. You reject society, acting like a hippie in your saris that smell of incense. But you're no different from us. You've money and class. You claim to be the poet. An independent woman. Yet here you are, acting the part of a perfect fifties housewife: home with the baby while the husband is off earning money. You say we don't have to play our roles. The point is, we play them without even meaning to."

Livy arrived at the beach to find that Joy had thrown up the seawater she had merrily swallowed on a dare. Livy collected her troops and took them back home for warm baths and a bowl of applesauce for Joy, and they were just fine. No questions asked about their father. They didn't miss him a bit. Livy contemplated the resilience and short memories of children as she powdered and dressed. They would be better off without him. No more crass jokes. No more hint of an accent that she had found so attractive, thinking he'd had French or Russian influence, only to find out it was a Tennessee drawl. Livy tried on different clothes, making an honest assessment of herself in the mirror. All her clothes still fit. She had a more angular look to her than she had in years before, but the magazines liked that. So did the men, who still turned to look as she walked by. She had only to snap her fingers and remember not to slouch, and her life in New York would be quite gay, with none of the puritanical crap she'd had to deal with before she got married. If—IF—she got divorced, she would have huge amounts of fun. And hard work, of course. She looked forward to the challenge. It would liven her up, improve her complexion, all that running about.

She sat down at her dressing table, in front of her brute of a magnifying glass mirror. A spritz of perfume. Her pearl necklace. Coral lipstick. She looked herself straight in the eye and told herself that this was an opportunity. In many ways, she felt like a kid given the keys to the car. Tickly feeling in the stomach. Heart fluttering. Freedom. It would be her own choice what to do. No one else would tell her how to live her life. It would all be up to her.

No one else would help.

She would be all alone.

And then Griffin slammed open her bedroom door and announced that they had still to decorate the Duncan Hines orange cake with lemon frosting that they had baked that morning.

The task probably should have been done before the baths. Squirts of yellow, red, and blue writing gel mixed together into what appeared to be a green-black bruise. An enormous disappointment to them all, until Livy suggested they cover the cake with Sarah Perkins roses, at which point the bruise became a lovely background of leaves and a live ladybug for luck. With great care, they carried the cake to the maternal house for cocktails, Griffin in his fireman pajamas, Joy in her "Cindy Lou Who Christmas" nightie, and Livy in her favorite sky blue muumuu. Livy left the cake and the children in the kitchen, where they were to eat dinner with their cousins and be entertained by their grandmother. Gussie appeared thrilled, if harried, to be in their midst, serving them. The children shrieked, shouted, and laughed, adoring their grandmother's teasing, and somehow food remained on the plate or went down their gullets with none of the whining and lobbing that went on when Livy led the assault of string beans and hot dogs. It was a shame. Her mother spent so much time and energy with the children. She had such potential to do other things. Livy felt grateful that she, herself, still had her life and times ahead of her. She would do things her mother had never dreamed of—which led her to wonder what her mother had dreamed of, and why she tolerated what she did. Granted, toleration served a purpose: avoiding the headache and stress of a divorce. But it was ironic. Everyone talked about Livy's marriage, when really it wasn't Livy who should get divorced but her mother. There was nothing to be ashamed of, after all. Society wasn't so frumpy about divorce these days. It might be quite liberating.

Livy stepped into the dining room to make herself a much-deserved drink. The sliding door to the patio had been left open by the children, letting goodness knew how many mosquitoes and other bugs and things in. Ever the responsible adult, she slid shut the screen first, then addressed the sideboard liquor cabinet. It stood open. The martini shaker beaded with the sweat of melted ice cubes. A sliced lime, an open tonic bottle, and a half-empty bottle of gin. All proof that the cocktail hour had begun. Livy reached for a glass and the gin and listened to the children's voices in the kitchen blend with those of the adults in the living room. Familiar noises. The conversation of her siblings and their spouses. The crackle of Winston's radio. He sat, Livy knew, in his chair at the other side of the room from the others. A man of routine, he arrived home from his euphemism of a job, raging against his boss, and then, over his whiskey, listened to the news. The family could only hope that he wouldn't hear something to set him off on the subject of communism or civil rights. He could entirely ruin the cocktail hour.

"Stunned?" Auggie's voice carried into the dining room. "But she's perfectly aware that her marriage is a failure."

"She's just afraid she'll have to work," Alyssa said. "Though God knows what kind of job she'll be able to get. She's no skills or qualifications."

"She just hasn't figured herself out yet," Nan said.

"Certainly, she has," Alyssa said with a laugh. "She's known since she was a girl. She is a woman of leisure. Reading historical fiction all winter next to a cozy fire, and sunbathing and toiling in her garden in the summer. I wish I could do that."

"You can," Auggie said. "You choose not to."

Livy silently toasted her brother. His support meant the world to her. An extra splash of gin and a squeeze of lime.

"I choose to challenge myself, and accept that I have to work for a living," Alyssa said. "Father, please turn down that radio. I can hardly hear myself think."

"Hello," Livy said, stepping into the room with a smile and a look to let them know she knew perfectly well that they were discussing her and didn't care one bit.

"How am I supposed to hear, if you children shout so," Winston demanded. He wore black pants and his maroon velour smoking jacket.

"The reason you can't hear it is you've not put in your hearing aids," Alyssa replied with her self-conscious air of being entirely unconscious of her beauty. Livy felt plain next to her.

"Livy!" Winston barked. "Where is your dear mother?"

"In the kitchen enjoying her grandchildren, Father."

"She should be here, relaxing with a drink."

"Rest easy. She's in something close to heaven." Livy raised a brow of tolerant amusement as she sat on the low bench in front of the fireplace. She set her drink down next to her, hugged her knees, and looked about her: Nan and Auggie on the couch to her left; Renny and Alyssa on the one to her right; and her father at the other side of the room, by himself. "Aren't we all a dressed up and handsome group? Nan, your sari is glorious; the saffron color is perfect for you."

"I'm afraid it clashes with my sunburn," Nan said, leaning against Auggie, whose arm was around her shoulder. He smiled down at her. His profile was positively Grecian, and Nan did have the color of a cooked lobster, having got far too much sun for one so fair-complexioned. Auggie touched a long, elegant finger to the white band on Nan's nose where her dark glasses had rested and kissed the top of her head. She snuggled closer. Alyssa toyed with Renny's hair. He lay lengthwise on the couch, his head in her lap, coddling a drink. Livy's heart felt squeezed such that she could hardly take a breath. Everyone else had somebody. Quite suddenly, she missed Ed and wished with all her heart that he would call.

"What happened to you, Renny?" Livy asked.

"Moved one too many boxes from the back room," he groaned.

"It's nice and tidy. You did a good job on it."

"How do you know?" Alyssa asked, her voice sharp.

"That's where I put the cake," Livy replied.

"That's my study now," Alyssa said. "I hope you didn't get frosting on my books."

"Study?" Livy repeated, her gut tensing.

"She's made herself a room of her own," Nan said.

"But that's what you need," Livy said, flushing with irritation at the way Alyssa took over everything. "And what about Auggie? He wouldn't have to drive to New Haven every day if he had a study."

"I don't mind," Auggie said.

"Nan does," Livy retorted, causing Nan's burn to brighten. "She hates how you leave her with us all day."

"That's not exactly true," Nan protested.

"Nan is coming with me next week," Auggie replied.

"And who's to take care of Emma?" Alyssa asked, alert. "She's still breast-feeding."

"Easy enough to cure her of that, and Nan will get more done if she comes with me." He smiled at Nan, who smiled back, uncertain.

"Gussie!" Winston boomed from his chair, his hands clutching the arms. His children glared at him. "Gussie!"

As if on command, the kitchen door swung open and the children came running through, racing each other across the living room and up the stairs. Only Max stopped, to tell his grandfather that his grandmother said she'd be out in a minute and to please stop shouting.

"And have you nothing to say for yourself, young man?" Winston asked, stern as could be. Max hesitated, then dove in to tickle his grandfather, who grabbed him by the waist and swung him, shrieking with laughter, upside down in the air. Released, Max ran off to join the other cousins upstairs, where, judging by the sounds of large objects being dropped at regular intervals, they were guillotining their Barbies and G.I. Joes. The smell of roasting chicken came from the kitchen. Renny struggled to sit up.

"Livy?" Auggie said. "I got a letter from Ed today. He says if you sign those last papers, everything can be tied up with a bow by the end of next month."

"At which point, I'll join the ranks of gay divorcée?" Livy smiled brightly. Her hand shook slightly as she sipped her drink.

"What are your next steps to be?" Auggie asked. "He's not going to be able to pay much of an allowance, and—"

"Exactly!" Livy interrupted. Another quick smile and sip. "Divorce is expensive. Our bills will be doubled. I'll have to go back to work, and then who will take care of the children? It's not reasonable at all that I go back to a full-time job."

"It's the only reasonable thing you can do," Alyssa said.

"I am thrilled at the prospect of working," Livy snapped, furious that this conversation was taking place in front of Alyssa. The fact was, Alyssa left Livy feeling entirely insufficient, and doubtful that she might accomplish anything near to what Alyssa had. Getting herself through college and into law school, all the while taking care of her babies and a part-time job at the Women's Center. Who could keep up? Not that there was a competition. It was just that Alyssa's presence shrank Livy's. Compared to Alyssa's—which she was certain Ed did, compare the two sisters—her own life appeared provincial and uninteresting. Livy decided, then and there, to call the local college for a course catalogue. She would study something challenging. Part-time. That would allow her to pick up a few jobs modeling.

"I've been desperate," Livy said, only recognizing it as she spoke, "to go back to work, but the children come first."

"Mummy can take care of them," Alyssa said, her eyes a brilliant green against her tan, her entire self glowing with health.

"You might consider our mother a babysitter, but I won't." Livy glanced toward their father and lowered her voice. "I think it's high time Mummy be left free to do whatever she wants, and not be tied to this house and its goings-on. Besides, how can Mummy babysit if we're in New York?"

"New York?" Auggie repeated.

"Yes," Livy said with satisfaction, finally able to get them to listen to her. "I intend to spend the next bit of time catching up with my old friends in the city. I've still got their numbers. Remember how upset they were when I left? They called me for months afterwards. I'll maybe get my old job back, or something like it, with a higher salary. I told Ed and he thinks it's a grand idea. I'm surprised, Auggie, he didn't mention it in his letter. More money, less stress, and the best part is that I'll be independent and not so needy of him. In which case, why go through the expense of a divorce? We'll just have to get married again. It'll be a whole new life for us."

"Pie in the sky," Alyssa said. Livy slammed down her drink on the table.

"Why are you always so damned negative about everything I say and do?"

"I'm not being negative. I'm being realistic. It's been nearly eight years since you've lived in New York."

"The budget you gave to Mummy and me last week was very helpful, Livy," Auggie interrupted. "It makes clear that at your present rate of expenditure, you'll have nothing left but your house by the end of next year. At that point, like it or not, you will be a thirty-two-year-old, unattached female who is out of touch with the work you used to do in New York. Jobs are not going to tumble into your hands. You have your family and friends, of course. You couldn't starve if you tried. But you have to act soon, or you will slip into precisely the kind of humiliating dependence you abhor."

The baby started crying. Nan got up to go attend to her needs, and wouldn't that be nice? Livy wished that hunger or wet diapers were *her* only challenges. Emma had no idea of life's toils. No idea of what her future held. Poor child. No wonder she wept!

"A bit late in the day to be talking about dependence," Alyssa said.

"Presently," Auggie said, holding a hand up to silence her, "your life is quite comfortable, with your gardening and teas and books. But in a couple of decades, your life will have become tedious and dull. At the very least, *you* will be tedious and dull if you don't find a job that keeps you interested and interesting."

"You certainly have been talking with Ed," Livy said, lighting a cigarette. Wasn't that exactly, word for word, what Ed had said to her? It was cruel and unfair of him. She had never wanted to quit her job, only everyone—himself included, and her mother in particular—had insisted. And now she bored him. But wasn't she exactly the girl he had married? Which had led him to say, "Yes, that's the problem."

"Why are you so mean to me?" she had asked, bursting into tears. He had made no move to comfort her. Just as on their wedding day, when she had caught him kissing Alyssa. A harmless romp. They had laughed. She realized it was silly of her to cry, and so she had apologized. And, years later, apologized again for being boring. For being exactly the girl he had married. She was sorry.

"Don't apologize," Ed said. "You're always apologizing."

"I'm sorry. No, I'm not sorry. I just don't know what I did to cause you not to talk to me."

"It's what you haven't done, Livy."

A mean thing to say, which had caused her to say mean things, too, and now he had been gone a week and not a phone call or note and her family was talking about her as if she could not take care of herself.

"The problem," Auggie continued, "is the type of job you'd be interested in usually begins at a low pay, and at an apprenticeship level. Which is something you don't believe you should have to endure."

"No, I don't." Livy dabbed her eyes with the bottom hem of her muumuu.

"Just because she feels entitled doesn't mean—"

"Hush, Alyssa. She's had a rough time of it, and doesn't feel up to getting a job at all. I want to facilitate her reentering the work force. Barring the miracle that you are able to land a fifty-thousand-dollar-a-year job—and you are, of course, free to try, Livy, but you haven't yet."

"Entirely for lack of trying," Alyssa said, and Livy felt so frustrated, so judged, that all she could do was stick her tongue out at Alyssa.

"The foreseeable result of what you are doing, Livy," Auggie went on relentlessly, "is that in about a year you'll have to put your house on the market, and that will put you on our dole, no matter how tactfully we all try to hide the truth. It is my view, and Mother's, that everything should be done to avoid this."

"Agreed," Alyssa said.

"If you don't mind, you are talking about my life." Livy stubbed out her cigarette with determination. She was not to be pitied! She was not pathetic. She would never sell her house. Never. "I think I might have a chance to put in my two cents."

"Livy," Auggie said gently, and the rage she had been feeling disappeared. He was only trying to help—and if she were angry? A breathtaking thought. He would not want to be around her. She didn't want him to leave. She appreciated his help, needed it. Only sometimes, it felt awful. "I can only imagine how afraid and trapped you must feel."

"I certainly do," Livy said, chin trembling, tears trickling. She took the napkin he held out to her. It was too depressing after such a lovely day.

"Mother and I have discussed it," Auggie said. "We have a proposal that would allow you to find a job that meets your requirements. I have a salary of sixteen thousand dollars. This is enough for most of our friends to live on. The only difference between me and them is Nan's small inheritance, which allows me a certain flexibility. If you will go out and get a job of the sort that will keep you occupied, Mother and I will supplement your salary to the amount of my own. If you earn nine thousand dollars, we will each give you three thousand, five hundred, for a total of seven thousand. Plus any cost of living increases I get. The increment will be paid monthly, starting when you start work. It will be paid by a bank so that we won't forget and you won't have to ask. When your salary reaches mine, or when you stop working, we stop paying. You may treat it as a debt if you wish to, but you may also forget about it. There will be no conditions on how you spend it."

"What did Ed say about this?" Livy sniffed. "He isn't one to accept charity. Nor am I."

"This is an investment, Livy, to help you make a fruitful life for yourself. And to avert the horror and expense of bankruptcy."

"Auggie," Alyssa said. "This proposal of yours ensures Livy's dependence on you. None of us trust she can make it on her own, least of all herself. She has to prove she can do this on her own, or she'll continue to flounder."

"You are entirely unaffected by this offer, Alyssa," Auggie retorted, "other than as a beneficiary of the result."

"I won't do anything until I talk to Ed," Livy said with a mounting sense of panic. "You can tell him that, Auggie. He has to call me. I have to talk to him. You've no idea how important it is that I talk to him."

A crash in the dining room.

"Heavens to Maude." Gussie's voice echoed in the dining room, and a brown flash ran into the living room. A squirrel, chattering loud reprimands, jumped onto the back of the couch and up onto the mantle. As it ran a full circuit of the room, Gussie came in, slamming shut the door to the dining room behind her. A lamp toppled off a side table as the squirrel leapt from it to the stairs, immediately twisting away as the children, shouting warnings, tumbled down the staircase in pursuit of Tipper the Siamese cat, who had a mouse in its mouth.

"Freeze!" Gussie shouted. The children did. The cat disappeared under the couch but came out immediately, attracted by the sound of the squirrel. It stood on its hind legs, chattering furiously, on top of the grandfather clock. Tipper crouched, his tail swishing the floor.

Winston reached to open the sliding door to the patio. A moment of hush. The mouse dropped out of Tipper's mouth, lay there, stunned and panting. Tipper placed a paw on its tail.

"Towels. The towels." Gussie pointed to the pile of damp, sandy towels that had been left by some negligent someone at the bottom of the stairs. "Flap them about, children. Stay exactly where you are and mill about making noise. The last thing we need is a squirrel in the bedrooms. Winston, you might want to step away from the sliding door so you won't scare the beast off."

At which words, Tipper leapt.

The next minutes consisted of pandemonium, the end result being the squirrel escaping out of the house with Tipper close behind, the mouse disappearing to who knew where, and a hairball mushed between Alyssa's toes. Everyone collapsed in laughter, which led to a game of ha-ha, all of them lying prone on the floor, heads on tummies.

"There is nothing like this," Livy said, wiping her eyes, when finally they had put the room to right and returned to their cocktails. "It's nice to know that, even when one has left one's parents' home, there is always a place to come to where you can cry so hard you laugh."

Everyone was silent for a moment until Nan asked, "You mean laugh so hard you cry, don't you?"

"Why yes," Livy said, reaching for her drink. The ice had melted, watering it down. Staring into her glass, Livy wondered out loud if she had left her oven on. She had better check it.

The path between the two houses at the end of the day. Moonflowers glowing. The dew covered grass cooling her feet, making way for the cushion of pine needles and cones, dry and occasionally pricking. From the goldfish pond came the peepers' peep and the bullfrog's sonorous burp. In such idyllic circumstances, it seemed unnecessary to debate Auggie's proposal. Nonsense, of course. She could support herself, whatever Alyssa might say. Ed would support her until her own work sustained her. The only question was, what kind of work would suit her?

She arrived into her wide, open living room that blended into the kitchen where she refreshed her drink. The stove, of course, was off. Leaning against the counter, drinking, she stared out to the harbor. The village was ablaze with the reflection of the sunset. Livy took a deep, sighing breath of contentment knowing that behind her, out of her sight, was the glorious, setting sun. Breathless beauty. How blessed she was, having all this! If Ed decided not to share it with her? If she had to divorce? She adjusted her posture, stood up tall. She was not afraid! She would be fine.

A knock on the window startled her. A blur of white. She walked to where an albino hummingbird hovered, knocking itself against the glass. Bizarre. It held itself before her as if it wanted to tell her something. It wanted to get in. She couldn't wait to tell Ed! He loved hummingbirds for their cocky ways, their competitive brutishness, and rapid wing beats. Territorial bastards, he called them, just like himself. He was terribly jealous of other men's attentions to Livy, and there would be other men. Of course there would be. Then he'd regret it!

She cranked open the window but the bird flew away. The phone rang, jarring her. She smiled, though, as she walked to answer it. How often had it happened that she would be thinking about Ed and he would call or appear? She picked up the receiver, anticipating the sound of his voice. She could almost feel the rough stubble of his beard, and that grin of his that made her giggle just seeing it, and the smell of his breath, a mix of tobacco and gin. Even the thought of his kisses left her quite breathless. She determined to do exactly what he told her to. Divorce wouldn't be all bad. They would be friends. She could count on him again. Life would be good. With just that confidence, she answered the phone.

The police. How ridiculous. An accident. She clutched the gay divorcée's garb that she had just donned, gripping it around her throat, as if that might stop the introduction of this new fashion line: the drab rags of a merry widow, because a car, alcohol, and Ed. Impossibly, he had been killed.

Seeds of Doubt
October 1973

The light from the television and the fire snapping in the hearth gave the living room a cozy glow, though the smoke from Livy's cigarettes added a hint of back room deals being made, if a person had a suspicion of such. Alyssa did. The silence that had fallen on the room upon her entering it had been deafening. It evoked a familiar feeling of curiosity: what did they know, and what did she not? Alyssa studied her family. Livy and Gussie sat on the couch opposite that in which Nan and Auggie sat, each looking into their drinks as if into the future. Eleven-year-old Emma, dressed in her new pink tutu, was perched on the couch between her parents. Perfect posture. Her slender legs and arms crossed at the ankles and wrists, respectively. Her feet, elegant in their lengthy boniness, pointed. She was the epitome of a young girl's self-importance and determination; now that her parents were home—they'd arrived just that morning—Emma hoped they would take her to get her ortho-pedist's approval to begin *en pointe* work. Alyssa shuddered to think the damage the girl would do to the house practicing *pirouettes* and *pas de bourrées*.

"Vice President Agnew has resigned," Gussie said, setting down her drink with satisfaction. At sixty-five, she was still at the top of her game, far more so than her friends, who had all seemed to fade and hunch in the last few years. "*Nolo contendere*."

"It's too bad when someone refuses to admit his guilt," Alyssa said, thinking more of her own client than of Agnew.

"I suppose everyone deserves a fair trial," Auggie said, glancing down at his daughter. Emma smiled up at him, reminding Alyssa of herself at that age. Skinny. Blonde. Enamored of her parents. Poor Emma. Auggie and Nan's absence had exposed the girl's dependence on them. She had yet to develop the solid grounding that good parenting gave a child. Such as Alyssa's own children had received. Gus, Max, and Julia might reject, rebel, and call her a fat cow, but the reason they dared to push her was because they knew she wouldn't give up on them. She would be there for them when they needed her. Alyssa, of all the family, knew how important it was to provide a child with enough love to last through the years. Her own parents had given her that.

At first. Until they had fallen off their pedestals. Which of course, all parents do, eventually. It was a part of being human. A matter of timing.

Auggie and Nan had bad timing. *Pliés, frappés*, and homesickness had been Emma's preoccupations for the two months that her parents had traveled in Europe. It was gratifying, seeing her so happily ensconced. Happily? Rather she clung, as if that might prevent another departure. Alyssa could appreciate the bruised feeling of not wanting to be left behind.

"Of course everyone deserves a fair trial, Auggie. Agnew and myself included." Alyssa tossed him a stiff smile.

"I am pleased, Auggie and Nan, that you are staying through Christmas," Gussie said, preventing Auggie's response. "We'll be able to catch up with one another."

"Your letters were so newsy, we feel as if we didn't miss a thing," Auggie said, and then turned to Alyssa to ask the inevitable question. "When is Renny to arrive?"

"Soon enough." Alyssa flopped into a chair. Her slacks cinched her waist, an unpleasant reminder that her metabolism had come to a screeching halt when she had children, such that now, at thirty-seven, she had to exercise huge restraint, only pecking at meals while everyone else indulged. "He's paying homage to his battle-ax of a mother."

"You should be more respectful of Mrs. Jones," Gussie said.

"But she is impossible. I assume you've heard the most recent to-do, Auggie. Mrs. Jones came to visit Renny and me at the Providence house, determined to be miserable. Three days in, she up and left. I say we are well rid of her."

"Alyssa, you've been married nearly twenty years," Livy said, and the toning of the years shocked Alyssa. Twenty? Years? "She's family."

"I'm tired of Renny," Alyssa snapped, and then, not quite ready to leave it at that, continued. "He acts like a sycophant around his mother, and leaves me to wait on her hand and foot. *Alyssa, dee-ah, the fi-ah is too hot. My room is too cold.* She is impossible, nattering on all day. Every morning, I presented her with her grapefruit, and each time, she complained. *I prefer the sections cut in-di-vid-dually, not the whole cut into four pieces. Alyssa, dee-ah, please. As I said yesterday, I would prefer you not cut up my grapefruit. I find the way you hack at them to be quite violent. Please don't bother yourself with it. I will take the time to cut my own grapefruit tomorrow.* As if she were making a great sacrifice, cutting her own grapefruit. The third morning, she stood up and walked out of the house and down to the train station. She refused to speak to Renny, other than to tell him to ship her things overnight to her New York address. She hasn't contacted us since."

"Did you apologize?" Emma asked. "You said a person should always apologize."

"I did nothing wrong, Emma."

"Neither did I," Emma replied. A bad case of early-onset adolescence. Alyssa looked to Auggie, who looked amused, and to Nan, who was reading a book of poetry and was, as usual, lost in her own little world. Emma had no parents to butt up against, and so it fell to Alyssa.

"Emma," Alyssa said, gently, as she sat forward in her seat, "as I tried to explain this afternoon, this house is for everyone's use, not one or another person's. That requires mutual respect of everyone's needs and space. Children should go outside to run about, not through the kitchen when people are trying to work. I have a very important case."

"I was excited to see Mummy and Daddy. And I wasn't running. I was dancing. I wanted to show them how much I've improved since they've been gone."

"I remember the days when your children ruled this house, Alyssa."

"Exactly, Mummy. It belongs to all of us. I was only pointing out that there might have been a better time to jump about. Ballerinas such as Emma have to be more careful."

"I am a ballet dancer, not a ballerina. I have to earn that title, Aunt Alyssa," Emma said firmly. "I don't deserve it yet. But I will. Someday, I'll be a prima ballerina. And I'll knock down these walls, put barres along that wall, and dance all day long."

"I hope you'll move the lamps out of the way. Then you won't have to worry about breaking them like you did my favorite mug today," Alyssa said, and then added, "You have a lively imagination, if nothing else, Emma, thinking you're going to get the house."

"She just might, Alyssa."

Alyssa looked to her mother, stunned. After such a frustrating day in her study, unable to use the phone with any privacy, the suggestion that she might not get the house felt to be too much. Her body prickled. Yet, even with everything seeming to be against her, Alyssa managed a smile.

"Of course, that's for you to determine, Mummy."

"It certainly is," Gussie said, and there was a shortness in her tone that suggested she was still ruffled about Mrs. Jones.

"For the record," Alyssa lifted her chin. "I've written several letters of apology. Mrs. Jones won't read them. There is no forgiveness in that woman."

"You've always had issues with her," Gussie said.

"She has issues with me." Alyssa felt the heat rising in her cheeks.

"I had a good chat with Mrs. Jones today, Alyssa. Your mother-in-law is a very thoughtful person. She cares deeply for her son, just as I do for my children. We only want your happiness."

"Of course, Mummy," Alyssa said with foreboding.

"Renny is a good man."

"Yes, Mummy. He is a good man."

Alyssa left it at that. After all, she couldn't explain—not to her mother—the lack she felt with him. Had always felt. The wistful yearning for someone else and the awful sense of having missed her opportunity. Not just one, but many.

"I bet nothing much different happened than ever," Livy said, settling back into the couch, comfy as could be, her long, slender legs crossed, the upper one swinging lightly. "I'm sure Alyssa did nothing intentionally."

A wave of gratitude washed over Alyssa. Livy's blue eyes, set off by the cobalt blue of her silk shirt, appeared bright and kind, understanding, as she tilted her head and looked up at Alyssa with studied curiosity and concern. It was her older sister there. The one whom Alyssa could respect and talk to. The one she missed. Alyssa wished with all her heart that she could depend on Livy, confide her secrets to her. But it seemed that whenever she did, those confessions came back at her as accusations and evidence, and as the saying went, *Fool me once, shame on you. Fool me twice . . .*

"You and your mother-in-law are both entitled," Livy said. "No small wonder you can't bear each other. There's not enough for the two of you."

"That's not true," Alyssa said. Her protest was met by the clink of ice cubes and quiet sips. Tears welled in her eyes. Alyssa reached forward to cut a slice of cheddar cheese and make a sandwich between two Ritz crackers. No attempt to see her side of things. Just like Mrs. Jones when Alyssa had told her about the case she was working on.

"It is important to the partners in my law firm to have their prosecutors work as defense lawyers," Alyssa had told Mrs. Jones. "They think it makes for better prosecutors, knowing how the enemy thinks and all that. But I will never understand how I'm supposed to prove doubt when the man reeks of guilt."

"Are you sure you haven't missed something and he's innocent?" Mrs. Jones asked. "Maybe you're asking your client to admit to being guilty of something he didn't do."

"But he did do it."

"Well," Mrs. Jones had said. "I hope you will at least consider the possibility. After all, facing the electric chair would turn a guilty man's conscience, whereas an innocent, upright man might go to the chair on principle."

"The man is a wife beater and a drunk."

"That doesn't make him a murderer. God forgives a bad temper and drink," Mrs. Jones said.

"Then God is a misogynist," Alyssa said.

"All I am saying is the man might have a pure soul."

"He has no conscience. He thinks killing his spouse, just because he's bored with her, is acceptable. Lou Wilkes." Alyssa indulged herself. Even the thought of Lou left her weak-kneed, and so to say his name . . . "Lou is a partner at the firm. He's the one who encouraged me to take this case. A crackerjack lawyer. I don't know what I'd do without him."

Alyssa took a breath. To stop the floodgates. The temptation to tell all, even to Mrs. Jones, was that great, because the only time Alyssa felt truly alive was with Lou, his eyes admiring her, his lips and fingers exploring. To think she had hardly noticed him until he had offered to buy her dinner at an Italian restaurant that took an hour to get to during rush hour traffic—an hour of anticipation, a touch of fear, worth every second once a week for seven months, and Renny never knew. Oblivious fellow. His name should have warned her. Renald Jones. He had turned out exactly as she had hoped he wouldn't, and now—after all she had done to transform his fantasy of sailing the open seas into the more profitable navigation of Wall

Street—he had decided to quit his job and build an off-grid house. As if he would save the world. As if that might save his marriage.

"Lou and I were talking the other night, and we agreed that this case is a perfect example of why marriages should end after twenty years," Alyssa said. "A person should be able to opt out, rather than feel so trapped that they want to kill the other person."

Mrs. Jones had stared at Alyssa for so long, and with such an odd expression on her face, that Alyssa wondered if she'd had a stroke.

"Marriage can be a challenge," Mrs. Jones finally said. A sip of tea. "Why isn't this Mr. Wilkes trying the case if there's so much at stake?"

"Conflict of interest. He knew the woman who was murdered."

"Then how can he be advising you?"

"My job is to separate out the emotions. He said I have to prove I can put myself above sentiment."

"Then I'm sure you'll do just fine. You're always so logical and dispassionate." Mrs. Jones hesitated and then added, "At work."

"Yes, I am." Alyssa sat up, put off by the qualification. "I'm just grateful that he's willing to advise me."

"I'm sure you are." Mrs. Jones set down her tea. The teaspoon clinked against the fine china cup. "Renny is quite excited about the new house, Alyssa."

"It's an anachronism, isn't it? Husband builds wife a house where they live happily ever after? Never mind the fact that we have Mummy's house."

"You are always saying you want your own place in Poquatuck. A place where you can be free to put things where you will. That's what one's own house is. Why are you so threatened by the idea? It's not as if having your own house pushes you out of the family." Alyssa didn't respond, but her heart fluttered, overwhelmed by the prospect of the expense and commitment, and the fact that it did, indeed, feel like a conspiracy to push her out of the family. "Of course, Renny'll need your help. Without you, he would be quite lost."

"Nonsense," Alyssa said, bracing herself. "That's what everyone says about Livy, and it's not true either. The two of them are perfectly fine on their own, only they are never given that opportunity. They are trapped in a limited view of themselves. They need to overcome their fears and pettinesses, move past them. Like my client. If only he'd admit what he did, I might be able to save him."

". . . I find self-righteousness to be an ugly trait," Mrs. Jones said.

"Yes, it is. It's difficult to defend," Alyssa agreed, not daring to say more because Mrs. Jones sat there, self-righteousness incarnate. A controlling woman, who knew nothing of the law, questioning and doubting her. It had been infuriating to think of as Alyssa hurried to prepare Mrs. Jones's breakfast the next morning. And now, again, everyone blamed her, as if she had done something wrong.

"Gussie!" Winston stood in the threshold of his room, leaning heavily on his mahogany cane, which appeared too spare to support his height. Seventy years old, his faded maroon evening jacket and dark gray slacks hanging from his frame. Short, wiry white hair, sparse on his head. Thick glasses magnifying his eyes. He was old, but still loomed. A wave of nostalgia swept over Alyssa. He didn't judge her. He still believed in her. For what that was worth. It had used to be worth something. She looked around, wanting to grasp them all, hold them tight and unchanging. She couldn't bear how things changed. Her aged parents, her aging siblings, her children, all grown up and out of the house. The only thing she could count on was the continuity and solidity of the house.

"When will my dinner be ready, darling?"

"At seven, just as it always is," Gussie said, not looking in his direction but rather at the television screen as he limped through the room, aimed for the dining room and liquor cabinet. "In the meantime, we are having a peaceful cocktail hour."

"Good luck, with those Commies and Arabs trying to bring us to our knees with their oil shenanigans."

"For pity's sake," Gussie said. She grabbed the blab-off button: an extension cord, at the end of which was attached an on/off switch that controlled the sound of the television, invented by Gussie for just such an occasion: Winston's interruption. The sound blared on. Mr. Cronkite reported on the most recent Arab/Israeli war. The question of who had attacked whom was worried, and its effect on *détente*. The Middle East chaos. It was all about oil. Money. Everyone in a panic, wanting more, instead of being sensible.

"Texas Tea, Arab-style." Livy intoned the hillbilly jingle at the next commercial break. "That's what this is all about."

"It's got less to do with oil than with history," Alyssa said, because coming from Livy it didn't sound right. "A people's wish for self-determination. They're entitled to it."

"And who are 'they'?" Auggie asked, ever the devil's advocate.

"That's the million-dollar question, isn't it?" Alyssa replied, tossing a pistachio shell at Auggie, who batted it to Emma, who caught it. In the background, ice was crushed and clinked into a glass. Bourbon poured into a jigger, three times, and into an old-fashioned glass. A cherry dropped in, stirred with a finger, sucked on. Winston stepped back into the room, cocktail tray in hand. He paused to lean on the television. Alyssa admired his tray, with its pile of cheddar cheese goldfish, and his drink, a short tumbler with etched pheasants, sweating and full.

"I will be in my room, listening to the radio and looking forward to a delicious home-cooked meal," Winston said. "Not any German-cooked cabbage and potatoes."

"I would choose Italian pastas and Hungarian goulashes over meatloaf any day of the week," Auggie replied, proving once again that father and son were fundamentally unable to let things be.

"Don't insult your mother's cooking," Winston said. "And if that's the case, why do you come back looking like they've starved you?"

"Calories work differently over there."

"They fiddle with your food. Damned terrorists. If it were up to me, I'd shoot down the next plane that gets hijacked."

"That is a gratuitous statement, Father," Livy said. "What if Auggie and Nan were in the plane?"

"A sacrifice I'd make."

"You'd be devastated," Alyssa said.

"That's what sacrifice means. Giving up what you love most." A pause for them all to contemplate what he had just confessed. "Isn't that true, Emma? That's what you and your friend talked about in the car all these weeks. Sacrifice for what you love."

"Yes, Gramps."

"Stand up when I speak to you, young lady!"

Emma jumped up to attention. Winston stared at Emma from beneath his bushy brow, and Alyssa remembered how terrifying and delicious it had used to be when he had looked at her that way.

"You missed your parents, Emma," Winston said. "You missed them mightily, but you did it for your dance. You worked hard and improved immensely. Congratulations."

"Thank you, Gramps."

"The tutu becomes you," he added. Emma glowed with pleasure, leaving Alyssa to wonder what would have happened if Emma had chosen to travel with her parents that summer instead of taking the intensive ballet class. Of course, she hadn't. She wouldn't have, being entirely obsessed by the activity as she was. Not even the temptation to go to the Bolshoi Ballet had distracted Emma from her determination to stick with her dance. *I will go to the Bolshoi when I dance there with Nureyev.* Her youth and confidence had convinced the adults around her. She would stay with her grandparents while her parents left for what had suddenly become a second honeymoon. None of them had realized until too late how challenging for Emma the separation would be. Now that it was over, Emma had made it clear there would be no such separation again.

"Winston!" Gussie said. "It is nearly six thirty. Here is Mr. Cronkite to say good night."

The sound rose up. Winston headed to his bedroom. The rest of them listened as Mr. Cronkite recognized the tragedy of Vice President Agnew's fall, and it was sad. As sad as their father's stubborn unwillingness to listen to common sense. The door shut behind him. The ship's clock chimed five times. Six thirty. Right on schedule, the telephone rang, announcing the start of his weekly chat with his *friend*. They were just friends now. Part of the family routine. Tsks and sighs. The television was turned off.

"I am going to finish preparing dinner," Gussie said, with a sharp look to Nan and Auggie, whom she had told, in no uncertain terms, what to do. Nan shut her book, using her finger to mark the page.

"Emma, your father and I were so sorry to miss your dance recital," Nan said.

"That's okay," Emma replied, her words belying the previous week's tears when she had realized they would not be there. "You can come to the Halloween dance we are putting on."

"Yes, well." Nan glanced at Auggie, who said, "We are so glad to have you back with us, Emma. Why don't you and your mother go upstairs and have a nice talk while she unpacks?"

After taking a moment to glare her rebellion at her husband, Nan looked to her daughter. Her irritation relaxed into a grin. She held her hands up for Emma to take hold of, pull her up. The two jostled and bustled and laughed each other up the stairs, leaving the siblings to have a nice talk of their own. Alyssa decided that it was as good a time as any to begin preparing herself and her family for life post-Renny. With Lou.

"Mummy needs to get away," she began. "You can see that Father is wearing on her."

"If Father catches wind, he'll throw a tantrum about how lonely and deserted he'll be."

"You know perfectly well, Livy, that he complains but is perfectly fine when she's gone," Alyssa said. "She would adore to go to Europe, and I intend to make it happen."

"Europe?" Auggie frowned. "I wish this idea of travel had come up while Nan and I were there. She could have stayed with us."

"I suggested it," Livy said, "but Alyssa wouldn't be bothered."

"I beg your pardon, Livy. Mummy doesn't like to travel by herself," Alyssa retorted. "As soon as this case is done, I have vacation time. She and I could fly to Paris and visit the Finers. I asked them about it last night and they're thrilled by the idea. That will leave me free to go off on my own. To Venice. I haven't been there since I was a girl."

"What a nice vacation for you and Renny." Alyssa blinked, her visions of Lou in a gondola interrupted by Livy's tone of voice, full of false generosity and envy. It was grating, the way Livy glamorized Alyssa's life. In Livy's eyes, Alyssa had everything: the perfect job, the perfect husband, perfect children. That idealization left no room for Alyssa to be herself. When Alyssa walked into a room, Livy seemed to crumple, as if, just by her presence, Alyssa deprived Livy. Sometimes, Alyssa felt guilty for existing. At others, she couldn't bear the claustrophobia of the comparing of one to the other. Alyssa would be her own person, whether it took from Livy or not!

"Don't plan my life for me," Alyssa snapped. "Renny isn't coming. It will be an expensive trip, with oil prices going up the way they are. Mother needs to be careful with her money. Her pockets aren't bottomless."

"But you'll be paying your own way, Alyssa," Auggie said.

"Why? It won't be a vacation, taking care of Mummy."

"If her pockets aren't bottomless, as you put it," Auggie said, "then she can't afford a trip to Europe for two."

"She could if she didn't have to pay for someone else's property taxes," Alyssa snapped. Livy sat up.

"Mummy doesn't pay my taxes," Livy said, her voice tense. "I do. That's why I move back into this hell house every summer, to rent my house for the taxes."

"As if living here is a sacrifice!" Alyssa said. "You get to spend quality time with Mummy, and it doesn't cost you a penny."

"It doesn't cost any of us," Auggie said. "This house being our home."

"The difference is, Livy has her own place right across the way," Alyssa said, resenting that he used her words out of context. "Given to her by Mummy, along with everything else. The house. Her taxes. Her trip to California. Her food and cigarettes."

"Trip?" Livy asked.

"Her schooling. An English Literature degree? She'll be able to talk to Nan about her esoteric poetry, and that's about it. I had to put myself through law school, Auggie."

"You had a full scholarship," Auggie pointed out.

"Because I applied for one."

"I did, too," Livy said. "I'm just not as smarty pants as you. Do you mean the trip when I went to retrieve Ed's body? That's the only trip I've ever taken. His company reimbursed her."

"Not the money she lent Ed to get away from you," Alyssa snapped.

Livy stared at Alyssa, not a freckle to be seen. Auggie put his face in his hands and groaned. Alyssa wished she had not said what she said, and she hated how she acted around Livy, but the feelings rose, the comments flew, and there was nothing like her family to bring Alyssa to her lowest self.

"I don't know anything about that," Livy said. "But if you feel I owe Mummy money, I will figure out a way to pay her back."

She drained her glass and stood, pausing to check her balance. Bizarrely, for a moment she reminded Alyssa of a bog person whose desiccated body has been pickled in acid, showing every line of pain and worry. Alyssa was overwhelmed by regret. As Livy tottered off to the bathroom, all Alyssa wanted was for her sister to revert to the lovely girl she had used to be, instead of the difficult, brittle one she had become.

"To hold that trip to California against her after all these years is worse than the damned grapefruit," Auggie said. "You swore you would never bring that up. The money was a gift, not a loan, and it was at your behest that it was given. We all hoped to get Ed back on his feet. It was not to help him leave. That money is not owed by Livy."

"No, it's not."

"She is entirely innocent."

Alyssa held very still, allowing Auggie's words to buffet her.

"Is she?"

"She had no idea about it. None of us know what happened to the money. It was just gone."

"Gone," Alyssa repeated, remembering Ed's call and the devastation she had felt because instead of investing it, as he had promised, starting a nest egg for their life together, he had proven he didn't care. He had destroyed her hopes to lead a different life than the one she was living. "He lost it gambling in Tahoe, Auggie. The night he died. Every last penny, and then some. I paid off his debts."

Auggie stared at her. She shrugged.

"I should have expected that you'd take Livy's side, Auggie. You always do. I'm the evil one, and poor Livy can't take care of herself."

"She can, in her way. What baffles me is why you act so surprised when people do exactly what you could have predicted. You expect what you want, without taking into account who a person is. You seem to think that if you point out their faults, they'll change."

"I've no idea what you're talking about."

"Because you don't want to understand, Alyssa."

"We need to have a discussion about this house," Alyssa said changing the subject because the one they were on was pointless. "You have always said I am unaffected by all the money going out to various members of the family—and non-members." Alyssa paused to allow Auggie to contemplate their father's expenditures. "The fact is, I have never taken a penny from Mummy, whereas she paid for your university schooling, dipping into the principal. She does the same, and has been for years, for Livy. Without that principal to earn from, Mummy has lost money. You paid her back, of course, but without interest. Livy, we all know, is never going to repay her. Don't scoff, Auggie. You know it's true, and it's fine. I only hate to think of the stress it causes Livy, knowing that. I want to alleviate that stress. It isn't good for her. My idea, to make things even, is for me to get the house. That way, you two don't have to feel bad about not paying Mummy back. At least, what's been borrowed up to now. Mummy can set up a trust for me. She's going to live for years more, and with a QPERT she can pay off all the taxes, so I'd get it free and clear."

"Which?" Auggie said.

"What?"

"Which do you want, the trip or the house?"

"They are not mutually exclusive. The one makes up for the past and the other anticipates the future. What I am saying about the house isn't disinheriting anyone, you know. It is only rectifying things. I don't think I should be punished for being the responsible one. It's like home owners who maintain their house, having to pay more taxes. It should be the other way around, don't you think so?"

"All quite reasonable," Auggie said, and Alyssa couldn't tell if he were being straight or cynically resigned as he finished off his glass of wine. "What about Emma?"

"What about her?"

"I don't want the house, but she might someday," Auggie said—then added, with a wry smile, "For her ballet studio."

"This is residential property. She can't run a business from here."

"Hello!"

Alyssa startled and turned around to see Renny slouched in the doorway. He looked worn out and dowdy in the old suit he wore, given to him by his mother.

"Renny, it's good to see you." Auggie stood. The two men shook hands, both tall and elegant, and Renny still with a full head of hair, slightly graying. It gratified Alyssa that the two got on so well.

"Welcome home," Renny replied with genuine affection. He clapped his hands together. "I'm all for a drink. Shall I freshen yours, Auggie? Alyssa, your mother asked for your help."

Help? How exhausting. To think that her mother had used to be a source of strength and advice on everything from fashion to child care. But life had become complicated, and Alyssa couldn't depend on her anymore. Their conversations had changed. Now, when they sat down to chat, Alyssa was the advisor, assisting her mother in all her financial, legal, and household decisions. Always the responsible one, while Auggie was off on sabbatical in Europe and Livy was in her cups. It felt to be too much as Alyssa made her way into the kitchen. The trip. The QPERT. It all made sense, yet—when she said it out loud—didn't. If only she could talk to Lou. Wouldn't it be nice if he would call? He would calm her frustration, turn her foul temper into laughter. The kitchen door swung shut after her.

"Father will be shouting for his dinner shortly," Alyssa said, glancing at the kitchen clock.

"Would you prepare his tray?" Gussie asked as she poked frozen string beans into the saucepan. Alyssa proceeded to set up a tray with silverware and a napkin, salt and pepper mills, a plate and bowl, and wondered why she always had to help while everyone else got to lollygag.

"Please do not bang things about so much, Alyssa," Gussie said, and then added, "It was good to see the Finers last night, wasn't it, though Kitty didn't look well."

"She's recovering from cancer, Mummy."

"I only hope he dies first. He would be devastated if he lost Kitty. I hate the thought of it. Men are not so adept at getting along as women."

"Many men have survived the loss of their wives." Alyssa pointed out a fact that she counted on, and what frightened her was that even Lou was beginning to fail her. He was pulling away. In response, she clung to him, dreamed of him, wanted him that much more.

She lifted the lid of one of the pots rattling on the stove. Campbell's tomato soup.

"Do you remember when Cook just up and left without a word?"

"Her name was Susan, Mummy. You really do need to work on remembering the names of your help."

"I always assumed that your father had said some ridiculous something that was the final straw." Alyssa's hand remained steady as she picked up the soup ladle. "She left me with just two hours before my dinner guests arrived, and my Julia Child cookbook.

Rather like Mrs. Jones. As if something had happened that caused her to reach her limit."

"Think what a wonderful cook you are as a result of Susan's leaving," Alyssa said.

"Where's my dinner?" Winston's voice boomed. "I'm hungry."

"He is impossible, Mummy," Alyssa said, slapping the ladle down, flushed and frustrated.

"Winston knows what he's doing." Gussie hung up her apron. "He is stubborn and demanding because it gets our attention. It serves his purpose. I'm not sure what your stubbornness does. You seem always to do the opposite of what you should do to get what you want. I worry that it will do irreparable damage. Some are not so fortunate, you know."

"We have all been fortunate, Mummy."

"And yet you look at life with expectation, not gratitude. It is making you bitter. For all his faults, your father is not that."

The door swung shut after Gussie. Alyssa placed the soup bowl on the tray. A few slices of cheese, more crackers. A glass of milk. She carried her father's dinner out to the living room and presented it to him.

"Is this everything you need, Father?" Alyssa sat down on the couch next to him. Winston unfolded his napkin as he admired the tray.

"This is lovely, dear. Thank you."

"How is the soup?" Alyssa asked.

"Delightful," Winston said. "It's the perfect temperature. Please tell your mother she has outdone herself again. A magnificent cook. Your brother does not appreciate her. None of us can sufficiently. Where has she gone off to?"

"Right out there on the patio with Livy and Renny." Alyssa stared out the window at the reflections and shadows of the lighted area. Her heart fluttered as Livy touched his arm. There was a solidity about Renny, his handsomeness, his athleticism, his wry wit and kindness, and wouldn't it be just like Livy to steal him away? "Do you see them?"

"Ah, yes. Getting their fresh air."

"They are trying to get away from your shouting, Father," she said, straight-backed and on the edge of the couch, balanced between the living room and the patio where the others were enjoying themselves. Renny was a sweet man, and so what if he weren't the brightest bulb in the pack? At least with him she could be entirely herself and be accepted. She knew that. They had not spent enough time together lately. She missed him.

"You really should try to be less difficult, Father. It's obnoxious how you yell."

Winston held his spoon still, halfway between the bowl and his mouth. He smiled, his eyes glinting with mischief, and she knew he was about to reminisce about past meals, when he and his brothers had used to hide under the dining table and play pranks on their parents' guests. One time, though, he had come down, famished, only to find a slice of Melba toast and water at everyone's place, which they all ate quite solemnly, and then out they went for a five-mile hike. Winston slurped his soup as he spoke, ate another cracker and cheese, crunching them as he told Alyssa how he had arrived at the doorstep of their house, exhausted, hot, and sweating, and burst into tears of frustration and hunger. He was so hungry. His parents and brothers laughed at him, merrily tapping him, as they led him into the dining hall, where there was an enormous Sunday dinner laid out.

"It was April Fool's Day, Alyssa," Winston said, finishing up his soup and patting his lips dry. "My father loved a good prank, and my whole family knew me well. They knew how much I hate being hungry."

Alyssa's eyes teared in sympathy. She hated to be hungry, too. She was always hungry.

"You should put that story in the book we gave you for your birthday. It's important for them to know who you are, Father."

"They already know that, don't they?" he asked, to which Alyssa gave no reply.

"You must miss those times," she said instead.

He finished off his drink. "I have your mother and you children. It's all I could wish for."

Alyssa stared at her father. Was he kidding? But, of course, he had more than that. He had his other life. She had never appreciated why. Now she could. He had made his life choices and stuck by them. He had gotten exactly what he asked for. Alyssa had only to ask.

Renny returned to the living room. He did not join her but sat down on the long, embroidered footstool in front of the fire, hunched over his drink. Alyssa took a cracker from her father's plate.

"I'm having a terrible time with this case," she said, in hopes that Renny would respond.

"You always say that, dear," Winston said, looking over at her with a nod and a point of his spoon. "You get the jitters, but in the end you do a brilliant job."

"Thank you, Father," Alyssa said, focusing on him. He still thought her perfect. Her chin quivered. She wished she still thought the same of him.

"That's right," Renny said. "You have only to remember that it's not about right and wrong, but the law."

He held out an envelope to her, as if it were a lesson she would have to learn. She walked across the living room. Her heart pounded, as if she were on a gangplank and below her were dark, tempestuous waters, cold and full of danger, and no lifeline. No forgiveness or hope. She opened the envelope. A letter from Mrs. Jones's lawyer. The letter should serve as notice, and be sufficient proof of intention that Renny not contest the will when Mrs. Jones passed. Renny had been disinherited. Mrs. Jones had left everything to Alyssa in trust. If ever Alyssa left Renny—divorced him, picked up a lover, etc.— then all the money would go to charities, not least of which was the Foundation Against Domestic Abuse.

"Renny, this is entirely wrong," Alyssa said, as a wave of emotion overwhelmed her. "What about the children? I won't stand for it. I thought you were going to talk to her."

"I did. She gave me the option of divorcing you."

"I beg your pardon?" Alyssa whispered, the blood rushing to her face. "What right has she to interfere in a perfectly good marriage?"

And as she spoke, she heard her mother voicing the same words. A perfectly good marriage.

"Is it?" Renny asked, and he had the strangest look on his face, so full of frustration and pain, as if he might cry. So like a child who had been left behind one too many times. Alyssa's heart fluttered. She stared at her husband. Poor man. She raised a hand to touch his unshaven cheek with the tips of her fingers, expecting to find what she looked for: doubt. Instead, to her horror, she saw trust.

"But what did you decide?" Alyssa asked, stepping back.

"I'm here, aren't I? You get to choose."

To stay, or leave Renny with nothing? What kind of choice was that? There was no choice. How like her own mother's *arrangements*. Alyssa was condemned and with no recourse. She was trapped, and her fantasies of a life with Lou? She almost reached out to physically grasp the moment . . . that had already gone by. Too late. Silly. One couldn't grasp a moment, anyway. Only, she had counted on Lou to save her.

Alyssa thought of her client. Was this how he had felt when she had walked into that small, dingy attorney-client room at the prison? The buzz and blinking of a fluorescent lightbulb about to blow out. His outrage at the accusation had flared. He had looked at her and said *I won't have a woman represent me.* It always shocked her when someone treated her so stupidly. She had assumed it was a prejudice against her as a woman. In fact, now, as she thought about it, maybe just by looking at her he had sensed that she had taken from him the only chance he had: his presumption of innocence. Because Lou had first presented the case to her. Conflicted himself, he had introduced the case to Alyssa from the perspective of a prosecutor, which was how she was most familiar with dealing with her work: from an assumption of guilt, not doubt. What no defense lawyer should do.

"Marriages take work," Renny said, putting a hand on hers. "We've had a lot going on."

"Yes," Alyssa said, holding back the horror of her failure. Alyssa shut her eyes against a wave of nausea. The situation with Lou had brought the personal into her work life, and what had the result been? Her client's outrage had burned down to resignation because he knew Alyssa's convictions would send him to the gallows.

Dinner was ready. Everyone got their trays and served themselves, returning to the living room. Alyssa took her time, slowly filling her plate, reviewing, step by step, actions made and life's unfairness. The pieces fell into place. She had not fully reviewed the forensic evidence, and the last report, just the day before, had been so full of typos, each more irritating than the last, such that the words hadn't come together. Until that moment. As she put one soggy green bean, and then another, onto her plate. The memory of her trysts with Lou, her rejuvenating—redemptive—fantasies of another life with him, now felt like a grueling gauntlet that she had run. In retrospect, she saw how each of their meetings had exhausted her because his wit was sharp with resentment and bitterness. Every time they had been together, he had challenged her, pushed her arguments away from innocence, compromising her. Meatloaf on her plate, and his brilliance lost its allure because she had believed in him, and he had failed her. He had set her up to lose, and she wondered, was it only for the case that he had asked her out to dine? Had he never really loved her? She reached for a piece of garlic bread. And another.

Alyssa returned to the living room and sat down next to Renny. Close enough to feel the warmth of his body. She might have fantasized about being free and going off with Lou, but the fact was, she was able to think such things only because she had Renny to depend on. Until that very breathless moment, she had had no idea how much she needed him.

Gussie pinched some salt from her tiny salt saucer and sprinkled her food. "The exterminator needs to be called. Auggie, will you deal with him?"

"I'm afraid I won't be able to," Auggie said, glancing at Nan, at whose feet sat Emma. "Reality has set in. We have to get back home."

"What, what?" Gussie looked at him, her eyes wide and glittering. "You can't leave. Emma has only just settled into the school, all her new friends. And her ballet classes."

"She has her friends at home," Nan said, buttering a piece of bread, leaving her daughter to stare into the fire, her expression unreadable. Except by Alyssa, who imagined Emma felt as she did. Crushed. Her plans for the future destroyed. Life entirely out of her control. But then Emma stood up, her hands at her sides, her back straight, her eyes wide and fierce as she looked from one to the other parent. Neither of whom seemed to know how to help her. Alyssa couldn't fathom how they could not. It was so clear.

"You promised me before you left this summer that we would stay here. That I could attend the Academy," Emma said, her face flushed.

"Emma, you cannot expect to get everything you want in life," Auggie said. "You might as well learn that lesson now. You are only eleven. Your mother and I have work to do and that means we have to go home."

"No. I have to stay here and attend the Ballet Academy in New Haven. Why don't you get a job at Yale, Daddy? You're smart enough, and then you could drop me off on the way in."

Auggie paled. Alyssa cringed, knowing the sensitivity of that subject; he had never risked applying for a job at Yale. What if he didn't get it?

"Don't be ridiculous," Auggie said.

"I'm not being ridiculous. You are. I have to attend a ballet school where I will be trained correctly."

"There are scads of bored Russian ballerinas running around

town at home. Nan will find you a good teacher, Emma, and take you to your ballet lessons."

"We will, Emma," Nan said, her voice sharp as she stared at her husband, not her daughter. "Remember? We promised to take her to her lessons."

Emma watched her parents, alert to their silent debate.

"I would have to be taken to classes every day," Emma interrupted them. "And we'd have to find the right teacher, one who knows how to teach. Thea's mom knows how. She found Mrs. Siminoff. You'll have to call her so that what happened last time doesn't happen again. Remember? The last teacher you found me almost destroyed my feet by starting me too early *en pointe*. If I hadn't strained my ankle, he might have ruined me forever. Everything depends on how I'm taught. It's who I will be. Do you understand that?"

"We understand, Emma," Auggie said, taking Nan's hand and giving it a squeeze, when it was Emma who needed the reassurance of touch and presence. "When we get settled back home, we'll figure it out."

"But why can't we stay here?" Emma persisted, and Alyssa stared down at her plate, knowing the girl would not get what she wanted.

"Auggie, ballet is not a passing whim for Emma," Gussie said. "She's been studying since she was six, and now she has gotten into this Academy, I don't think there's a question. Of course she should stay here."

Emma glowed under her grandmother's support, relieved because if Gussie supported something it usually happened.

"I am going to practice my *échappés* for class tomorrow," Emma said, confident that the debate was at an end. She headed off to her room.

"Mother," Auggie said, "I don't want you to waste your time driving Emma to New Haven."

"Winston and Thea's mother both enjoy driving the girls to classes. And I will get to have the pleasure of Emma's company."

"A child needs her parents," Nan said. Emma's progress up the stairs stopped. She looked back at the adults.

"Where were her parents this summer?" Gussie retorted. Silence, and then the discussion proceeded. Alyssa watched the shifting emotions on Emma's face: confusion making way for recognition. She would stay. Then horror and fear, because her parents would leave. Again. And then bafflement, because how could they leave her, and why?

"Auggie had been to boarding school for eons by the time he was her age," Gussie said. "Emma is a big girl now, aren't you Emma? So beautiful and tall and slender. The perfect ballet dancer. You are well on your way to doing great things."

Emma looked to her parents, who agreed. It was decided. But Emma was not ready to lose them. She struggled to keep them on their pedestal. Her perfect parents. Just as Alyssa had kept Lou on his. He had failed her.

"So I will stay?" Emma asked, to clarify that she was getting what she wanted, and what she would gain and lose. "Mom and Dad will go home. Because they have their work to get done." Her chin went up. She would do it. It was the right thing to do. "This way I won't be in their way. And I'll be able to get my work done, too."

"It's wrong," Alyssa said in Emma's defense, even as her own defenses failed her. Because how justify such a sacrifice? Work filling the void of insufficient love. A future of having to prove herself good enough. Of grasping for more. She would end up with nothing. An emptiness that grows inside, fathomless. However would the child survive? "She shouldn't have to choose between her parents and her ballet. She needs them both. If this summer proved nothing else, it is that she is not ready to be on her own. She was so happy to see you, and now you've ruined everything."

Alyssa burst into tears because Emma would give up her parents, just as Alyssa would have to give up Lou.

"What in heaven's name is wrong, Alyssa?" Gussie asked.

"Maybe she's afraid." Everyone looked over at Emma.

"What did you say?" Gussie asked. "Afraid? Of what?"

"Of nothing," Emma whispered, her eyes tearful even as she

tried to smile. Alyssa controlled her sobs, beating back the depths of panic with a grateful wonder at Emma's understanding. The devastation of nothing echoed through her. How had she missed it?

Alyssa stood up and took a deep breath. Excusing herself, she walked, then ran, back into the kitchen and to her study, where she searched for and found the typo-filled report. There it was. Nothing. The man had said he felt nothing when Alyssa had asked him about his children. He would lose his children, and it was all in the perspective: nothing as in not caring, or nothing as in being lost in the empty depths of the pain and fear and desperate yearning for what would be lost? Flipping through the case folders, this time reading them with the man's innocence in mind, she turned the personal back into work. Her humiliation rearing back into a lash of determination and rage because she would not be made the fool. Her client was just like herself. And Emma. He, too, risked losing something irreparably, and Alyssa would save him. He would get off and regain custody of his children. And Lou couldn't stop her, because she had found what she needed: doubt.

Mumpsimus

The church bell tolled, the tones reverberating through the crisp noon air. A rippling, gray-blue cloud skirted the horizon. Gussie and Emma lifted their faces up to the sun. It warmed them. The blast of a train's horn. Gussie opened her eyes just as someone stepped out onto the porch of the house. Gussie and Emma both squinted to see. A man. Then another. A woman joined them.

"I never noticed all those sprawling mansions around us," Gussie said, fiddling with the clasp of her purse as if debating whether to open it. "Those enormous lawns. It's foolish to leave yourself exposed to the elements."

"People buy the land for the water views, Gram."

"It's perfectly obvious the water is there. There's no need to show it off. Mercy! Where has Livy's house gone off to?"

Emma looked at the spot where Livy's house had used to stand, with its dark brown barn board A-frame. The new owner had knocked it down, then dug a foundation for a five thousand-square-foot house. There it sat, unbuilt.

"It's hard to see unless you close your eyes," Emma said, quietly. Gussie's chin lifted ever so slightly. A pause to allow for them both to contemplate that space, and what might fill it.

"Oriental Bittersweet used to be a catalogue item," Gussie said. Her voice sounded choked. She cleared her throat. "Mother ordered a few cuttings, and they arrived in a brown package. I hardly noticed them growing, shaping the landscape. Such a busy life. Raising the children, marrying them off, and then the grandchildren running along the paths that Winston cut through the trees and bushes, down to the beach to swim and collect their shells. Except for the occasional stubbed toe or knocked head, I always knew you children were safe, somewhere in those thickets. Winston spent so much of his time cutting and hacking at those vines, but they comforted me."

"They killed your plants, Gram." Emma reached over to snug the coat up around Gussie's chin, a buffer from the breeze.

"Just suffocated them a bit," Gussie replied, pushing Emma away impatiently. "I kept them under control."

"Kind of delusional."

"What is?" Gussie snapped.

"Controlling nature. Thinking we can control anything. I mean, you can be successful for a while but, in the end, nature wins."

"I've always believed one can overcome nature."

"Isn't that like pretending not to be who you are?" Emma asked with a sideways glance.

"No. It's being your best self. We have tendencies and weaknesses, but they can be overcome."

"We can try, anyway. I certainly worked to overcome mine."

"You were a lovely dancer, Emma. The way you used to hover over the stage, floating. As if there were no such thing as gravity."

"I worked every day so as to give that impression. I can still feel the ache in my muscles from those hours of practice, and the sense of relief and regret when I peeled off my slippers at the end of each day, soaked in sweat, knowing I had to do better. Especially once I was in the Academy. I mean, I'd given up Mom and Dad. I had to prove it was the right thing to have done. If it were, maybe I'd get their attention. I never really did."

"Certainly you did. You were exceptional. All my children were," Gussie said. "From the day they were born. I knew how they would be."

"You've always said that. It makes everything seem inevitable. As if we don't have the power to change."

"How they would be, not what." Gussie's eyes moved, watching the rapidly changing landscape as the people stepped down the porch steps and strolled across the lawn to the paths that wound through the plantings that she and Winston had planted thirty . . . forty . . . fifty years before. "It was for them to determine their lives."

"Was it?"

"*Dicentra spectabilis*," Gussie replied.

"Bleeding hearts?"

"Yes. Always weeping, but they spread and grow. God created us to feel pain and understand what joy is relative to it. The key is not to go barreling forth without thinking how your actions might affect others."

"That would be the key, Gram. I wholeheartedly agree."

Gussie turned herself full around to Emma. "Who are those people?"

"My real estate agent with one of her customers." Emma forced herself to meet her grandmother's fierce assessment. "It's not a surprise, Gram. You know I put it on the market after Thanksgiving. Until now, no one's looked at it. I can't get rid of it."

"You have to own the house before you can be rid of it."

"I do own it."

"Don't be so literal." Gussie sniffed. "You've denied it from the day you got it. Renovating it. Renting it. Then disappearing, as if by not using it, it would go away."

"Denial serves a purpose. I wanted to get used to not having it. To prove that it's not so much a part of me that I'll be crippled without it."

"And what's the conclusion? But, of course, you're back."

Emma opened her mouth to deny it, but there she was. Back.

"When my real estate agent called last night to say this guy might buy the house," Emma said, "I panicked. I realized I've spent so much time and brain space rebelling against owning it, that I haven't dealt with what it will be like not to have it anymore."

"You have no idea how much you'll miss it. Fortunately, it's not too late. You haven't sold it."

"All these years, I might have seemed to be denying it, but, in fact, I've clung to the house, so afraid of the consequences of letting go that I never considered the consequences of not."

"Exactly. That's why you won't give it up. We don't give up on what we need." Gussie struggled to stand. Emma held up a hand to assist her. Gussie steadied herself on wobbly feet, leaning heavily on her granddaughter even as she looked about, as if by looking away she would be there, not here. "You aren't one to give up what you love."

Emma allowed for a silence before responding, "No. I'm not one to give up what I love. Not lightly."

Again, Emma paused, as if debating whether to throw down the gauntlet she held. In the past, she would have kept it. But in the months since Thanksgiving, there had been nothing in the world she'd wanted more than to challenge her grandmother, even if in a backhanded Michaels way. "But you taught me how to, Gram. It's like we were saying before. It's easy to reject what, or whom, you love. You have only to raise yourself above so it won't seem to matter. We just have to pretend we don't need it, which we're so good at, aren't we? If it's the right thing to do?"

Gussie didn't respond at first. A brow raised, a hand raised, and she rapped Emma hard on the side of the head.

"Ow!"

"Go away."

"This is a public dock," Emma said, rubbing her head and frowning.

"You talk too much. I want to be alone."

"You already are," Emma snapped.

"On the contrary. I have God to help me. I had only hoped . . . I didn't want to live too long. I woke up this morning—" Gussie abruptly let go of Emma's hand and began to shuffle her way out of the gazebo. "For pity's sake. You wanted the house. You were thrilled to get it."

Gussie proceeded forward. A gull coasted, wings spread on the stiffening breeze, searching. Emma walked up to and alongside her grandmother, held a hand out to Gussie, who ignored it. The pace was slow as they approached the sun-bleached dock, littered with crabs' legs pecked empty by gulls. They stepped onto the dock. The sun warmed the air as Gussie leaned against a pylon.

"You're right, Gram. And I do love the house. It's part of me. It will always exist exactly how it was when I was eleven, living there with you and Gramps that summer. Dad called the upstairs a claustrophobic rat warren with its low ceilings, small rooms, and weak lighting. But I adored it. When the cousins were all there, bedsheets became togas, and blankets became Indian buffalo hides, and then there were the "dress-ups." Yours and Livy's and Alyssa's old party dresses and shawls and hats and high heels."

"My bedroom," Gussie said. "So sunny. The sea air perfuming everything. The overstuffed twin bed with its white cotton bedcover. I would love to rest there, just one more time."

". . . And I would love to dance."

"The difference is," Gussie said, "you can. You didn't have to give it up. You could have continued."

"Oh?" Emma held herself still and thought how a person could be told something, again and again, but not hear it. Because she didn't want to . . . wasn't ready to . . . couldn't . . . wouldn't hear, until one day, this day, a shift, and the little snippets of conversation and vague feelings coalesce, and nothing is the same. She could have continued . . .

"Maybe," Emma said. "Or maybe, sometimes, we give up what we need and then our task is to learn how to accept that."

The breeze, light against their faces. A dinghy bumped up against the dock. Life proceeded. The construction workers had returned to their jackhammering. An endless shriek from a child trapped on the spinning wheel of the playground by his older sister, who kept turning it around, fast, then faster, chaotic and out of control. Gussie cleared her throat as if she were going to say something. Instead, she dropped abruptly down onto the dock, to sit. Emma stared down at her and wondered how she would get her grandmother up from so tenuous a position and back to a hot tea and blanket. But it was done, so Emma joined her. They dangled their legs over the edge, Emma worrying about splinters puncturing the back of her grandmother's bare legs.

"Mrs. Siminoff used to encourage us," Emma said. "When we had trouble learning something, she'd say challenges are to make you stronger, not to push you away. I guess I didn't have what it took."

"But you did. That was the puzzle. You wanted the role of Giselle so desperately," Gussie said. "What was so special about it?"

"It's one of the best roles in ballet. You have to be the best. Not just a dancer but an actor. *Giselle* covers the gamut of emotions. The idyllic innocence of the first act. A young peasant girl's love of dance and for a young prince, his betrayal, her madness and death. Then the second act and the underworld of the Wilis, ghosts of jilted women who died of heartbreak and now seek vengeance, forcing men to dance to their deaths. Their dreams crushed, they wait for their next victim, and then comes Giselle. Albrecht betrayed her, but still she loves him. She saves him. It's about the beauty of the soul, Gram, love and forgiveness. Who wouldn't want to dance that? Every time I go to see it, I have to stand in the back because I can't sit still."

"Well, I look forward to seeing them," Gussie said.

"The Wilis?" Emma asked, still in the glades, dressed in white, floating.

"Everyone who has passed on. I want to talk to them. Really talk."

"Gram, if they're dead, how are you going to—"

"If your Giselle can forgive, then I can talk to my parents in Heaven," Gussie interrupted, flustered, making a move to get up and realizing that it wasn't so easy. Or, perhaps, that moving wouldn't change a thing. "And Lawrence and Kitty. Winston will be off somewhere in the hinter-clouds playing football. I worry, sometimes, that they won't recognize me, I've changed so. But then, when I sit still, I remember that I'm the same inside and always have been. That young woman who thought she knew best."

"Death doesn't scare you?" Emma asked.

"Not at all."

"Does life?"

"What a question!" Gussie scoffed. She adjusted her posture and took a deep breath in. "So long as you live the life you were meant to, there's nothing to be afraid of." Gussie hesitated before continuing. "It's a sin to tell others how to live their lives. We have to make our own choices, be our own master. Then your errors are your own and good fortune is yours forever. You've been the master of your fate all along."

Emma shook her head no. Gussie's chin went up. She studied Emma. "Would you have made a different choice?"

"Without a second thought. I was going to succeed, Gram. I knew I was different from the other girls."

"You had real talent. We were all so surprised when you gave it up. Just like that. A snap of your fingers and it was over."

"Was it a snap of my fingers? It felt more like seppuku." Emma's phone rang. She looked to see who it was, then stood up and walked, heel to toe, up the dock. Sabers and muskets threatening, she answered the phone.

"Where are you?" Conner asked, his voice familiar and warm, concerned. She closed her eyes to allow its rich tone to soothe her.

"I'm visiting my grandmother." Emma held her breath, waiting for his reaction.

". . . In Florida?"

"No." She bit her lip, her heart pounding for no good reason she could think of, but there it was, arrhythmia. "She lives in Poquatuck Village, Connecticut."

"You told me she lives in Florida." Emma opened her mouth to speak but realized there was nothing she could say. A deadening silence fell between them. Uncomfortable, because that had never happened before. They usually had something to say. Or maybe

Emma had always filled the silence, and now she didn't have the energy to. The void grew, seemingly insurmountable, and she wasn't sure if he were still there, and was afraid to ask because what if he weren't?

And if he were?

"I read through the pink binder you left," Conner said. "You never told me you were a ballerina."

"A ballet dancer." Emma corrected him, not wanting to be taken for what she had never been. "I did tell you. You sniggered."

"I don't snigger."

"When I told you I was going to the ballet, you scoffed. You hate ballet. All that taffeta bouncing about, skinny legs. It's pretentious and ridiculous. You'd rather drink beer and hang out with your carpenter and painter friends."

Conner didn't respond at first.

"You know Ron?" he finally said. "The macho guy you dislike so much because you think he doesn't like you? He was a dancer when he was a kid. He didn't have the body for it. Sound familiar?"

"I have to get off the phone," she said.

"I'm not going to let you run away from this, Emma."

"It's not for you to dictate."

"You're right. But if you don't want to work this out, I need to know that now," Conner said, and he sounded just like he did when a client had a change in plan: indifferent to the change, but needing to know its effect. "Are we going to see each other again?"

"Do you want to?" she asked.

"Of course I want to. That's not the question, is it?"

Emma squeaked. She didn't usually make strange sounds, but she squeaked in order to breathe and to admit the truth. She had been the one leaving him, not the other way around, and, like her grandmother, she'd done it because it was too risky. To have. To love. Nothing was enough, and safer, because love dies, leaving only the memory of Conner's arms around her and of the house, an Edenesque ivory tower. It burned, collapsed around her. And what would

Mumpsimus

be the consequence if she admitted she cared? That she regretted? That she would stay?

Conner asked if he could come meet her. Emma gave him directions to the dock, then closed her phone, holding it between her two hands exactly as if she were praying, hoping, which she wasn't. Rather, as she returned to her grandmother, she thought how she used to dream she could breathe underwater, and now she could hardly breathe in air.

"What in heaven's name happened to the second floor?" Gussie laughed, a puzzled, lost laugh, looking before her with baffled wonderment. "We have to get to the cellar. God and Mother Nature are against us. And the kitchen is gone. The wind groaning."

"Gram, what's going on?"

"Auggie is trying to get back in." Gussie hesitated, her eyes watering. She looked over at Emma. "Imagine if Winston hadn't caught him. Afraid and dripping wet from the rain, wanting to cry. The children said I couldn't take care of him. They insisted we put Winston in that nursing home. They thought it would free me, but I visited him every day. It was the only thing that made sense. It took an hour and a half out of my life to drive to his bedside, to sit and wait. So afraid of losing him. All of them. I told them, *Kill me before I end up . . . here*." Gussie blinked and a tear trickled down her cheek. Emma reached to catch it, but Gussie caught her hand, held it, as she tentatively felt her way through the past. "All my life, and now Lawrence."

Gussie breathed in, then out, a white cloud of air.

"Cigarette smoke," Gussie said, brightening. "He's coming to tea. I have to be back at the house in time for tea."

Gussie fell silent. Emma contemplated the brain's passages as Gussie's world came up and down and around her. Was this journey like sleepwalking, dangerous to touch, to awaken from the echoes of the past, with no one to fall back on? Nothing but a house full of love and suffering, gone. Smiling, then thoughtful. Returning.

"Gram," Emma said. She touched her grandmother's arm.

"What?" Gussie started.

"You're wandering."

"I've a right to wander," Gussie said, two bright red orbs coloring her pale cheeks. "I'm . . . how old am I?"

"Eighty-seven."

Gussie looked at Emma wide-eyed, blinking.

"Where was I?"

"You were talking about a hurricane."

"The '38 hurricane. Awful. We nearly lost Auggie." She pulled the coat around her, irritably looked about, orienting herself. She cleared her throat. With a nod of her chin to the Dyer Dhow rocking in the water at their feet, "How is your boat?"

"I don't own a boat."

"No," Gussie said, raising her hand to pat her hair. "Of course you don't. You study ballet. You want to be exceptional."

Both women sat quietly while Gussie caught up, remembered that ballet was over and done.

"Did you, Gram? Did you have a secret wish?"

"Not so secret," Gussie replied. "I hoped to make the world a better place than when I arrived here. To be someone special, important. My mother said I couldn't be but I wanted to be Joan of Arc."

"Being burned at the stake is a hideous way to die."

Gussie glanced at Emma, a brow raised.

"I intended the heroine aspect, not the martyr's," Gussie said.

"That's good." Emma adjusted the coat on her grandmother's shoulders. "I've always felt sorry for martyrs." Emma paused because wasn't that how she lived her life—as a flagellant, punishing herself for her deficiencies and destroying her wish to have with the powerful knowledge that she didn't deserve? "They sacrifice their lives for something that doesn't exist."

"On the contrary. It exists in their hearts and minds. We most of us can only do small things. We might not change the world, but if we do what we do with our hearts, that's enough."

"Is it?"

Gussie eyed Emma.

"We can't change the past, Emma."

"No, we can't. But if we could, what would you change? If you could do it again, what would you do differently?"

"Well! That's a question for the books. I'm not the same person I was. There are things I've learned along the way. It's unlikely I would make the same decisions, though who can say? Life comes in, wreaking havoc on carefully laid plans. You do things you would never have imagined you would do. You see something and wish you had done it, knowing you wouldn't have. You didn't. After all, many have failed in their life's purpose. Everyone can't be a Joan of Arc."

"It isn't your fault there were no kings to save, Gram."

"There was Archduke Franz Ferdinand of Austria," Gussie retorted. "I was six when he was assassinated. A bit young and in the wrong part of the world, but I remember being terribly disappointed that I couldn't help. I felt responsible for the First World War, as if I might have prevented it. I had a vivid imagination as a child. Not so much as an adult."

Gussie fell silent.

"You've been my hero, Gram. Ever since you offered to let me stay with you and Gramps that summer so I could continue with Mrs. Siminoff. And then convincing Mom and Dad that I'd be okay if I went to a college for dance instead of *real learning*. Never mind the fact that you knew how to get chewing gum out of hair. How to dress. The house was always open and welcoming. You knew exactly the right thing to say to make everything better. All my life, I've known you'd be there, telling me the right thing to do. I counted on you, Gram. I always believed that you, anyway, believed in me."

Gussie blinked.

"Heroine," she said. "A female hero is a heroine."

"Right," Emma said, letting the criticism pass by. "That was you."

"It didn't feel that way. More like a blind reaching out, hoping it was for the best, and trusting in God. We can't go back. But it takes work. Hard work not to look back."

"Mumpsimus," Emma said. "Do you know what that means? It's something people do. We cling to the past. Afraid to lose. We try to avoid change, which is impossible because change is inevitable. It's the only thing we can count on. By denying that, we're only blocking new beginnings."

"It's a shame to live that way. I have never understood why Lawrence, and then Auggie, spent so much time on things long dead and gone."

"They thought the past might teach them something," Emma said.

"How go forward if you're constantly looking back? Regretful. It's so easy to do. The last time Lawrence and Kitty came for dinner? It was a comfortable evening. We had known each other for so long. We could relax and be ourselves. Even Winston. He enjoyed Kitty so much. She amused him, allowing Lawrence and me to have our chats. I could talk to him in ways and about things I couldn't with anyone else. We discussed everything, debating different ideas. I did not know I would never see him again. When they left, he didn't say good night as he usually would. He said good-bye. As if he knew. Such a negative phrase. Other languages hold hope. *Au revoir. Auf Wiedersehen*. To see again. Good-bye is so final."

"Do you know what's so cool about languages? They each create a different way of looking at the world. The way the ideas are formed determine the perspective, and how you go about life. When Dad and I traveled that fall after . . . everything . . ."

"After I broke my foot and you took such good care of me."

Emma nodded. "Dad and I talked about how amazing it would be to know every language there ever was, how vast an understanding you would have, but still not know everything. Because people will do the strangest things."

"Did you see the snowball Auggie gave me for my birthday last year?" Emma looked over at her grandmother and was startled by the deep flush in her cheeks, the glitter in her eyes. Gussie worked her mouth as if chewing over the memory. She stared out to the breakwater, the piles of granite that ended in a strip of beach with a high tide mark of salt and sun-dried seaweed, black and crunchy on the sand, driftwood, lost buoys, and empty shells. Gifts from the ebbing and flowing water of Long Island Sound and the ocean.

"A lovely present, a snowball in July," Gussie concluded. "It melted. We agreed that that was the beauty of it. We knew it would melt. Fearing to lose something allows us to appreciate what we have."

"That fear can warp us, too," Emma said. "We might act a certain way, do something to avoid losing something, when maybe it's better just to let it go. If only we dare."

Gussie fidgeted, looking off but holding still, as if listening, waiting. She grasped Emma's hand, held it tight. They watched. An osprey coasting on the winds, hunting, diving. A Boston whaler roaring into the harbor, its bow raised up, banging against the waves, slowing to a putt. Emma wondered if there were something inside herself that, if gently blown on, could flare up, fill and warm her insides; or would that thing merely die out, a flicker not given the chance to live, left to drown in tears unshed until too late?

Maturity

Coals of the Heart
June 1982

As Auggie drove the car behind the funeral home's limousine, he was seeing the end of his father's life, and it gave him perspective on his own. To calm the uncomfortable flutter and tightening in his chest that that perspective caused, Auggie assured himself that he was different from his father, whose only usefulness had been pulling vines out of trees, and stumps and stones out of the ground. Auggie was a polyglot, a world traveler and professor, an author of five books and scores of scholarly articles. He signified. He mattered. Through his work, the only standard worth bearing.

Granted, one can't judge a life until it is over. Only then can its final and lasting effects be known. One's death could be noble, comic, or pathetic. The last being his father's. Winston's hulk of a body had withered, then one night he had benightedly wandered off. Gussie had been distraught. To save her from further distress, Auggie, Livy, and Alyssa had agreed to put Winston into a nursing home. The vines had grown back. More granite pierced the ground. The end. Sad. His father's life had had no effect on Auggie's life, and his death? None either, other than taking up this late spring weekend better used correcting the galleys for Auggie's most recent book.

So then why the sense of incompletion, an emptiness that blossomed, dark and ominous? As if a slender string had held up a curtain, frail yet necessary. The string was gone now, and Auggie couldn't bear how everything seemed on the verge of falling apart.

Though of course he could bear it. He was bearing it. He had no choice but to bear it.

"Why would Mummy want to go in the car with Kitty and the Cunninghams and not with us?" Alyssa asked from the passenger's seat, looking like a plump, discontented child, her beauty padded by forty-six years of a nibble here, a bite there. She had lost all self-restraint, and had gained those deep furrows between her brow, her mouth in its permanent frown. Auggie wondered if Nan were right: was Alyssa so unhappy with how her life had turned out? How, when she had so much—one might say too much? Granted, that could be said of them all. Time passed. Life didn't necessarily follow the path one had expected or hoped for, and then it ended. He knew that. Nan claimed he didn't feel it. "She dislikes the Cunninghams."

"Because with them chattering away, it's easier to be with herself and avoid talk with Kitty," Livy replied from the backseat. His pretty Livy. She had shriveled, her slenderness now a gaunt angularity of face, her skin mottled with freckles and wrinkles. She lit a cigarette.

Alyssa grimaced and opened a window. Emma, sitting next to Livy, closed her eyes against carsickness. What would it be like if the three women were all the same age, his sisters back to their youthful, hopeful selves? Like Emma at nineteen: healthy, athletic, elegant, and unmarred by worry or bitterness. Her presence made the changes in his sisters almost hideous.

"Kitty asks such probing questions, doesn't she?" Livy continued. "So warm and personal; one says things one would never have intended. I think that's why Mummy has avoided her these last years since Lawrence died."

"Has she really?" Alyssa asked. "I hadn't noticed that at all. They have tea together once a week and are planning a trip when all of this settles down."

"Well, you might think all is well, but I'm worried about Mummy," Livy said.

"I'm worried, too," Alyssa snapped.

"Will you two never outgrow this petty bickering?" Auggie asked.

"I'm not bickering," Alyssa replied. "I am only pointing out that there's a certain fight that's not there anymore. Father irritated her to no end, but he gave her something to butt up against. Now there's nothing."

"I'm sure Mother will be fine," Auggie said. They drove into the cemetery and along the paved paths to the gravesite. "She is only adjusting. After over fifty years of marriage, she has to reinvent herself."

"Exactly what I had to do when I lost Ed," Livy said, and her chin quivered, her eyes teared up. Auggie glanced at Alyssa and was gratified by a refreshing glimpse of her young self as they exchanged a look of mutual understanding of Livy's drama, and the care and restraint required when faced with it.

"It's a drag that Gram broke her ankle," Emma said.

"A real nuisance," Alyssa said. "How is she going to take care of herself?"

"Emma, you're going to be around, aren't you?" Livy said.

"No. I have to be in New Haven."

"You could help if you don't get that part, Emma," Alyssa said. "Weren't they supposed to call yesterday?"

"I'm going to get it. The audition went great. I'm the best one in the company," Emma said, not vain or smug. Only confident. She did not doubt herself. She took a deep breath. A smile. "I've worked hard apprenticing with this company. I deserve it. If I get to be the soloist in *Giselle*, I'll be principal ballerina material. I've proved I can do it."

"It seems to me taking care of your grandmother might take priority over hopping about a stage in a tutu," Alyssa said.

"Don't pay attention to her, Emma," Livy said. "You are a beautiful, talented ballerina."

"Of course she is," Alyssa said. "Which is why it would make no difference if she took off a couple of months."

"It would make all the difference. One day off takes a day to recover. Two months off, I'd never catch up. At my age, and at this point in my career, I can't afford that. There's no way."

"Fine then," Alyssa said. "Only Mummy will need help from someone. She can't go upstairs alone with that ankle."

"Don't look at me," Livy said. "I've taken care of her my whole life. I won't give up my safari."

"You will go on your safari," Auggie assured Livy; the timing of their father's death had been inconvenient for all of them, but Auggie had managed to make it all right. "I will drop you at the airport tomorrow, and Griffin will be waiting for you at the other end."

"I sold my gold coins for this, Auggie. I know, Alyssa, you think that was silly of me, but what are they for but just such times? A person needs to live their life."

"I thought Mrs. Potter was going to stop by to help," Emma said. "If we move Gram into the downstairs bedroom, she'll be fine."

"Move into her dead husband's room?" Livy asked after allowing for a long pause.

"It's been the guest room for five years," Emma replied. "What's the big deal? And if it's so important, Alyssa, why don't you help?"

"It's my vacation time. Renny and I are working on the house up north."

"Of course," Auggie said. That was what Alyssa and Renny did these days, build houses. They never settled but kept moving about, as if afraid to be still. Auggie couldn't blame them for that. It was not comfortable or useful to be still. What might they find? As for himself, it went without saying that he had to get back to work. And Nan would be returning soon. He had to be there when she arrived. "Emma, it does seem as if you're the most convenient option. Everyone else is busy."

"So will I be," Emma snapped. "Very busy."

"If you get the role," Alyssa said.

"Here we are," Auggie said. He parked the car, leaving the spot nearest the gravesite for the Cunninghams. Other cars followed, a long line of them, attesting to Gussie's popularity. It was a relief to Auggie to know that she had a network of friends she could depend on, not just himself.

"And a beautiful spring day, it is," Livy said as they got out of the car. She used the car window as a mirror, adjusting her blue silk scarf around her neck and the belt of her stylish cashmere sweater coat around her waist. Satisfied with the result—though how she could be given the skeletal effect of her body, Auggie didn't know. But she was content, and who was he to judge? He watched her as she opened the back of the car and began to address the floral arrangements: the flowers to be put on Winston's grave, the bouquet she left every week on Ed's, and shears to trim the rhododendron surrounding the Willards' family plot. A woman stood in the clump of cypress near them, reading the gravestones. Auggie wondered if she were one of those gawkers who attend funerals of people they don't know. Was it the life or the death that fascinated them? Or was it the passage from one to the next—hope and activity to a closed book?

"What could Livy be thinking, clipping now, at the funeral?" Alyssa asked. "I told her Renny would do that last week and she wouldn't hear of it. It's infuriating how she says she'll do something and then doesn't. Everything according to her ease and convenience."

"I'd be willing to bet that if you had offered your own services, and not Renny's, she would have accepted the offer," Auggie replied, watching as their mother approached them. She was her regal, handsome self, in control as she had been forever. Her hazel eyes alert and clear, her teeth gritted against life's assaults, the most recent being the necessity of leaning into her crutches. And then he saw it, what his sisters had been talking about: a sadness and bewilderment, one Auggie knew she would not admit even to herself because admittance meant letting in. Letting in meant it existed. Existence meant it would take over, and how function without the person one had depended on without even knowing it for years and years? How function without them? The very idea left Auggie breathless. How would he dare leave his mother alone with that feeling? What would she do all by herself? What would he do?

Auggie berated himself. Making up stories again. Ever since Nan had left him, nearly a year ago, his imagination had too often predominated, conjuring fantasies of what was and what might be, sentimental stuff that he would be embarrassed to admit to anyone. Except Nan. Perhaps. She might be amused. Or angered. She had used to get so angry at how he dismissed his feelings. But how not to dismiss those uncomfortable sensations? They needed to be controlled, not encouraged. When it came to feelings, the only thing he was sure of was Nan. Who was not a thing. She was . . . gone. Her absence was telling. He missed her.

"How was the drive, Mummy?" Alyssa asked Gussie. "You look pale."

"Auggie, tell her she may stay," Gussie said in response and with a glance to the woman in the cypress trees who watched the coffin being removed from the limousine. "And that she need not worry about the money."

"Mummy, we should discuss this at another time," Alyssa whispered. "I can't with good conscience allow you to continue those crippling payments."

"You're my legal counsel and Power of Attorney, Alyssa, not my guardian. I am perfectly capable of making my own decisions. She is my responsibility. I won't have her homeless. Winston would have wanted it. Go on, Auggie."

Auggie stepped forward. He had not meant to be slow in his response, only he had not placed the woman at first. Ridiculous of him. Rather dense, but he was tired, distracted by a rush of adrenaline that left his knees weak, his body shaking, as he stepped up to her.

"You have his eyebrows and height. You must be Auggie," she said. "I'm Gloria."

"Of course," he said. Of course, he thought. She hadn't changed that much. The passage of time had not aged her but given her character. No longer the plain version of his mother he had always thought of her as, Gloria had taken on a solidity and confidence. Gray hair dampened the red, making it a brown blonde. An almost elegant stature for one who had so comfortably plumped. Her eyes, though, jarred him. They seemed to see more of him than he saw of her, and so he shifted his focus to her forehead, though it was not he who had anything to hide or be ashamed of.

"Mother wants you to know that you are welcome to stay," he said.

"I don't need or want her permission."

Auggie didn't reply and wondered what she had thought of the letter he had written to her years ago, expressing his outrage and demanding that she leave his father alone. He had spent hours editing that letter, trying to express exactly his feelings, contracting, until he had it down to one or two sentences, which, now he thought of it, he had burned. Why bother to send them? His father would only be angry. His mother mortified. Some things are best left unspoken. He had returned to his studies.

"When you people put him in that place, it meant I could visit him anytime." Gloria smiled in Pyrrhic victory. "You never thought of that, did you?"

"I don't think we cared," Auggie replied.

"I wish I could say the same." She flushed. "I always stood yards behind Gussie and you children. Winston knew how much you counted on him. Your mother especially. She depended on him."

"No, she didn't."

Gloria looked at him, askance.

"You wouldn't like that?" she asked.

"It's not for me to like or not. It's a fact. Either way, it would make no difference to me."

"It made all the difference to him," she said. "Like it or not, he loved you. That's why he built you that cabin. He thought it would be a good compromise. He knew you didn't like being in the big house. Whether it was because of him or that it was your mother's jurisdiction, who knew, but the cabin was to have given you your own place. The way he put it was that you would be apart from the family, yet a part of it. I told him it was a waste of time and money, but he would do it. Stubborn man. He convinced himself that she would be happy about it too. Of course, she wasn't. She wanted you closer than that. He was so disappointed that you rejected it. At least until he realized how happy it had made your mother that you chose her. That was what he wanted, for her to be happy."

Auggie stared at Gloria. Had he chosen his mother? Not consciously. No. Choice had nothing to do with it. His father had always been all wrong. So it was not by choice but rather by default because there had been no commonality between father and son. Except, perhaps, the wish that Gussie be happy.

"He thought he had made her happy?" Auggie asked. "How could she be happy with you in the background?"

"You don't think I was a convenience to her?"

"Convenience?"

"I kept him occupied, leaving her free to do what she would. Even so, she knew he was there. He never left her."

"It would have been better if he had."

"Your mother didn't think so, insisting he stay to prove a point. Plain stubbornness," Gloria said. "Unforgivingness."

"Unforgiving?" Auggie repeated. "My mother unforgiving, tolerating you all these years? Putting up with Father's duplicity? Just to show you how unforgiving she is, she wants you to know she will continue the payments."

Gloria started, then laughed and shook her head.

"Does your mother really think that's why I've stuck around all these years? I don't need the money and never have. I've worked for my living. Unlike your mother, I didn't have everything handed to me on a silver platter."

Auggie bridled at this second slight. Or was it a prick of shame that he felt? After all, it was true. His mother had never earned a dime. Was that a fault, or a fact? Was she guilty for having lived in favorable circumstances? For having wasted all her talents and potential? Because that is what Auggie had to admit as he stood there. The glaring fault in his mother. What had she ever done? But Gloria. She, too, had been given favors. "What about your house? Father bought it, didn't he?"

"He was old-fashioned that way. He felt he should be taking care of me, providing for me. Dear man. He was kind and thoughtful. Always there when I needed him. Listening to me, advising."

"I hardly recognize the man you describe," Auggie said, though he did: her description was that of the father he wished he had had. Auggie hesitated and then said for no particular reason—to fill the space, perhaps—"I used to imagine that my mother and you would become friends. You would move in with us, into the room off the kitchen."

"The maid's quarters?" Gloria mocked, and Auggie thought how strange it was to want something from someone that the person can't, or won't, give. Something important, necessary. He had imagined, as a child, that with it he might do things he otherwise couldn't. Stranger still, at the gravesite, to find that the hope that Gloria might give him something had become a vague feeling that she owed him. But what was to be done? He ignored the feeling in the pit of his chest, the warm eddying from his heart that spread so uncomfortably.

"Someone wants your attention."

Auggie turned in the direction Gloria indicated to see Nan walking toward them. A quick breath. For a heartbeat, he felt alive, until Nan became Emma. A slender version of Nan. In her requisite black leotard and flowing skirt. Exuding vitality and life. Her posture proud, each step a statement of beauty and awareness. Emma's physicality, how muscle moved bone, contrasted with his own more . . . intellectual consciousness. Her expression of life intimidated and fascinated him. If he allowed himself, he could have watched her move about all day long. Instead, her presence left him tense, unsure of what to say to her. What had they to talk about, she so lost in her dance and he in his books?

"Everyone's ready, Dad." Emma held a hand out to Gloria. "Hi. I'm Emma. Were you a friend of Gramps's?"

"Yes," Gloria said as they shook hands. Two hands clasped. Auggie stared. So brief a contact, so warm and natural. "I came to see where he'll be."

"He's back at the house," Emma said. Auggie started.

"Don't be ridiculous, Emma," he said, irritated that she would say such a foolish thing to a stranger.

"He probably is there. He loved his home." Gloria tilted her head, studying Emma. "I'm glad someone understood that. It's nice to know about you, Emma." Gloria smiled to herself and then turned to Auggie. "I'm sorry if I disturbed you and your family, Auggie. Thank your mother, but I'll come back later, after the ceremony. Good-bye."

Gloria held out her hand to shake, a hand that, hours later, he would still feel in his—very small, very warm and soft. Like Nan's. He hadn't been able to respond to her. Nan had called him a cold, superficial man. Not stupid, but superficial, and he couldn't understand why. *Exactly my point*, Nan had said, crying. But her tears had not been sad. No. She had been angry. She had thought of herself as an independent artist, only to find that she had fallen into society's mold of mother and wife, words she had spat out like curses. She believed her life had been wasted spent in marriage. His throat had been too painfully tight to argue the point. The car door slammed. Such finality. He watched as she drove off, pulled after her as if attached by some cord because he had not told her . . . He wished he had said . . . Auggie didn't know what to say. He had said nothing and regretted it, even as she left him behind. And now, again, a car door shut. A good-bye. Not "see you again" but good-bye, gone. And again that sensation of being left, and what had he done?

When he felt this way as a child, he would lie on his stomach and watch the ants dragging dead wasps into their sandy hill homes and the particle-sized red mites scurrying on multiple feet—and to where? Why? The bugs had put his life into perspective. In the grand scheme, he was as insignificant as a grain of sand. On the other hand, within his own life's scope, if mites and spiders were so self-important as to seem irritated but undaunted when a finger blocked their ways, then how dare he not achieve? Auggie, too, could overcome unfortunate circumstances, such as his father. By thinking. Working. Achieving. Which was probably why he was feeling so uncomfortable. Auggie was not accomplishing anything standing there in the graveyard, and a sense of panic rose up at all the time wasted. He had to do something to hold back the sense of repulsion and shame. Without purposeful work, he had nothing to fall back on, and still the weekend to get through.

"Are you okay, Dad?" Emma asked.

"That was my father's girlfriend." Emma started. Had she not known about Gloria? But she must have. It had been whispered about for years. "I wonder why she came. A rather pedestrian woman without much to say. She never had our expectations."

"How enviable."

"What?" Auggie asked.

Emma shrugged. "She has no rules to follow. Nothing to risk. No one to fail."

Auggie frowned at Emma, nettled by her nonsense.

"Let's get this over with," he said, and marched toward the gravesite and the gathering of family and friends. His sisters stood on either side of Gussie, supporting her. Or maybe she was supporting them. And Renny, looking exactly the same as he had at his wedding—not coincidentally, given he was wearing the same suit and standing next to Alyssa, ever her guide and helpmeet. As to the next generation, last Auggie had noted them, they'd been children going off to boarding schools or to their swimming and tennis lessons at the club. Now here they were, a tall, handsome group of adults with their various spouses and lovers, all chatting as if at a cocktail party, not a funeral. No one took note of the coffin. It sat next to the hole, leather straps beneath it, waiting for the lowering.

"Well?" Gussie looked at him expectantly.

"She said it's not necessary."

"Pride before the fall. I'll take care of her. Whether she knows it or not, she needs me."

"You mean the money, don't you?" Auggie asked.

"Of course," Gussie snapped, chin up, tears jiggling alarmingly on her lids. She lifted a handkerchief to her face. To sneeze? A sob. Her shoulders shook. His mother crying. Women did. Nan had. Watching his mother, he wondered if she felt the same as Nan. Anger, not sadness? Regret . . . relief? Seconds passed. His curiosity and pity shifted to irritation. It seemed undignified for Gussie to stand there crying with the rest of them just watching. He touched her arm. She pushed him away. Her tears disappeared. No tears, and for some reason, Auggie wished he had gone off in the car with Gloria.

The ceremony proceeded. The preacher's toning a familiar rhythm. Assurances and rituals created to soothe the faithful and bereft. Auggie reviewed the work he had to get done. He formulated a schedule, strict and exact. By clarifying what he would accomplish and when, he gained assurance that his life would right itself. Soon. His confusion was calmed by this repetitive review. Only a moment of panic when the dirt thudded on the coffin. The sound interrupted his rumination with its sense of finality. Winston would be buried, even though the ground into which the coffin had been lowered gave off the distinct smell of his room, fresh sawdust and freshly dug up dirt. The smell raised images of revolutionary guns, antique ceramic soldiers, forced marches, cold showers. His father in the coffin, knocking to get out. That powerful, tall man with his huge hands and broad shoulders. That gruff ignoramus, bellowing, vitriolic. How Auggie had hated him. How much he had wanted to love him. Wanted his love. A feeling only half felt, a thought not fully formulated before Auggie reminded himself that he had to confirm his airline ticket back home. Perhaps Nan would have returned by then. He might talk to her.

The family invited everyone back to the house for luncheon.

Correct protocol, Auggie supposed, but a bother. The caterers Gussie had been persuaded to hire doled out sandwiches, cookies, and coffee to everyone who entered the house. To be out of the way, Auggie stepped into the room off the kitchen. The junk room. Alyssa's study. The maid's room. He would stay there for a while because he had nothing to say to anyone and the feeling was reciprocated, he was sure. The odor of cat litter and mold mixed with laundry detergent. He picked up a book. One of Alyssa's old law texts. There was nothing else, and so he opened *The Law of Mergers and Acquisitions* and read. Something to focus on. The undertones of talking in the kitchen. His sisters. About their mother. Emma. Responsibility, priorities, meanness. Silence fell when Emma came into the kitchen. Had anyone called?

Auggie needed fresh air but couldn't face them. He opened the window. The creeping roses with their sharp, nettle-like thorns tore his jacket as he climbed out. He left it on the stone wall and headed over to the garage. Cool, dank air, smelling of gasoline and cut lawn, wafted out. His eyes adjusted as he walked past the clutter of old lawn furniture, sailing accoutrements, and rusted garden tools to his father's work bench. In Winston's day, it had been Knickerbocker Grey-organized, the glass jars aligned and full of nails and screws, the boxes of bolts, caps, and dowels alphabetized. Winston could find exactly what he needed, picking out a tiny washer with his enormous fingers without knocking everything down around it as he did in the house.

No longer. The jars and boxes had been overturned. The drawers opened and rummaged through. Auggie turned his back on the chaos. Someday, it would all have to be disposed of. Even his father's tractor, there in the first bay of the garage. Cobwebbed and rusty. Auggie remembered perfectly the day it had arrived. The family had been preparing for a trip to New York City. Auggie had been six, and his father had lifted him up to sit with him on the nine-hole metal seat of the dark lime green 1936 John Deere. Auggie had loved how the green of the body had contrasted with the bright yellow axels of the rubber wheels. Two small ones in front, two enormous in back. The tractor huffed next to the maturing chestnut tree that grew up next to the driveway. The tree's leaves had rustled as the tractor lurched forward, chugging past Gussie's garden with its orange roses and red and white peonies, bumping over the rocks that rose out of the crabgrass lawn, following the winding paths to the beach, where Livy shouted for him to join her. Alyssa, the baby, wailed. Winston had stopped the tractor and stood up. Towering and strong, he'd lifted Auggie onto his shoulders so they could both see over the bulwark of beach roses. The top of Livy's head. The waves. The salt air. The depths of the ocean. Auggie had felt safe sitting on his father's broad shoulders. He had trusted his father, depended on his strength and love.

All of which betrayed the discomfiting contrast between euphoric recall and reality, because, so many years later, Auggie found it hard to believe he had felt that way about his father. Who had built him a cabin. To express his love? The cabin must have fallen in on itself by now. Auggie admonished himself, and wondered what had come over him, that he would want to see it, as if returning to it might accomplish anything. But he did.

What if there were no light or dark? Nan might have asked if she had been with him as he walked along the path that had been kept so nicely pruned. By whom? *No sunrise or sunset. If the world stopped turning, would there still be time? Would we grow old? I love that idea. Time stopping. Everyone the same age.*

Overpopulation, he would say. And Emma, *We're mortal.*

Nan would laugh. They would have laughed together at the thought of mortality and how silly a word it was. Mortal. Mortal. Mortal. Tasting the word and what it signified, the passage of life and its relevancy. She had accused him of not valuing her poetry. Untrue, though he found the rawness of it too flagrant, the images of the psyche expressed in physical violations. He missed the simple haikus of her earlier years. They held more self-restraint than rage and regret, which were uncomfortable.

He stepped onto the porch of the cabin. A radio played. There was someone inside. Emma. She was dancing. Ballet slippered, still in her black dress with its full skirt that swirled and wrapped around her as she turned one way, then another, as if wildly searching. He watched, transfixed. Her every movement so exact and true. So free and uninhibited. Her body flowing through life, and life through her body, capturing all he had never been able to express. All he had never dared to do. Tears and happiness. Love and tears. She was crying. He realized he was watching her die, and nearly slid himself into the black hole he avoided. A terrifying panic. He wanted to reach out and touch her, as if that might save them both. He stepped forward. His presence broke the spell. She stopped. Both disoriented. Embarrassed for having been caught in such an intimate act.

"Is there a call for me?" she asked, breathless, her face glowing with her activity. And hope. She looked to him as she had so often as a child, as if Auggie had something for her. Strange. He had nothing to give.

"No," he said. She shrugged, and gave a smile full of tears that would not fall. She would not let them. Familiar. She reached to turn off the cassette player, then looked around the cabin, shivered.

"It's so cold, I was trying to get warm," she said. "Whenever I've felt upset, or lonely—like when you and Mom traveled without me?—I've come out here. I didn't miss you as much here."

"You didn't miss us at all. We used to come back from trips and you'd act as if you hadn't noticed we were gone. You would talk nonstop about your dance and what you'd learned."

"I didn't want you to think I'd made a mistake, choosing to dance. I mean, I had missed you and Mom so much. I couldn't give up ballet too. Or maybe I sensed how unhappy you were, and didn't want to make things worse by being too needy."

"We weren't unhappy. Your mother and I have a wonderful marriage. She's just going through a hard time. A lost lamb. She'll come back."

Emma stared at him as if he had entirely missed some point, and

257

he had never understood his daughter's dislike of travel. "You know, I would have given my eyeteeth as a child to do the traveling you might have done. The opportunities you gave up."

"I'm not you," Emma said with a quick smile. She picked up a leather notebook that lay, dust-covered, on the desk. Standing up, so straight and tall. So sure of herself. "It wasn't dislike. If I had traveled, I'd have missed other opportunities. Dance. I needed to dance. If I danced, I'd be somebody. Special. I thought you'd be proud of me. Someday, anyway. It's been a fight all along. You've never thought it was that important. I've always gotten the sense you looked down on it."

"Not true."

"No? I guess that's good to know. I used to dread the days that Thea's mom couldn't drive us to class because then Mom would have to, and it felt as if I were stealing something from her. I knew she had better things to do with her time than waste it watching my dance class. It was easier to stay with Gram and Gramps." Emma indicated the notebook. "The cousins gave Gramps this for his seventieth birthday. He was supposed to write down his stories so we'd have them when he wasn't around. Like now. So that we might know him."

"His stories were tedious," Auggie said.

"Maybe," Emma replied, slowly turning the pages. Auggie ran a hand along the oak shelf, admiring the tongue and groove cuts, imagining his father sitting in the cabin, penning his stories with those calloused, clumsy hands, and growing teary-eyed at the thought that, when the grandchildren finally read them, he would be gone; that the words would not give him what he wanted, because his family—Gussie, Auggie, Livy, and Alyssa—were talking about him up at the house, scoffing. Auggie winced. He didn't want Emma to think that way of him. He wanted to help her, be there for her in ways his father had not been for him.

"Your grandfather wasn't very good with words," Auggie said. "Sad. Thinking of him trying to write. Insignificant events, but they must have meant something to him."

"He was probably trying to say something," Emma said. "Sometimes I say something, and it's interpreted entirely differently from what I meant, and when I try to explain? I only dig myself in deeper, even more misunderstood. I end up feeling totally out of it."

"Out of what?" Auggie asked. "You have to be more specific with words, Emma. They're powerful. You have to be clear."

Emma stared at Auggie.

"Unacceptable," she said. "I imagine that's what Gramps felt like. Isolated and misunderstood. That's what I love about dance. I don't need words to express myself. I just am. I'm not limited by my head."

Emma looked at him, and he looked back and had no idea how to respond. He could only feel frustrated, because what was she trying to tell him?

"There's an intellectual component to ballet, Dad. Physics. And it requires . . . self-control. There are all kinds of rules and steps to learn. I remember when Gram took me to my first class with Mrs. Siminoff. There was something familiar about it. No questions. No whys. All that was expected was obedience and loyalty to the master. Mrs. Siminoff was so clear with her directions. She'd correct mistakes and show how it was done, rather than just telling it. She always said that if you followed the rules and taught the body the movements, such that they became a part of the body, like breathing, you'd learn how to surpass your own limitations, because then the soul would be free to take over. You could be free to escape your self."

"Isn't it time you stopped trying to escape? You're nearly twenty, Emma. You need to start settling down. Why not work on your law school applications today?" Auggie asked.

"Alyssa says law school is great if you want to practice law. Otherwise, it's dry as toast."

"It will teach you how to think."

"That's right." Emma knocked her forehead lightly with the heel of her hand. "I knew there was a reason I should go to law school. It'll get me away from the stupid dancers I hang out with."

"If you don't want to go to law school, don't, but you have to do something. You need a real job to occupy you. You can't just dawdle through life."

"I'm not dawdling. I've been dancing professionally for two years now. I've been written up in articles. I sent them to you. Did you bother to read them? *'Just short of the angels.' 'Evocative of what we all might achieve and be.' 'Transformative.'* That's me, Dad. But not yet. I still have work to do. It's never done. If I stop now, it'll be forever."

"A self-fulfilling prophecy."

"Fact. The competition is huge. Why don't you believe me? Dad, I'm a dancer, and I'm going to be a Prima ballerina." Emma picked up her radio-cassette player, hugged it to herself as if someone threatened to take it away. As if, if she didn't hold tight, it would be lost forever. "I thought that money was to allow us to pursue dreams we might not be able to otherwise. I thought it was the right thing for me to do all these years. Now I find out everyone's been thinking it's a waste. Bounding around a stage like a startled deer. That's what Livy said. They were talking about me in the kitchen. Even Livy thinks it's a good idea for me to stay with Gram for a while."

"It will be hugely helpful, Emma," Auggie said, as the tension in his neck let go. Emma valued Livy's opinion. The decision had been made. "It will be a huge relief for me to have you here. You'll be company for each other. Just while your grandmother is getting back on her feet. It will be dull here, of course. I've never been able to accomplish much. But you'll heal from your disappointments. And you can practice here in the cabin, and go back in the fall."

Emma started to go up on her toes, an age-old habit of pirouetting, as if the movement helped her to think. But she held herself still, looked around. There was something different about her. A sloppiness. She wasn't holding herself as she usually did.

"So you think it's hopeless too?" she asked.

"They haven't called. Obviously, you didn't get the part. Worse things could happen."

"No, Dad. That is the worst. For me. But then, I guess I was fooling myself all along."

"No. You are very good. But you can't expect perfection."

"That's all I can expect. If I didn't get the role, then why bother to continue? If I can't make it in some minor league company—it's not the New York Ballet, after all, right? Maybe if it were, it would count with you. It's humiliating. Thea and Vlad. I'll never be able to face them again."

"You only need to put your priorities in order," Auggie said, trying to comfort her in ways he had not Nan. "You can't fight reality. If you want something different, you have to change."

"You're the one who doesn't change. That's why Mom left. Because your work comes first. You totally ignore her for months, trying to finish your book—then, when you do, you pop up from your study wanting to take her out to dinner. Expecting her to drop everything. People need more than that. Books. They need community and recognition."

"Don't worry, Emma." Auggie looked back at her, staring directly at her forehead. "Your mother will come back."

"No, Dad. She won't."

Auggie turned his back to her. Something in his throat. He castigated himself. He did not understand what they were talking about, change. How was he supposed to change? What was he supposed to do. *Change?* Didn't they understand? Didn't Nan sense the risks he took every time he stepped away from his desk? Away from the calm and control of his office, life took over. Life, with all its inconsistencies. Order. He could breathe in order. In order he knew what to expect.

But not without Nan. It had been Nan who had provided at least some succor from life's chaos. Her acceptance and love nurtured him, held him safe. With her, he could risk breathing in and out, dare to feel, just not too much. And the idea of his life going forward without her? Such isolation terrified him. Though not as much as the alternative. He had to get back to work. And maybe that was why Emma was upset. It was different for her. His books were always there, waiting for him. Emma had to count on other people. She needed them to work with and dance with. And so this must be uncomfortable, to have that succor removed. Auggie stood up straight. He knew how to comfort Emma.

"Don't worry, dear heart," he said, turning back to her. "Three months isn't a long time. You'll go back at the end of the summer."

But Emma, too, was gone. She was running up the path to the house, and did she think that might save her? Did he? Confusing. To stay. To go.

Auggie walked back toward the garage, breathing carefully, noting the dangerous sensation percolating to the surface: how much he missed those who had not been in his life, in part because he hadn't dared let them in.

As he walked along the stone driveway, he looked across the field to the harbor, listening to the constant, steady honk of the foghorn bidding good-bye as lobster boats chugged out to sea. He thought of the first time he saw Nan, at a party of Livy's in New York City. She had worn a black and white, strapless dress and held a glass of champagne, her eyes so dark and alive and exciting. And before her, in Germany, Pat. Her laughter had been so free-flowing and infectious. He had felt uninhibited with her, and entirely acceptable. He wondered at the memories. So many what-ifs. And here he was, the same but safe.

An adolescent osprey chirped, riding the breezes, occasionally tipping, clumsy. Not far away flew its parents, responding, showing it how to swoop and lift. A natural exchange of chirrups back and forth, constant, guiding, and Auggie envied that osprey and wanted to own the warm calm of that scene. His shoulders relaxed. He didn't want to move. He wanted everything to remain as it was. Like his father, who had put up a large peg-board above his work station. Winston had placed hooks at regular intervals and then drawn the outline of the tool that was to go on that hook. Even the youngest child knew where each tool should go. Even so, everyone laughed at Winston's requests, and gradual insistence, that things be returned to their place. They had all scoffed at him as he raged in his search for this tool or that. But Auggie had to admit that he had understood his father's frustration. He liked to have things in their place as well.

And yet, and yet. Night after night, drinking bourbon, lecturing endlessly about those *asinine liberals*, those dreadful *Chi-Coms*, the insidious *dole*. How relate to someone who refuses to listen? Auggie hoped that those aspects of his father that might be in him had been buried too. He wanted to lie down on his stomach and watch the ants, his mind and body empty and unthinking, numb. Stomach not churning with an unsettling nausea. Heart not caving in on itself. Breath not sounding like the waves in a conch shell. Lie on the belly and dream and hope and not have to know. That he couldn't return to the past or change it. He had acted as he acted, expected what could never be, and by expecting doomed what he had hoped for. Life proceeded. Do with it what one does, and then die. Everyone dies. Even he would die someday.

But he imagined he was six again. On a tractor. His father present. The water lapping the beach.

Divisions
February 1990

Livy stared out the living room window of her mother's house. (In Livy's mind, it would always be her mother's.) It was winter. Everything looked dead. But the familiarity of view—the village and the breakwater, the distant horizon—allowed Livy to imagine a kind of quiet in the future, a sense of control in chaos. Their mother moving to an assisted living home; Auggie . . . terribly sick with cancer; and Alyssa grasping for more, always more, in the division of things; and should she laugh or cry? That was the question Livy asked herself as she packed her share of the pink roseate porcelain. She decided to laugh. Her infectious laugh. Then it would be like the old days when everyone was happy. They used to get along so well!

"This is like a game, isn't it? A game called . . . mitosis." Livy smiled, delighted to show off what she had learned in the biology class she was auditing at the local college. "Dividing into two, four, six cells, a repeat of what was before."

"Meiosis," Auggie replied.

"What?" Livy asked, jarred by his correction. She looked over to where he sat in his wheelchair, leafing through the list of things to be divided. Efficient as ever, and able to concentrate, though so very sick. Everyone dies, of course, but not Auggie. He had to be her buffer from Alyssa's grasping, even now, when gray-faced and coughing. Livy winced as his upper body thrust weakly forward. Her tummy growled incongruously. How dare she be hungry at a time like this?

"Meiosis," he repeated. "Sexual reproduction, not cell division. We aren't recreating identical houses but recombining them into new ones, and it is up to us, Livy, to decide what the new will be."

"How do you know so much about everything?" Livy asked, miffed less by the fact that he seemed to have already thought out her idea than by his suggestion that she had to choose what the future would hold.

"I read a good deal and have excellent retention," Auggie replied, and looked thoughtfully into space. He smiled at some memory or other, showing a hint of the brother with whom Livy used to dance, cutting through the crowds, both of them tall and slender, his left hand holding up her right high in the air as they whirled around in circles, he leading the way, tunelessly humming. Never again. Livy's chest squeezed. She missed her brother. Their youth and her . . . beauty. She had been beautiful once.

"This has all gone too far, too fast," Gussie announced. Livy turned to find her mother dragging an armchair in from where it had been placed next to the dumpster. Both arms broken. The seat gone. How was it that everything around Gussie aged but herself? Certainly, her wool dress hadn't survived the years so well; what had happened to her mother's sense of fashion? "I won't stand for it anymore."

Alyssa stood up with the help of the fire poker. She was lopsided and limping with the strain of a bad back.

"Mummy," she said. "What are you doing with Daddy's old chair?"

"I caught Emma throwing it into the dumpster," Gussie said, carrying the chair over to the fireplace. Rather, holding the back of it, leading Emma, who carried most of the load, by the proverbial nose. Emma's eyes looked swollen, as if she had been crying. No surprise. Gussie had developed an edge in the last years, and Emma seemed to be the lightning rod.

"We agreed at dinner last night that it's not worth saving, Mother," Auggie said. "Don't you remember?"

"Of course I remember," Gussie snapped. "But reality is quite a bit different from talk."

Emma set down the chair. Her jeans and sweatshirt hung formlessly from her too-slender body and were covered with the sawdust and mess of the garage. Without a word, she headed back out. Where she found the energy, Livy didn't know, and because Emma wasn't talking, one couldn't ask. They all stared after her.

"She's an odd duck," Gussie said, looking around for someplace to sit. There was nowhere. "Throwing away tradition, silent as a sphinx as she drifts from one thing to another. It's as if she doesn't want to be acceptable to this family. It's awful to see someone floundering, especially one who had seemed so directed. She was such a marvelous dancer."

"It's too bad she didn't stick to it," Alyssa said. "I find it bizarre that after all those years of hard work, she just gave it up without a second thought."

"But Emma thinks about it all the time," Livy said. "She told me she misses it, every, single day."

"Then why not pick it up again?" Auggie asked, and his voice exposed his worry and frustration. How hard it would be to have to *leave* before he could see Emma . . . a success!

"She said she's not good enough, Auggie."

"With that attitude, she'll never be good enough at anything. She's twenty-seven. She has got to choose something."

"I agree, Auggie," Gussie said. "She mustn't just wade through life. I think I had better remain here until she figures herself out. I thought this move was the right thing to do, but I was wrong. Emma can stay with me until she gets her feet on the ground. A graduate program, or a business venture."

"Mummy, the reason she's not got her feet on the ground," Alyssa said, "is because she lives here. She needs to move to where there are people her age and things going on."

"That is what you said to me about moving. You're wrong. I've made this place my home. People come to me. I'm not moving."

"You've already bought the new apartment," Livy pointed out, struggling with the confusion of feelings that their mother's announcement caused. Familiar. So often their mother would change her mind and off the entire family would go, jibing in a direction previously undreamt of, and how adjust to yet another change?

"I'll sell it," Gussie said. "People flip property all the time, and profit from it."

"No, Mother. No," Alyssa said, the self-appointed diplomat these days, now that Auggie was ill. Her voice had the shrill quality it took when events turned unexpectedly against her best interests. There always seemed to be an agenda behind Alyssa's actions, but for now Livy was grateful her sister was there to take the proverbial bull by the horns. "It is too late. We are not speculative buyers, and we have gone too far into this to turn back. This was your decision. You said it would make sense to divide up things now, and to move to a smaller place. There will be less to clean. You won't have to cook. Remember? You said you've cooked for sixty-plus years, and are glad to be done with it."

"Have I been particularly forgetful lately that everyone seems to think I don't remember things? I know the arguments," Gussie snapped. "I hear them in my sleep. They're all excellent reasons, none of them dealing with the fact that the new place is all wrong. I'm not at all convinced by it, and until I am, I'm not leaving this house. It's my home. I've lived my life here. Why would I ever give it up?"

"You aren't giving it up," Alyssa said, looking at their mother wide-eyed with surprise. "The house will always be here. Just like you said it would be for me when Renny and I were debating whether to build. You said I could come back anytime. And it's true. And the familiar things will be here, or at one of the other houses, for you to see and touch. It will be just like old times."

"Mother," Auggie said. "You've been excited about the move. What's changed your mind?"

"I already said. The reality of it."

The discussion continued. Livy quietly closed up the box with the plates and marked it with a black Magic Marker. She stood up, feeling efficient and responsible, and glad not to be involved in the discussion. It wouldn't affect her either way. Whether her mother stayed or went, Livy intended to move on, break out of her rut. She wasn't quite sure how, but she would do it. It was time. Past time.

"It's too late," Alyssa concluded, gently but firmly. "I'm afraid we have to stick to your decision. We can't go changing with the wind."

Gussie stared at Alyssa, quite suddenly drooped. She lifted a hand to her throat, over her heart, and looked around her. Cardboard boxes scattered about, half-filled with the books and bric-a-brac collected over the years. Side tables, lamps, chairs, and paintings that had been separated into three groups, one each for Alyssa, Livy, and Auggie. The couches disposed of: one to the dumpster outside, and two to the basement of Alyssa's house next door, built nineteen years ago, thus sandwiching the maternal house between the daughters'. The remaining couch, claimed by Auggie for Emma, sat buried under the blankets, bedsheets, and pillows from the upstairs linen closet. How awkward, to have dissected their mother's house so blatantly. It seemed cruel— yet to reverse things? To return each item, laid claim to by one or the other sibling, back to where it had been for years on end? Impossible. It was, indeed, too late. Nothing would fit anymore. Livy pitied her mother. How awful to have given up something only to find that it had been a mistake. A huge mistake that could not be undone.

"I have been thinking of your father in that nursing home," Gussie said, thereby gaining her children's full attention; their father had been dead eight years, after all. Why would she be thinking about him? "I don't want to outlive my shelf life. I am counting on you to be sure that I don't. I want to walk gracefully into old age, and die a noble death. It is an empowering thought, isn't it, to control one's death?"

"Isn't it life we have to control, Mother?" Auggie asked.

"I am quite tired," Gussie said in response. "I've a meeting at the apartment. Window treatments. I'll be back afterwards for a nap."

She began to wend her way through the maze of things not in their places, heading for the kitchen and presumably the driveway, the car.

"Why not nap at your new place, Mummy?" Alyssa suggested, putting on a cheerful tone, as if speaking to a child about the treats they will get once the medicine is taken.

"Because I am coming back here to sleep in my own bed," Gussie replied.

"Have Emma drive you if you are tired," Alyssa suggested.

"She drives too fast."

"Livy will take you, then," Alyssa offered.

"I beg your pardon?" Livy flushed.

"I will drive myself, thank you."

The door swung shut after their mother.

"Livy," Auggie said. "Did you not talk to her about the car?"

"Why would I?"

"Because you insisted you be the one to talk to her. Why else?" Alyssa fumed, once again laying the blame squarely on Livy. It was always Livy who got blamed when things didn't work out for Alyssa, who had used to be so lovely and adorable. A beautiful, frail little thing, all gurgles and giggles, whom Gussie had allowed Livy to help dress and play with. Livy had wanted to protect Alyssa back then. Save her from anything terrible or scary. But with the years, it had become harder and harder to feel love and affection. Instead? Irritation and outright anger. Livy admitted it! She felt angry at her sister, because Alyssa needed so much. And paid no attention to anything Livy said. It was as if Alyssa didn't trust or respect her opinion. Even Livy's suggestion that the couches be donated to the Salvation Army had been rejected by her *dear* sister, who claimed the couches only needed to be repaired, and so to Alyssa's basement they went. To sit until they rotted, for all Livy cared. And now the car.

"It's cruel to take away the car," Livy replied sensibly. "It's Mummy's freedom, and with all the changes, it's the one thing she has control of. I did try to bring it up with her. She promptly moved the conversation to the last time she got stopped by the police and what a zippy car he had. A Camaro. She wants one for herself."

The only sound in response to Livy was Alyssa's chewing of a handful of M&Ms as she hovered over the jewelry that their mother had laid out that morning after breakfast. Each piece had been put in a clear plastic baggie with a tag telling its description, history, and worth in red pen. They lay like white jellyfish on the low coffee table—it was Auggie's now—near the hearth. The fire had died down to embers; all those cheerful fires they had enjoyed, cocktails in hand, removed to the past. The poor house. It felt so stark, dim, and chill.

"It is only too bad her view will be of the parking lot," Alyssa said.

"Emphasize the positive, Alyssa," Livy retorted, annoyed by her sister's fondling of each packet. "It's convenient. Her friends won't have to walk as far to their cars."

"And that will remind her that she wants to have a car, too."

"A new one," Livy said. "And why not?"

"Livy, we've discussed her driving before," Auggie said, exasperated. "Mother's driving days have got to end. We all agreed that was to be one of the benefits of living in town. She won't have much use for a car. Being rid of it will ease her financial burdens."

Livy stood up. She could hardly breathe for the tightness in her throat and the vast pity she felt for her mother, who only wanted to live her life.

"Another benefit is that you'll be able to use Mother's car," Auggie said. "On the assumption you help her get to her appointments and shopping."

"I beg your pardon." Livy startled as the sympathetic, protective feelings she felt toward her mother warped into resentment of her continued presence. "I am not her chauffeur."

"The price to be paid if you're to use her car," Auggie said. "It could be a weekly event for the two of you, Livy. You'll do all your shopping together and have a gay old time."

"How very convenient," Livy said, pressing her lips together to stretch them smooth into a smile. She had to smile, not purse. She had noticed the ruts lining her lips.

"Now that that's settled, shall we do the jewelry?" Alyssa asked.

"You already asked Mother about the jewelry, Alyssa, and she said no," Auggie replied, his voice harsh, if weak. "Please stop dredging for the answer you want."

"Selfish cow," Livy added, unable to resist, but quietly, so no one would hear.

"What did you say?" Alyssa asked.

"Nothing."

"I only ask about the jewelry, Livy, out of concern for my daughter. Julia is going to be heartbroken when she finds out Emma got Mummy's pearls."

"Keep asking Mummy, and Julia won't get anything." Livy walked over to Auggie to adjust the blanket around his legs, mere sticks in his voluminous forest green sweatpants.

Alyssa didn't respond, only continued her study of the various baggies, reading their tags, as if by touching, knowing their value, she might possess them. Livy wished she could tell Alyssa that having the jade ring or the diamond watch would not solve anything. But likely as not, that would start another disagreement, and Auggie's shoulders already sagged. Even his hair, flattened and sparse, seemed exhausted.

"I thought this time was to be for the three of us, not our children," Alyssa said. "Emma has moved in here lock, stock, and barrel. She couldn't take over fast enough when she found out she's to get the house."

"Don't be unpleasant, Alyssa," Auggie said. "I am the one who moved here *lock, stock, and barrel*. Emma is here to take care of me because I've limited energies. She's been an enormous help to all of us."

"I certainly don't mean to be unpleasant." Alyssa crossed her arms. "I am only concerned for Emma, who should be off living her own life."

"You've already said that, Alyssa," Livy replied. "Have you ever stopped to think she *is* living her life? She is helping her father. They've been having a wonderful time together, drawing up plans for the renovations. It's certainly not for you to judge the rightness or wrongness of that."

As if on cue, the swinging door opened and Emma came out. She went directly to her father and picked up the pad of paper and pen. She began to write a note. He sighed, looking at his daughter with a medley of concern, sadness, and frustration, because Emma was still not talking. It had been four months, and only Livy knew why. Emma and her boyfriend, Loren—where Emma had found him, Livy had no idea, but he was the worst she'd come up with yet—had come to Livy's for tea. They had sat on her patio and enjoyed the Indian summer weather, the view of the harbor, and Livy's garden. Emma and Loren had been to the ballet *Sleeping Beauty* the night before. Loren went on and on about how absurd it was to waste one's time watching tutus running about on skinny legs.

"Emma? What did you think of it?" Livy had asked.

"It was amazing," Emma had said, her eyes shining, for once not adapting herself to Loren in an attempt to mollify him. Rather she was her old self, glowing and excited, all hand gestures and motion; life. "Thea was magnificent. I was so proud of her. She floated across the stage. Her pointe work was perfection. The Rose Adagio? Wow. She's totally mastered everything she used to be challenged by. Although she did get a little lazy with a couple of her leg extensions."

"You could have done better?" Loren asked.

"Certainly, she could," Livy had said. "Emma danced circles around her. I used to weep watching you dance. You expressed yourself so beautifully."

Emma smiled. "Thanks, Livy."

"Do you miss it, Emma?" Livy asked, reaching over to touch her. The girl looked suddenly so sad.

"Every day. But I can't think about it. Mrs. Siminoff always said you have to stay in the present."

"If you miss it, why aren't you dancing?" Loren asked. Emma shrugged. "And the martyr reveals herself. That's the problem with you privileged people. You have dreams but you don't know how to carry them out. Without starvation barking at your door, you don't have the motivation to act. You never learn that you have to sacrifice to get what you want, instead of sitting around waiting for things to come to you."

Emma stared at him, slumped in his chair, fingers interlaced across his skinny chest. Miserable wretch, Livy thought, stubbing out her cigarette. Granted, Livy enjoyed bantering with him about philosophy and life's meaning at exactly the right comfort level for both: she the willing and curious student, he the patronizing teacher. But she didn't have to tolerate his base meanness. Livy reached for her pack of cigarettes and a lighter.

"Actually, Loren, when I gave up dance, I sacrificed everything I ever wanted," Emma said, her voice a whisper. "There's nothing else I've ever cared about as much. Except, maybe, Gram's place. It's not that it was too hard. Just pointless. I'd never be what I wanted to be. I thought I was close, but then the dance company—I wasn't good enough to be cast in a ballet they were putting on."

"*Giselle*," Livy said.

Emma nodded. "Ballet is an elite club, Loren," she said. "Once you're in, you'll do anything to not give up your spot. I had to be perfect. If I wasn't good enough for a small dance troupe, I was doing something wrong. I had to change. So I took the summer off to help Gram out. I was determined to work harder than ever that summer. But I couldn't leave the house because Gram might need me, and every time I started in, warming up or stretching, she'd call for me. I couldn't not go. I mean, that was why I was there, right? To help. In between doing things for her, I was lucky to get in an hour or two of work. It was so frustrating, because I knew I was losing it. All I could see were the mistakes. It got to the point that I couldn't bear to watch myself. It was too painful. So when Dad asked me if I wanted to do some traveling with him, it was a relief to stop dancing. Sort of."

Emma fell silent, staring out to the horizon. "The worst part is that Gram didn't even really need me that summer. Gram doesn't need caretaking."

"Entirely untrue," Livy said, sitting up and feeling almost angry at Emma for saying such a thing. "She would be lost without us. We will always be grateful for your help that summer."

"Don't try to make her feel better, Livy. It's a perfect excuse for Emma to sit around and feel sorry for herself," Loren said. "Blaming her grandmother, when she just said she chose to leave because it wasn't worth her precious time. Now she takes part-time jobs and brags about it, as if she's something special, earning a wage, which is what most people have to do. You don't even consider the fact that you're stealing a job from someone who really needs it, Emma."

Emma stared at him, the color drained from her face.

"Like yourself?" Livy asked, smiling, though her hands shook with fury. She knew perfectly well that Emma had been paying his bills for the past year because he wouldn't deign to get a job that didn't pay him to sit around and act the part of a *philosophe*, all negativity, absurdity, and poverty. Never mind that loan. Loren looked at Livy, his chin jutting forward.

"I wouldn't lower myself to menial labor, whereas Emma will do anything to prove she's impoverished."

"What makes you think she isn't?"

"Oh, please. You people reek of privilege. How else can you afford these mansions on the water?"

"Ours are modest homes that have been in the family forever," Livy said, as gracious as she could be under his crass, misdirected assault.

"That's right," he said. "Cry poor when you've millions socked away. It's a power play."

"I thought it was a trough." Emma's chin quivered. "You called us pigs at a trough."

"If that's the case, you've enjoyed bellying up to it, Loren," Livy said, flushing, and then, though knowing she shouldn't, continued. "Certainly, you didn't say no to that money Emma gave you to pay off your school loans."

Livy stopped herself, regretting . . . but too late. Loren sat up, glared at Emma.

"You promised not to tell anyone," he said.

"Fifty thousand dollars is a lot of money."

"In other words, your precious money comes before me?"

"I'm sorry. I needed to talk to someone."

"The only person you should talk to about my personal affairs is me. Have you any idea how humiliating this is for me? Never mind the fact that you insisted I take it. Now I owe you and you expect me to act at your bidding. Going to idiot ballets and restaurants that make me sick to my stomach when I see the bill. People could eat for a week on one meal. But I'm supposed to smile and make you happy, kowtow to your wishes." He sniffed. "You're not the person I thought you were, Emma. You're greedy and selfish."

"That's not nice to say, and is entirely untrue," Livy said.

"That's right." Loren reached for a gingersnap. "Circle the wagons. Go on the attack. That's how you do it, right? Ya know, in ways, you're no better, Livy. You are either very smart or very stupid about money. OW!"

Emma had taken the butter knife and nailed his hand to the table. She kept it there, not cutting the skin but stark in her hold, saying nothing as he ordered, then asked, then pleaded with her to let go. After a full minute, Emma had lifted the knife, drawn it against her throat, stood, and walked away. She took the car, leaving Livy to endure Loren's umbrage while they waited for a cab to pick him up. By the time he had made his way to Emma's apartment in Providence, she had put all his things on the street, changed the locks, quit her job bartending, and caught a bus to California to visit her mother, arriving in time for them both to fly back to be at Auggie's hospital bed: he was riddled with cancer. To nurse him, Emma moved into the New York City apartment he had lived in since his separation from Nan, and then to the family home. All done without a word, her silence growing more complete. Emma's muteness made sense to Livy. She was lonely and voiceless in her life. What was there to say?

"We know, Emma," Auggie said, sitting up. He was better when Emma was around. At least, he tried to be. "Your grandmother insisted on driving herself. Just into the village." Auggie continued to read her notes. He smiled, laughed, and even though the laughter became a cough, Livy could see the gratification Emma felt at having caused at least a moment of joy. "You're right. There isn't a stop sign in the world that she doesn't want to drive through."

"We should get back to work so we're done by the time Mummy gets back," Alyssa said. "It's unpleasant dividing and choosing in front of her. Livy, it's still your turn."

Livy focused her attention on the objects on the two card tables. She touched the slender iron vase, its handles, sculpted lilies. The brown ceramic jar with its bumpy exterior, smoothed by glaze and years. It had held thousands of cookies. The gold-rimmed picture frame—gaudy, but Livy adored the picture within: of their parents dressed for a white tie affair, young, vibrant, and in love. Of all things.

"Isn't it interesting about material things?" Livy asked, attempting to articulate the tug of her heart for her father. Or was it her mother? Maybe the past. It was too awful how old they had all become. "They last so much longer than we do, yet have no significance without us."

"Would you just get on with it?" Alyssa urged, nervous as a cat, as if all would be lost if the choosing didn't proceed. Looking at her, Livy felt . . . pity. She could not imagine, or perhaps imagined too closely, the relentless deprivation her sister felt. She'd had the world handed to her, but hadn't the capacity to appreciate it. Livy had talked to her therapist about it. They had concluded that Alyssa had the "poor relative syndrome," viewing the world from impoverishment. It must be unpleasant to always feel she had less than everyone else, even when she had gotten more.

"But there is too much stuff, isn't there?" Livy tsked, attempting to reveal to Alyssa the riches. "Maybe we should throw everything away and take ourselves out for a nice lunch."

"If you don't want more, Auggie and I will divide the rest. I'm sure I can find a place for everything, somewhere."

"Not in this house, Alyssa," Auggie said.

"Why not? It's still the family house, and always will be if I have anything to do with it, which I do."

Livy noted Emma's response—a startled and wide-eyed look to Auggie. She stared at her father, waiting for his rebuttal. He only gazed down at the list of objects. Emma turned to Livy who shrugged, entirely helpless, because she, too, sensed what his silence portended—that Emma would share ownership of the house once Auggie went the way of all flesh. Through trench warfare and attrition, Alyssa's argument that Emma couldn't afford the house on her own had prevailed. Livy clenched her hands into fists as her gut coiled, a ticklish braid of spite against Alyssa, pity for Emma, and relief that it would be her niece, not herself, who would have to deal with Alyssa in the future. Livy had given up her share to Auggie to repay him. She felt very strongly that she didn't want to be in debt, and was glad the house would go to Emma. Two-thirds of it, anyway. Auggie had hoped for an alternative. To avoid burdening his daughter, he had even suggested selling the place. Of all things! Unthinkable. Livy put her hands into her sweater pockets. She was, frankly, disappointed in Auggie. He was wrong to allow Alyssa to manipulate him. He should have found another way.

"House, smouse," Livy said, giving a reassuring smile to Emma. "And we aren't going to throw these things away. Don't look so concerned, Auggie. I was only speaking in hypotheticals. I can take care of myself. You need not worry about *me*," she said, with the implication that he should consider Emma, who had run out of the room. Without a word, and it was perfectly clear why she wouldn't speak. Speaking was like eating: once she started, she might not be able to stop. Words were powerful. Words might express such rage. They might kill. "Whose turn is it?"

"For God's sake, it's yours!" Alyssa said. Auggie shut his eyes.

"I'll take this." Livy chose as quickly as she could so as not to be bothersome to him. The parrot bookends. Alyssa chose a huge Tiffany vase. And around and around they went, making exhausting, endless choices. Alyssa got more flushed and upset with each of her siblings' choices. Livy felt more cloyed, nearly ill with all the stuff. Auggie picked the copper sundial, greened with age. Livy clapped her hands, knowing how much Emma liked it. A shadow passed over Alyssa's face. But it was Livy's turn. The phone rang. Livy pointed to the brown ceramic cookie jar.

"No!" Alyssa's frustration exploded. "I was going to choose that."

"Then why didn't you?" Livy snapped as she walked over to answer . . . but the phone stopped ringing. A voice. Someone had answered it in the kitchen. Their mother must be home, and making tea.

"We agreed to divide things up so that we'd be compensated equally," Alyssa said. "I am taking price into account, whereas you people insist on choosing the most sentimental items."

"I don't see why I can't choose as I want. I'm an adult, and perfectly capable."

"It's not fair, Auggie. It makes no sense to put things that have no financial worth in with those that do."

"I guess we have to decide for ourselves what's of worth to us," Livy said,

"Just take the brown jar, Livy," Auggie said.

"But I want it," Alyssa said. "It's one of the very few pieces that has sentimental value for me. I haven't gotten anything that really means something to me yet."

"Your opportunity knocks. It's your turn," Auggie said. "Livy, try to pick some things of worth, otherwise, Alyssa won't get anything, nothing at all, of sentimental value."

The sisters both frowned at him, uncertain which of them had been judged most harshly.

"Go ahead, Alyssa," Auggie said.

She hesitated, then reached for the old ship's clock. Auggie, in turn, chose the champagne flutes that their mother had picked up for a song at a garage sale.

"But this makes no sense that you should get them. You won't even be around to use them." Alyssa stood in the middle of the room with a trembling chin and teary eyes.

"Oh, for God's sake, take everything," Livy snapped. "That's what you want, isn't it? You're worse than the children used to be at Christmas, surrounded by mountains of gifts but disappointed and looking for more. You're unbearable."

To put the proof in the pudding, Livy allowed herself to burst into tears. It was too awful that it was Alyssa who would be left and not Auggie. She refused to be stuck with Alyssa!

A crash. The champagne flutes. Emma had somehow come into the room and swept them off the table. Glass broken and shattered at their feet.

"Still alive?" Emma asked, and before they could respond, she continued. "Gram's been in a car accident. She's being taken to the Lawrence & Memorial Hospital. A family member has to get there as soon as possible."

"That's impossible. She just answered the phone in the kitchen," Livy said—but, of course, it hadn't been Gussie but Emma who had answered, and how surprising. A wave of dizziness. Livy sat. On the floor. It felt solid. It wasn't moving the way everything else did, so abruptly changing.

"Livy," Auggie said, his voice like a ghost's. She stared at him through blurred eyes, trying to pay attention as he directed the next hours of their lives. Alyssa was to retrieve a copy of Gussie's living will upstairs in the closet file cabinet and leave immediately. Livy would help him into the bedroom and settle him in while Emma changed out of her work clothes. Emma would drive Livy to the hospital once the hospice nurse arrived to take care of Auggie.

"Give Mother my love, Alyssa," Auggie said, to send her on her way. Alyssa hesitated, a tear trickling down her cheek.

"I didn't mean what I said earlier, Auggie," she said, kissing his cheek, then turning to hug Livy. Soft and kind, adorable. How comforting it was to have her little sister back. "This accident of Mummy's puts it all in perspective, doesn't it? None of this stuff really matters. I'm very sorry I've acted so beastly."

"People say things when under stress that they would never say otherwise," Livy said, happy to forgive and forget. "And certainly don't believe."

A heartbeat's silence.

"Well. That's the beauty of being sisters," Alyssa said. A flutter of a smile. "Under other circumstances, we'd refuse to see each other. I mean, we aren't best friends or anything. But here we are forced together, again and again, to learn something."

"And what might that be?"

"God knows, but we do keep coming back for more."

Pale but steady, Alyssa hurried off, the living will clutched in her hand. Livy stepped forward, wheeled Auggie to their father's old bedroom. She wobbled as she helped him to get from the wheelchair to the bed, made sure his medications were within reach, got him some water and the phone. He leaned back in the pillows, gray with exhaustion. He closed his eyes, his breathing short and irregular. The fluttering sensation returned to her throat, her heart. The uncomfortable feeling of having forgotten to do something, and now not being able to. Yearning to the point of nausea, as when Ed died in the heyday of their love. Three decades later, Livy was only just climbing out of the shock of it, and now this!

"What did you say, Auggie?" Livy asked.

"Why do we come back?"

"Because we're family and love each other. No matter how much we irritate and frustrate one another, at the very depths of our mis-understanding is what we've shared. Our history binds us. It's in our blood." Livy contemplated the wisdom of her very own words, feeling it even as she spoke. "And then, of course, there's Mummy. I'm sure she will be fine, Auggie," Livy whispered. "It's hard to imagine, otherwise."

Auggie didn't respond. Livy couldn't tell if he had fallen asleep or was just thinking. She couldn't bear the thought that he might be feeling as she felt every day and every hour. Afraid to be alone, facing an unknown future, and he in a body that would not heal! Skin like paper from the radiation. Infections, more tumors, and what wouldn't she do to protect him from the accompanying thoughts and fears? But one couldn't escape. No one could. Everyone mortal and creeping around the edges of an isolation that shriveled the soul, pretending everything was fine though oppressed by the emptiness and fear of life passing by and unable to stop the breathtaking changes. Losing Auggie. And now her mother. Was she already dead? What would life be without Gussie?

Livy hugged herself, wanting to cry. To hurt. To fight the bizarre sensation welling up, the lightness of a burden removed. Livy blinked, admitting for a moment a truth that she kept buried: Without her mother, she would be free to do *anything she wanted*. She would not have to consider her mother's demands and needs. Nor worry if her mother were lonely or bored, which she never seemed to be, buzzing from church meetings to garden clubs to bridge games, or collapsed happily in her chair with her letters and the phone. Yet the minute Livy had prepared herself for a quiet dinner at home and a good read, the phone would ring, and there would be her mother, asking if Livy wanted to come out for dinner or go to the theater. Her mother, screaming for attention and company. How could Livy say no? Her mother needed her. Imagine having one's life back! And money, to boot. She would travel to all the places she had read about over the years, renewing the jet-setter existence she had had with Ed when they had been so deliriously happy. She would meet interesting people who would get her a job as a consultant to the fashion magazines. She would make her own schedule, just enough work and difference to keep her busy, living the life she had expected. The one she deserved.

Auggie shifted his body, trying to get comfortable. Her tummy gurgled, and Livy caught a glimpse of a frighteningly old woman—herself—in the mirror. The sight caused her sense of levity and lightness to pitch. Her olive corduroy pants and knee-length cardigan sweater, which had seemed so fashionable when she put them on, made her look fat, repulsive, as depths of love and hate coiled around her, a noose tightening, deservedly condemning her because how dare she hope for such a loss? Such a hope might kill.

Emma came in, dressed in her running clothes, with belly bag and car keys in hand.

"Are you okay, Dad?" Emma asked as if she had never not spoken. He nodded. She touched his hand. "The nurse is due here any minute."

"Go ahead. I'll be fine."

"I can stay if you want me to." Emma voiced exactly what Livy wanted to say. It would be preferable to sit in the quiet of Auggie's room, the world screaming and swirling around them, and they safe and snug.

"Alyssa shouldn't have to make such decisions alone. You'll be more helpful at the hospital keeping my sisters apart." He tried to smile as he patted Emma's hand. She started to speak, but what good were words? Words couldn't save him. She couldn't help him. She was, in fact, quite helpless.

Livy got into the passenger seat of Auggie's VW bug. The leather smell, the sea mold. The motor's chug.

"I remember when Auggie bought this car," Livy said as Emma put it into gear and off they went in a swirl of dust. "1975."

"I was thirteen. Learning *en pointe*. It hurt like hell. I wanted Dad to come save me. I used to listen for the motor, hoping he'd come pick me up and whisk me out for lunch or some crazy thing like that. He never did."

"He had to work."

"What does that matter now?" Emma asked, her voice sharp. She could be quite fierce. Attacking her father as if he had done something wrong. Of course, she was upset, maybe even angry, at life. Not Auggie. One couldn't be angry at Auggie. That would be like being angry at one's mother. And what had she ever done wrong? Guilt and a sense of her own meanness washed over Livy. All those bad thoughts she had had. The wish that her mother would—Livy couldn't even think it.

They were quiet as they drove down Bittersweet Lane. When they reached the railroad tracks, Emma stopped the car. As the family had for years, they lowered the windows and listened. Livy held her breath. Train blast or silence? Emma hit the gas pedal. They crossed over the tracks. It always felt so dangerous! They made it across, passing the old oak on the side of the road with its scar where Auggie had crashed learning how to drive a stick shift at age thirteen, then up onto Route 1. They picked up speed on the old highway. A new road shot off to the west, leading to a new series of houses where the old Charles farm used to spread for miles, now divided. The train tracks paralleled the road to the east, across alternating lawns and marshes, and the ocean stretched beyond. A fried seafood diner where there used to be a field full of horses grazing. A dead possum on the roadside. An omen? They reached I-95.

"Loren was right, you know," Emma said, her hands at ten and two of the steering wheel, effective and in control as they rocketed up onto the highway. "I do lack that *je ne sais quoi* that motivates people. Every time I start something, I get all excited about it, but then lose interest when the real work begins. Strange. With ballet, I loved the drudgery of it, the repetition. It was so clear why I was doing it. Whereas now, everything is just a drag. When Loren said that, I realized that I must have been looking for an excuse to quit. That I wanted to quit because it was too hard, that I'm just plain lazy."

"Don't be ridiculous. You were heartbroken."

"And so I came back here to heal. Thank goodness I had this

place. Although we don't heal here, do we? In one's imagination it's an Eden, but stay here, live here, and the reality sets in. We heal in a pustulant way. We fester. That's why Dad doesn't want me to get the house."

"Of course he does. You're just making up reasons not to take it. Pustulant? For pity's sake, don't be so bitter. You need to live your life, Emma, and be grateful. We only have this one. Be content with it. Mediocrity is perfectly okay, if that's what suits you."

"I am better than mediocre," Emma said, fiercely, and Livy remembered when she had felt that way. "I've failed my potential. That's why I don't go backstage to visit with Thea after seeing her dance. I go to every show I can, but have never dared say hello. It's too humiliating."

Livy didn't reply. Emma was determined to be unhappy. Looking so closely at one's actions was uncomfortable. Acting or not acting. . . Looking back at your hopes and dreams strewn on the path of life was a wonderful way to make yourself miserable. Livy refused to do it. Far better to be in the present and looking to the future, with all its potential!

"I wonder if she did it on purpose," Emma said, after a while. "By mistake."

"What?"

"Gram and this accident. The hospice nurse, Rosemary, told me that she thinks we need our illnesses."

"Need them?" Livy looked at her and wondered at how easily Emma had fallen back into communication. Talking again. It must be like drinking. "Who needs to be sick?"

"It's not a conscious thing. According to her, physical sickness is an outward manifestation of something that's going on inside us, and it's up to each of us to decide whether we want to deal with it or not. She thinks illness gives us an excuse to relax, to finally let go of our safety nets. Like Dad calling the nurse in again and again. He's so used to holding everything in. He wants to connect but doesn't have the words to express himself."

"That's ridiculous," Livy said. "He knows all those languages, and he's so intellectual. He puts everything together so nicely. Did you know his nurse in the hospital had read all his works? She had found them transformational. An entirely new perspective on history and the world. She said they had determined her life. When he pointed out to her that she is a nurse, not an historian, she said, *Exactly. Thanks to you, Sir. Self-determination.*"

"I guess," Emma said, after a while. "I think Gram is having more trouble with this move than we give her credit for. Maybe she's asking for something."

"She has always gotten exactly what she wanted," Livy replied, her chin trembling. She stared out the window. A blur of tears. She gritted her teeth and smiled. "Everything she's wanted. I've made sure of that. I just hope she isn't in pain."

"That's what I'm talking about. Maybe she can't express her pain." Livy looked at Emma, buffaloed by what she was saying.

"Mummy is a very strong woman. If something is bothering her, she might not say it out loud. In fact, she won't. But she makes perfectly clear what she needs."

The highway was full of enormous trucks, passing, buffeting the VW. Emma's grip on the wheel tightened as she focused on getting them to their destination alive.

"Which would you prefer, Aunt Livy," Emma asked, "to be in chronic pain or to die?"

"Our family has a high threshold for pain," Livy said, getting a Kleenex and her pack of cigarettes out of her black satchel.

"Meaning?" Emma asked.

"It doesn't hurt as much," Livy said, and blew her nose. "We think of it as uncomfortable, not pain, per se."

"It's still pain."

Livy laughed her delighted "ha!" of a laugh. Her bracelets jingled. "Emma, your expression is priceless," she said. "So severe and serious. Such a stoic."

"Me the stoic?" Emma said. "You're the one who says you don't feel pain."

"High threshold, I said. We can live with pain." Livy lit her cigarette with the car lighter.

"In other words, you choose chronic pain."

"It's not a choice, is it? People live in pain or die of it. *C'est la vie.*"

"No one dies of pain," Emma said. "They just want to. Like Gram."

Livy filled her lungs with smoke. The word *transference* came to mind. Livy reached over and gave Emma's hand a squeeze. It was icy cold. They took the exit for New London and began the series of turns one took to get to the hospital.

"How is your therapy going, Emma?"

"Did you know you can't just numb part of yourself?" Emma asked in reply, her eyes shuttering. "If you try to shut down one part of you, your whole self shuts down. Shut down sadness, you won't feel happy. Shut down anger, you won't feel joy. My therapist fired me because I didn't know that. She said I wasn't taking therapy seriously. I'd change the subject just when we were getting to something. Laugh when I should have cried. Or just as I was leaving, I'd mention some major point. Mostly, she said I wasn't telling her things, and that when I did get around to talking about anything that mattered, about the feelings, it was all from the head, so what was the point of continuing?"

"That's ridiculous, *from the head*," Livy said. "What does she mean?"

Emma shrugged. "All I know is I felt like an eel."

"You are a wonderful, caring, warm person, Emma." Livy bristled. "That therapist should be sued. What right does she have to say all that to you?"

"You can't sue a therapist for telling the truth," Emma said. Her eyes filled with tears as she smiled. "That's what you pay them to hear, isn't it?"

"My therapist holds my hand," Livy said, admiring the boniness of her fingers and wrists, and her webs of blue veins. "She sees exactly how I am, and allows me to be."

"Isn't the point of therapy to go to the next step, and change?

That means being aware of how we are, and that's the worst part," Emma said, her voice slightly raised, as if to be heard above a din. "Not knowing you're doing it. How weird is that? The mind goes along, doing things behind the scenes that we've no idea about, or we do but don't want to think about it. Or we might want to but we can't control it. Even though we think we're in control."

"My, my," Livy said, lighting another cigarette, though she had one smoldering in the ashtray. "All this talk and no thought to Mummy. How mean of us. We should pray for her."

Emma stopped the car at a stoplight. She stared ahead of her, not moving even after the light turned green.

"Emma? The light."

Emma looked at Livy.

"We are talking about Gram, aren't we? She said she wanted to walk gracefully into old age and die a noble death, to control death. She's like us, trying to control what we can't control. We starve. We run. But we can't control life or death. The only thing we can control is ourselves, and can we even do that?"

They fell silent for the rest of the trip. Emma offered to drop Livy at the entrance, but Livy insisted they go in together. Parking, and the walk, gave Livy a few more moments to compose herself. She wanted to be perfectly together for the upsets to come.

They followed the receptionist's directions to an elevator. Up two floors. Down halls reeking of antiseptic fighting the putrid smells of digestion and illness. A flutter of her heart, nervous anticipation of what she knew was to come. A fifth sense. Her mother, lying on a gurney bed, the front of it raised so she could breathe. An oxygen mask over her swollen face. Eyes closed. Swaddled in sheets and blankets, tubes sucking and pumping in and out of her shrunken body. Emma was right. That was exactly what her mother didn't want, tubes! She wanted a noble death, and Livy determined that she would fight Alyssa on that. She knew Alyssa wouldn't let their mother go. Their mother, who was struggling to breathe her last as a nurse pushed open the door and stepped aside.

The window was bright against the dimness of the room. Alyssa's head bowed.

"Is she dead?" Livy stepped forward, braced for the news. Alyssa started and looked at Livy. She smiled wryly and pointed to their mother. Sitting up in bed. Eyes open, a Band-Aid over her left eye, black and green.

"Imagine it!" Gussie expostulated, hopping mad. "The policeman gave me a ticket! For pity's sake. Anyone could fall asleep at the wheel."

Livy burst into tears as the reality hit her. Relief, of course, not disappointment.

"Isn't this a happy surprise?" Emma grinned. She gave her grandmother a kiss on the cheek. "The nurse on the phone gave me the impression you were a goner, Gram."

"Mother was being difficult," Alyssa explained. "She has a bridge game this afternoon and every intention of going to it, broken rib and black eye notwithstanding."

"Mummy, you hate those games," Livy sniffed. She looked for a Kleenex. This was all so . . . usual. "You make any excuse not to go."

"That's when it's my prerogative."

"In any case, we found a compromise," Alyssa said. "I called Kitty and they're delaying the start by two hours. It will be a dinner instead of tea."

"Are you up for it, Gram?" Emma asked. "A broken rib must be uncomfortable."

"Oh, they've bandaged me all up," Gussie said, smiling brightly. Her front tooth was missing. "It doesn't hurt a bit. Besides, the bone is only bent, not broken. Those young doctors have no idea. I'll mend soon enough. There's certainly no sense in lolling about feeling sorry for myself. How is Auggie?"

"Fine, Gram. He's home resting. Alyssa, did you call to tell him Gram's okay?"

"I haven't had a second," Alyssa replied, flushing at what she took to be criticism.

"Dear boy," Gussie said. She stared out the window. Squinted her eyes. Her chin trembled. She blinked. "Such a beautiful, bright sun. It makes my eyes water."

She patted them dry with her bedsheet. None of them answered. Rather, they all got busy organizing who would do what. Emma excused herself to call her father and run home. Which Alyssa said was crazy, to run fifteen miles with two perfectly fine cars. But that's what Emma did, she ran—and, as Livy told Alyssa, it wasn't for her aunts to judge.

Preparations for transferring Gussie out of the hospital and to the assisted living facility of The Harbor View were briefly hindered by Gussie's insistence that she be allowed to go home. Alyssa and Livy deferred to the doctors, who took the brunt of Gussie's wrath. Alyssa followed the ambulance to The Harbor View while Livy, heartbroken for her mother, drove the VW back to the house. She stopped in to check on Auggie. He was sitting up, watching the nurse rip apart a paperback copy of Vol. II of *Remembrances of Things Past* so he would have manageable pieces of the book to hold up and read.

"Everything is fine," Livy said, sitting down on the bed next to him. She told him about their mother's broken rib. Her black eyes. The tooth.

"You know, Auggie," Livy confided. "I found the hospital fascinating. There is so much going on. All the patients coming in and out. The doctors talking about this and that case and what was to be done. It made me think what a good doctor I would be. I so like to help people. I think I might apply to medical school." She smiled, excited by the prospect and looking to Auggie for validation. He said nothing. In fact, he wouldn't meet her eyes, causing a recognition on both their parts. Tears sparked in Livy's eyes. He didn't believe in her.

"Of course, it's a good deal of hard work to get into medical school, and it will cost money. But if we talked to Mum—"

"Livy," Auggie interrupted, and touched her hand with his. It felt like ice. "I can't help you anymore. I'm sorry."

"But I'm an idiot to go on like this." Livy laughed and stood up, her heart crushed and mortified and maybe a little afraid. "You've had a big day."

"Our dreams of grandeur," he said, and indicated for her to sit back down. "Livy, do you remember that awful weekend years ago—the club dance?"

"When Father was such a baboon. How could I forget it?"

"Was he so bad?"

"Don't sentimentalize the old man, dear brother."

"I wasn't going to. I only wonder. We were so convinced she would leave him. Live her own life."

"I figured that out ages ago, Auggie. She never intended to leave. It's too comfortable. She's been quite content."

"It's hard to challenge oneself here. One falls into an eddy of life. Finding all sorts of troubles where most people wouldn't have the luxury to look. Sometimes, I think that none of us have . . . fledged. We've never truly broken free from here. I don't want Emma to get stuck too."

Livy sat up, tense at the implicit condemnation of her own choices.

"Stuck?" she asked. "That's an odd word choice. Emma's thrilled to be getting the house. The two of you have been having a grand time drawing up plans for the renovations. Besides, I certainly don't know of any options. The house has to be dealt with somehow. It's only too bad Alyssa and Renny built their house. It would have made the most sense for Alyssa to get this one. For myself, I'm just glad not to be in debt. I don't owe anyone anything and intend to keep it that way."

Livy gave a firm nod of her head and felt proud of herself. She had stood her ground, though Auggie looked at her as if she had done something wrong. As if she had not understood him at all. "Don't worry, Auggie," she added to comfort him. "Emma will figure things out for herself, just as we all have."

"Have we?" Auggie asked.

"Of course. Though I do wonder," Livy said, feeling suddenly quite outraged—judged and angry!—"how in God's name we got to be so old? I was supposed to have done things. I know that. Everyone expected so much of me. So did I. Remember how full of hope we were?" Then the flare of frustration died into a sense of helplessness. Livy shrugged. They sat quiet until Livy suppressed a yawn. "Oh, my. I can't think, I'm so tired."

"And I'm so tired, I can't read," Auggie said. "I have only my thoughts. That's never happened. I've always had something to occupy me."

"I'm sorry, Auggie. Shall I read to you?"

He shook his head, and she realized that wasn't what he had meant. She waited quietly for him to explain, when what she really wanted to do was go home to a hot fire and a cold drink.

"When you bring things down to their essence, it really is just about the day, isn't it? And the people," Auggie said. "I was more fortunate than I'd any idea about. I had two great loves. Pat and Nan. Only I wasn't able to appreciate them. Too busy avoiding what they offered me."

"Pat?" Livy repeated. She stared at Auggie. He had a look of such surprise, like a young boy holding up a grain of sand as if it signified an entire world that he had just discovered. But that thought dissolved into a sense of significance and importance, because, for the first time ever, she was there to comfort her brother while he cried. His shoulders shook in such a way that she thought he might die right there in her arms. She felt grateful to be there for him, if afraid because she was used to it being the other way around, and how uncomfortable it was to hold another's pain. She would never want to feel such pain. And yet, as he lay back in bed and she tucked him in, he looked at peace.

She turned out the light and hurried home. It was dusk. The cold air clipped her nostrils shut. A squirrel rustled the leaves. An owl. The wind worried the evergreens as she stepped into the stillness of her house. The cold pine air followed her in, cutting the stale smell of sour milk and wood ashes. Her coat, mittens, and gloves dropped onto the grayed white Formica tile floor. Chipped, broken, and one entirely missing. The place was falling apart, but who had time to fix it? No messages blinked on the answering machine, and medical school did seem like the answer. She had been such a help to Auggie just now, and always read the Science section of *The New York Times*. She would be able to support herself, at least once she got through the schooling bit. Auggie need not worry about her!

Livy poured herself a drink, then leaned against the kitchen counter. The dusk view of the harbor, the sun reflecting on the village, and the whitecaps of the glistening blue-gray water. Her children flitted through her mind: Griffin, in the Peace Corps in Congo; and Joy, living with her boyfriend somewhere in California. She would call them about their grandmother later. Maybe tomorrow. After she had begun the process of applying to medical school. Livy took her drink and moved to light the fire that she had laid before going over to her mother's house that morning. How naive she had been! How much she had grown and learned since then. It was incredible to think of all that could happen in one short day. A brief and overwhelming thought: filling out the applications and calling around to have her transcripts sent. Would she have enough science credits?

If not a doctor, then a nurse. Nurses did more of the caretaking, and with all her years of taking care of others, she had life experience for her resume. Finally—she could feel it!—she was taking her life into her own hands. She would do what she wanted to do— she should volunteer to be a candy striper. That way she could start immediately, and create no debt. Auggie would be so proud of her!

She struck a match. The paper caught fire, burning the twigs, the flames reaching up to blacken the wood. She thought about Auggie, and what it must feel like to be really dying. His vast intellect contemplating the past and future. Those tears. What had Emma said, something about needing sickness? Ridiculous thought. She wouldn't think about it. It was too depressing. The fire caught. Nice, dry wood. Cheerfully snapping, a sound to keep her company as she picked up her book, her drink, and headed for her favorite place in the world. Her secret place. Not even her therapist knew. Only her best friend, Boodles. Gin. The only thing she could really count on.

Livy stepped into her coat closet and sat down in her seat, a Revival-style armchair with a down comforter over the back, and her mink coat, bought on sale years before. The softness of its embrace brought tears to her eyes, it was so unbearably comfortable. She took a deep breath. Mothballs and cedar, a tad of mold lingering in the clothes hanging above her, the aromatic smell of gin. She set her drink down on the floor next to her ashtray and reached into the coat's pockets. A spritz of perfume, a smear of lipstick, her pearls. Fully prepared, enveloped by a sense of safety and control, she stared out at the wall-to-ceiling plate glass windows, through the reflection of the fire burning, to the wind blowing across the black, ruffled waters.

A knock. On the sliding door into the kitchen. She didn't want to see anyone! Livy stubbed out her cigarette and turned off the light. The kitchen door slid open. Emma called her name. Livy listened, eyes wide, fingers pressed against her lips, debating. She could just step out of the closet, act as if she had been looking for something, but then she would have to talk. And the gin smell. She wasn't supposed to be drinking. Livy reached out and slowly shut the closet door to just a crack, listening to Emma's movements in the living room. The fire burning. Livy's fingers clenched into fists. The fire would give her away! Emma's footsteps came across the room to right outside the closet. Livy could see Emma, beet red from her run, the sweat dried by the heat of her body, her eyes red from the salt, seeming to look directly into her own eyes.

"Livy?" Emma said. She looked so sad. All that talk about Auggie. Owning the house with Alyssa. Death all around. Livy girded herself. She should help Emma. Clearly Emma needed an older, wiser person to lean on.

But no. To Livy's relief, Emma backed off and away, out of the house through the kitchen. The door shut behind her, leaving Livy alone. A toast with Boodles. Some difficulty lighting her cigarette because her hands shook so, and she must have forgotten to wind the clock because the house was terribly quiet and still. A flash of discomfort and confusion, abject fear. A welling of tears that might overwhelm if allowed to fall. But it was only pity. Livy pitied Emma, who had yet to learn as Livy had learned to live. Like Tibetan monks. They live in bliss because they recognize life's emptiness. They live on nothing at all, and have learned to like it.

Having reminded herself of that, Livy opened her book and began to read.

Thanksgiving
November 1994

The luxurious smell of onions, celery, and carrots caramelizing in hot, melted butter permeated the kitchen. Alyssa gave the vegetables a quick stir, then returned to frosting Livy's birthday cake. For old times' sake. Ever since she was a child, Alyssa had made a Duncan Hines Devil's Food cake for Livy's birthday. Every single year, even if it wasn't convenient. It had been a tradition—and here was the cake, frosted and decorated, but no Livy to protest that she didn't like chocolate. Only the rest of the family, gathered so that the day wouldn't seem so lonely and empty. Alyssa's throat ached with tears. For all the conflicts she'd had with them, her siblings had been the only two people in the world who had truly understood her. She missed them, and regretted her quarrel with Livy those last months. If only Alyssa had followed Auggie's age-old advice to be more generous. Which, as she licked the frosting off her fingers, Alyssa resolved she would be on this first Thanksgiving Day that Livy wasn't there to enjoy.

The beep of the kitchen smoke detector announced the roast turkey's doneness just as Auggie's 1975 VW Beetle chugged round the curve of the drive; Emma considered it a point of pride to keep it going. Alyssa opened the oven door. A wave of intense heat. A car door creaked open, slammed shut. Alyssa lifted the turkey onto a clean platter and scraped all the crunchy pieces of flesh and skin from the pan, saving the juices for later. Footsteps crunched on the frosted gravel drive and up the gray slate sidewalk. She tested one small piece. Perfection. The door into the kitchen opened where the porcelain double sink used to be. The smell of cold and dead leaves whirled in, freshening the warmth of the kitchen and dining room.

"I'm home!" Emma announced, flushed and excited, her arms full of grocery bags and packages, a knapsack on her shoulders. Tall and lanky, as were all Michaels women, Emma had her mother, Nan's, disorganized air, with her hair half out of her ponytail and the bags dropping out of her arms more than being set down. "I'm so glad you're already here, Alyssa. You've made it so warm and cozy."

Niece and aunt hugged, genuinely glad to see each other. Alyssa stepped back and watched, wide-eyed and with growing alarm, as Emma began to unpack her groceries. The makings for an entire Thanksgiving meal. Emma chatted: she had seen her cousins walking but knew there was too much to do to join them; she had gone to see her former dancing friend, Thea, dance, and invited her to Thanksgiving dinner; and she had a twenty-eight-pound turkey, dressed and ready to go in the car, did Alyssa think that was big enough? Then she noticed Alyssa's turkey.

"What's that?" Emma asked.

"The Thanksgiving turkey, of course. Farm fresh, free range, and thirty pounds. It cooked faster than I thought it would. But at least it's ready. We're to eat at two o'clock. Why have you brought all this food?"

Alyssa indicated the glut of food that now littered the kitchen island counter. Emma held very still as she looked around, this time noting the roasted vegetables, the sweet potatoes topped with marshmallows ready for browning, all the baked goodies, the salad, the creamed onions . . . Alyssa turned off the heat under the now caramelized ingredients for the stuffing.

"We agreed weeks ago that I would host Thanksgiving," Emma said. "Dinner is to be at six."

"Gus and Crystal have to leave by five o'clock to catch their flight," Alyssa replied, busying herself by covering the turkey with tin foil, crimping the edges.

"I don't know anything about that, Alyssa. You were the one who wanted to eat at six. You said you'd tell everyone. I told you I'd be here at eleven unless I heard otherwise. Here I am." Emma spoke with all the sensibility of Auggie, making the facts line up to prove Alyssa wrong. It felt accusatory and unfair. After all, Emma was never around. Alyssa had practically forgotten that she was coming, and now here she was, breezing in without a boo.

"Emma, I haven't heard a peep from you in weeks and weeks."

"I have a phone. You could have called."

Alyssa smiled with as much resolution and generosity as she could muster.

"I'm sorry for my part in this misunderstanding. However, I have a full house to worry about. I couldn't risk there being no food."

"Well, we don't have that problem now, do we?" Emma put on a quick, offended smile, then picked up her knapsack. "I'll take my things upstairs, then figure out what to do with all the extras."

"Upstairs?"

Emma looked at Alyssa, her eyes shuttered. "Yes. To my room."

"I already said. The house is full."

Emma stood silent for a breath. Two.

"No one asked my permission to stay here," she finally said. "Except Gram. I told her she could stay in the study."

"Impossible. The grandchildren have their tents all set up in Daddy's room. Joy is in the front guest room. Pam and Julia are in the back room."

Emma marched through the dining room into the living room and up the stairs. Alyssa hesitated and then decided it might be best to go with her. When they reached Emma's room—what had used to be Auggie's room, combined with Livy's room into a master bedroom and bath—Alyssa had to admit that, if looked at from Emma's perspective . . . Alyssa could appreciate the surprise, if not the accompanying wrath.

Months before—it had been that long since Emma had been back—Alyssa had decided it would be rejuvenating to spend a night in her old family home, test what it felt like to sleep there after all the changes Emma had forced through. Alyssa had brought clean sheets and towels, and a book. It had been fun, in a heart-breaking way, to figure out where, exactly, Livy had used to sleep, and to move the bed there. The next night, she'd replaced Auggie's worn-to-the-nub Turkish Kilim with her own father's deep piled, American-made rug. Softer on the feet. A better lamp. Some clothes to change into. The room had gradually become more familiar as Alyssa's belongings replaced Emma's. Renny had admonished her, but life in that other house wasn't as comforting. She wasn't herself there, with him, and it was luxurious to have a bed to herself, space to breathe, and the ability to do whatever she wanted to: stay up late, get up early. For the first time in her life, she felt in control. As if her decisions were hers alone. Staying at her childhood home had, indeed, been rejuvenating. Certainly, it had not felt as if she were doing something wrong, which was how Emma made her feel, staring into her bedroom.

"Where did you put all my things?" Emma asked, walking over to the bed and picking up the photo of Alyssa's children when they were children that was on the bedside table.

"In the attic. I didn't want anything to get broken by the grand-children. Emma, you can't expect things to be exactly the same if you arrive from out of the blue after months of not being around."

"Actually, that's exactly what I can expect. It's my house. If anyone stays here, they are supposed to tell me, and pay a ten-dollar fee per person per night to help me pay for keeping the house in toilet paper and olive oil."

"Well." Alyssa felt her face flush. Would Emma actually charge her that usurious fee? "If you plan to stay the night, I'll change the sheets and move next door."

"Don't bother. I'm not staying."

Alyssa bit her tongue. If Emma didn't intend to stay, then what was all the to-do about? The beep of a car's horn sounded.

"That will be Renny with Mummy," Alyssa said. Neither woman moved, each waiting for the other. In the end, Emma left to go downstairs. Alyssa adjusted the picture frame and plumped the pillow on the bed. Her hand shook slightly. She felt fragile. At loose ends. Everything had been going so nicely, all peaceable and calm, until Emma showed up. What could Alyssa have done differently? She had no idea, but felt sick about the whole interaction.

Misty-eyed, Alyssa headed downstairs, leaning on the railing that still bore the claw marks of her mother's Siamese cat, Tipper. As she crossed the living room, she looked out to the porch and was startled to see two men standing at the fire pit, drinking beers. It took her a moment to place them. Max, of course, pale and distinguished, with the same debonair manner and slenderness as his father, Renny; and Gus, shaven-headed, solid, and square-jawed. It jarred Alyssa to think that those two towering males were her sons. She still expected her skinny, red-faced little boys to run around the corner, hiccuping with the joy of being chased by Renny, holding high a bucket of water. She regretted the soft down on their chins almost as much as the loss of the companionship of her siblings and her misunderstanding with Emma, whom she could hear outside on the driveway side of the house. Emma and Renny were reminding Gussie of how it had used to be before the renovations. Four years ago. Had it already been so long since the walls were torn down, entrances moved, the familiar replaced with the strange? A fierce resentment welled up. Alyssa had warned Emma, and now it had come to pass: Gussie's voice sounded befuddled and upset as they stepped into the house. Gussie was preceded by her walker—a convenience more than a necessity, customized as it had been by her grandsons with hooks and baskets. It was convenient, too, for those around her. A quick study of the walker's incidentals indicated the length of time Gussie intended to stay. Alyssa grimaced. An overnight bag.

"Hello, Mummy." Alyssa stepped forward, overwhelmed and half-resentful of Auggie and Livy for being dead and so well out of it. It fell on Alyssa's shoulders, Gussie's expectation that she could stay the night, even on days when she was invited only for tea or Thanksgiving dinner. Before, when Livy was alive and Alyssa could teach by example, the responsibility had been satisfactory, proving Alyssa's generosity of spirit as opposed to Livy's resentful one. But now her mother's demands had begun to grate on Alyssa's nerves. Especially with the added necessity of a rubber mat on the bed. "What a treat that you're here. I'm sorry I couldn't pick you up myself."

"We had a fine time," Gussie said as Renny helped to take off her coat. "Renny took me to see Livy's place, now her house is gone. What a deep hole they have dug for their basement. I was scared to go anywhere near it."

"It must have upset you terribly," Alyssa said, looking at Renny, bewildered that he would do such a thing.

"Not at all. I wanted to see it. It's a lovely site for a new home," Gussie said. "I just don't understand why they would build so low. The first hurricane will have them swimming."

"Gram?" Emma leaned toward Gussie discreetly. "Why don't we go to the bathroom?"

"Go ahead," Gussie replied, walking through what had used to be a wall separating the kitchen from the dining room. Now there stood a granite island counter. It was shaped like an eggplant, with a raised countertop for people to sit at while others worked in the kitchen or relaxed around the dining room table. Alyssa had chosen the raised counter as the place where the desserts would preside: the apple crisp, the chocolate-pecan and lemon meringue pies, the chocolate cake and gingersnap cookies. She had not been able to decide what to make and so made them all, and now had the pleasure of watching her mother pick up a gingersnap with her knobby fingers. Gussie bit into it. Her eyes closed briefly with contentment, and for a moment Alyssa saw her siblings—their eyes, their brows, the moles on their right nostrils. They all loved and appreciated such a small thing as a cookie. Alyssa's eyes teared. Her nose flared. The distinct odor of urine marred the sugar and spice smells of the kitchen.

"Are you sure, Mummy? Sometimes I find I have to go even when I don't think I do."

"Isn't it lovely in here, warm and cozy?" Gussie smiled in stubborn response. "The delicious smells."

"It is going to be a wonderful day," Alyssa replied with a smile of her own, and then added, "It's a shame you can't stay the night. Every room and bed is taken up both here and at my house."

"There's always room for one more," Gussie said. "It's much more fun if one stays in the thick of it."

"Mummy, I'm sorry." Alyssa girded herself. She would have to be firm. "You'll be comfortable and welcome until the grandchildren go to bed, but then I will have to drive you home."

Alyssa's smile brightened as Gussie's faded.

"This is my home," Gussie said, her jaw fixed.

"We have had this discussion before, Mother. You live at The Harbor View now. You moved years ago."

"I was forced to move, kicking and screaming."

"Oh, for pity's sake, Mother," Alyssa said. "That wasn't how it was and you know it."

Gussie looked at Alyssa. Her posture straightened with disappointment. Alyssa reached for a canister of peanuts. Her mother had done this her entire life, asked for, and it was done. She was the most fortunate woman Alyssa knew, and still her mother asked for more.

"I am incredibly grateful that you are here to enjoy another Thanksgiving meal with us, Mummy. Just not overnight. I can't do overnight. It's too much all by myself, and after cooking this entire meal. I'm sorry."

"Don't take it personally, Gram," Emma said. "There's no room here for me, either."

Alyssa looked at Emma, stunned. "How can you say such a thing? I told you I would clear out of your room if you wanted it. It's no trouble at all. Of course there's room for you."

"Just like you used to say to Gram."

"An entirely different situation. She is more than welcome, but she can't just pronounce when she's coming and for how long."

"I invited her, Alyssa," Emma said.

The sliding doors rolled open. Ruddy-cheeked and invigorated by a long walk in the fresh air, the family swarmed into the open layout of the dining room and kitchen, shouting greetings: Max's wife Betsy (Alyssa's good daughter-in-law) and their children, Milly and Elise; Gus's children, Olive, Benjamin, and Winston; Julia with her partner Pam; and Joy and her gaggle—five children. It seemed irresponsible these days to have so many, but the acorn didn't fall far from the tree, and there they were, Livy's grandchildren: Eddie, Chris, Lila, Augusta, and Bill, all shrieking for the attention of their great-grandmother, who adored it, patting each child on the head and saying his or her name.

"But where's the birthday girl?" Gussie asked, looking around. "I want to wish her a happy birthday."

"Livy's dead, Gussie," Betsy said, matter-of-fact and efficient as she took the pillow Emma slipped her to be used to guard whatever chair Gussie chose to occupy. "She died last Halloween. We were all here for the funeral. Remember? We agreed to have Thanksgiving together this year."

"Oh, yes, of course," Gussie tsked. "How silly of me to forget. But then where is Griffin? Is he dead, too?"

"In Congo," Alyssa said. "He stayed there after his stint with the Peace Corps. The government employs him now."

"Really!"

"Don't you remember?" Alyssa pleaded with her to remember. "He got married there."

"Not to a darkie, I hope."

"Mummy! You met and loved her, and their two beautiful children."

"Of course, I did." Gussie smiled gamely as she tried to dredge up the memory. "It's a shame they aren't here. Griffin makes the best cocktails, and I would love a drink."

Max offered Gussie his bartending expertise and arm. Off they went to the liquor cabinet, now located in the living room.

"Not too strong, Max," Alyssa called after them. Her chin trembled as the rest of the family followed, three-year-old Lila pushing Gussie's cart. Alyssa waved off offers of help. After all, who could help? What Alyssa wanted was her mother, the mother who had used to be politically correct and unprejudiced; who had read *The Christian Science Monitor* for its objectivity; and had joined the Hemlock Society so as not to live too long. Alyssa wanted that mother back. She wanted her back now.

The doors between the living room and dining room closed to keep the fireplace in the living room from sucking all the heat out of the dining room. The liveliness of conversation on the other side of the wall contrasted sharply with the silence in the kitchen.

"I'm going to bake some rolls," Emma said.

"We don't need rolls," Alyssa replied, and indicated the three loaves of garlic bread that she had prepared that were ready to pop into the oven.

"Alyssa, you've already taken over the whole meal. The least you can do is let me bake some stupid rolls."

Be generous, Alyssa reminded herself. She would be more generous if it killed her.

"You can make anything you want to, Emma. It just seems as if there is already too much."

"There's never been a problem of too much before."

They were quiet while Emma put away everything she had brought and added her prepared foods to Alyssa's, as if there would be a contest between them. Alyssa washed the turkey pan with a scrubby, the pan banging against the sink, and wondered at Emma's relentless worrying of who had what, where, and how much. Alyssa made room in the oven for Emma's *rolls*. They looked dull and tasteless as Emma removed them, one pasty white blob after another, from the pan they had been rising in and put them onto a cookie sheet.

"It must be hard for you to see Gram getting old," Emma said.

"Mummy's practically normal," Alyssa said sharply, putting the kettle on to boil. She got out a large stainless steel bowl and set it down too hard on the counter next to the stove. Two bags of Pepperidge Farm stuffing. The cooked vegetables. More butter.

"It's strange," Emma persisted. "She can be entirely with it, then boom, off she goes into the hinterlands."

"It couldn't have helped matters for Renny to take her to Livy's."

"Gram said it looks like it used to when she was young, now they've cleared it. Who would have guessed Livy had such a fantastic view?"

"I would have. This whole area was pasture land when I was a girl," Alyssa said, and then took the opportunity to put Livy's wish for a view into perspective. "I never understood why Livy didn't maintain her property. She'd clip and trim the bare minimum to keep the path clear down to the beach, not wanting to harm all those junk shrubs and bushes, and yet when it came down to that magnificent spruce, she had no mercy."

Emma didn't respond. Alyssa tried to think what else to say, because somehow and once again, she felt as if she were the one at fault, the small-minded, unpleasant one. Down to the last breath. Because Livy had claimed that the only thing she wanted was a view of the harbor from her bedroom, and so Alyssa had had to fight to save the towering spruce tree blocking it. The tree was on their mother's property, after all, not Livy's. But one day, Emma, in a snit, had gone out and chopped it down. Just like that. As if she owned the place! Which, of course, she did, but if Emma had contained herself, the tree would still grace the property. Livy had died only two weeks later. For most of those last days, she had stared out at the view, the water sparkling, the horizon suggesting all the possibilities it had ever had, unattainable though they were. Even now, Alyssa could see Livy's expression, so like her girl self: quietly awed by the fearsome beauty of the world. It would have been best for Livy to die facing out like that, but the stairs. She had had to be on the first floor of her house in the end, and the guest bedroom was in the back, quite dark and chilling, smelling like a wet basement.

Alyssa had gone to see her that last morning. Livy was facing the wall, her mouth open as if she were surprised. It had been such a surprise to think that Livy wasn't there anymore. Alyssa was so used to her. All her wonderful qualities. Even her struggles exemplified Livy's Pollyanna perspective of life as fun. Full of curiosities. Which had led to her expensive dabbling in erudition. The B.A. in English, followed by one in biology, then botany. Her final excursion: playing the part of candy striper, as if it were her job to make people happy. Life a game, and so evanescent. Livy had passed, leaving Alyssa full of the regret at that silly tiff, like so many things in Alyssa's life that she wished she could redo.

"Livy loved her plants," Emma said, spraying the rolls in preparation for the oven. "She had an appreciation of the little things in life. A wonder at them."

"It seems one should do more with oneself than wonder," Alyssa said. "Of course, that was Livy. She never really grew up. I was always the one having to be responsible. I wish that, for one minute, she had been a stronger person. It would have made all the difference."

"Everyone can't be as efficient and together as you, Alyssa," Emma said, and it was as if being that way were a bad thing, the way she said it. "I wish the new owners had given her more time. I feel as if Livy were rushed away."

"I think they showed great restraint," Alyssa countered as Emma took over the oven. "It's been nearly a year that they've owned it. It was full of dead squirrels. The downstairs had flooded. The house felt as if it were dying. I couldn't help but think how decadent it is, not living in a house you own."

The oven door slammed shut.

"You're right," Emma said. Alyssa stiffened at her tone of voice. "I've been thinking that, too. How decadent it is for me to own a house like this and not live here."

"I wasn't talking about this one."

"When I'm not here and think about this place?" Emma continued as if Alyssa hadn't spoken. "I get homesick. I think of how pleasant it is. The light-filled, wide-open rooms. So many places to read and nap and entertain. And the land, with all the specimen trees and bushes that Gramps and Gram planted. And, of course, the cabin. I spent hours and hours in there, stretching and practicing. In my imagination, this place nurtures and heals. It's a refuge."

"Of course it is. It's home, even with all the changes. It's the place to come back to when life overwhelms us."

Emma looked over at Alyssa, who was thinking about her bedroom upstairs. Not the one she had tried to recreate but the original room. The sunny, front bedroom, before it became her mother's. Before misunderstandings and loss. When she was a girl, and happy.

"That's what I imagine," Emma said. "That's why I was looking forward to today. I thought being here at the house, hanging out with everyone, would be like old times. But the reality is, I come here and there's no room for me."

"Don't be ridiculous."

"I'm not being ridiculous. I don't use it except for an occasional holiday and a week or so in summer. The cousins use it, and you do." Emma paused, as if to make a point. "But not me."

Alyssa frowned.

"That's your choice, not to use it, Emma. You sound just like Livy, complaining about having to move back here every summer so she could pay the property taxes on her place. She never appreciated how lucky she was to have somewhere to go."

"It must have been confusing for her to move back."

"Confusing?"

"I remember her saying something about it. She had moved back here for the summer, or maybe she had moved back into her place again in the fall. But she touched the rim of her glass with a finger, frowning, as if she were debating some deeply philosophical question, and said, 'What makes a place home?' She said she thought of home as the people. She never missed the place so much as the people, the sense of them inside her."

"Maybe because she never left the place," Alyssa said. "The place is what holds the memories. That's why this house is home."

Emma smiled, if crookedly. "Then why do I feel lonelier here than anywhere else in the world?"

"Maybe for the same reason I miss the people, even when they're sitting right next to me," Alyssa replied, her voice catching as she realized that her sense of isolation and misunderstanding was now forever because those she most wanted to be with, connect to, were gone, and had she ever really known them, or they her?

"I just found out that the house I live in up in Providence is going to be sold in the spring," Emma abruptly announced. "I don't know what to do. Where I'm going to live. My first thought was to come back here."

Alyssa held herself still. Emma move in? A jarring thought.

"Why would you do that?" Alyssa asked and proceeded to state the obvious. "You live in Providence. It makes no sense for you to move here. Why not buy the Providence house yourself? You could use the money that old boyfriend of yours, Loren, paid you back for the down payment."

"That was five years ago, and I used it to pay for the renovations on this place."

"Well." Alyssa thought of all that money wasted on renovating a perfectly good house, and of the FedEx package that had arrived for Emma a few days—weeks—before. Alyssa had meant to call her about it. "Maybe some money will come your way out of the blue. Then you could buy the Providence house."

"Alyssa, I can't afford two places. The only way I could buy Conner's house is if I sell this place."

"That would be stupid," Alyssa snapped.

"I know," Emma said. "I can't imagine letting it go."

A brief silence, and then the doorbell.

"It must be your friend Thea, Emma." A voice. Gussie's. She

stood in the threshold of the living room, leaning on Gus, both with drinks in hand, and Gussie's with far too generous a pour. Alyssa could tell by the darker-than-blond-brown color. The glass tilted. It might spill at any moment. Alyssa wondered how long the two of them had been there listening. She tried to remember what had been said. "After all these years, Thea is back. How lovely."

Introductions, or reintroductions, all around. Emma was nervous and awkward, clumsy, as she tried to help Thea with her coat. Gus took over, flirting with the attractive, petite woman—slender, with a long neck that seemed longer being at the end of such a straight back. Gussie suggested they all remove themselves to the living room where they could relax. Emma hesitated, glancing over at the oven.

"I'll take out the rolls for you," Alyssa promised. "I have to finish the stuffing, anyway."

The others left. Alyssa straightened her posture and took a deep breath. She put the stuffing into a casserole dish, covered it with tin foil, and set it next to the sweet potatoes. Everything was ready to be warmed and browned in the oven as soon as the white-as-ghosts rolls were done. She stared into the pan of giblets simmering in water and remembered how Auggie had used to tease her with the pope's nose. The sound of his laughter echoed in her mind, along with the jingle of Livy's bracelets, and she could almost smell the toasted sugar donuts smothered with butter that they had used to eat as children, sitting at the sky blue table and drinking cocoa that warmed and soothed any hiccups of the day. Her siblings had supported her, until they grew up and went away.

Alyssa removed a gingersnap from under the Saran wrap. It melted in her mouth, calming her. She studied the dining table, enlarged by the cousins that morning with a card table and covered with a white linen tablecloth. Betsy and Joy had set it with the family silver and delft plates. Crystal glassware. Silver salt and pepper shakers. Another cookie. Alyssa verified that the name tags were where she wanted them. Everything was where it should be. It was difficult without her siblings, but life was what it was, the past was impossible to change, and one could only go forward as the sun set. It was getting dark in the dining room, only shadows and smells, and another breathless moment filled with all the absent voices: her siblings, her father, Ed. Alyssa straightened a fork, a plate—all hers now. Things she had always wanted for herself. She had them. So why didn't she feel better? Why did she feel so unhappy and alone?

In the living room, the family had sprawled. Crayons and construction paper occupied the children, while the adults had gathered on the other side of the living room, enjoying the fire and perusing the family photo albums that were scattered about, piled on tables and laps. Conversations flowed, separating then coming together. Alyssa drifted from one to another, feeling as if she were playing jump rope, unable to find the exact right time to jump in without a foot catching. She ended up behind the couch nearest the staircase, looking over her mother's shoulder.

"Who is that fatty?" Gussie pointed to a photo.

"That god-awful orange bridesmaid's dress," Alyssa said, flushing as she remembered how tight the damn thing had been. "It was all wrong for my figure and coloring. Why is it that bridesmaids' dresses are always so hideous?"

"Brides want to look their best, in comparison," Crystal said, all diamonds, bleached hair, and bosom. Alyssa tried to smile. Certainly, Crystal had wanted to look her best on her wedding day. Poor Gus. A dreamer and poet as a child, he had been transformed by his materialistic and, frankly, low-class wife into a high-powered venture capitalist and . . . Republican. There was no other word for it. The only redeeming factor was that Alyssa's father would have been proud of Gus, Alyssa knew, and how sad that Winston wasn't there to see his progeny. Gus would have bonded with Winston. They could have consoled each other. After all, one believes what one believes, but it is nice to have supporters.

"I hated Mrs. Siminoff at first," Thea said. She and Emma sat on the staircase, as they had as children. Their postures perfect, elegant.

Both so self-aware, as if they were part of an elect, privileged group. Which, Emma had always pointed out, they were. They were ballet dancers. And here they were again, so many years later, indulging in a tête-à-tête. "Her teaching style rubbed me the wrong way. She was so strict."

"I guess that's why I felt so at home with her," Emma said. "Gram and Gramps were all about rules and duty, so her classes felt familiar."

"Your grandfather used to terrify me," Thea said. "Remember how quiet we had to be when he'd drive us to class in the morning?"

"Until we started reading the *Lord of the Rings* series aloud. He used to drive faster at the exciting parts."

"A rough transition, from Frodo to barre work."

The two women laughed. Alyssa imagined what it must be like, to meet again after so many years and such an . . . *abrupt* break. To return so easily to how it had been. At ease with themselves, knowing at heart what they wanted.

"We were lucky to have Mrs. Siminoff. Whenever I go to see the ballet?" Emma said, flushed and excited in a way Alyssa hadn't seen her excited in years. Of course, Emma hadn't talked about her dance in so long. "My body still remembers the movements. I can't do them anymore. But it remembers the precision of the motion."

"Never look back. You don't need to. You already know it," Thea repeated, and Emma joined her in Mrs. Siminoff's mantra and parting words to them when they had left her instruction.

"Trust yourself, too," Emma said. "You had to trust."

"You never had a problem with that, Emma," Thea said. Emma started, looked over at Thea, curious.

"No?" Emma asked. Rhetorically.

"This is Uncle Joe," Gussie said, indicating a photo in the book on Renny's lap. "An oddball. He used to eat enormous amounts at all times of day and night but was skinny as a rail. He was on the *Titanic* when she went down."

"That's too bad," Renny said.

"Why? He didn't die," Gussie said. "He met his second wife on the boat and lived to be ancient. Irascible man. He treated everyone terribly. Winston used to say that no gentleman survived the *Titanic*. It drove Uncle Joe batty—which, of course, Winston adored to do."

"It's terrible to think," Joy said, with her mother Livy's pensive concern, "all the rich surviving while the lower-class citizens were trapped in the lower berths."

"Survival of the fittest, Joy." Gus leaned back in his armchair, his voice dominating the room. Alyssa caught herself wishing he didn't talk with such a superior tone of voice.

"No, dear. It was survival of the rude," Gussie said. "Gentlemen stepped away to allow the women and children to get into the lifeboats first. So a man who survived was not a gentleman. Exactly as Winston said. People knew the rules back then."

"Ah, the good old days, when people knew what was expected of them." Gus grinned. "All you needed was the right bloodline. Now, no one cares who you are, only what you're worth. I was listening to an interview the other day. The interviewer and interviewee—both rich and famous—were falling over each other to prove they had earned their money, had begun life dumpster diving. They didn't want to be mistaken for some trust fund baby."

"They certainly didn't learn their manners, flaunting their poverty," Gussie said.

"Manners don't matter anymore, Gram, any more than bloodlines do," Gus said, looking into his wineglass. "It's how much you have."

"Then why do you go to the club, Gus?" Max asked. Alyssa braced, not wanting the day to be ruined by an argument. "You grumble about going, but you certainly keep up those connections. Is it to be sure your kids know the right people to schmooze with and marry?"

"Why not give them what opportunities I can? I'm not one of those bleeding-heart liberals who give away all their wealth and only leave their kids ten thousand bucks on principle. That's plain stupid. If you die before they've made it through college, they're fucked. Excuse me, Gram."

"People who do that are trying to equalize things," Joy said.

"By screwing their own kids?"

"Maybe by challenging them to make it on their own and not have to spend their lives worrying if they can support themselves or not."

"No kid of mine is going to worry if they can support themselves, because they're going to have plenty. And Joy, one person raised in wealth getting dumped in the gutter isn't going to change anything. Never mind the fact that even without money, he still has something over someone raised in the projects. Like us. Just by being raised in this house, we've been exposed to life experiences most people only dream of. We can do day labor, blister our hands, but we know how to act in certain circumstances, how to speak. We exude privilege. It's in our blood."

"It's more an attitude, isn't it?" Thea asked, not looking at anyone in particular, though anyone could see by Emma's reaction how pointed and directed her words were meant to be. "The ostentation a person puts on, thinking she's so special, holding herself above and apart, and yet she's the one who loses out. She misses opportunities because she's too good for what she's doing, meant for bigger and better things."

"I don't do that," Joy said. "I'm no better or worse than the people with whom I work."

"So why do you hide who you are?" Max asked, then continued over Joy's protestations. "Just the other day, you were telling us about some cultural exchange you participate in. Hispanics telling of their traditions. Mexicans. African Americans. Many from challenging, dare I say *poor*, backgrounds.

"Impoverished financially," Joy said. "But they have rich lives. Enviable. So full of history and customs."

"So you listened to your co-workers tell of their experiences, but did you tell them about yours?"

"Why would I? It's dull as mayonnaise."

"I think you're mum about it because you're ashamed."

"I just don't want to embarrass anyone," Joy said, flushing.

"Who would you embarrass? Them? There's no reason for them to be embarrassed. Or would you be embarrassed by your privilege? For exposing yourself for thinking, at heart, that you're better than them?"

"Save your psychoanalysis for your patients, Max," Joy said, rolling her eyes.

"I'm happy eating bonbons all day while other people toil," Crystal said. "We would toil if we had to, but we don't. Be happy. Everyone isn't so lucky."

"You're talking to a roomful of WASPs, Crystal," Betsy said from where she sat with the children. "With every sliver of decadence comes a healthy dose of Protestant guilt. We have to earn what we have in this society. We don't deserve."

"I've always believed that," Emma said. "That I had to earn what I got. I never thought I was entitled."

"But you were entitled, weren't you?" Thea asked.

"It's in our nature," Betsy grinned.

"We had a discussion about nature once. Not the birds and the bees or Latin names for plants, but in terms of how we are," Gussie said. Everyone turned, waiting for her to continue. "Lawrence Finer. One of his visits, eons ago. He had just met my cousin Kitty and was saying how alike she and I were, though we had grown up apart."

Alyssa held still. The smell of wine in the nose. The sensation of her family around her. Her adored Auggie, probably home for some vacation or other. Livy, so elegant and enviably slender. Their father, gruff and grumbling, reminding her of the furnace with its clanks and bangs, slightly irritating but necessary for warmth and safety. Her mother, of course, around whom they circled, younger then than Alyssa was now, so many years later, trying to celebrate when so much had gone by.

"When we were all very young," Gussie continued, "we talked about how family can affect us in ways we've no idea about."

"Exactly," Max said. "It's part of you. If you deny your past, you can't live your future."

"Then we're as trapped as in the old days," Emma said. "Fated by birth."

"Nonsense. Self-determination. That is what Auggie talked about," Gussie said. "Within certain boundaries, of course. And money helps. It would be naive to think it doesn't. Oh, there is Livy."

Gussie pointed to another picture. Alyssa looked at it, not seeing it, trying to remember where she had put that Federal Express package, because it was true. Money did help. It would.

"She was sick as a dog that night," Renny said. "Livy, Ed, and I had been all over the city, starting with cocktail parties on through to closing our favorite bar. We ended up at Ed's studio, fooling around with the cameras to see what would come out."

Alyssa stared at the photo of Livy protected by the two men standing above her—Ed, drink in hand, looking directly into the camera with his devilish black eyes and square face that was just on the edge of being pugnacious but was, in fact, surprisingly kind. Just like Gus. And Renny, same old Renny, with a cigarette, face up to the sky, blowing smoke. Livy sat in a full-skirted dress in a chair, hands devotedly clasped at her heart, staring down at the floor.

"Wasn't she lovely?" Alyssa asked, possessive and proud because that was her older sister. "Livy."

Alyssa whispered her name, and for a moment that name signified the willful girl who would sneak out with her boyfriends, boys who took the risk of getting caught by Winston with a gun; men who escorted her around New York City, willing to do whatever it took to amuse her because Livy was fun and exciting and beautiful and smart. Alyssa used to adore Livy. She would have done anything just to be in her orbit, watching the rakish, irresponsible, but independent side of Livy, rarely seen in later life, now irretrievably gone. Alyssa missed her at the oddest times:

as she compared the young Livy to her memory of the old Livy's Dickensian-waif's pinched face, her clothes sagging off her skeletal body.

"That was the night Livy and Ed got engaged," Renny said. "December of '53. Ed was home on leave from the army."

"You've your dates mixed up, Renny," Alyssa said, removing the photo from the album to look at it more closely. "I was dating Ed then. Livy and Ed didn't meet up again until the spring of '54, at Mummy and Father's twenty-fifth anniversary party."

"Livy had been dating Ed for ages before that." Gussie turned the page. Renny sucked his tooth.

"No, Mummy, you have it all wrong. I was dating him. They hadn't seen each other in years. It was at your twenty-fifth anniversary party that Ed said he and Livy had started talking and something had clicked. He wanted to take her out again. I know that's when it happened because Ed was supposed to take me to the Hinkley wedding and I ended up going with Renny instead."

"A fortuitous turn of events," Renny said, finishing off his drink. Alyssa dragged her eyes up from the photo, forced a smile.

"It certainly was, Renny. We had a wonderful time, too," Alyssa said, trying to think of her perfectly good marriage. Her mother-in-law. Choices that were not choices. "You are always such fun."

"Wasn't that weird?" Julia asked. "For Uncle Ed to date one sister, then the other?"

"It was odd," Alyssa agreed, looking down at her hands, the photo. Smiling, at times, took such effort, as when remembering the humiliation, and her envy of Livy. Alyssa had always felt left out around her, the wallflower, deprived of any hope of being so lively and exciting. Until Livy had changed into what she had become. And yet still she took. Over time, Livy had taken more and more, even as she had seemed to push away, an unbearable, sucking neediness. Even now, there wasn't enough for the two of them.

"I was used to Ed being mine. He was my consort. We had fun together. We went skinny dipping once. I lost my brassiere." Alyssa shivered, feeling again the nakedness, and the slap of cold water against hot flesh. "I did like him."

"He wouldn't have done for you," Gussie said. Her voice, again so crisp and certain. Knowing right and wrong. "You'd more important things to do, Alyssa. If you'd married Ed, you wouldn't have continued at college. You'd have spent your time keeping him in line instead of studying. Renny was a much better match. A home boy who worshipped you and let you live your life."

"My life, Mummy?" Alyssa asked, looking at her mother. Her mother, who had wanted to go to college.

"You didn't understand that, of course," Gussie said, shaking her head. "Such hysteria I've never seen. The absolute end of the world. Your eyes were so swollen, I didn't think they'd ever come back to normal."

"Imagine if it had been Livy," Alyssa snapped. "Queen of histrionics."

"But it couldn't have been Livy. That was the point," Renny said, and his breath was warm with whiskey. "You were so sweetly self-involved, you didn't see it. You only cared if someone else got him. Particularly Livy. Whereas she needed him. It was delicate, but Auggie convinced Ed."

Alyssa stared at the page of photos in front of her mother. Bunches of people from decades and decades before. She had no idea who they were. Strangers. Blood relations. They passed, and what was left but the memories, and it was just like Auggie had used to say: memories are fictions made up by individuals, each with their own interpretation, and so maybe it was only Alyssa who remembered the night that Ed had tried to break off with Livy. Livy, in tears, shrieking that Ed should be free to do what he wanted. Winston bellowing that he'd marry Livy or face the consequences. By then Alyssa was engaged to Renny and too proud to turn back. And Gussie had sat silent, letting Winston effect what she wanted.

As for Ed, he had been pale, shaken by all the drama, but he'd managed to keep his perspective and sense of humor. Winston had connections. Class. That was why Gussie had married him. Winston could drop his daughters at their debutante balls still dressed in his janitor clothes because, after all, he was Winston Michaels. And so, after the wedding, Ed got his job with *The New York Times*. He deserved it, of course. He had earned it. The job of his dreams, a house by the sea, and, every so often, a romp with Alyssa. When she least expected it, he would be in front of her, kissing her in a way that left her wobbly with the memory. Just to prove that he could. That he was free. Doing what he wanted. He had chosen it.

"I always knew it was something like that between those two," Alyssa said, her hands shaking as a near lifetime of assuming *I didn't get* turned into *I could have had*, and then, *Maybe not*. "They got married so soon afterwards. Of course, I wasn't interested in marriage. I'd seen what it did to you, Mummy."

"Didn't you get married before Mom and Dad?" Joy asked.

"Gus was a healthy preemie," Gussie said.

"Both of your daughters were fast in those days," Renny said, thoughtful and unperturbed. "But Alyssa was the beauty. Auggie knew that I'd do anything for her. He only wanted your happiness. That's all any of us wanted for you. But there's always been something else on the horizon that you wanted. As soon as you got one thing, you wanted something else. Like a kid in a candy shop, grabbing until you were sick."

"You've had too much to drink, Renny," Alyssa admonished.

"Look on the bright side, Alyssa," he replied quietly. "If you'd married Ed, you'd have been the widow all this time."

"I'd have played my cards differently," Alyssa retorted, even as she realized she had played them exactly as her mother had. She had married to prove a point. She had married a safe man who did not threaten her soul, and then stuck by it. For better or worse.

Renny toasted Alyssa with debonair indifference. As he had so often in the past. Alyssa wasn't sure what to do. Blood rushed to her cheeks. Saltwater in her eyes because she was so exposed. What else did Renny know that she'd had no idea about? What else might he have tolerated? Alyssa looked at him whom she had counted on to save her. Like all those other men. She had thought she was in control. Maybe they had controlled her. Their needs and wants. She had given them everything and they had given her nothing back, though she stood there, waiting, with open arms. Giving and then rejected—yet, like a child, still hoping and going back for more. As deaf and blind as Livy had been with money. So self . . . self-righteous. At which thought, Mrs. Jones came to mind, and Alyssa wished. She had an overwhelming urge to go to her mother-in-law, who had been dead for so many years, and beg her for forgiveness.

Alyssa stared numbly down at her mother until, slowly, she realized Gussie was looking over at Emma and Thea, listening.

"It's time for me to retire," Thea was saying to Emma. "I'm thirty-four. My body can't do what it used to. The younger dancers aren't including me in their discussions. I want to leave while I still have control and choice."

"That makes sense," Emma nodded.

"Part of me can't wait not to have to struggle and work so hard, and yet I can't imagine what it will be like. Who am I if not a dancer? I'm afraid that, without the structure and routine I've lived with all my life, I won't exist. I'll lose myself."

"I know that feeling," Emma said, and she was relaxed, safe with her friend. Alyssa sensed that she was ready to confide what she had never been able to.

"No, you don't," Thea said. "You've no idea. You didn't need dance the way I have. You just gave it up, whereas I did what we always dreamed of. I danced. It has been my life. I would never have given it up if I had the choice. That's where you and I are different. Just being in the *corps de ballet* would have been enough for me. Whereas you . . ."

Thea scoffed. Emma stared at Thea. Alyssa watched, sensing that the gauntlet, thrown down so long ago, was to be picked up.

"I went to see you dance Giselle that summer," Emma said, trying to be gracious. "You were stunning. Absolutely beautiful."

"Not as good as you would have been, Emma. And I didn't even want the part."

"Easy for you to say." Emma flushed. Alyssa cleared her throat but with no intention of saying anything, because, thinking back, into the confusion of the past, she realized that sometimes betrayal is done with the best of intentions. And that the helpless reaching back to change everything . . . was impossible. And after all, it hadn't been Auggie who had found the compromise that night when Livy and Ed "met." It had been herself. She had had to prove she didn't care. She didn't care. Alyssa bit her lip to stop the trembling of her chin. Wanting so badly to do it all again. Wanting to be different. Just wanting, and wishing she could save Emma from this pain of understanding. Because the two of them were the same that way. They had both had their dreams in their grasp. They just hadn't known it.

"It's never made any sense to me, Emma," Thea said. "You had always been so determined. You worked so hard. And then you just walked away. One day we were working together, and the next, you were gone."

"I had to take care of Gram."

"I didn't buy that then and I don't buy that now," Thea snapped, unleashing the raw hurt of past rejection. "A dancer doesn't just quit. We'd been best friends. Our entire lives, from when we were seven and eight years old, we were together. Directed. We knew exactly what we—"

"I didn't want to be in a club that didn't want me, okay?" Emma interrupted. "I wasn't good enough."

"You acted as if you were, snubbing us the way you did."

"Snubbing?"

"All the grace and musicality and nimbleness of the greatest ballerina," Gussie said. "It was a second-rate company. Emma was better than that."

"We were her only chance, Mrs. Michaels," Thea said.

"Exactly, Thea," Emma said. "That's what you have no idea about.

I knew I wasn't entitled to it, but I was so sure I had gotten the part. I was devastated when I didn't."

Alyssa held her breath. Thea frowned.

"You did get it," she said. "We all knew I'd be principal ballerina the next year, but everyone in the company pushed to have you dance Giselle. Roger finally relented. I was so excited when I called to tell you. You never called back. You just came in the next day and quit."

"You called?" Emma said, staring at Thea, and there, right in front of Alyssa, was the Federal Express package. Right there next to the fireplace. Alyssa reached for the package, relieved. The panacea.

"Yes, I left a message."

"Who answered the phone? Who took the message?"

"Emma? This is addressed to you." Alyssa handed Emma the package. "I found it on that pile of junk mail."

Alyssa moved toward the dining room and kitchen. She partially rolled shut the living room doors behind her, looked back through the crack. Emma and Thea talking, a cabal, and Emma perhaps feeling how Alyssa felt: a sense of loss and betrayal. And there was Gus, paying no attention to the dramas around him. Gus, who looked just . . . exactly like his father. And Max. So handsome and good. In the kitchen, she tested a green bean and thought of the day, years ago, when Max had come home from his job at a restaurant and announced that he had set a lobster free. Not just any lobster, he said. This one had kept trying to escape. It would climb out of the basket. Max had caught it three or four times making its way across the floor. How kill such a will to live? And so he had announced at dinner that night what he had done: he had taken it to the town dock and dropped it back into the water.

"Did you remove the rubber bands from its claws?" Gus had asked, calmly cutting a piece of bloody steak. He chewed, watching his brother paling in deadly silence, uncertain, sick at heart, and that was how Alyssa felt as she fiddled with the foil over the turkey, testing one small piece. She began to slice it, carefully placing the pieces on a serving platter. Alyssa imagined Emma would have opened her FedEx package by now. She would be reading the letter it held. From the law firm executing Gloria Wilson's will. Alyssa had seen the woman's obituary in the paper, and recognized the firm's name when the package arrived. Now there would be enough money, perhaps. One door opens and another closes. Something like that. Alyssa had to maintain a sense of humor and perspective, and food, at least, made sense. All her life, food had helped. As a child she was always hungry and would hide donuts and cookies in her room to eat late at night. She was so hungry, it was hard to stop. She wanted, and before she knew it, the bag or container would be empty. And she wouldn't really remember eating. She wouldn't have appreciated the taste and so wanted a little bit more. Another bite. The movement became habitual. Chewing and swallowing calmed her.

But not today, because Emma came running in, whooshing past her to the oven. Smoke. Something was burning! Emma grabbed some oven mitts and pulled out a tray of black charcoals. Her rolls. She turned on Alyssa.

"Not even rolls?" she said, tears rolling down her cheeks. "I wanted one thing and you ruined it."

"I'm sorry, Emma. I forgot."

"Because you didn't care enough to remember."

Emma stormed past her, carrying the tray outside so the rolls wouldn't smoke up the house. Betsy and Joy came into the dining room, turning on more lights. The bustle of the last-minute preparations proceeded, the realization that Livy had always made the gravy. Betsy, Crystal, and Julia argued around the stove about their differing memories of how she had done so. The gravy ended up with too much flour, and was lumpy to boot. In fact, nothing was quite right as the various platters were set on the sideboard. Alyssa's body itched. She stood in front of the turkey, protectively reaching back to be sure it was still there. Still warm. She wanted to scream as the others poured into the dining room, taking over.

"This house is built on a chestnut tree," Gussie told her

grandchildren as she sat at the head of the table with the help of Max and Betsy. Everyone circled her. Moons around the sun, extinguished in her presence. "I planted it the year I turned eighteen. When I came back from Europe, it was almost as tall as I was, then Winston went and cut it down. It was in the middle of where he wanted to put the foundation for the house. I was fit to be tied, and he didn't understand why. He had no idea. He tried to replace it. He planted a stick of a sapling. It grew into the chestnut tree that spreads itself across the driveway now. Hard to believe. Seed casings all over the lawn from that little stick. Winston had thought it was the sweet kind, an American chestnut. I knew immediately. I'd had a lesson on chestnut trees as a girl. I was furious with him, but couldn't say why. I wasn't quite sure myself. Silly. There was no reason to be so angry, though I didn't realize it at the time. You see, the roots of that sweet chestnut tree were still there. They still are. I know they are because we all like each other. That's what is so wonderful about our family. All families love one another, but we like each other. We gather here under this roof and have such fun. We always have, and always will. Won't we, Emma? You do such a good job of maintaining this place."

"Where is Emma?"

"She was here a minute ago."

"Her friend Thea had to leave. Emma was saying good-bye to her."

"She has all the luck, doesn't she?" Joy said. "First the house and now the money."

"Money?" Alyssa asked.

"The Fed Ex package. That Gloria woman died," Gus said. "She never spent the money Gram sent her. Left it all to Emma."

"She must have known Emma loves this place as much as Winston did," Gussie said.

"No more whining about land rich, money poor," Joy said. "Now she can keep the place."

"Not if she was broke before," Gus said. "Do the numbers. Gram paid Gloria a couple or three hundred dollars a month for, what, twenty years? Depending on the bank and what kind of account she had, she made maybe 4 percent interest? That's chump change."

"It's tens of thousands of dollars," Joy said.

"Like I said." Gus shrugged. "That would keep this place going for a year."

"Do you think she'll sell?"

"I wouldn't blame her," Max said. "Gifts like this place come with a cost."

"Why don't you buy it, Gus?" Alyssa asked, her heart fluttering. "You've the money."

"Just because a person can afford it doesn't mean a person should," Crystal said with an iron smile. "If Emma doesn't want the headache of this place, why would Gus?"

"We can't let it out of the family," Alyssa replied. "It's where we come together. We depend on it."

"Why not gather somewhere else?" Renny asked thoughtfully. The enthusiastic reaction around the table to his suggestion nauseated Alyssa. She listened as the children named off all the places they might meet, and the things they could do, a rotating family reunion.

"It wouldn't be the same," Alyssa said, with an eye to her mother. What would happen to her mother, left all by herself?

"Maybe that would be a good thing, Mom," Max said.

"The children are hungry," Betsy said. "Gram, do you want to give the blessing?"

Gussie did. She spoke directly to God, greeting him like an old friend, recognizing absent family and friends, and asking for His good graces. She concluded with the traditional toast that she had made at so many family occasions.

"To happiness," Gussie said, her hand shaking as she raised her glass, her eyes tearful. "And other more important things."

Livy and Alyssa had used to exchange raised brows and secret smiles during that toast. Alyssa couldn't remember why. A secret joke between them, and if only Livy were there to remind her of the punch line.

"Cheers to that . . ."

Everyone picked up a plate, setting their glasses on the table in an unorganized fashion, not one of them choosing the place Alyssa had chosen for them.

"What happened to the turkey?" Betsy asked, holding the foil cover that she had just removed. The carcass had been ravaged, as if clawed, ripped apart, hunks of it gone.

"Looks like a cougar got it," one of the grandchildren said, setting off screams of excitement and shouts for a hunt. Alyssa flushed, wondering. It couldn't be . . .

"I don't know what could have happened," Alyssa said over the mayhem.

"Throw it out, Gus," Crystal said. "The cat probably got to it. It's unsanitary. There's plenty of everything else."

Plenty? Was there plenty? Alyssa backed away. She wanted something. Her drink. She excused herself. Not that anyone noticed as she walked out to the living room. In the dark, made darker by the bright light and the cheerful discussions going on in the dining room, she headed toward the stairs. A movement. Someone near the fireplace. Tall and angular as Auggie. The sound of Livy's bracelets. Emma staring into the embers, poking them.

"Hello!" Alyssa said. "Everyone was wondering where you'd gone to." Alyssa stopped, realizing that Emma had, of course, heard the conversation. "What are you doing here?"

"I was just wondering the same thing," Emma said, jabbing the dying fire. "But then, I've nowhere else to go. All these years. I thought it was safe. I thought I was acceptable, even though I wasn't good enough at the one thing in the world that I wanted. I've been stuck and ashamed and wallowing here. Now it turns out I was good enough. But it's too late. I'll never be able to be what I had hoped to be. And I don't understand how . . . why no one told me. Not even Dad." Emma set down the poker and zipped her coat.

"I'm out of here. Please be sure to leave a key in the usual spot. I'm calling Sally at Seascape Properties tomorrow. She'll need to get in when she comes to look around."

"What are you talking about?"

"I'm selling this place, Alyssa. I'll have a moving truck come in a couple of weeks. Please have your things out by then. I won't be back. I'm never coming back."

Emma's voice choked—or maybe it was a laugh? She was smiling, after all, though tears rolled down her cheeks. She shook her head, shrugged, all very confused. "Where am I going to go? I have nowhere to go."

Alyssa's heart welled in sympathy and she stepped forward to comfort Emma, who sounded so lost, like a child peering into darkness, her understanding of the world destroyed. But Emma backed away from Alyssa and left. Out the side door and onto the patio, jumping off and running down the path to Livy's. Alyssa hesitated, then reached for a duffle coat that had been left on a couch and followed Emma. To convince her how crazy it would be. To explain. Though how to explain what had happened so long ago?

She limped over to Livy's land along the path, just as in the old days. Only slightly overgrown. It would take more than a year for that decades-old path to disappear. The memories of the cool dirt and soft pine needles on bare feet. The frog pond. All so real. In the crisp November air, the breeze through the yews whispered, and Alyssa felt a desperation—a hope—that when she came through the woods the path would open up to Livy's house, brightly lit, with her dearest sister and brother there to welcome her.

Instead, (of course, what could she have been thinking?) Alyssa stepped into a chilling, black expanse, with not even a star to light it as the past yawned up around her. All that time gone, wanting, and the darkness was no different if her eyes were open or closed. A lifetime of solitary confinement, and she had no buttons to throw.

Alyssa stepped toward the edge of the foundation hole. She had called it Bittersweet Lane's very own Grand Canyon when she had first seen it. What would it feel like to fall in? If she tripped and fell, who would save her? Alyssa opened her arms to the darkness. She had always been convinced it was empty, not daring to see how full it was: of terrors and dreams, now lost potential. She shouted for Livy. For Auggie. For all her lost loves. Hoping they would support her, alleviate this terrifying fear of losing the only thing she believed in: the house and all it symbolized—family, love, and connection. In response, it was Renny who came running through the woods to save her once again. He held her so tightly. She thought he would crush her. In fact, she realized, he was the only one who understood her, who might teach her that it was safe to let go. She dared. She looked into that darkness, he holding her hand, and she laughed and laughed at what a close call it had been.

A Forever Home

A rainbow, shimmering but definite, stretched from the ocean beyond the breakwater, over and across the harbor, to the house. It ended on the roof, a colorful arc that the people walking the property didn't see. Being in it, they couldn't perceive the frail and short-lived beauty that existed. For a moment—a passing moment—that Emma and Gussie observed, breathed in, and watched disappear.

"Strange," Emma said, "how people can pass out of your life. It's as if they never existed—until one day you realize that, even gone, they've filled your life. Taken it over. You've made their same mistakes, and try as you might have to go in the right direction, the same thing that stopped them has stopped you."

"Is that all you have done these last months?" Gussie asked after a moment's pause. "Molder and ruminate? The only thing that has stopped anyone in this family was the limits of their imagination."

"I suppose you're right. I never imagined my family would sabotage me."

"Nonsense."

"Is it? You knew how much it meant to me. How could you not have told me Thea called?"

"For the obvious reason that I was protecting you."

Emma stared at her grandmother.

"Protecting me from what?"

"Yourself." Again, silence as Emma tried to process the

contradiction. "You wanted more than the lead role in *Giselle*, Emma. You wanted to be principal ballerina. You always had, and you expected that one went with the other. Well, they didn't. It was better for you to move on when you did. You would have been even more devastated than you already were when they passed over you. We didn't want you to be disappointed."

"You were the ones who were disappointed. You thought the company wasn't good enough for me. I had to do better."

"Of course you did. And you would have if you had stuck to it."

"That was my intention, to continue. And Robert's. The artistic director. He was very tough. No one was entitled to succeed. But he knew I could do it."

"If he had wanted you to continue, why did he stop correcting your mistakes? I'll tell you why. He wanted to ruin you. He was determined to push you out."

"Gram," Emma said, studying her grandmother with a degree of disbelief. "You saw me dance with their premier danseur, right?" Gussie didn't respond. "I looked ridiculous. He was five feet four inches. I towered over him. But he was a great dancer. They couldn't lose him."

"So they gave you the role of Giselle out of pity. A consolation prize before they cut you."

"No. Robert knew that, if I danced Giselle, it would buff up my resume so that I might audition for other jobs in companies that took taller dancers. Giselle and my future did go together, Gram. It wasn't pity. They gave me the part out of love. They loved me enough to give me my dream. But I didn't know that because I thought I hadn't gotten the part.

"The night of Gramps' funeral was the worst. I wrote my resignation letter. Pages full of excuses and pleas. What could I do? How could I improve? But I knew I couldn't. I had tried my absolute best, and, apparently, it wasn't good enough. As I edited and cut, I went from humiliation to defensiveness, then anger. I convinced myself that I didn't need them. I came to believe what you believed:

they weren't good enough. Second-rate. Fools to have rejected me. I was determined to get another gig without their help. I'd go to New York. Balanchine had just died. They'd be having auditions soon. I laid it all out. It was perfect. My resignation letter was one line. *I quit.* The next day, I handed Robert the studio key and my letter."

"I find it hard to believe no one came up to congratulate you. Then the cat would have been out of the bag."

"I didn't give them the chance. I wouldn't—I couldn't—look anyone in the eyes because I was so ashamed. Heartbroken. But I presented myself as cold and haughty. I hid myself so well that not even Thea could tell. *Not good enough?* she asked as I walked away. I thought she was being cruel. In fact, she knew I had the part, and there I was, quitting, as if the company were irrelevant. I assumed she was saying I wasn't good enough. Because I was like you, Gram. I didn't ask questions. No one knew to stop me from giving up the one thing I could count on."

"Your dance," Gussie said.

"No. Myself. I stopped listening to me that day. It was a mistake to leave. I would have done anything to stay, because I knew better, Gram. If I weren't good enough for them, who was I good enough for? I wanted to stay because it wasn't minor league. It was my life. My friends." Emma paused, staring at the house and seeing herself walking away, the days of regret and justification, the dearth. "It wasn't just not getting the part. It was making the break. I would have had to leave eventually. Thea would be the prima ballerina when Chloe retired the next year. We all knew that. But if I'd danced Giselle, or even in the *corps de ballet,* I'd have had time to mourn. I would have left, because I was too damned tall, but, at least, I would have learned how to let go. And maybe how to forgive."

Gussie startled. Emma sat up, took a deep breath as she looked around her, felt the tinge of cool in the afternoon air. Waited.

"I'm sorry," Gussie said. "I'm sorry you didn't get to dance that last time."

"Me too. I'll never know what I might have been, or done."

Gussie cleared her throat. "You should have carried on with your New York plan."

"I did. I tried to keep in shape that summer, and when auditions were called I went to New York, terrified and without an ounce of self-confidence. I went into the auditions and peeked in. One look and I knew that I was all wrong. I had been taught in the French School method. All about fluidity and elegance. Romance. Balanchine dancers move quicker and . . . I didn't have Balanchine arms. And I didn't have the confidence and energy I would have had coming off of *Giselle*. My audition was a flop, and then Dad asked me to travel with him. So you see? It would have made all the difference."

"That's not a reason to blame the house. It's not the house you're trying to escape. It's nothing to do with the house. Imagine where you would be if you hadn't had it to fall back on."

Emma's throat tightened, swelling with a silence held for too long. A resistance reared up, an urge to run away. She remained still. For the first time in years, she listened to what was in her heart: not the should-do, but the want-to. She bent low, anticipating the sense of failure and shame that usually twisted inside her, braiding into the guilt of disappointing her grandmother. Instead, nothing.

"The mind is cunning," Emma said, feeling a lightness in her heart as the impossible suddenly became the only possibility. She might not want to disappoint her grandmother, but if she didn't, she would be failing herself. Again. And in the end? Gussie wouldn't be there to help. "It can convince you that you still need what you let go of long ago."

Gussie shifted, uncomfortable. "You should use the money that you got at Thanksgiving to support the house."

"It's not the money, Gram," Emma said.

"Certainly it is. That's what you've been talking about, with all your goings-on about privilege and shame and passing."

"No, Gram," Emma said, as, like a black number eight fortune ball, her future rose up with absolute clarity. "I've been talking about home, and connection. I have always wanted a connection between the past and the future."

"That's what the house is. You won't dare to give it up," Gussie said, triumphant as she spoke the words already spoken so many times before. Gussie looked at Emma, challenging her, even as Emma broke free. Gussie couldn't stop her. Gussie's fear had no effect on Emma's resolve, because it was Gussie who did not dare.

"Certainly, I never would have dared," Gussie said. "The rules were clear and unbendable back then. I didn't know to break them."

"Maybe you didn't want to break them badly enough. That's what I've been figuring out, Gram. Do I want to change badly enough?" Emma remained still as her grandmother's panic rose up around her. Emma stayed, knowing that it was her grandmother's, not hers.

"I've never really left dance, Gram. Dance is and always will be a part of me. I think back to when I was little and watched the older dancers practice, and how fascinated I was, how determined. And then, over the years, when I was the one practicing and all the little girls and boys waiting for their class to begin would watch me. They were rapt. They knew what they might do if they worked hard, and I was proud to be able to engage them, pass along the tradition of ballet to another generation. They didn't mind my mistakes. They knew one had only to correct them. Again and again. It's hard to be perfect. I worked so hard. And now Thea is starting a ballet school. She's asked if I'll help. I'm going to give her the Gloria money, Gram. Because I am going back to what I wanted to be. I might not do exactly what I dreamed of doing. But I can still achieve something."

"If you give up the house, you'll be left with nothing and no one to take care of you. Just like my Aunt Lucinda. And Livy. Poor Livy."

"We all make our choices, Gram," Emma hesitated, testing blindly where her next steps would fall. "The way we have been—*I* have been—isn't working anymore." Again, she paused to listen. "This morning, walking through the house, I felt as if it were watching me. It was listening, waiting to see what I would do. As if I had betrayed it somehow, leaving it alone for so long, and empty. Most of the furniture is gone. The rooms echo. The heat is on low, so it's freezing cold. I thought how it was just a house. Not a home."

"It's as much a home as it ever has been," Gussie said, her voice sharp with rebuke.

"I imagined it was offended, angry, so I had a conversation with it," Emma continued, leaving her grandmother's words to dissipate. "I told it what a great house it's been. I told it I didn't mind all its faults, its cracks and peelings and mold. I shared with it some of the memories I have. Those sand castles that you let us build in the living room. All those big parties you threw, and Gramps buying the girl cousins camellia corsages, and how you'd both pin them on our dresses so carefully, so proud of us. And playing card games on the dining room table on rainy days. I told the house how lucky we've been all these years, but that it's time to let it go. It isn't the expense. It's because I can't move forward if I keep it. We have to let go, Gram."

"Sky diving," Gussie replied. "My seventy-fifth birthday. Up in the sky in the plane. I was turning around to tell the man I had changed my mind when he pushed me out. Plummeting through space. The deafening, rushing noise. Screaming in terror, and then the abrupt jolt and silence when the man pulled the parachute open. He caught me screaming. I'd always been afraid to scream."

"Like in New York?" Emma dared to ask.

"Auggie got lost there," Gussie said.

"It must have been terrifying."

"Like going to a beheading and realizing you are next in line."

"Or having your home sold, and nothing you can do about it."

"You want to backtrack, do it all again."

"But do we? For years, I have wallowed in a rut of if-only. What and who would I be? But that's not the question, is it? It's who am I and what will I do *now*? I have to move forward. Choices are not always pleasant, Gram. If only because we've so many options. It's hard to know which to choose."

"On the contrary, our choice is perfectly clear."

"Not ours, Gram. Mine. It's not your choice this time. You don't have to choose. The change has already happened. You have only to accept. I'm selling the house to a CEO of some big corporation. He's the guy who bought Livy's place. He's negotiating with Renny and Alyssa to buy theirs. He wants to join the property together, Gram."

Gussie leaned against a pylon, using it as a crutch. A moment of panic as Emma wished she had said nothing. Then she remembered. She couldn't save her grandmother, only herself.

"We are more capable than we give ourselves credit for," Gussie said. "Never forget that. And what a lovely thought. The property will no longer be divided. That's all I wanted. For everyone to get along. We can only hope he will love and enjoy it as much as we've had the good fortune to do. Maybe we will all become friends."

"I don't think so, Gram. We have different . . . principles. He wondered what the deal is with the 'shack.'"

"Do you mean Auggie's cabin?"

"No. Alyssa's house."

Gussie burst into laughter, a forceful, full laugh that Emma had not heard in years. Gratifying. There was her grandmother, as vibrant and alive as she had ever been. Not helpless.

"From blue blood to white trash," Gussie said, smiling cheerfully. "That's too funny. Alyssa must have been fit to be tied. The crassness of that attitude, and toward a perfectly fine home. I don't imagine she'll have much sympathy for a person who thinks like that. Maybe she'll find a way not to sell to him. You can find reasons and reasons not to accept an offer."

A long pause, during which they reached the end of the dock and stood to watch an osprey hunt for its dinner, hovering above the water, motionless but for the beating of its wings, abruptly diving down, smacking the water, and then coming up again, grasping its prey.

"The buyer is very tall," Emma said. Gussie glanced over at her.

"It takes all kinds."

"I imagine being as tall as he is could leave him feeling out of place in the world, uncomfortable in his own skin," Emma said. "I can appreciate that. That's how I felt when I had that last growth spurt and was suddenly four inches taller than Thea. I imagine he'd want to slouch all the time. Crazy thought, isn't it, to have to stoop in your own home? Not being able to stand up and be?" Emma stopped under her grandmother's glare. "I'm trying to give him the benefit of the doubt."

"Why?" Gussie asked.

"He only wants the land, Gram. He intends to knock down the house."

A moment. Time stopped. Emma appraised her grandmother's demeanor.

"Good luck to him," Gussie said, her dander up, not to be challenged. "Mother Nature tried her hand at knocking it down in 1938. Look what's happened to her as a result. Humanity has no mercy."

Gussie pushed Emma away. She walked quickly, stumbling, down the dock. She tripped as Emma rushed to her side—too late. Gussie fell.

"Gram, are you okay?" Emma knelt, an arm around her grandmother, lifting her up. Gussie leaned on Emma as they stepped off the dock and returned to the gazebo's bench. Emma examined the damage. "Your knee is all scraped, and your hands."

Gussie looked past her.

"I need to sit."

"You are sitting," Emma said, looking around for help.

"My purse."

Emma ran to collect her grandmother's purse and her own knapsack. When she returned, she sat next to Gussie, berating herself for the harm she had done.

"You always said you'd tear down the walls," Gussie said, her nostrils flaring.

"But I would never tear down the house, Gram."

"Instead, you sell it to a man who will do it for you."

"That's life, isn't it? Generations come and go. What in your day was unspeakable is commonplace now. For better or worse. But if we make it through, which we will, so long as we keep breathing—if we survive the change, Gram—we'll be in a different place."

"A place you will have chosen, not I."

"No. You chose to leave the house to me. You could have left it to Gus, or to Joy."

"He wouldn't have afforded it, and she couldn't. Just like their parents."

"Exactly. I was the only logical one. And you know why, right?"

Gussie refused to answer at first. Emma studied the deep lines around her grandmother's mouth, the leavings of lips pursed against the intolerable. But with the ruffling of the water by the breeze, the comfort of the view, and her granddaughter, she admitted it.

". . . Permission. I knew you would ask for my permission."

Emma took her grandmother's hand. It shook, so fragile and thin. Elegant and warped by arthritis.

"I'm sorry, Gram, to disappoint you."

". . . You couldn't disappoint me if you tried. You are exactly what I hoped for. You appreciate how fortunate we have been." Gussie lifted a shaky hand and swept the view, the horizon. The hand closed into a fist and fell to her lap. "It's just as you said. If we went back, it wouldn't be the same."

"Like watching a movie of your favorite book."

"Exactly. Ruined."

"So it doesn't matter what happens going forward."

"I wouldn't go that far." Gussie sat up. A deep breath. "When I woke this morning, I had a most uncomfortable feeling in my chest, Emma. A painful squeezing, as if something unbearably heavy had sat on me. I thought fresh air would help, getting away from that place. It got worse when I sat down here. I could hardly breathe for the pounding of my heart, and assumed I would be found dead of a heart attack, an old woman on a wooden bench with seagull dirt on my shoulder. Alone. Then you arrived. I don't know what I would have done . . . Imagine, if Auggie had married that German girl. You wouldn't be here. So you see? I wouldn't change a thing. How would I dare? I was who I am. If anything was changed, I wouldn't be me. I wouldn't have you." Gussie squeezed Emma's arm, almost too tightly, clinging. "Tell me now, what is your favorite color? The one that helps you feel at peace with the world."

Emma closed her eyes and imagined it.

"The deep, dark blue of the sky before dawn," she said. "The stars are dimming. Venus is shining to the east. The horizon only just beginning to lighten. It's quiet and peaceful, with none of the day's noise or confusion. I know Conner is asleep and safe. And the cat's on the end of the bed. I know the day will proceed. But for the moment, with the cobalt blue sky, there are no expectations. I have everything I need, and I try not to think how I will lose it."

Gussie nodded. Her grip had loosened, her hand resting lightly on Emma's arm.

"A lovely color," Gussie said. "Lucky girl. Did you see the moon this morning?"

"A crescent, but you could make out the outline of the whole."

"I've always thought how the phases of the moon are like life. The question being, are children full moons who retreat to a crescent, the past falling into darkness? Or do we begin in darkness and end up entirely exposed? Like the land used to be all those years ago when I had a lesson on life's expectations." Gussie paused, her memory a boat stuck on a rock breaking free, floating away on the ocean of thoughts and feelings.

"I was never strong enough," Gussie said. "God knows you are."

"Strong enough?"

"To let go," Gussie said with a quick smile. She shoved something round and hard into Emma's hand. "Here. It's yours. Don't hold on too tight or you'll crush it."

Emma glanced at her grandmother, and then at the chestnut in her hand. Brown and smooth to the touch.

"Thank you, Gram. For everything."

"You are most welcome." Gussie took hold of Emma's free hand and held it. "Is that Alyssa calling?"

Emma looked around, saw that Conner and Alyssa were walking across the parking lot towards them.

"Yes," Emma said.

Gussie turned herself around to look too. "Your young man?" Gussie asked. Emma nodded. Both women sat up and took a deep breath. "Well then. We've had such a nice little chat, haven't we?"

"Yes, Gram. It's been a wonderful chat."

"Ginger biscuits would have been nice."

"Next time," Emma promised as, together, they stood up and turned away from the view.

Acknowledgments

Immeasurable thanks and love to my writing mentor and friend, Lois Silverstein. Thank you for your tremendous faith, encouragement, and patience. Thanks also to friends who took the time to read the various drafts of this book as it developed over years, particularly Nancy Rhodes, whose support and optimistic energy have influenced all aspects of my life. And how can I not mention my mother and sister, my sun and moon, and Carl, my true north.

About the Author

© Joanna Eldredge Morrissey

Tory McCagg earned a M.F.A. from Emerson College's writing program in 1989; her thesis and novel *Shards* won the Graduate Dean's Award. Her short stories have earned various honorable mentions. Tory is an accomplished flutist. She divides her time between Rhode Island and New Hampshire. You can see and read more about her at her website www.torymccagg.com.

SELECTED TITLES FROM SHE WRITES PRESS

*She Writes Press is an independent publishing company
founded to serve women writers everywhere.
Visit us at www.shewritespress.com.*

The Belief in Angels by J. Dylan Yates
$16.95, 978-1-938314-64-3

From the Majdonek death camp to a volatile hippie household on the East Coast, this narrative of tragedy, survival, and hope spans more than fifty years, from the 1920s to the 1970s.

Our Love Could Light the World by Anne Leigh Parrish
$15.95, 978-1-938314-44-5

Twelve stories depicting a dysfunctional and chaotic—yet lovable—family that has to band together in order to survive.

Beautiful Garbage by Jill DiDonato
$16.95, 978-1-938314-01-8

Talented but troubled young artist Jodi Plum leaves suburbia for the excitement of the city—and is soon swept up in the sexual politics and downtown art scene of 1980s New York.

Cleans Up Nicely by Linda Dahl
$16.95, 978-1-938314-38-4

The story of one gifted young woman's path from self-destruction to self-knowledge, set in mid-1970s Manhattan.

The Geometry of Love by Jessica Levine.
$16.95, 978-1-938314-62-9.

Torn between her need for stability and her desire for independence, an aspiring poets grapples with questions of artistic inspiration, erotic love, and infidelity.

Hysterical: Anna Freud's Story by Rebecca Coffey
$18.95, 978-1-938314-42-1

An irreverent, fictionalized exploration of the seemingly contradictory life of Anna Freud—told from her point of view.